On the Internet, the terrorists hide in plain sight.
On the streets, counterintelligence takes them down.
But the bad guys need to get lucky only once...

CI: HOMELAND THREAT

On the rooftop, DeLuca tried to think of a strategy. The sniper had them pinned down.

"We have a laser on top of the Tobin Bridge," Hartshorn yelled out. "I just don't know if it has a clear shot."

"Do it!" DeLuca said.

Hartshorn called on his radio. "They've got the building," he said. "But they don't see anybody on the balconies. They're saying he's firing from somewhere inside the apartment."

DeLuca knew a trained sniper would do it that way. "I'll have to get him to come out, then," he said. "Tell them to get ready."

"What are you going to do?" Mack asked.

"The only thing I can do," DeLuca answered. "I'm going to surrender."

He took off his shirt, then his white T-shirt, and waved it in the air overhead. Then he stood up with his hands over his head.

He looked up to see the man in the apartment, walking out onto the balcony. The shooter waved, as if to say, "So long"—and then reaimed his rifle at DeLuca . . .

ALSO BY DAVID DEBATTO AND PETE NELSON

CI: Team Red

CI: Dark Target

CI: Mission Liberty

CI:Homeland Threat

DAVID DeBATTO
and PETE NELSON

WARNER BOOKS

NEW YORK   BOSTON

The characters and events in this book are fictitious. Any similarity to real persons, living or dead, is coincidental and not intended by the authors.

Copyright © 2007 by David DeBatto and Pete Nelson

Cover design by Jerry Pfeifer
Book design by Stratford Publishing Services, Inc.

Warner Books and the "W" logo are trademarks of Time Warner Inc. or an affiliated company. Used under license by Hachette Book Group USA, which is not affiliated with Time Warner Inc.

Warner Books
Hachette Book Group USA
1271 Avenue of the Americas
New York, NY 10020
Visit our Web site at www.HachetteBookGroupUSA.com

Printed in the United States of America

First Printing: May 2007

10 9 8 7 6 5 4 3 2 1

We dedicate this book to what's left
of the true American soul.
Let's restore what we've lost
while we still can.

CI:Homeland
Threat

Prologue

HILTON HEAD, SOUTH CAROLINA

"Nobody in Holland has a short game," the man in the bunker off the tenth green said as he addressed his ball. He waggled his sand wedge above the Titleist, making sure the club head didn't touch the sand. "The short game is all about playing lies with the ball above or below your feet. But there are no hills in Holland. Did you ever get a chance to play a Dutch course when you were with NATO, General?"

Alexander Wagner had made a career out of suffering fools, but there was something particularly difficult to bear about this fool from Amsterdam. He talked too much. He thought he was cleverer than he was. He'd also lost six balls already and hadn't taken a penalty for one of them. Wagner couldn't abide men who ignored the rules, in golf or anywhere else.

"Never had the time," he replied.

"General Wagner's dropped his handicap by eight strokes since he started working for us," Wagner's partner, Dennis Stirling, said. Stirling was CEO at Trans-Delphi Electronics. Stirling was in the habit of improving his lie whenever he thought nobody was looking. Wagner's wife had urged him not to say anything about it. He also despised Stirling for the ridiculous amount of money he'd spent on his custom-made Japanese Yonex clubs, but again, his wife had counseled silence on the matter. "If we're not careful," Stirling told the Dutchman, "we're gonna lose him to the Senior Tour."

"Wally gets all the credit," Wagner said, referring to the club pro, who'd joined them for the back nine. Wally was a good man who did his job and didn't initiate idiotic banter or drop names, though he'd played with all the greats, including Nicklaus and Palmer, when he'd been on the PGA Tour. He kept his mouth shut when you hit a bad shot and didn't correct you unless you asked. He'd make a good aide, Wagner thought.

The Dutchman hit his wedge, skulling it to the right, where it smacked the lip of the bunker and rolled back down the sand. Wally shot Wagner a quick glance.

"You see?" the Dutchman said. "No short game. I have told you."

"We give visitors one mulligan per nine," the general heard himself saying. He hated mulligans. He hated people who took mulligans, and he hated it when a golf partner offered him one. He wondered if TDE was paying him enough to compromise his integrity this way. He smiled. Actually, they were. They were here because Stirling wanted the Dutchman to buy $40 million worth of guidance systems for the Dutch air force. Officially, Wagner was here so that the idiot from Holland could say he'd played golf with someone famous. Privately, he was here to beat the 82 he'd scored the last time he'd played the course. If the Dutchman wanted to degrade himself by cheating, that was up to him. Wagner had never held the

Dutch military in high regard anyway. "Dutch military" was virtually an oxymoron.

The Dutchman's next shot flew over the green and rolled into a bunker on the opposite side. Everyone waited, because he was still farthest from the pin.

"Somebody forget something in the clubhouse?" Wally said, eyeing a golf cart approaching from the tenth tee. "Count your head covers."

Wagner saw the golf cart approaching as well. He reached in his pocket and took out his cell phone to make sure he was receiving a signal, wondering if somebody was trying to reach him and couldn't get through. He had plenty of reception. He'd informed his office as to his schedule and had asked not to be disturbed unless it was important. Perhaps whoever it was had a message for Stirling.

There were two men in the cart, both dressed in the white coveralls of the groundskeeping crew. They had a cooler behind them on the cart. Maybe it was the bar cart, bringing Bloody Marys, though usually the bar cart was driven by attractive young women in tank tops and short shorts.

The two men appeared to be Mexicans, Wagner noticed. Odd, because all the other groundskeepers he'd seen were black. He noticed, at the last moment, and too late, as the cart suddenly veered and headed straight for him, that the men were Arabs, young, with oddly ecstatic expressions on their faces. He didn't run, instead wielding his putter like a baseball bat, though he doubted he'd have a chance to use it.

The cart was ten feet away when the bomb went off.

When the Dutchman rose from the bunker on the far side of the green, he found only a crater in the green fifteen feet deep, the titanium-carbon-boron composite head of Stirling's custom-made Yonex driver, and a human foot wearing a brown-and-white saddle-shoe-style FootJoy golf shoe he recognized as belonging to Wally, the pro.

CORAL GABLES, FLORIDA

Peter Masland was in his garden, picking tomatoes for his omelet. When he popped one into his mouth to test its ripeness, a Red Sweetie cherry tomato the size of a Ping-Pong ball, the flavor burst across his tongue, powerful enough to make his cheeks pucker. He filled the stainless steel colander to the halfway mark, discarding the tomatoes that were cracked or discolored.

He eyed the new bed he'd prepared at the southeastern corner of his property, near the fence, and wondered if it was too soon to call Lieutenant Colonel DeSilva. DeSilva never seemed to mind the calls from his old boss, and Masland was wary of abusing the privilege, but after relying on DeSilva to answer his questions and address his needs for over twenty years, it was hard to stop. He wanted to grow his own tea, nothing fancy, one English or Irish breakfast tea and one green, an oolong or Darjeeling. He'd asked the woman at the garden center why it was that nobody grew their own tea, and she didn't know, suggesting it had something to do with *Camellia sinensis* not liking certain climates. But you could grow anything in Florida. He'd called DeSilva and asked him if he could find the answer. The lieutenant colonel said he'd put somebody on it and get back to him. "I hope it's not too much trouble," Masland had said. "Not at all, General," DeSilva had said, but Masland knew DeSilva would never complain.

He went down to the dock, to make certain everything was ready. His friend Thomas was coming over later that afternoon. The two men planned on spending the day on the water. Masland had served with Thomas in Turkey, years ago, before Thomas took early retirement, passed over for promotion after pissing off the Pentagon and able to read the writing on the wall. "Join me in Florida when you're ready," Thomas had said. "They've got bonefish down there that'll pull your arms right out of their sockets."

He stood on the end of the pier. Seagulls squawked from his neighbor's dock. The water lapped at the shore. High overhead, he heard the drone of a small private plane.

His cell phone chortled. He answered it. It was his wife.

"Onion or garlic?" she asked him. "They're out of raisin."

"Do they have sesame?"

"Onion, garlic, plain, and whole wheat," she said. "That's it."

"Onion," he said.

"Do you want a coffee?" she asked. "Hazelnut or French roast?"

"Hazelnut."

"Decaf."

"Regular."

"Peter," his wife said. "I shouldn't have to be the one reminding you of what the doctor said."

"Decaf," he agreed.

He was walking back to the house, feeling the pain in his right hip that he'd felt, off and on, since taking a piece of shrapnel there as a young captain in Vietnam, defending the perimeter of Landing Zone X-Ray at Ia Drang

Valley during evac, November 14, 1965, waiting for 1st Air Cav to arrive. He could still remember the day, the smell of cordite, the noise, and perhaps because he was lost in memory, he noticed too late that the small private plane he'd seen overhead had circled back, flying in low, as if about to land, though to Masland's knowledge there wasn't an airfield nearby. Strange. When it reappeared from where a grove of palm trees obscured his view, he looked to see if it was an amphibious plane, but the aircraft lacked landing pontoons, nor did it have the shape or girth to indicate the ability to belly-land on water.

Strange again.

Was he lost? In trouble? Making an emergency landing?

He pulled out his cell phone and dialed 911, prepared to notify the authorities, but waited to hit the send button on his phone.

He watched again as the plane turned, corrected its course, turned once more, and then leveled off, coming in lower and lower, headed, he realized, straight for him.

He felt frozen, unable to move, grasping only at the last moment what was actually happening. Due to the angle of the sun, he couldn't see, through the windshield of the plane, who was flying it.

Time slowed, then seemed to stand still, and then he took the full force of the collision with his body as the plane smashed into the ground, obliterating itself in a massive fireball.

ABINGDON ROAD, OXFORD, ENGLAND

The debate had gone well, Admiral McNulty thought, but he'd known it would. The students at the Oxford Union debating society had been bright and attractive, and in particular the girl, Hannah, who'd been assigned to escort him to dinner at the Three Castles Inn, and then to the Oxford Union, where he'd taken a position on the podium opposite a young fellow named Ian Leofranc Engraham, the president of the debating society and a formidable opponent. Engraham was articulate, well-informed, charming, and glib, and the admiral had pounded him into the ground, arguing against the proposition, "Resolved: That the United States Should Get Out of Iraq Immediately and Should Never Have Invaded in the First Place," and winning by a vote three-quarters in favor of his position, from a crowd he knew was predominantly antiwar going in. His speaker's bureau told him the fee they'd offered wasn't worth the bother, but his political action committee told him Oxford was huge—if you scored big there, they said, the whole world sat up and paid attention, and he'd scored big. He'd taken a briefing from Barnett at the War College in Newport on the newest global policies, and he'd rehearsed his talking points with a focus group the PAC put together, and he'd even flown to CENTCOM in Tampa to make sure he had the latest data. At the reception in the Union bar afterwards, a don from Christchurch College had asked him if he'd be interested in teaching a course in military history, but the admiral told the don he had other plans for the long term. When Hannah got him a drink and whispered in his ear, "My God, I do believe you have to be the sexiest man in England tonight," he knew his short-term plans were set as well. She'd suggested her place. What happened on tour of duty stayed on tour of duty—that didn't change when he made admiral, and it didn't have to change, now that he was retired. The only difference was that this time, he'd brought his wife along, but she'd begged off attending the reception, saying she had a migraine, and walked back to the hotel.

He saw the taillights from the girl's sports car flare up ahead as she rounded a curve.

"She's speeding," his driver said, smiling in the rear-view mirror. "I think she's in a hurry, Admiral."

"Youth will be served," the admiral said. "Don't follow too closely. I want to play hard-to-get."

He reached into his pocket, found his pillbox, and slipped a Viagra into his mouth, coughing first and pretending it was a throat lozenge.

The road led up Hinksey Hill, past a manse called Woodside, and another called Abingdon Cottage, a third called Aubreyston, each estate with stone posts marking the gated drives. Hannah had said she'd rented a country house with a friend, rather than live in college, but the friend was away for the weekend. "She'll be sorry she missed out," Hannah had said. "And I'm not talking about the bloody debate."

A rich girl. Irish. McNulty liked rich girls, and especially rich girls who talked dirty, and looked like Hannah did, red-haired and built, with a sense of utter confidence, so certain that she knew what she was doing. There was nothing sexier. She'd said only that her father worked in government. McNulty hoped he didn't know the man, but there was a chance he did. He'd served in London for twelve years as the Pentagon's chief liaison with MI6. Anybody in Parliament he hadn't met, he'd probably at least read a dossier about them. It didn't matter, but it was good to be careful (after what happened to Clinton, his political adviser had warned him about keeping his sexual adventurism in check), so he'd made a call before leaving the reception to an old friend from the ministry, a man he knew he could trust for his discretion, and asked him to pull the girl's file. He was hoping the friend would contact him before he got busy with Hannah, because after that, he wouldn't be taking any calls. If the man didn't reach him, it was all right. He'd get the information later.

They rounded a corner and saw where Hannah's red sports car had stopped at the top of the hill, her hazard lights flashing.

The driver slowed, pulling up behind her.

"Something wrong?" the admiral said.

"I can't tell," the driver said. "Do you want me to get out?"

"No no," the admiral said. "Just wait."

They were in the middle of nowhere, stone walls and hedgerows edging the fields to either side. The sky was overcast, and a slight drizzle had begun to fall, typical English weather, McNulty knew. Perhaps she'd stopped to use her cell phone, before driving out of range.

Then he saw it, a dead deer lying at the side of the road. Back home, the damn things were a nuisance, overpopulating the countryside thanks to all the goddamn Bambi-people who'd been passing restrictions on hunting. She must have hit the animal, and that was why she'd stopped.

He got out of the car, meaning to speak to her and console her. He hoped this wasn't going to blow his chances of getting laid.

He'd walked five paces and was standing in the headlights of the big Jaguar sedan, when suddenly the red sports car took off at top speed.

"What's wrong with her?" the driver said, getting out of the car and standing in the opened door.

"I think she's upset," McNulty said, watching the tail-lights fade into the night. He looked again at the deer. Only then did he notice a length of wire, about a foot, protruding from the dead animal's anus.

"What's that doing there?" he thought.

It was his last thought. The bomb inside the carcass went off, blowing the admiral's car twenty feet into the sky, killing him and his driver instantly. Police called to the scene later found pieces of the car blown a hundred meters from the scene of the explosion and traces of C4 in the residue.

BOUNDARY WATERS CANOE AREA,
CRANE LAKE, MINNESOTA

Retired U.S. Marine general Mike O'Hara was fishing when the first shot knocked him into the water. As he fell overboard, the wooden canoe it had taken him nearly twenty years to build in his "spare time" flipped.

He took refuge beneath it, collecting his wits, breathing the air trapped inside the turtled boat. At first he thought some sort of rock had fallen on him, though that was impossible. It soon occurred to him that he'd been shot. He assessed the damage. It appeared to be superficial, a flesh wound that had torn across the surface of his left shoulder, painful, but not enough to put him down.

He slowed his thinking, to summarize and extrapolate.

He'd been fishing, casting in the weeds for bass. The sun had set half an hour earlier, the sky a deep purplish pink in the west. He'd told himself he'd give it three more casts before paddling back to his cabin, where Emily was waiting to clean his catch and cook it for dinner. Emily probably had a pitcher of martinis ready. He'd been fishing off the point at the eastern end of the property, and the shot had come from somewhere to the west, either from the cabin or from the shore along the opposing peninsula. If the shot came from the cabin, it meant that Emily was already dead. If it came from the far point, she could still be alive.

Then two more rounds crashed into the boat, splintering the bow, and neither time did he hear the crack of a rifle. That meant the shooter was a professional, using a weapon prepared with a silencer and probably a flash suppressor. The two shots had blown the bow clean off the boat, indicating a large-caliber weapon, maybe even a sniper's rifle. That meant a powerful scope, and probably night vision capabilities.

He was not defenseless. Beneath what remained of his boat, he found his floating tackle box, opened it (experience had taught him to keep the box locked and closed after dumping a canoe once and losing all his gear), and took out the .45 Colt automatic he kept in it, sealed in a plastic bag, the weapon used to drive off marauding bears, which were plentiful in these deep woods along the Canadian border, a wild unpopulated country, and that was the problem—the closest neighbor was four miles down lake. There was no one to swim to for help.

It meant he was going to have to handle this alone.

He took a deep breath, dived underwater, and swam to shore, just as two more shots splintered what remained of his beloved wooden canoe. There were large rocks along the shore that made for good cover, along with the reeds and lily pads in the shallows sheltering the bass he'd been trying to catch.

He surfaced, hiding behind a rock, and turned. Where his boat had been, he saw only his tackle box floating, and then a final round hit and sank it.

The shooter was a marksman, he now understood, but a cocky one, taking shots that weren't certain, and in doing so, giving away his position. O'Hara now had a pretty good fix as to where the shots were coming from. The eastern promontory, dubbed Gilly's Point, after his grandfather, who'd built the cabin, ended at a solid granite ledge that rose eight feet from the water, Em's favorite place for picnics, with an old Ojibwa pictograph on the ledge that tourists sometimes anchored off and photographed. He moved furtively through the snakegrass, then took a deep breath and dived underwater again, swimming around the ledge until he'd made it to the far side, where it was safe to emerge.

He moved deep into the woods and circled toward the cabin, running. Emily had made fun of him for wearing camo when he fished, even though he'd shown her a study in *Bassmaster* magazine that said fishermen in bright colors caught fewer fish than fishermen who wore more concealing attire. Now he was glad for it.

He moved quickly, keeping to the darkening woods, certain that the assassin was moving too, but where? Closer, to take another shot? Or was he done for the day, in retreat, thinking his job was finished? The sniper had seen a body fall. O'Hara doubted the sniper saw him once he'd hit the water. For all the sniper knew, O'Hara was dead. Perhaps he was breaking down his weapon even now, hiking out, back to his boat or his ATV—or maybe he wasn't finished. A horrible thought occurred to O'Hara. Maybe, now that his primary target was eliminated, the shooter was moving more leisurely on his secondary target—Emily.

O'Hara doubled his pace, racing to reach the cabin. He was a strong man who stayed in shape by running marathons and Ironman competitions. His wound hurt, but it wasn't enough to slow him. He felt the adrenaline rising within him—the fuel of battle, someone once described it. He considered firing three warning shots, but Emily wouldn't know what that meant. She was so innocent, not naïve, but inexperienced, certainly in all things military, and she rarely asked him about the things he'd done as a marine, not that there was much he could comfortably tell her. They'd only been dating for two years, since he'd got back from Afghanistan, but he knew she was the best thing ever to happen to him.

When he got within view of the cabin, he saw her. She was standing on the porch, gazing out on the lake, enjoying the first stars of the evening. She was wearing a bright yellow fleece vest against the evening chill, and a white Irish cable-knit sweater, blue jeans, a white headband. He saw her lift her coffee to her lips. Cream, two Sweet'N Lows. He saw her take a sip.

Then her head disintegrated in a spray of blood as sniper's round tore through it at 3,000 feet per second.

He'd seen people die before, men he cared about, but this was different.

This was no war zone.

This couldn't be happening.

He knew better, knew he should have held, but instead he ran for Emily, as if to catch her before her body fell, as if that would matter or make a difference—as if he could still save her, and as he ran, he screamed the word "No," filled with a mindless rage that was absolute. He didn't care if he drew fire—he wanted the shooter to show himself, and fight him, man to man . . .

The first shell caught him in the gut. As he staggered, a second round caught him in the neck, dropping him to the ground. It must have done some nerve damage, he concluded, because he could no longer feel his legs or his arms. He couldn't move.

He saw a figure emerge from the woods in the distance, a man, dressed in hunting gear. He saw the man raise a rifle and aim it at him.

It was the last thing he would ever see.

And in Boston, Massachusetts, in an underground parking garage, a woman crossed to her car.

Shots rang out.

A body fell.

Chapter One

DELUCA WAS ABLE TO GRAB THE RINGING telephone at his bedside before it woke his wife. He slept more lightly than she did, a habit he'd picked up in Iraq, if not before then. He glanced at the clock on his bedstand. It was twenty minutes after five. Nobody calling at that hour would be calling with good news.

"DeLuca," he said.

"Good morning," the voice said. "Captain Martin with General LeDoux's office."

DeLuca had spoken with Martin a hundred times before, but Martin was the sort of guy who needed to give himself a full introduction each time he called, a formal military sort who followed the book at all times, but an okay guy.

"What can I do for you, Captain?" DeLuca said. He took the mobile handset into his study. The sky was becoming light in the east, overcast after a night of rain, the air coming through the window screen fresh and damp and full of ozone. Glancing out the window, he saw a pair of deer, sniffing at the tulips his wife had planted in the garden. He'd made a slurry from raw eggs and painted the flowers, upon the advice of his friend Walter, who knew about such things. The slurry was working—the deer turned away. Some people thought they were cute. He thought of them more like rats on steroids.

"Bad news, I'm afraid," Martin said. "There's been some activity. All in the last twelve hours or so."

"What kind of activity?" he said. "Where?"

"Minnesota, South Carolina, Florida, and England," Martin said. "Three retired generals and an admiral have been attacked. And possibly something in your neighborhood. I can't really give you a full briefing, right at this moment. We're still gathering intel, but we've only just got wind of it. General LeDoux wanted to schedule something for later in the day, but it looks like some of our retired stars are being targeted. And/or their families."

"In my neighborhood?" he asked. "In Boston?"

"We're not sure," Martin said. "There's been a homicide. No details yet. We were hoping you could look into it."

"A homicide?" he said. "Why are you calling me?"

"It's military," Martin said.

"The MPs handle crimes by military personnel."

"We don't know the killer," Martin said, "or killers, but it appears to be a terrorist attack on U.S. soil against a military target. Global coordination has been suggested. The Pentagon wants to get CI involved. They're still discussing to what extent, but they want you to scramble."

"Okay," DeLuca said. "Who and where?"

"Boston Common parking garage," Captain Martin said. "It's Katie Quinn. General Joe Quinn's daughter. We can tell you more at the briefing but right now, we'd like to get you on the scene ASAP. We just picked it up a little while ago, so it's pretty fresh."

"I'm about twenty minutes away," DeLuca said.

"We'll talk to you after you've had a look," Martin said. "We sent a car to General Quinn's house too. We might want you there as well, but we'll let you know. First things first. Sorry to have to wake you."

"It's all right," DeLuca said. "I had to answer the phone anyway."

DeLuca grabbed an armful of clothes, dressed quietly in the downstairs bathroom, and left his wife a note on the kitchen table to tell her something had come up and to call him on his cell.

He found his B's and C's in the drawer of his desk where he kept them, then took his service Beretta from underneath his mattress and donned his shoulder holster, the weapon concealed beneath his jacket. A familiar feeling came over him. In the fifteen years between getting out of the army the first time and reenlisting after 9/11, he'd served with the Boston Police Department. He knew the drill, too well.

He was on the road minutes after hanging up the phone, on a steamy summer morning where the humidity and the temperature were both already in the low eighties. Traffic at that hour was light. He took the Northeast Expressway over the Tobin and then 93 south into the "Big Dig," the massive reconstruction effort that, over the last fifteen years, had successfully taken Interstate 93 and sunk it into the ground, the expressway now a tunnel beneath downtown Boston, costing the city a mere $14 billion, which was only $12 billion over budget. He emerged at the Summer Street exit and took it to Tremont, circling the Common once to see where a squad car blocked the garage entrance on Charles Street, and parked finally on Boylston at a meter, walking across the park to a kiosk where an elevator and a stairway led down into the garage.

He'd walked the Boston Common a thousand times as
a detective. The rain had stopped, but the sidewalks were
still puddled. He recognized a homeless guy he'd known
only as Marvin the Moon Man, who liked to sleep in the
cemetery and who was, at this early hour, sitting on a
bench in a Thorazine haze, talking to himself. In another
hour or two, Crazy Larry would be playing the bongos
by the baseball fields. There were probably already Emerson College students smoking pot in the Public Garden.
DeLuca noted the irony—the last time he'd visited the
Boston Common had been to attend a political rally for
retired U.S. Army general Joseph Quinn, who'd been running for president. General Quinn had spoken of how he'd
come from Boston originally, traveled the world to serve
his country and come home to Back Bay, and how he
would nevertheless be willing, if called upon, to move to
the White House to serve his country again. DeLuca had
known General Quinn since Gulf One. He'd always liked
and respected the general, for how he'd carried himself in
Desert Storm, for the way he'd led the coalition of forces
in Kosovo, and for how he'd always respected and stood
up for the common soldier. DeLuca would have voted for
him in a heartbeat, had General Quinn won his party's
nomination, but he hadn't. Now, if Captain Martin's information was correct, the general's daughter lay dead in
the garage below.

He found the crime scene on level two, in the northwest
corner of the garage, four squad cars with their flashers
flashing, a forensics van, and a number of unmarkeds. At
this hour on a Saturday morning, the garage was nearly
empty. A uniformed officer stopped him as he approached

and told him no one was allowed to get any closer. De-Luca showed the officer his badge and credentials and asked him who was in charge. The uniform told him Lieutenant Morrissey was in charge but that Captain Wexler was there too.

"The army is involved in this?" the cop asked.

"You got it. You said Billy Morrissey?" DeLuca said. "I thought he'd be up in New Hampshire ridding the rivers of unwanted trout by now."

"No sir," the uniformed officer said. "He's still with us."

Morrissey was talking to a junior officer. DeLuca approached and waited for Morrissey to look up. He smiled when he did.

"Hey, Billy," DeLuca said, shaking the hand of his old friend. "Thought you did your twenty."

"Hello, Lieutenant," Morrissey said. "Long time no see. Or what was it when you were in the army? Sergeant?"

"I'm still in," DeLuca said. "Promoted to chief warrant officer, if you gotta know. Who else is still around besides you?"

"Couple guys," Morrissey said. "Me, Doyle, Finn, Kaz Takata, Difranco, Lapinski, a couple others. And Wexler, of course."

He nodded toward the man standing by the garage toll-booth.

"Why's Wexler here?"

"I don't know," Morrissey said. "Scoring points. I'm just trying to stay out of his way. Maybe he was in the area."

"At five a.m.? He still an asshole?"

"Did the Sox win the Series?" Morrissey said. "Yeah, he's still an asshole."

"You know what I heard about how the Sox won the World Series? Their lucky charm?" DeLuca asked his friend.

"What?"

"They had Ted Williams's head in the cooler," DeLuca said. "Keeping the Gatorade cold."

"I bet it was smiling too," Morrissey said. "You here on army business?"

"I'm afraid so," DeLuca said. "Counterintelligence."

"What the fuck's that mean?" Morrissey asked. "You're against intelligence?"

"Don't make me out like Frank," DeLuca said. "CI is sort of the army version of the FBI. Except with more toys. Something goes wrong inside the army, we look into it."

"Like internal affairs?"

"Not exactly, but sort of," DeLuca said. "We're also who they send into the fifth world to find the guy who knows the guy who knows the guy who's causing problems. Sort of like working a drug gang from the street up. Except with bombs. Katie Quinn?"

"Behind the car," Morrissey said. "I didn't think the army got involved in civilian matters."

"We do since 9/11," DeLuca said. "The Patriot Act gives us a bit more leeway. To be honest, they haven't told me yet why I'm here. There's apparently some question as to how civilian this is. I think they also wanted me because I know the father."

"General Joe?" Morrissey said, walking slowly.

"I worked his security detail, Gulf One," DeLuca said, walking with him.

"Yeah?"

"They knew he wasn't going to sit still behind a desk when the ground game got going. He was out there in the dirt with everybody else. They wanted me to make sure he didn't fall into the wrong hands."

"You like him?"

"Yeah, I like him."

"He talk much about his daughter?"

"Not much, actually," DeLuca said. "What can you tell me?"

He knew that to Morrissey, even though they were friends, Morrissey nevertheless saw him as a Fed, and cops didn't like Feds, for a wide variety of reasons, mainly for how they took credit for everything and treated cops like subordinates.

"Not much," Morrissey said. "She got off work at four-fifteen and walked to her car."

"Working where?"

"You obviously don't have any trouble sleeping," Morrissey said. "If you did and you were awake in the middle of the night, you would have heard her radio show. *Sports Nation.* They do it here but it's syndicated nationally. Six-ninety AM, WSPO. It's her, a guy named 'Dan the Man,' and the producer."

"She was on air last night?"

Morrissey nodded. "Reporting the nightly scores, but she also used to join in all the chitchat for the female perspective. The show goes until five, but her last segment is taped so she leaves at four-thirty. They talk about whatever's going on in the sports world and steroids or whatever and they take calls."

"Anything unusual about tonight's show?" he asked as they approached the body.

"We're getting a transcript, but no, we don't think so. She was shot about a quarter to five. The shooter was waiting for her, here."

"He didn't follow her across the park?"

"Doesn't look like it," Morrissey said.

"So he knew her," DeLuca said. "And he knew her car. He knew where to wait."

"Maybe," Morrissey said. "Probably."

"Robbery?"

"Her money is missing from her purse but her credit cards are there. She isn't wearing any jewelry, but we don't know that she wore jewelry, so that don't mean it was taken."

"Security cameras?"

"Disabled."

"Disabled?" DeLuca said. "When?"

"Last night."

"How?"

"I'll show you," Morrissey said. He led DeLuca to the cement pillar in the center of the garage's northern end where the security camera was mounted. DeLuca saw that someone had used a short length of plastic rod and duct tape to hang a small mirror in front of the camera lens, one end of the rod wedged into the gap at the top between the lens body and the camera housing. The rod was bright red, and a cross section of it would have revealed the shape of a four-leafed clover.

"What is that?" DeLuca asked.

"They're called K'NEX," Morrissey said. "It's like the new Tinkertoys. They sell sets for kids in practically every toy store. I got some for my grandchildren."

"You got grandchildren now?" DeLuca asked.

"Two," Morrissey said. "Twins. Cameron and Maeve. Born right around when you left. Anyway, you can make any shape you want with 'em and they're pretty strong. Once the mirror was in place, you'd still see the garage, but from a different angle. You'd have to be paying wicked-close attention to even notice the view had changed. I got guys in the security office right now looking at the video. The license plate numbers all start to reverse around three-thirty. We oughta be able to get it exactly. The downtown bar traffic is pretty much over after two-thirty or three—the guy in the booth said nobody comes in between three and five."

"Stairwell cameras?"

"We're looking," Morrissey said. "It rained last night, so all you had to do was keep your umbrella up and no one would have seen a thing. We're trying to figure out what car might have been parked under the camera—whoever rigged it would have had to stand on something. If we find the car, maybe we get shoe prints on the hood."

"So it wasn't random," DeLuca said. "The shooter knew."

"Maybe he knew what he was going to do, but not who to," Morrissey said. "To whom," he corrected himself. "How about Scott—you got grandkids yet?"

"Scottie was serious about a girl a while back, but she didn't like the lifestyle," DeLuca said. "Being an air force wife isn't for everyone."

"How's Bonnie?" Morrissey asked.

"Bonnie's all right," DeLuca said, not really wanting to get into it. "Cameron and Maeve, huh?"

"He's a cupcake," Morrissey said. "She's a terror. Usually it's the other way around."

"Can you show me the body?"

"I can show you what's left of it," Morrissey said. "You're not going to like what you see."

"I didn't expect to," DeLuca said.

Morrissey led DeLuca around to the passenger side of the car, a 1999 Honda Accord coupe. The body lay face-down in the space between the car and the garage wall. There was a broad spray of blood and brain tissue staining the wall. The body itself had been covered by a blanket, pending the arrival of the Suffolk County medical examiner, who was expected shortly.

"The shooter fired across the car," Morrissey said. "Standing right there, maybe six to eight feet away. On the driver's side."

"So why is she on the passenger side?" DeLuca asked. "This is her car, right?"

"Maybe she's trying to hide?" Morrissey said. "Though she was standing straight up when she got shot and not ducking. We think she turned her head away at the last second. It's a little hard to tell."

"Because?"

"There's not much left of the head," Morrissey said. "CSI pulled a slug out of the wall. The hole in the concrete was three inches wide and six inches deep. It looked like somebody hit the wall with a sledgehammer. They're gonna run the slug to make sure, but the guy who had it said he was guessing it was a .50AE 300 grain jacketed hollow point. We thought forty-five but he said it was more, and he's pretty good—he's usually right. You can tell from the spray pattern that it was something significant."

"Fifty cal?" DeLuca said. "What'd he use—a Sharps rifle?"

"Smith and Wesson makes a new fifty-caliber Magnum," Morrissey said. "Four and a half fucking pounds of gun. On the market for about a year. Just under two grand. The ads talk about how the thing can stop a grizzly. You just don't see a lot of grizzly bears in the Boston Common parking garage."

"That's because they've all been shot with fifty Mags," DeLuca said.

"There haven't been too many sold," Morrissey said. "We're looking at recent registrations."

"I won't hold my breath," DeLuca said. Perhaps someone who'd bought and registered an S&W .50 had reported one stolen—a weapon that large and that expensive would be something thieves would want to steal, but it was still a remote possibility. "Can I have a look?"

"Brace yourself," Morrissey said. "This is like getting hit point-blank by an elephant gun."

He pulled back the blanket. DeLuca saw a torso, and a neck, and the lower part of the skull, and a fray of connective tissues. The rest of the head had been dispersed against the wall and floor, where a large pool of blood had collected. The beam of Morrissey's flashlight revealed a number of white teeth and bone fragments scattered in the corner of the garage, amid the blood and gray matter.

"Jesus Christ," DeLuca said. He'd seen worse, in Iraq, the results of .60 caliber machine guns and mortar rounds and RPGs and IEDs, but that was war, and that wasn't the daughter of someone he knew. She was wearing a white skirt, stained where her bowels had released post mortem, and a pale blue top under a navy sweatshirt, still damp where the rain had reached her beneath her umbrella, which was collapsed but not snapped shut in her left hand.

Her car keys were still in her right hand. "Do you mind?" he asked Morrissey, who shrugged.

"It's all been processed," Morrissey said.

DeLuca bent down and took the car keys from her hand. He pressed the unlock button on the remote door opener attached to her keychain. The remote worked fine.

"Why's she on the passenger side?" DeLuca said. "What do you make?"

"You tell me," Morrissey said.

"She knew the shooter," DeLuca said. "She was going to let herself in the passenger side. He was going to drive. Just before she gets into the car, she looks up, sees the gun, turns her head away, blam. Why doesn't she toss him the keys?"

"No idea," Morrissey said. "Wexler makes it a mob hit."

"Why?"

"You should ask him," Morrissey said. "He's going to be the case officer on this."

"Terrific," DeLuca said.

"Sorry," Morrissey said. "That was decided before you ever got here."

Frank Wexler was talking to a uniformed officer and looked up as DeLuca approached. DeLuca knew Wexler had seen him arrive, but all the same, Wexler feigned surprise.

"Look what the fucking cat dragged in," Wexler said, turning to the uniformed officer next to him. "Here's something you can tell your grandchildren. This is famous Lieutenant David DeLuca, formerly of division A. You kill any A-rabs in Iraq, DeLuca, or you just there to hang out?"

"Morrissey said you make this a hit," DeLuca said, ignoring Wexler as much as was humanly possible while still talking to him. "You wanna tell me why?"

"No, I don't want to tell you why," Wexler said. "What would compel me to tell you why?"

Wexler had been annoying before, and nothing had changed in the interim. He was an idiot, and being patronized by an idiot was a little like getting kicked in the shin by a chipmunk, but after a few years, even that could get irritating.

"I don't know—courtesy?" DeLuca said. "I'd buy you a copy of Emily Post but you'd probably eat it. I'm here for the army, Frank. The victim is the daughter of a general. You wanna wait until Halliday tells you you have to help me, or you wanna get a head start on that?"

Wexler looked at Morrissey, who nodded toward him.

"Single shot, right in the melon, inside twenty feet," Wexler said. "You know the profile."

"It's fifty cal,'" DeLuca countered. "Hitters use twenty-twos."

"Maybe in your day," Wexler said. "These days, even preschoolers got nines."

A fifty-caliber would have made a roar like one of the cannons on Bunker Hill, a sound that would have been magnified, inside a huge underground parking garage. Hitters worked in public because sometimes they had to, but they still liked to keep the attention they drew to a minimum. Maybe the new fifties came with silencer options. He'd have to check.

"You said it was a pro, not a gangbanger," DeLuca said. "What's the motivation?"

"Sports book," Wexler said. "Last year, Katie Quinn called fifteen out of sixteen Patriots games and the spread too. I'm thinking she was costing the wrong guys a lot of money. Even in Vegas, once her show went national.

Steve Wynn tried to hire her to handicap for him. That's as much as I'm going to say, but do you really think I'd waste my time if I didn't have good solid reasons?"

"I don't know, Frank," DeLuca said. "You might. Four top-level retired military brass and a general's daughter get hit all on the same day. You don't find that odd?"

"Rule number one," Wexler lectured, "things happen at the same time don't mean they're related. Maybe I have reasons to believe my own theories. Why is it that you doubt me so, DeLuca?"

"Call me old-fashioned," DeLuca said. "I like to wait for all the information to come in before I form any theories. Kooky, I know."

"You're not a cop," Wexler said. "You're a fucking Fed. If they make me talk to you face-to-face, I suppose I'll have to, but until I hear from the commissioner's office, I think I'll keep my thoughts to myself."

"Next time they make us talk face-to-face," DeLuca said, "I'll try to remember to bring a chair for you to stand on."

He was returning to speak with Morrissey when a black sedan pulled up. DeLuca recognized the medical examiner, a man named Mitch Pasternak, who'd taken the position after DeLuca's old friend Gillian O'Doherty vacated the position. Pasternak was smart and capable. DeLuca hadn't spent enough time with him to know if he liked him personally or not. He'd farmed work out to Pasternak when he needed to bypass the endless paperwork and bureaucratic delays that were inevitably a part of working with the army forensics labs at Fort Gillem in Georgia and Fort Shafter in Hawaii. Pasternak appeared to be puzzled by DeLuca's presence. DeLuca explained, briefly, what he was doing there.

"She's General Joe's daughter?" Pasternak said. "That sucks. I followed his political campaign pretty closely—I don't remember seeing her on the podium with him."

"I don't remember either," DeLuca said. "I know I don't have to say this, but if you could be particularly thorough with this one, I'd appreciate it."

"You got it," Pasternak said, turning to Morrissey. "They told me some assembly was required—you wanna show me?"

"Over there," Morrissey said, gesturing over his shoulder with his thumb. "Watch your step."

DeLuca turned to Morrissey. "I don't think my old password is going to work anymore," he said. "Do you have any problem with providing access to the department reports?"

"I don't, personally," Morrissey said, "but that sounds like something I'd need to check on before I could give you a good answer."

"I understand," DeLuca said. "You mind if I have a look at her purse?"

"Not at all," Morrissey said.

He was looking for a picture of her, something he could show around if he needed to speak with neighbors or potential witnesses. The only photograph he could find in her purse was the one on her driver's license. Katie Quinn favored her father in appearance, more than a little, and that was not necessarily fortunate. DeLuca used the digital camera in his handheld to copy the photograph, as well as to briefly record the crime scene. When DeLuca showed the driver's license picture to Marvin the Moon Man on his way back across the Common to his car, asking Marvin if he'd seen that person in the park in the wee hours of the morning, Marvin said, "Who's that guy?" Marvin said he'd spent the night under the Colonial Theater marquee on Boylston to get out of the rain and hadn't seen a thing.

When DeLuca called LeDoux's office to give a preliminary report, Captain Martin asked him to hold and then put LeDoux on the phone. DeLuca described what he'd seen, sparing only the more gruesome details.

"I'm flying to Boston tonight," LeDoux said. "I'd like to get together and talk about this if you don't mind."

"I don't mind," DeLuca said. "You want to meet first thing tomorrow?"

"Tonight," LeDoux said. DeLuca was supposed to see a movie with Bonnie that night at the Burlington Mall. Outside of the military, someone might have said, "Unless you have other plans," but General LeDoux didn't have to make any such accommodations, and DeLuca understood. "They're giving us a room at Hanscom. Ten o'clock?"

"I'll be there," DeLuca said. "Can you give me anything? Big picture? Al Qaeda or somebody else?"

"Too soon to say," LeDoux said. "It's Web-based. I'll fill you in when I see you. In the meantime, I have another favor to ask. It's going to be tough, but we need somebody to brief Joe Quinn. Just tell him what you know, from today. We'll give him the rest. There's a chaplain there now, but you knew Quinn personally."

"I can do it," DeLuca said. "I wish I didn't have to, but I agree with you."

"We might want Quinn with us tonight," LeDoux said. "You can tell him if you want. Captain Martin will give you the details."

*   *   *

The dogwood trees on Marlboro Street had lost their blossoms, but the street in Back Bay, a block off Beacon, was still one of the more spectacular addresses Boston had to offer. The distance from the general's home to the Boston Common parking garage was less than a mile, and yet after speaking with the general for a few minutes, DeLuca had the sense that the distance between General Joseph Quinn and his daughter was considerably greater than that. A chaplain who identified himself as Captain Jahns had answered when DeLuca rang the bell after climbing a flight of granite steps from the sidewalk and standing before a massive mahogany door. Stepping inside, he smelled coffee coming from the kitchen and accepted the offer when the chaplain asked him if he wanted a cup. Jahns said General Quinn would meet him in the front study, which featured built-in bookshelves carrying leather-bound volumes on military history, a large walnut roll-top desk, and a chocolate-colored leather recliner where books lay bookmarked in a pile on the floor, that morning's *Boston Globe* still unopened on the leather ottoman. On the walls, DeLuca saw a portrait of Ulysses S. Grant, another of Robert E. Lee, and a third of Eisenhower, as well as photographs of General Quinn shaking hands with presidents Reagan, Bush I, Clinton, and Bush II, as well as foreign leaders Tony Blair, Vladimir Putin, Corazon Aquino, Helmut Schmidt, and others. He saw framed certificates from the companies on whose boards the retired general served, including Boeing, United Defense Industries, Raytheon, Allied Worldwide, Dynacorp, Anteon International, Anheuser-Busch (supplying Budweiser to U.S. bases around the world except in Islamic countries) and the Actel-Simmons Corporation, the third largest construction company in the world, behind Bechtel and Halliburton. Actel-Simmons was busy in the reconstruction of Iraq, though if DeLuca remembered what he'd read in the paper accurately, General Quinn had been brought in originally to stanch the bleeding of cost overruns at the Big Dig, a feat he'd accomplished in short order and one of the things he talked about in his presidential campaign—after getting a project like that under control, he'd joked, running a country ought to be a piece of cake. His opponents successfully spun that to imply that sitting on the board at Actel put him in the pocket of the defense industry. Old soldiers didn't fade away anymore, not when they could be paid a consulting fee by defense contractors who needed someone with a top security clearance who could pick up the phone and get people at the Pentagon to answer it.

The general was dressed in khaki slacks and a white shirt, unbuttoned at the neck. The only other time DeLuca had seen the man in civilian clothes was from the rostrum at his campaign rally, where the general had worn a black suit, red tie, and white shirt, offsetting his head of white hair, cropped short. He looked distraught and invited DeLuca to sit.

"When they told me you were available and looking into things," Quinn said, "I was glad to hear it. What can you tell me?"

This was a man who'd lost loved ones before, both family members and men who'd served under him. He was not a stranger to bad news. DeLuca had delivered some of it personally before, when a team Quinn had sent forward fell to an IED left on the infamous "Highway to Hell" where a hundred-mile string of destroyed vehicles marked Saddam's retreat from Kuwait during Desert Storm. Quinn had served as an infantry lieutenant in Vietnam and had been awarded a Silver Star when he'd declined to be evacked with his wounded and stayed behind with his men in a battle where he and his complement took heavy fire. Again, his political opponents made it look like he'd been the only American military leader to lose a battle. DeLuca knew Quinn as a man who'd ridden a Bradley to the front line at the launch of Desert Storm, before anyone had any idea that Saddam's vaunted Republican Guard was in fact a big bunch of pussies—Quinn was as honest as he was brave, and he had more integrity in his little finger, in DeLuca's opinion, than some entire corridors at the Pentagon.

"Can I get you anything?" the retired general asked.

"The chaplain is getting me coffee," DeLuca said. "I'm fine, thank you, sir."

"Have you had breakfast?" Quinn asked. "I'm not sure what we have but we could probably get you something."

"I'm good, sir, thank you," DeLuca said.

"What can you tell me?" Quinn asked. "Please. You don't have to spare me any details. I need to know everything." He sounded calm, resolved. DeLuca suspected this was something of an act—who could hear such news of his own child without collapsing inside? "All I know is that Katie was killed. When I called Washington to see what we could do, I gather they ran my request through INSCOM and kicked out your name. You used to work with Boston PD, isn't that right, Agent DeLuca?"

"Almost twenty years," DeLuca said. "You can call me David if you'd prefer."

"And you know people there?"

"I do," DeLuca said. "I ran into an old friend this morning."

"I heard you were in Iraq," Quinn said. "Who were you with?"

"Four Hundred and Thirty-eighth CI,'" DeLuca said. "Knocking on doors."

"I heard you'd done very well," Quinn said. "You're still CI?"

"Still CI," DeLuca said. "Special assignment. Trying to line up with DHS, but that's still shaking out."

"What do you know about Katie?" Quinn said. "Please. I need to understand this thing."

"Well," DeLuca said. He'd been rehearsing what he was going to say for the last thirty minutes. "I can tell you that I don't believe she felt anything. Her death would have been instantaneous. One bullet, about here." He put a finger on the back of his head. He did not advance his theory that Katie had turned to see the gun, then turned away, because it was only a theory. "Fifty-caliber, from close range."

"Fifty?" Quinn asked. "Why?"

"We're not sure," DeLuca said.

He didn't have to explain to General Quinn what a fifty-caliber shell fired from close range could do to someone. It was a very small thing to be grateful for, but he was glad he didn't have to. Perhaps the hardest part was over.

"About what time?"

"Between four forty-five and five, they think," DeLuca said. "Boston Common parking garage, level two."

"And who?" Quinn asked. "Or why? Do they have any idea?"

"They don't," DeLuca said. "They're looking at the security video, but they don't expect to find anything. I hate to ask you this, but there's some indication that she might have known her killer. He was apparently waiting for her in the garage, but she might have been letting him into her car. Can you think of anybody she might have known who could have had a reason to wish her harm? Anyone at all, going back as many years as you want."

Quinn considered his answer.

"Katie and I weren't close," he said finally. "Lately. I should correct myself and say her mother and I had a bit of a falling-out with Katie, about five years ago, over some lifestyle choices she made that her mother and I couldn't approve of. I think my daughter and I last spoke at her mother's funeral. So I guess I don't know how to answer your question."

DeLuca waited to see if the general had anything further to say, a clarification.

"Maybe if you told me what the falling-out was about," DeLuca said, "it might help. It's been my experience in homicides that you never know what's going to lead you somewhere. You look for anomalies. I had a case, years ago, when a girl's hair smelled funny so we tracked it to her new boyfriend's shampoo. You can't tell, so you just keep digging until you have more than you need, and sometimes it falls together and sorts itself out."

Quinn again thought for a moment before he spoke.

"It had to do with her sexual preference," he said. "She was very private about it, and we were grateful for that. It was something we had to consider when I decided to declare my candidacy. I left a message to ask her for permission, but she never returned my call."

"Permission?"

"To expose our . . . private lives," Quinn said. "At a certain point, you can no longer guarantee privacy."

"Do you know who her partner was?" DeLuca asked.

"Partner. That makes it sound like a business, doesn't it?" Quinn said. "Someone named Claire. From Northampton. We don't know her last name. We have an old address. But apparently that ended a few years ago when Katie moved back to Boston. We didn't accept Claire, and Katie never forgave us for that. You have a wife and a son, as I recall."

"I do," DeLuca said.

"Then you know that a military man's family is often forced into a kind of duty they didn't choose. I moved my family twenty-seven times in thirty years. I know that when she was growing up, Katie wished I'd been home more. As did Eleanor. I know they both had to make sacrifices they didn't want to make. I'm not sure that the lifestyle thing wasn't some kind of rebellion against that. Against me. To get back at me. And I probably deserved it. If that has anything to do with why I've lost her, I will never get over the regret I feel right now. I'll never forgive myself."

"General Quinn," DeLuca said. "May I speak freely?"

"As I recall, you always did," Quinn said. "I'm a civilian now. You can speak to me any way you wish."

"Thank you, sir," DeLuca said. "I know there's a school of thought that says people make a choice as to their sexual preference, and I suppose some people are actually halfway between one expression of it and the other, or encompass both, to where maybe they do have an actual choice of how to behave, but not of who they are. It's been my experience that most people don't choose, any more than they can choose their hair color or the size of their ears. I'd be very surprised if she decided who to be in love with, just to get back at you. That's sort of an emotional mission creep that doesn't make any sense, to me. When you fell in love with your wife, I imagine you did it because it felt right for you and you alone. You weren't really thinking about your parents, were you? It's not something you consciously decide."

"I'll take your point into consideration," Quinn said. "Isn't it true that a good part of the time where homicides are concerned, it's often the romantic liaison who's suspected?"

"I'd say that's generally true, yes," DeLuca said. "That's definitely something I need to look into. And as I said, there are indications it was someone she knew, so that tends to increase the odds. For the record, just to correct any misinterpretations, in my experience as a cop, there's no correlation whatsoever between sexual preference and homicidal tendencies. The vast majority of homicides involve heterosexual perpetrators."

"I called Phil LeDoux, just before you arrived," Quinn said. "The general has asked me to attend a briefing tonight. Do you have any idea what that might be about?"

"I do," DeLuca said. "But I should let him explain."

"Well, I'll see you then, I suppose," Quinn said. He paused. "I was going to ask you what you thought the odds were that you'll catch the killer. I don't suppose you can answer that."

"No, I can't," DeLuca said. "The guys BPD have on it are pretty good. They seem to think it may have something to do with organized crime."

"Organized crime?" Quinn said. "What do you mean? You mean the Mafia? I didn't think those people were still around."

"They're still around," DeLuca said. "BPD hasn't told me their reasons yet, but I'm sure they have them. And I'll be there to help them with whatever means the army can bring to bear."

"I'll make any phone call you need me to make," Quinn said. DeLuca nodded in response. "Is there anything else I could do for you?"

"Do you have any recent pictures of Katie?" DeLuca said. "Something I could show around when I ask people questions?"

"I don't," Quinn said. "Katie had something of an aversion to having her picture taken. She always did. She felt cameras were unkind to her, I'm afraid."

"All right then," DeLuca said. "I'll see you tonight. I'm sorry for your loss." He'd never seen the general so much as bowed before, but now he seemed broken, shaken, and lost. It was possible that if he stayed there much longer, DeLuca would see General Joe Quinn fall apart, and he didn't like to see his heroes fall apart, if he could help it, so he said good-bye and walked to his car.

The briefing was held at Hanscom Air Force Base, which was, like most air force bases, nicer than the average army base, with new buildings and shiny-clean facilities. General Philip LeDoux was accompanied by his aide, Captain Martin, as well as by a tech specialist who'd set up a PowerPoint. The conference room was at base headquarters, with walls adorned with framed color photographs of vintage and new aircraft and a large rosewood conference table. There were plain yellow legal pads on the table, a cheap ballpoint pen atop each, and glasses to use to drink water from a crystal pitcher.

Joe Quinn was wearing khaki pants and a windbreaker over a black polo shirt. He was only in his sixties, and looked like he could still kick the ass of anybody who worked for him. DeLuca arrived at the briefing room at the same time that Quinn did. Quinn looked better than he had that morning, DeLuca thought, but not much better. He'd shaved, and his bearing was a bit more erect.

"I'm deeply sorry for your loss, Joe," LeDoux said. "I speak for the entire Pentagon on that."

"Appreciate it, Phil," Quinn said softly. "Words fail to express. It's kind of otherworldly. Not like anything I've been through before, really."

"I can't imagine," LeDoux said. "Unfortunately, it's part of why we're here. Why don't you have a seat? Agent DeLuca, by the way, is someone I've known since we worked together in Germany as very young men, sitting in a Quonset hut listening to East German officials bitch about how Jimmy Carter had pulled out of the Olympics. Agent DeLuca is fully read on and part of a army counterintel special ops team we're putting together under the director of intelligence. He works directly for me, and I asked him to step in this morning and to be here tonight. David, anything new since this morning?"

"I've been spending a lot of time on the phone with my friends at Boston PD," DeLuca said. "Crime Scene hasn't come up with much, I'm afraid. It's definitely a fifty Magnum, so that may lead somewhere, since there haven't been a lot of those things sold yet. There's apparently nothing on the security tapes and no prints on the mirror they used to blind the main camera. This wasn't an impulse killing, obviously. They're searching for other crimes that used mirrors, but they've got nothing so far. The main detective on the job still thinks the shooting may be a mob hit. He hasn't convinced me yet, but he hasn't really told me why he thinks that either. He says your daughter was pretty good at picking winners, so he thinks somebody running a sports book was trying to keep her quiet. To me that sounds like inviting more trouble than you need, but I could be wrong about that."

"Let me tell you why we're here," LeDoux said, "and then we can strategize. Actually, I'm going to bring in a tech specialist to help with the presentation, but we're going to have to teleconference him in because right now he's at the Pentagon. Here's a familiar face for you, David."

A small window appeared in the upper right-hand corner of the plasma screen.

"Joe," LeDoux said, "this is Captain Scott DeLuca with INSCOM/JTIOC. He is also Agent DeLuca's son."

"Good evening, General Quinn," Scottie said. "Hey, Dad."

"Hey, Scooter," DeLuca said. "Captain Scooter, I guess I should say."

"Captain," LeDoux said. "Proceed, please."

They saw four slides simultaneously, photographs of Generals Al Wagner, Pete Masland, Mike O'Hara, and Admiral Ted McNulty.

"You haven't seen any of this on the news yet because we're sitting on it as hard as we can, but it's going to come out very soon," LeDoux said. "These four men were killed within the last twenty-four hours. In order, a car bomb—actually a golf-cart bomb—an attack by a small private plane, a sniper, and a roadside IED. Admiral McNulty was killed in England but the other three were domestic. The attack on Mike O'Hara included his wife. Because they were formerly high-ranking military personnel, CI has been directed to become involved. This comes from the White House. Four attacks in four different parts of the world, all within thirty minutes of each other. They're still pulling together the forensics. We think this is what's coordinating it. Captain . . ."

The next slide was the home page for a Web site, with the letters/numbers "I-4-N-I" rendered in a large decorative font in English, and above it, the same phrase in Arabic, though DeLuca could speak Arabic considerably better than he could read it. In the center of the graphic was the image of a seven-headed snake.

"Eye for an eye," DeLuca read. "And the logo is what?"

"That's a hydra," Scottie said. "In Greek mythology, it was a monster that lived in the swamps of Lerna, in Argos. Cut one head off and immediately another would grow in its place. Deadly breath. Eventually slain by Heracles."

"I knew there was a reason why we sent you to college," DeLuca said.

"Also used to describe a single-node motherboard with multiple orbiting nodes," Scott added, "Intel server board SE7520BD2, Xeon800, dual Giganet, VGA, CPU usually a 2x Xeon 2.8GHz, FSB 800. For whatever that's worth. It's a state-of-the-art Netgear array."

"Many heads," DeLuca said. "Multiple attacks? Is that what it's trying to say? This is a new terrorist Web site?"

"You got it," LeDoux said. "Vengeance is mine. Nothing new about terrorist Web sites, right?"

"There's, what, two thousand of them?" DeLuca said. "And change?"

"More," Scottie said. "We're over four thousand and counting. About three-quarters of them hosted right here in the U.S. A lot of ranting and raving, and until now, maybe the most dangerous function they've had was to raise money. We've got people monitoring all the chat rooms and posting deceptive messages and so on, but so far, they've been relatively harmless, or at least harmless enough that we'd rather monitor them for intel than shut them down. Martyrs get their faces on the Web after they blow stuff up, and it's a good way to disseminate your basic decapitation videos for free or sell them, but no serious damage done."

"Until now?"

"Until now," LeDoux said. "You want to try it in Arabic?"

"English, please," DeLuca said.

Scottie clicked on the English-language icon. They saw:

A CALL TO ACTION:
Brothers! Martyrs! Soldiers of Islam!
Wherever you are, we are one, in spirit and in deed. The Jihad needs you! We need you. The time for talking is over. The time for action is now. We are many millions strong, but know that you and you alone can make a difference as an individual.

Below is a list of American military personnel, retired and active. They have sent bombs

down on your houses. They have killed your
children, your parents and your loved ones.
They are cowards who hide in the sky and send
missiles and bombs raining from above to destroy Islam. They believe they can defeat us.
They believe they cannot be touched.

THEY ARE WRONG!

Use this website to track them down and
kill them in their homes. Kill them, in the same
way that they have killed the people you love.
Any act of violence against them will be smiled
upon by Allah.

It is your duty to your people.

It is your duty to Allah.

"Just so you know," LeDoux said, "we have a dozen
briefings just like this going on right now, around the
country, for Hugh Sheldon, Tony Zinni, Barry McCaf-
frey, Dick Hawley, Wes Clark, Norm Schwarzkopf, Dick
Myers, Joe Prueher, Tommy Franks, Leightan Smith, John
Shalikashvili, and a number of others. This Web site was
up and running for about four hours before we found the
server and pulled it down, but we know they're going to
bounce it from one ISP to another. It'll be back. In four
hours, it received almost a hundred thousand hits, so somebody knew it was coming. We'd picked up the rumors. The
home text is Arabic, but my language people tell me it's
not very good Arabic, so we think the designer could be a
non-Arab, posing as an Arab. It's a MANGO, either way."

"Mango?" Quinn asked.

"Malign non-governmental organization," DeLuca said, decoding LeDoux's intel-speak. "Our foes in the GWOT. 'Global war on terror.' Is somebody thinking the attacks we know about were planned in four hours?"

"No," LeDoux said. "We'll get to that."

"The rhetoric is not so unusual," Scottie said. "'Allah has called upon all the oppressed people of the world and all the holy warriors, yada yada yada,' you know the tune. I'll go straight to the scary part."

Join The Martyrs

Updates

Find U.S. Military Targets In Your Area

Add A Name To the List

Ask The Bomb Doctor

Use Their Technology Against Them

Secure Communications

Weapon Sources/ Technical Support

How To Send Money

Organize A Cell

Support The Refugees

Daily News
American Admiral Killed in Oxford
Jihadists working in Oxford, England, have managed to assassinate retired U.S. Navy Admiral Tel McNulty in a daring night time operation *More* ⇨

Daily News
American General Executed in Florida
Retired U.S. General Peter Masland, responsible for the deaths of over 5000 members of Saddam Hussein's Republican Guard, was successfully executed *More* ⇨

Daily News
Sniper Kills U.S. Marine
While Fishing

Retired U.S. Marine general Michael O'Hara, former commander of U.S. occupation forces in Basra, was struck down by the strong and vengeful hand of Allah when a sniper found him at his vacation cabin. *More* ⇨

Daily News
U.S. General Alexander
Wagner Assassinated By Holy
Martyrs

A pair of Holy Martyrs brought vengeance and destruction to former U.S. General in Hilton Head, South Carolina. *More* ⇨

Links:

⇨ Al-Aqsa Martyrs Brigade @
http://www.kataebaqsa1.com
⇨ HAMAS (Islamic Resistance Movement) @ http://www.palestine-info.info
⇨ Hizballah (Party of God) @ http://www.nasrollah.org
⇨ Palestine Islamic Jihad (PIJ) @ http://www.qudsway.com
⇨ Hamas military wing, Izza Deen al-Qassam http://www.alqassam.info

"Let's see what the Bomb Doctor is up to today," LeDoux said. "Captain, if you would." Scottie clicked on that link. A page appeared displaying a simple question-and-answer format. DeLuca read quickly.

> **Dear Bomb Doctor,**
>   We recently lost our cache of C4 and anticipate a considerable wait to replace it. What can we use in the mean time? **Army of God**.
>
> **Dear Army of God,**
>   In order to truly help you, I would have to know what your intended target is and how you

hope to deliver the bomb to the target. You will want to make sure you use the right explosive for the project. Using an explosive that's too small for the task is usually worse than using too much.

For creating bombs using common substances:

You can make **napalm** by melting soap into gasoline. You will need to heat the gasoline in a double boiler over the stove (but remove the water once it boils to make sure the gasoline doesn't come in contact with the heat source). Add soap flakes or shaved soap bars (laundry or liquid detergent won't work) and stir until the mixture thickens. (click for details)

You can make a **fuel-air bomb** by taking a one gallon glass jug or jar and dropping into it 3 or 4 drops of gasoline, rotating the jar or jug until the inner surface is coated. Explodes when thrown against a hard object and equals about half a stick of dynamite—good for killing people in cars or small rooms. (click for details)

"I'm not making light of this," DeLuca said, "but this information has been on the Web for years. And in books like *The Anarchist's Cookbook*. I'm more interested in the target information."

"As are we," LeDoux said. "I just wanted to impress on you, first, that this thing is trying to be the Amazon or the Google of terrorist sites. The one-stop shopping place for bad ideas. Here's what is concerning us tonight. Scott?"

Scottie clicked, and they saw a gallery of photographs of U.S. military leaders, including all the men LeDoux had mentioned and others. Wagner, McNulty, Masland, and O'Hara already had red slashes across their faces.

"Anybody have a preference?" LeDoux said.

"Click on me," Joe Quinn said. Scottie obliged him. It led to another gallery of thumbnails, including pictures of the general's house in Boston, his summer place in Kennebunkport, his brother and his brother's family, his nieces and nephews, their addresses including maps, phone numbers, class schedules, weekly activities, and favorite places to go or favorite things to do.

"There's no picture of Katie," LeDoux said. "If that's what you were wondering. We're not sure how significant that is. On the other pages, we have family members, friends . . . The files are, well, let's just say astonishingly thorough. And it's all public information, stuff anybody with DSL and the motivation could put together, sitting in a jungle longhouse in the Philippines or wherever, with a satellite uplink and a little ingenuity. None of this is classified. You can use information Web sites like 411 or Infospace or Dogpile, high school yearbook Web sites, dating sites, government sites, genealogy sites, Mormon stuff, public records, credit reports. We had an IW team at DIA run an OPFOR last night to see what sorts of personal information they could come up with. It's not hard. All you need is motivation, and somebody out there has plenty of it."

"IW?" Quinn asked.

"Information warfare," Scottie said. "It's as black ops as it gets right now. New since you left, I believe. There are over two hundred people targeted on the I4NI site, each webbed to a dozen other potential targets. Somebody wants to strike back, and make it personal. Whoever is doing this has a fairly high understanding of the technology and the software involved. Information warfare is the obvious next step. Right now the gap countries where our many enemies reside are catching up technologically a lot faster than they are economically. It's not as asymmetrical as other ways of measuring. Insurgents in Iraq have already used the Web to post bounties on the heads of Iraqi leaders. A hundred thousand for Jaafari, last I checked. Fifty for Bayan Jabr. This is the same thing, on a global scale."

"Are they posting rewards?"

"Just the usual seventy doe-eyed virgins and all that," LeDoux said. "There's a 'Sponsor a Martyr' page where members can offer money for various targets, but when you go there, you get a message saying the page is not yet available. Sort of like putting a contract hit on eBay. We're waiting to see how they expect money to change hands, but we think they know that's the easiest way to get caught, so we're not sure how serious they are about that part of it."

Scottie clicked to the next slide, a diagram showing hundreds of small computer icons, connected by dotted lines to an icon resembling a central shepherd in one direction, and to a larger computer in a second.

"This is how computer crime works," Scottie said. "The smaller computers are called bots, or zombies. Just personal computers, like you or I use at home. They work as proxy servers. The central character there is the zombie herder. A bot is a computer where a program written by the herder has been surreptitiously installed. Spyware works this way. A zombie is like a virus, except it doesn't do anything until it's activated. Herders send out zombie programs, looking for bots to convert, hoping to infect as many computers at they can. People rarely know they've been infected. Herders even swap or trade bots in special chat rooms. The zombie programs are always evolving to slip past the firewalls and antispyware barriers and antivirus stuff. They act, we react, but it's tough because they always go first. So a zombie herder usually sends an e-mail through a proxy server to a corporation, saying pay us $25,000 by Friday or I'll attack your computers. If the person being extorted doesn't pay up, at the given hour the zombie bots come to life and start bombarding his system with messages and queries until his servers overload and he can't do business anymore. IWD says the biggest herds number in the six figures, so far, but that number is most likely growing even as we speak. Imagine if every computer in the Arab world were linked to act jointly against us. Imagine if instead of bots, they became sub-herders looking for bots to drive. We often don't know when it happens because a lot of corporations have figured out it's cheaper to pay the ransom than to have all your systems down for three or four days or hire somebody to protect you. We're pretty sure I4NI is a primary zombie herder, except that they're not asking for money."

"Meaning?" DeLuca asked.

"Meaning at the same time that our people were being attacked in Minnesota and South Carolina and Florida and England . . . and possibly Boston, the computers at DIA and NSA weathered a massive assault. There was no warning or note. They're just trying to hurt us. DIA's not even telling me how much damage was done or how long our systems were down—I've been directed to say only that we did not escape unscathed. We're not sure if it was meant to be a diversion from the physical attacks, or if it was the other way around. We think it was a test. Either they were testing their offensive capabilities, or our defensive capabilities, or both. We don't think we got the full force of what they can do. And we don't want them to know we have defenses other than the ones they've already encountered. The point is that these are the most protected computer systems in the world—if they could touch that, think of the damage they could do to our economy, attacking less protected business systems. They could target the stock exchange. Bank systems. Credit card companies. Equifax. Kmart. The Information Warfare Directorate in the basement of the Pentagon is taking it extremely seriously. They ran a tracesource program and, as I said, we've shut down the initial server, but there's a million servers where I4NI could have bounced to. Closing a server treats only the most minor symptoms."

"Were technology components involved in the other deaths?" DeLuca asked. "In Wagner, Masland, McNulty, or O'Hara?"

"We're looking," LeDoux said. "We think it's possible. Their locations and schedules were all posted on the site. We'd just as soon you stuck to secure phones until this is over, Joe. We just don't know."

"How does this connect to my Katie?" Quinn needed to know.

"We're not positive that it does, Joe," LeDoux said. "Her picture wasn't posted, and as Agent DeLuca has said, there appear to be other possibilities. The Web site is making a lot of different kinds of threats, but right now the main threat seems to be painting the targets for everybody else. Used to be, the public barely knew who our generals were, or if they knew, they had to wait until the history books were written to find out about them. Now the whole world watches. Maybe that's the price we pay for living in an open society. Some countries have secret armies where no one knows who the generals are."

"And you think Katie was targeted? Because of me?"

"Not because of you. You didn't do anything wrong. It's just too soon to say," LeDoux said. "That's what I want Agent DeLuca to find out."

"I do think it was more than a robbery or something random," DeLuca said. "Murder might not necessarily have been part of the plan—it could have been a kidnapping that went sideways. Maybe the Web site posting was a green light."

"I suppose they want me to be afraid," Quinn said. "I'm an old man without any grandchildren. I lost my wife, and now my daughter. If somebody comes to my house and I blow his head off, I'm not going to lose any sleep worrying about what's going to happen to me."

"We're not going to let anyone come to your house, Joe," LeDoux said. "You've worked with Agent DeLuca before. I want you to work with him again. David, I want you and your team on this. We've got other teams taking up other details, but since this is your backyard, I think you're the best person to handle this. I'll get you a copy of the Web site, and we'll keep you informed as to what we find. They're basically taking the Internet and using it against us. We can knock the site down, but the information is going to come back up somewhere. Meanwhile, our best lead, right now, in Boston, is finding the general's daughter's killer. Or killers. We're following every thread we have."

"If there's anything I can do to help," Quinn said.

"You should also know," LeDoux continued, "that we're going on orange alert as of tomorrow morning, based on some chatter we're getting from a variety of sources. Based also on this. As I said, I4NI wants to create the impression that it's coordinating a multipronged attack. Captain?"

Scottie clicked to another page on the I4NI Web site, where they saw a map of the world, with boxes over various cities across the map and large Arabic words at the top.

"This, believe it or not," LeDoux said, "is a page that gives visitors to the site a chance to click on the city they'd like to see attacked with a nuclear weapon. The targets getting the most votes in this country are Boston, New York, San Francisco, and Chicago. Globally, Tel Aviv ranks number one."

"Why is Boston getting voted off the planet ahead of New York?" DeLuca said.

"Some people are saying it's because the coverage of the Sox winning the Series was carried worldwide and made Boston a target as the All-American town."

"I knew there was going to be a downside," DeLuca said. "People are taking this seriously?"

"People aren't dismissing it," LeDoux said.

"Homeland thinks there's a chance something big is going to happen in the next six days," Scottie added. "A broad range of attacks, either on people, on cities, or on computers, or all three at once. If they successfully tie up our computers or take down SIPERNET or INTERPOL. NET, it's going to make it considerably more difficult to stop the other attacks, because then we're back to notepads and trench coats. The orange alert is not classified, obviously, but the rest of this is special access."

DeLuca couldn't help but feel proud of how well and how competently his son was handling his part of the briefing.

"So Joe," LeDoux said, "you work with David on this, okay? We've assigned security details to other generals and their families, so don't worry that you're getting special treatment—we're taking care of our own. David, pull in whoever you need for this. Captain Martin—as always, see that Agent DeLuca wants for nothing. General, if you don't have any further questions, the base commander wanted to meet you and to offer his condolences. I told him when we were done, I'd ask."

"Certainly," Quinn said.

DeLuca asked LeDoux if he could browse the Web site while he waited for Quinn to finish. Once LeDoux was gone, DeLuca clicked down into the "L" section of the I4NI Web site, where he saw, as he'd expected he would, a photograph of LeDoux himself. When he clicked on the image, he saw a page describing the general's family, including his daughter Elizabeth, who was a sophomore at Harvard. DeLuca made a note of the contact information. Whether LeDoux asked for it or not, he intended to make sure Elizabeth, who he hadn't seen since she was small, would be safe as well.

In the meantime, he had a killer to catch.

Chapter Two

"DAVY-BOY," THE VOICE ON THE OTHER END OF the phone said. "I heard you was back from Iraq. How's it goin', man? You come back in one piece?"

"I've been back for a while, actually," DeLuca. "Back and gone and back again. How are you, Jackie?"

The man on the other end of the line was his cousin, Giacomo. Jackie's mother, Eva, had sent her boy to live with DeLuca and his parents when Jackie was fifteen and DeLuca was fourteen, after Jackie's father died of cancer and Jackie became too much for Eva to handle. DeLuca's parents had tried their best to instill discipline and forestall delinquency in David's unruly cousin. DeLuca remembered it as the summer he'd gotten into more trouble than the rest of his life combined. Jackie had been a star on the high school track team, a distance runner who'd made all-state as a sophomore, but he'd let himself go since then. DeLuca had loaned Jackie a thousand dollars, five years ago, and hadn't heard from him since. He hadn't expected to be paid back. It seemed a small price to pay for the peace and quiet it ensured.

"I'm good, I'm good," Jackie said. "You?"

"I went through the windshield of a Humvee when we hit something," DeLuca said. "They have a serious street-light problem."

"That's great, that's great," Jackie said. DeLuca wondered how that was great. Jackie was never much of a listener. "Hey, Davy, you wanna have lunch or something?"

"I'm kind of busy right now, Jackie," DeLuca said. "I'm putting something together." He'd been on the phone to his team, Agents Dan Sykes, Julio Vasquez, and Colleen MacKenzie. They were flying in, and would be assembled by dinnertime. Walter Ford and Sami Jambazian, DeLuca's former partners on the force, both retired but both con-tracted members of the team, would be attending as well. He'd been trying to reach Morrissey, but no callbacks yet.

"Hey, it's noon, you gotta eat something, right?" Jackie said. "Let's get some calzones. I'll pick you up."

"Where are you calling from?" DeLuca asked.

"I'm on the cell," Jackie said. "I'm parked in front of your house."

DeLuca pulled the curtain aside. At the curb, he saw a black Jaguar sedan, and a man waving from the driver's side, smiling.

"Man," Jackie said, "what about that girl in the parking garage, huh? Too bad you're not still on the job. So wha-daya say? Lemme buy you lunch."

"Okay," DeLuca said, alerted now that this was more than a social call. "I'll be out in a sec."

When he turned, he saw his wife. She was wearing her gardening clothes.

"Who was that? Who's in the car?"

"My cousin Jackie," DeLuca said. "He wants to get something to eat. Should I invite him in?"

"No," she said.

"I didn't think so," DeLuca said.

"I thought he was in prison," she said.

"Looks like they let him out," DeLuca said. "What do you got going today?"

"Pulling weeds," she said.

"You pull yours," he said. "I'll have lunch with mine."

The was a dent in the passenger-side door of the Jaguar where Jackie explained he'd backed up with the door open and caught it on a curb. It didn't close all the way, but don't worry about it, he said. He was wearing sneakers, white socks, khaki shorts, a Hawaiian shirt with parrots on it, and a one-size-fits-all Red Sox cap that looked like it had been run over by an Abrams a couple hundred times, worn backwards. He'd been a good-looking kid, and it had been easy to score chicks, hanging out with him at Jones Beach back in the hot summer days of fourteen. The last time DeLuca had seen him, Jackie had looked like shit. Now he looked trim and muscled again. The word in the family about Jackie was, good heart, bad brain, and zero impulse control. He was tanned, his dark hair hanging down out the back of his cap all the way to the gold chain around his neck. He looked ten or fifteen years younger than he deserved to. DeLuca wondered how Jackie was going to play him. That he was going to play him was a given.

"It's great to see you," Jackie said. "You look real good. What, they didn't have doughnuts in Baghdad?"

"Wasn't in Baghdad. I was stationed north of there, at Camp Anaconda. I got back in shape when I reenlisted, after Eileen," DeLuca said, referring to his sister, who'd been working in the World Trade Center during 9/11. He felt something wet under his left arm and looked down to see the head of a small brown dog, the size of a large cat, with wiry hair, much of it falling in front of his eyes. The dog was smiling.

"That's Wesley. Wesley the Westy. Don't look at me—my ex-girlfriend named him, before she left me with him. He's okay—he just wants food. You'd think I never fed him. How's Tommy doing?" Jackie asked in reference to DeLuca's brother-in-law, giving the dog a shot with his right elbow to drive him into the backseat. "He was NYPD, right?"

"Tom's with Homeland Security these days," DeLuca said. His brother-in-law, after losing Eileen, had transferred from the post-9/11 NYPD terrorism task force when DHS was formed. Tom had always politely held his tongue, whenever the subject of Jackie came up. "You look good too. You lifting?"

"Some," Jackie said. "I'm running a little bit. Couple miles a day. I still got a gut but now it's surrounded by muscle. You know what my problem is? When I was younger, I had a silicone belly implant because I wanted to look more mature, but now I'm thinking of having it removed."

DeLuca smiled. Jackie had always been able to make him smile, even when they were in deep shit as kids.

"When did you start?"

"I started at Walpole," Jackie said. "I figured I might as well make something out of myself, if I was going to be sitting out a few years. Everybody in there was on steroids. You shoulda seen these guys. Fucking huge. You know what I like about the steroid thing in baseball? All my heroes are intact. You see what these pumped-up guys are doing now, like Barry Bonds hitting seventy-three home runs, and you say, what would Teddy Ballgame have hit on steroids? Or Mickey, or Hank Aaron, or Ruth, or whoever? And you can't answer the question, but you know it would have been more, so breaking those old records is meaningless. We'll never know. My heroes are intact. No one will ever beat 'em. By the way, I have it on good authority that before Jose Canseco started taking steroids, he was a hundred-and-thirty-five-pound East German female shot putter named Helga. That's how much that stuff changes you. I never touched the shit, but I knew a lot of guys that did."

They'd never talked about the reasons why Jackie had gone to prison, but DeLuca had pulled his cousin's file on his own, years ago. There'd been a shooting during a liquor store robbery where Jackie had been a witness. He knew the killer, but had refused to give the man up in court. DeLuca understood that Jackie's choice had been to hold his tongue and go to prison for contempt, or tell what he knew and be killed by the shooter, who was, according to the street and what DeLuca could find out, a hitter out of the old Anguillo crime family. Jackie had always been on the edge of things, working the angles, coming up with schemes to avoid becoming "a nine-to-five schmuck" and priding himself on knowing people "from all walks of life," meaning hoods and criminals and made guys and Cosa Nostra wannabes, among whom he took his place, as far as DeLuca could tell.

At a stoplight, the black Jaguar stalled. Jackie had to curse several times and hit the dashboard twice with the palm of his hand before the car would start again. DeLuca saw discarded racing forms in the backseat, amid the other debris, empty Styrofoam cups, McDonald's bags, crushed cigarette packs, and Wesley smiling from the center of the pile.

"How the horses treating you?" he asked.

"I'm about even, I think," Jackie said, repeating what all the inveterate loser-gamblers DeLuca had ever known always said, guys who'd lost their homes, families, and jobs betting on horses or dogs but who still somehow figured they were "about even."

"Well, that's good," DeLuca said, not wanting to get into it.

"Listen," Jackie said, "I had a question—you hear about Katie Quinn? The sports babe?"

DeLuca had been waiting for this. "The woman on the all-night sports talk show?" he said. "From the parking garage."

"Yeah," Jackie said.

"Why do you ask?" DeLuca said. "You knew her?"

"I felt like I did," Jackie said. "I've had insomnia for the last couple years. Since Walpole. You sorta sleep with one eye open. I've been listening to her show for years. Off and on. Didn't you used to guard her old man during the first Gulf War or something? I thought I remembered that."

"I did," DeLuca said. "How'd you hear about her?"

"You know, people," Jackie said casually. "People talk. I got a buddy whose brother is with BPD. You still doing counterintelligence? What is that? That like being an MP or something?"

"MPs just guard stuff," DeLuca said. "So what are people saying?"

"Nothing," Jackie said. "Just that it happened. So what's counterintelligence? Is that like the army version of the FBI?"

"Something like that," DeLuca said.

"You still know people on the force, though, right?" Jackie asked. "You were like their golden boy or something, right?"

"I still know a few," DeLuca said. "Except I'm a Fed now, and cops hate Feds."

"I hear that," Jackie said. "But if you had to, you could make a few calls, right? Let me tell ya, I wouldn't ask, but I got a friend who knew her, who sorta worked with her, and he was asking me if I knew anybody, so I thought of you."

"I thought you said you had a buddy whose brother was on the force."

"Yeah, I did, I said that," Jackie acknowledged, "but the guy, the brother, is a nobody. We were hoping, my friend was, that we knew somebody who had some juice."

"Who's your friend?" DeLuca asked.

"This guy, Freddy," Jackie said. "He's a real nice guy, real salt-of-the-earth fuck, but he heard about his partner Katie and he wanted to know so he called me because he knows I know people, so to speak."

"How's this Freddy know her?" DeLuca asked.

"They had a business," Jackie said.

"A business?"

"A moving business," Jackie said. "She was more like an investor. Anyway, I promised Freddy I'd ask, 'cause I owe him a favor. Actually I hired him as a mover, that's how I met him. But he's a real nice guy."

"Maybe I should talk to Freddy," DeLuca said. "How do I get in touch with him?"

"I'll give you his cell," Jackie said. "You could call his business but I don't think he's there. It's called Hard Moves."

"Hard Moves?"

"Yeah," Jackie said, handing DeLuca a card. "They guarantee to get your stuff out in an hour. It's for people in a hurry who don't care how much shit breaks. He puts together a crew of however many guys it takes, mostly unemployed musicians—you hear the one about the kid who tells his father, 'When I grow up, I wanna be a musician,' and his father says, 'Sorry kid, but you can't do both'? Anyway, I wrote down his number for you on the card. I'd really appreciate anything you could do. I'll give you my cell. I'm living on Hull Street in Copps Hill, but I don't have a land line. I figured, why bother? I talk on this thing all the time anyway."

When Jackie pulled the car over to the curb, DeLuca realized he was in front of his own house. Bonnie was on her knees in the front garden, pulling crabgrass from between the hostas.

"I thought we were going to have lunch," DeLuca said.

"Gee, I'd really love to, but I'm going to have to take a rain check," Jackie said. "I've got a bunch of errands, so I think I'll just eat at the drive-through. Hi, Bonnie—how you doing?" he called out.

Bonnie turned and waved, smiling insincerely, then went back to her work. DeLuca realized that Jackie was staring, somewhat longingly, at his wife's ass.

"Anyway," Jackie said, breaking his reverie, "I'll be in touch, then. I owe this guy, so I'm glad I could facilitate. Say hi to Scott. Is he home?"

"He's in D.C.," DeLuca said.

"Well, tell him I said hello," Jackie said before driving off. "I'll be in touch."

"Jackie," DeLuca said. "What's Freddy's last name?"

"King," Jackie said. "Freddy King. You'll like him. Thanks again."

From his home office, DeLuca called his friend Kaz at police headquarters and asked him to run a name for him. Kazuo Takata had been a detective who'd worked the Anguillo family with DeLuca, back in the eighties, and still knew more about the activities of Italian crime families in Boston than anybody on the force.

"David DeLuca," Kaz said with surprise in his voice. "I thought you'd moved on to bigger and better."

"Bigger, anyway," DeLuca conceded. "Where've they got you these days?"

"Chinatown," Takata said. "Because of my heritage."

"I thought you were Japanese," DeLuca said.

"I thought so too," Takata said. "What can I do for you?"

DeLuca explained that he was working the Katie Quinn case on behalf of the army, and that he'd gotten a strange call from his cousin, who was asking more questions about the crime than he had any right to. DeLuca asked Kaz if he knew what his cousin was up to these days.

"Jackie D.'s your cousin?" Kaz said. "So he's the black sheep?"

"It woulda been me if he hadn't filled the position first," DeLuca said. Takata asked him to wait a moment while he called up the file. He was able to confirm that there hadn't been any new entries in Jackie's file for over a year.

"Pretty much what I thought," Takata said. "I got a guy who has Jackie occasionally handling payoffs for a sports book on Commercial Street. Nothing heavy-duty. No collection or muscle stuff. Strictly delivering envelopes to the winners. They're probably paying him back for standing up at Walpole by giving him a job every now and then. And they know they can trust him because they know how scared shitless he was the first time. That would be how I'd read it. Jackie gets to hang out with people who think they're important and then he gets props from his peeps the next time he's having risotto on Hanover."

"Whose sports book?"

"Guy named Joey D'Angelo," Takata said. "Runs with Vinnie P.'s crew. I heard the books in this town took a huge beat when the Sox finally won the pennant. They've been getting rich on Red Sox Nation stupidity for years, so they were taking bets at thirty-to-one and better after the Yankees won game three nineteen to whatever it was. This is probably the only town in America where your team is down three games to the Yankees and the last one is a rout and the money is still pouring in on the Sox to rally. Who'da thunk, right? You can guess how Joey D'Angelo and all the others must have felt when the Sox took the next eight games."

"Serves 'em right for lacking faith," DeLuca said.

"What's Jackie have to do with Katie Quinn?" Kaz asked.

"That's what I'd like to know," DeLuca said. "I'm on the case since only this morning and already my phone rings. He says he knows her business partner and was asking as a favor."

"Why's he asking you?"

"Exactly," DeLuca said. "He told me he remembered that I worked with Joe Quinn during Desert Storm. Which may be true, I suppose. Jackie always remembers what he wants to remember. He's not stupid. He just wants people to think he is."

"What'd you do with Joltin' Joe Quinn?" Takata asked.

"Special protection unit," DeLuca said. "He had trouble staying in the Humvee, so we had to go with him. So Joey's with Vinnie Potatoes?"

"Vincent Pastorelli," Kaz pronounced. "He's a boss now. When you knew him, he was just a punk, I'll bet."

"You got it," DeLuca said.

"We heard he clipped a couple guys from Winter Hill," Kaz said. "I heard he baked them alive in a pizza oven because they called him a dumb pizza-eating wop. But that was just a rumor. Probably one Vinnie started himself. Though he is a psychopath, no question."

"Do you think there's a connection between Katie Quinn and the mob?" DeLuca asked. "That's what Wexler was saying."

"Wexler's not saying much to me," Takata said. "I heard there could be something. That's all I heard. Something about surveillance. I'd tell you if I knew more. Things are getting sort of compartmentalized around here. Wexler's already put it out that anybody who talks to you is on his shit list. I hate to admit, there are people around here who that matters to. He's in line. Nobody wants to piss him off."

"Thanks, Kaz," DeLuca said. "You mind if I call you again?"

"Not at all," Takata said. "I got my twenty in a month ago. I'm just finishing up a few things and then I'm gone, so I'm bulletproof around here."

"Where you going?" DeLuca said.

"Las Vegas," Takata said. "I know a guy who has a casino security business. They always need Chinese. Especially now that the Chinese tourists have money."

"And you, coming from the Tokyo part of China."

"There you go," Takata said.

DeLuca was surprised to find an e-mail from Walter Ford in his in-box. Walter had been a helluva detective in his day, and had been teaching criminology courses at Northeastern since retiring, the most patient, dogged, and persistent man DeLuca had ever met, and a good friend. He'd sent him a request only an hour earlier, asking Ford to pull together information on Katie Quinn, her telephone records, and whatever else he could find.

David,

Looking forward to seeing you tonight. It's been too long, plus I think I'm getting what my grandchildren call "very close" veins from sitting too much.

Attached, you will find Katie Quinn's phone records. I've run a cursory analysis and will be performing a more thorough one shortly. Of note, you will see, highlighted in red, the telephone numbers of a variety of local and national sports figures, including Danny Ainge with the Celtics, Theo Epstein with the Sox, Tom Brady, Curt Schilling, also Allen Iverson, John Elway, Jeff Gordon and a couple more, agents/publicists etc. One is a high school kid in Texas who they say has a 100+ mph fastball and he's only 15. This was something she did every day, to get the inside poop with the various teams for her show. Important here, I think, is that the average length of the calls that go through is about half an hour, meaning nobody was giving her the brush off, also that as far as I can tell, these are private numbers—she wasn't going "through channels" like some rookie. She knew people.

More significant, I think, highlighted in blue, you will find the names of sixteen men and one woman, all called in a block of time on the day of the crime between six and ten pm. I ran the names through SIPERNET, just to see what turned up. The names of all sixteen men turned up in the system as having restraining orders out against them by their wives or girlfriends, and the woman on the list recently took out a restraining order against her boyfriend. I logged into those sixteen names, and three I couldn't access, but with the rest, I cross-correlated their logs against Katie's going back a month. None had called her directly, but all of them had called the numbers, some repeatedly, of the women who'd taken out the restraining orders, and all of those women had called Katie. She had, by the way, a permanent block on caller I.D. on her home phone. I don't know what to make of this, but I think it's statistically significant.

Attached, as well, are her library and video store records. I have to tell you that I'm a little bit uncomfortable passing this on, only because to my mind it crosses a line, but this is what comes up when you punch in her name, so if everybody else knows it, you should too. I don't know if you've been keeping up to date, but as you probably heard, our handsome rock-jawed governor is positioning himself to run for president on the Republican ticket (obviously—duh) so he's trying to position himself in a variety of ways, claiming, for example, to be a "moderate" on abortion even though he's been on the record as opposing it for the last twenty years. The smart money says it'll never happen because the evangelical far-right would never recognize a Mormon. Anyway, germane to our purposes is that he has established a statewide database which he is calling simply Fusion which he hopes will make Massachusetts the most advanced state in the nation in terms of homeland security, because he's going to need to appear tough on terrorists etc. if he gets the nomination. They've got private 1099 sub-contractors from here to Haverhill working data-entry and MIS jobs to get the thing up to speed. Fusion (Commonwealth Fusion Center), when it's completed, will link all the public and many of the hitherto-fore (bet you didn't think I knew how to use the word "hitherto-fore") private records on residents of the state, including library book loans, video rentals, credit reports, telephones, medical records, charitable donations, travel (if you use EZ-Pass, they can figure out where you've been), tax returns etc. Raytheon got the contract to write the software, $2.2 mil. Some people are upset, but most either don't really know what's going on, or they think if it stops terrorists, then good. I have to say I find the added access useful, but it still creeps me out somehow. Maybe I'm just old.

Anyway, you will notice that Katie Quinn liked to rent lonely woman videos and romances. *Sleepless in Seattle*, *When Harry Met Sally*, *The Notebook*, *Rebecca*, *Love Letters* etc. Recently checked out books include many that one might describe as self-help, including *The Dance of Anger* and *Everything I Need to Know I Learned from My Cat*, a lot of self-esteem-boosting books, as well as much "chick-lit." The records are not,

I should note, up to date and there's a gap for the last three months. She also took out a book and a cassette tape on learning to speak Serbian (travel plans?) and one on writing your own will, whatever that might mean. Note that nowhere in her pleasure reading or home viewing is there anything about sports.

That's it for now. See you tonight.

Walter

DeLuca was about to log off when an Instant Message window popped up on his screen. It was from his son, Scott, at JTIOC Pentagon, "Jay-tock" in the new parlance, short for Joint Task-force Intelligence Operation Command, linking INSCOM to DHS.

CaptScottDeLuca: Busy?
DavidDeLuca: As ever. Your mother wants me to mow the lawn. Good job at the briefing, by the way.
CaptScottDeLuca: Sorry to interrupt but it's important. Go to www.I4NI.org/targets/deluca/hg756544.html immediately.

DeLuca clicked on the link, which brought him to the Web site General LeDoux had briefed them on earlier. On this particular page, DeLuca saw several images, including a crude pencil drawing of himself, which he recognized as the wanted poster that had circulated in the area of Iraq known as the Sunni Triangle, and around the town of Balad and Camp Anaconda, where DeLuca had worked, tracking down members of the Ba'ath Party and Saddam's regime on the black list, talking to people on the gray list and the white list as well. The wanted poster hadn't bothered him, until it got a man who'd borne a striking resemblance to him killed by a sniper during a raid on a house in the town of Ad Dujayl. They'd never found the shooter, though they'd found the person on the base who'd been supplying information to the insurgents. The second image was a photograph someone had taken of him without his knowledge, somewhere in Iraq, a pair of date palms in the background and DeLuca in his Kevlar and full battle rattle. That someone had taken his picture without his knowing it disturbed him, as did the paragraph describing him as someone believed to be a leader of a special ops team of intelligence agents.

What disturbed him even more were the other two photographs. One was of his house, taken from the street in daylight, beneath which was listed his address and home phone number, the name of the grocery store where he shopped, the closest theater, the Burlington Mall where he shopped, the church that Bonnie kept trying to get him to attend, the Blockbuster Video where they rented DVDs, the corner liquor store, and the names of both his neighbors. The fourth and final image on the page was a thumbnail of Bonnie. He clicked to enlarge. In the picture, she was wearing khaki shorts and a blue polo shirt with a red bandana on her head. He zoomed in one more time to be sure. He noticed the front porch in the background.

He looked out the window, to where his wife was still working in the garden. She was wearing khaki shorts and a blue polo shirt with a red bandana on her head.

The picture had been taken that morning, from across the street.

CaptScottDeLuca: You still there?

"Bonnie?" DeLuca called from the front porch. He scanned the house across the street, and the one next to it, and the gap in between them where, in the distance, a wooded hillside led up to a park. Amid the leaves, he thought he saw, ever so briefly, a flash of light, the sunlight reflected off the lens of a sniperscope, perhaps, or someone's sunglasses—or was that just his imagination? The hillside was the most obvious sniper position. He felt the hairs rising on the back of his neck. He looked up and down the street for car bombs, but all the cars were familiar to him, and there was no traffic. The neighbors had their trash and recyclables on the curb a day early—was there an IED hidden inside the blue plastic bin? The neighbors across the street always put their trash out early. It was part of what he didn't like about them. Still.

"What?" Bonnie called back.

A decorative stone wall edged his property, the wall at least a hundred and fifty years old, according to the real estate agent who'd sold him the house, though the house itself wasn't that old. DeLuca moved back and forth, keeping the brick column between himself and the sniper position while trying to present a more favorable target than his wife. She was pulling weeds from among the tiger lilies just inside the wall. If somebody had been waiting for a shot, and hadn't shot yet, it was probably because the shooter was hoping for a twofer.

"I want you to lie down," DeLuca said, still moving, his Beretta in his right hand, semi-concealed.

"Yeah, right," she said without looking up. "In your dreams."

Down the street, a kid on a skateboard was coming toward them.

"Bonnie . . ."

"Not right now, David, really," she said.

"Uncle Mike wants you to lie down," he interrupted. He hadn't used their private code word in years. During Desert Storm, in 1991, a time before every other soldier had his own personal SAT phone and could call home anytime he wanted to, the army had tried to limit and control the amount of information that flowed from the combat zones. E-mail had been strictly monitored, and soldiers had only fifteen minutes a day to talk on the phone, during which time a government censor would be listening in, ready to terminate any conversation that appeared to be veering into sensitive areas. DeLuca was never able to tell his wife exactly where he was or what he was doing, and when the conversation started to approach anything classified, he would say, "I'll have to ask Uncle Mike," or "Tell Uncle Mike . . ." and then they'd change the subject before they were cut off. "Mike" was short for "Microphone"—neither one of them had an uncle named Mike.

"What?" Bonnie said, pausing a beat before she understood, seeing the gun in his hand. She lay down on the ground, confused and scared. She mouthed the word "What?" again.

"Stay down and stay as close to the wall as you can until I tell you it's safe to get up," he said, taking cover himself behind the brick porch column at the top of the steps. The more thought he gave it, the surer he was that the attack would come from a sniper. If DeLuca moved to his right, he would be exposed for about ten or fifteen feet before the house across the street would provide coverage. Were this a more traditional military operation, he would have moved back into the house, perhaps used the back door to circle around and flank the hill across the street, but as it

was, he couldn't leave his wife alone. He was grateful for
the stone walls of New England, and for the brick house,
one Bonnie hadn't liked at first. He'd told her he wanted to
buy it because he'd painted houses to work his way through
college and swore when he became a homeowner that he'd
buy something he wouldn't have to paint, but deep down
he'd known, even then, that the world was full of wolves
both bad and big, and that houses that couldn't be huffed,
puffed, or blown down were good investments.

He had his cordless phone in his other hand and was
about to dial 911 when three shots clipped the brick near
his head, shattering the support column.

He hit the deck.

A ricocheting bullet or a brick shard smashed the picture window, sending glass flying. He hadn't heard a report or seen a muzzle flash, suggesting the shooter had
used a suppressor of some kind.

He waited a moment.

He lifted a pillow cushion above the porch railing, hoping to draw fire.

When none was forthcoming, he bolted across the street.
He gestured to Bonnie to stay down, took the street in a
second, the neighbor's yard in a few more, their little dog
yapping at him from the end of its wire run as he crossed.

He jumped the cyclone fence and scrambled through
the underbrush, sumac, dogwood, maple, losing his foot-
ing once in the carpet of decaying leaves. He ran up the
hill, toward the park.

He heard a car starting above him, and then the screech
of tires.

When he got to the top of the hill, he burst out of the
brush and ran onto the road in time to see a car speed-

ing away. He saw a white or possibly silver sedan, but it was too far away to tell the make or model. He bent over, hands on his knees, to catch his breath. Perhaps when he was younger, he thought, he would have run faster, would have seen the car.

Then again, when he was younger, he might not have recognized the danger as quickly, and then he'd be dead.

"Are you going to tell me what just happened?" Bonnie asked when he returned, rising and brushing the dirt from her shirt and shorts.

"I'd like you to pack a bag," DeLuca said. "I can come back if you forget something. I'll explain inside."

"David . . ."

"I'll explain inside," he said.

"David, you're bleeding," she said.

In the mirror in the front hall, he saw where a piece of flying brick had cut him above and behind his right eye. He went to the kitchen and grabbed a wad of paper towels to stanch the bleeding.

In his study, his computer had switched to screensaver mode, a picture of himself, Bonnie, and Scott when Scott was only four years old, the three of them posing on the deck of Barnacle Billy's lobster pound in Ogunquit, back in happier days, a Fourth of July vacation before 9/11, and before they had to cancel the fireworks to save the sand plovers. Behind the screensaver, there was a question on his computer screen.

CaptScottDeLuca: Dad? You still there? Everything all right?
DavidDeLuca: Sorry. Everything's good. I had to take care of something. Not to worry.

CaptScottDeLuca: You see the Web site?

DavidDeLuca: Yeah.

CaptScottDeLuca: We keep pulling it down but it pops back up.

DavidDeLuca: What do you make of the imagery?

CaptScottDeLuca: The ones of you and Team Red were random. Somebody taking pictures of you without your knowing it. Ten pictures, ten different cameras, two film that was scanned/digitized. The ones of Mom/house were 5 megapixels, 10x lens.

DavidDeLuca: Not a camera phone?

CaptScottDeLuca: They don't get that high. Yet.

DavidDeLuca: I'm thinking pix were downloaded to a BlackBerry/PDA/CIM or phone of some sort and sent wireless to post on the site.

CaptScottDeLuca: Good guess. There's a webmaster somewhere.

DavidDeLuca: Can you find out where?

CaptScottDeLuca: We're *trying.*

DavidDeLuca: Those pix were taken this morning. We had a visitor.

CaptScottDeLuca: What do you mean, "visitor"?

DavidDeLuca: No major damage. Mostly glass. Your mother is going to be staying at Caroline's, at least for tonight. I'm going to get her an encrypted phone until this blows over.

CaptScottDeLuca: I thought Caroline hated you.

DavidDeLuca: She does.

CaptScottDeLuca: Any port in a storm.

DavidDeLuca: Yup. There's relocation housing available at Ft. Bragg, so I'm going to send her there until this thing gets straightened out.

CaptScottDeLuca: Bragg? Mom hates Bragg.

DavidDeLuca: I know.

CaptScottDeLuca: The PX there is an entire shopping mall.

DavidDeLuca: She knows.

CaptScottDeLuca: I'll talk to her.

DavidDeLuca: Don't. We'll deal. Are *you* on the Web site?

CaptScottDeLuca: Not that I can find. So far so good. It isn't clear where I4NI is getting their data.

DavidDeLuca: It's out there. You can be tied to me. When I co-signed for the car loan on the MG, for only one example. I would not stay in your apartment, if I were you. Are you armed?

CaptScottDeLuca: You tried to tell me not to buy that piece of shit, but I wouldn't listen. Yes, I have a sidearm. I could probably get a room at the BOQ at McNair if you think that would make you sleep better.

DavidDeLuca: It would. Do it. I have to call the glass company.

CaptScottDeLuca: I almost forgot. You need to report ASAP to the head of the Intel Analysis Unit, East Coast FBI Joint Task Force on Terrorism. They were having conniptions when they thought we were end-running them. Don Massey, room 754, 7th floor at 2 Center Plaza.

DavidDeLuca: I know where the FBI offices are. Do I really have to work with the Feds on this?

CaptScottDeLuca: You *are* the Feds on this.

DavidDeLuca: I keep forgetting.

CaptScottDeLuca: Good luck. With Mom.

DavidDeLuca: Roger that.

Chapter Three

HE BOOKED A ROOM AT THE COOPER HOTEL, because he needed to be downtown, and moved the meeting scheduled for that evening there, contacting MacKenzie and Sykes and Vasquez and the others using his CIM, the new army-issued Critical Information Module they'd tested in Africa, a pocket PC that did everything his desktops ever did, though this one had a function the one he'd tested in Africa lacked, a ten-megapixel digital camera. The army planned to issue the CIMs with the intention of making every soldier an autonomous intelligence-gathering unit, recording interviews, taking pictures and biometrics of suspected insurgents, locations, that sort of thing. In theory, it sounded promising. In practice, DeLuca wondered just how much intelligence the army was going to be able to digest, given the problems with analysis at the current levels. In practice, he had reason to believe if you gave every soldier a digital camera with a satellite uplink, you were going to get an awful lot of pictures of people's asses and genitals.

When he stopped by the offices of WSPO 690 AM, on the top floor of a ten-story building in Haymarket Place, he was told that the tapes of the previous night's show had been taken by the police, and that if anybody inquired about them, they needed to go through Captain Frank Wexler. "Dan the Man," a.k.a. "Dan the Man the Sports Fan," a.k.a. "Downtown Danny Rhodes," generally didn't show up at the station until midnight, DeLuca was told. He was taping a TV show called *Red Sox This Week* at Fox, the receptionist said, and between then and the show, he was quite likely to be found at Murphy's Irish Steakhouse on Washington Street—did DeLuca need directions?

He didn't. He'd been to Murphy's a number of times before, the pub positioned more or less at the crossroads of downtown Boston, midway between Emerson College, the theater district, Chinatown, and the club district.

It was less than a mile to the FBI offices at 2 Center Plaza, so he decided to walk and take a cab back to the Cooper if he found himself in a hurry. He showed his badge and credentials at the security desk and told the officer he had an open appointment to see Don Massey. While he waited, he looked through the tinted bulletproof glass at the plaza, the courthouse, the JFK Federal Building across the way, and the Tip O'Neill Federal Building. He wondered, during an orange terrorism alert, how many of the people he saw on the plaza were actually undercover police. He noted the concrete security pylons and a conspicuous contingent of motorcycle cops. Even so, a centrally placed car or truck bomb of significant size could do more damage than what occurred at the Murrah Federal Building in Oklahoma City. They'd been discussing various plans to increase plaza security when he'd quit the force.

The officer handed him back his B's and C's and said, "Seventh floor, to the left." A man on the elevator who DeLuca made to be a young FBI agent was listening to music on his iPod. He was standing to DeLuca's left, staring up at the floor numbers as they illuminated.

"Did it ever occur to you that listening to music could be a security risk?" DeLuca said to the man, staring straight ahead. "What if I were talking on my cell phone about a plot to blow up Fanueil Hall? You'd miss the whole thing, wouldn't you?"

The man was completely oblivious. DeLuca looked directly into the lens of the overhead security camera that he knew was recording them.

"I think somebody should talk to this kid," he said. "I'd do it myself but I don't want to harsh his mellow."

He winked at the camera.

He found room 754 and announced his presence at the reception desk. The woman there was tall, just under six feet, DeLuca guessed, and strikingly beautiful.

"Would you tell Agent Donald Massey, if he has a minute, that Special Agent David DeLuca with army counterintelligence is here to see him? Thanks. And I could really use a cup of coffee if there is any."

The woman looked at him a moment, as if DeLuca had asked for more than he deserved, and perhaps she wasn't the kind of secretary who fetched people coffee, but he was exhausted and he needed a jolt of caffeine.

"Cream or sugar?" she asked him.

"Just cream," he said.

"I'll be right back," she told him.

When she returned, she carried two cups, handing one to DeLuca. DeLuca thanked her.

"I apologize if I've treated you like a waitress," he said. "I usually get my own coffee. I think I'm going through caffeine withdrawal."

"That's all right," she said. "I was getting a cup anyway. Does Mr. Massey know you're coming?"

"I gather," DeLuca said.

"What is this in regards to, may I ask?"

"The Katie Quinn case," DeLuca said, lowering his voice conspiratorially. "Just between you and me, they told me he's got his panties in a twist because I hadn't checked with him first, so I guess I'm here to eat crow."

"Just a minute," the woman said, entering the office.

DeLuca waited.

A minute later, the door opened and the blonde woman told him he could come in.

Once inside, he saw that the office was empty.

"You want me to wait in here?" he asked.

"No," the woman said, taking a seat behind the desk. "We can get started. I'm Dawn Massey."

She extended her hand. DeLuca shook it. He could have made an omelet big enough to feed the 27th Infantry from the amount of egg he had on his face.

"And you needn't concern yourself with the state of my panties," she said. "I'm fine in that department."

"Dawn with a 'w'?" DeLuca said.

She nodded.

"Apparently I've gotten some bad information."

"In your line of work," she told him, "that's more than a little concerning."

"I'm ready for my crow now," he told her. "Two helpings, apparently."

"You sound like you've eaten it before," she said.

"Actually, I think it's one of the MREs they gave us in Iraq," he said. "I do apologize for the misunderstanding. I actually came to be of whatever help I can."

"Well, that's good to know," she said in a tone he took to be more than a little condescending. She clicked for two seconds on the laptop on her desk, then folded the screen down to give him her full attention. "You can start by telling me why the army is interfering with my case. It's hard enough, working with Boston PD."

"Have you talked to General LeDoux, by any chance?" DeLuca suggested. "He might be able to answer that better than I could."

"I don't want to hear it from the Pentagon," she said. "I want to hear it from you. You're the one making phone calls and having your man Ford digging into computer records."

He was tempted to tell her he was also the one who'd been shot at that afternoon, and that the large Band-Aid on his forehead was not there for decoration, but he decided if she wanted to know anything, she would have to ask for it directly, unless she changed her tone.

"Yes, Walter works for me," DeLuca said. "I would respectfully suggest that if you want to know what Walter is doing, all you have to do is ask him. You don't have to put him under surveillance."

"I'm not so interested in your suggestions right now," she said. "My task is to gather intelligence on terrorist activities and write reports to the head of bureau counterterrorism. If I have to clear the way to do my job, I will."

DeLuca took two deep breaths. Massey's panties weren't just in a twist—her thong was a veritable pretzel. He'd learned that the best way to deal with angry people was to slow them down, and more than anything, to not get angry yourself. It had worked with countless angered and grieving Iraqis. It hadn't worked all that well with

Bonnie, negotiating her transit to Fort Bragg, but there were plenty of days when nothing worked with Bonnie. He took another deep breath, speaking in slow, measured terms.

"I think," he told her, "that if you and I aren't going to work together, then I should just leave now, but if we are going to work together, we need to start over. It's my fault for getting off on the wrong foot, but it's going to be your fault if we stay on it. Walter Ford was solving murder cases when you still had bunnies on your pajamas. And for the record, if you're having trouble working with Boston PD, then people like Walter and myself can help you. We were both on the force and we both know people there. So, do you wanna make nice and be friends, or do you want to chew me out? Because frankly, I get enough of that at home."

She looked at him for a moment.

"I agree with you about getting off on the wrong foot," she said at last. "I officially and personally apologize. The FBI doesn't have much experience, working with the army in domestic cases. And as far as I can tell, Katie Quinn is still a civilian domestic case. I spent the night getting up to speed on General Wagner and General Masland and the others, but even if the I4NI Web site targets military personnel, the fact that they're all retired makes them civilians, correct? And the FBI handles civilian crimes. Your jurisdiction is restricted to army bases. Or do I have that wrong?"

"I have a cursory understanding of the posse comitatus laws and the new allowances under the Patriot Act, but I'm no expert on jurisdictions or legal distinctions," DeLuca said. "I didn't mean to step on any toes. I was asked to look into the case by INSCOM. Plus, I used to work with General Quinn, so there's a personal connection. And for the record, I was shot at this morning, and I'm CI operational, if there's any question about whether or not only civilians are being targeted. I'm not retired. And there are men posted on the Web site who are still active duty."

"It's not that I don't want your help," Dawn Massey said. "I'm just trying to establish the ground rules. You were just at the radio station?"

DeLuca wondered who'd been following him, or how she knew.

"I was, but Dan the Man wasn't there. Frank Wexler has the tapes of last night's show. I was going to ask him if I could listen to them, but I'm not holding my breath waiting for him to cooperate."

"Why's that?"

"We don't get along," DeLuca said. "He's a turd. He's been kissing every ass in sight and sucking more— Excuse me."

"Don't edit yourself on my behalf," Massey said. "I grew up with five brothers. I'm no shrinking violet."

"Anyway, he was campaigning for a promotion, while I was being groomed by Commissioner Halliday to take his place. The mayor would have had to have approved it, of course. Anyway. Wexler hates me because he thought Mom liked me best. That I was getting special treatment. And I suppose I was. But it was only because I'm not a turd."

"Yes, but the real turds are always the last to know, aren't they?" Massey said. "If you don't believe me, I can give you the number of my ex-husband. And if it makes you feel any better, Frank Wexler and I don't get along either. He's telling us it's organized crime."

"I heard there's a connection," DeLuca said. "I don't know quite what, yet. It seems unlikely. I worked on the Anguillo thing, years ago, so I think I might know some of the players, if it was. I also, just so you know, helped put Mickey O'Brien away. You should know that, up front."

O'Brien was the FBI agent who'd gone to prison for taking payouts from the Irish mob in Boston, later tipping them off when the arrest warrants went out for them. The notorious criminal Jimmy Keenan, brother of the former head of the state senate and at one time the top mobster in Boston, was still on the run, thanks to O'Brien's tip. The crime they actually convicted the FBI agent of was taking $7,000 in cash from Keenan, money O'Brien had used to pay for an operation for his beloved dog, a ten-year-old basset hound named Buttercup (the papers loved that one) that had cancer. It wasn't exactly like O'Brien had lined his own pockets, but still, a bribe was a bribe.

"I have no problem with that," Dawn Massey said. DeLuca was still trying to get over how attractive she was, and how young. She was somewhere between thirty and thirty-five, his best guess, but she probably still got carded in liquor stores.

"What can you tell me about I4NI?" he asked. "Is it Al Qaeda, or somebody else?"

"What's your hunch?" she asked. "I'm curious."

"Somehow, I don't think so," DeLuca said. "It's like they're subcontracting the jihad. I don't know how much experience you've had with Arab terrorists, but it's been my experience that they all want to be the guy. I know that's a generalization, but it just doesn't seem like they'd post an address list 'to whom it may concern' and say, 'Go get 'em, boys.' I think they'd keep it among themselves. They want the credit. From Allah."

"Just so you know, up front, my father was the ambassador to Qatar and then Yemen," Dawn Massey said. "I grew up in the Middle East. I speak Arabic in four dialects as well as Farsi, French, and Italian, and I have a doctorate from Johns Hopkins in international relations. So I know a little bit about Arabs and Islam. And I suppose I agree with your characterization. We have linguists looking at the language on the Web site and deconstructing the text. The preliminary report says some of the grammatical and syntactic mistakes and word choices indicate the person passing himself off as an Arab may be Eastern European."

"Or *her*self," DeLuca said.

"Or herself," Massey agreed. "Right now, the site is worming itself onto the hard drives of whoever hits on the links. We can't stop the spread, but we added a spyware program of our own to the kernel codes, and we're already getting reports back on user loci for new bots. Obviously, copies of the original are still out there, but we think we got to it fairly early."

"That would be a nice list to generate, wouldn't it?" DeLuca said. "The names and addresses of all the people around the world who like to hit on a terrorist Web site. You don't think anybody would let something like I4NI proliferate, just to get that list, would you?"

"Agent DeLuca," Massey said. "I'm going to ignore that, because I don't think you really believe the FBI would put the lives of our retired servicepeople and their families in jeopardy intentionally."

"Oh really?" he thought to himself.

"What I do want you to know," she continued, "is that we can't suppress information, once it's on the Web, and it's been written to either self-replicate or download. We can't put the toothpaste back in the tube, but what we can do is make the toothpaste so toxic that nobody brushes their teeth again. This thing hasn't really gone wide yet, but it's only a matter of time. What we want, when it does, is for potential users to think, 'better not go there, because if I do, I'm going to be arrested.' That's the only way to kill a Web site. You make it poisonous and then you let the word spread, along with the virus."

"I was told the map page had over two hundred thousand hits already," DeLuca said. "That isn't wide? Four people already dead."

"Two hundred thousand isn't wide, even if the numbers are true," she said. "Web site hit totals are largely a meaningless statistic. And the four killings you're talking about were highly planned—those weren't teenagers, clicking on a Web site and finding a new way to spend an afternoon. Why four? Why not ten? Fifty? These were cells who'd been working their millions for months. The question is, who's coordinating it? FYI, we've been putting up bogus sites for years now, fishing for exactly the sort of data you're talking about. We're going to mine all the intel we can from a real site we're trying to shut down, because it would be irresponsible of us if we didn't, but we're not going to nurture a bad site just to mine it."

"I apologize," DeLuca said. "As someone with a big sheet of plywood where his living room picture window used to be and a wife in the process of relocating to Fort Bragg, it's a little hard to hear someone say they're letting the Web site that caused it spread."

"It's spreading," she said. "We're not *letting* it. There were nearly 651 terrorist attacks in 2004 and two thousand killed or wounded, according to the National Counterterrorism Center. We're not going to stop them all. Who do you think shot at you?"

DeLuca shrugged. "Judging by the slugs they pulled out of the wall and the size of the hole they blew in the brick pillar on my porch, I'd say it was a sniper rifle."

"You reported it to the police?"

DeLuca shook his head. "I put some of our own people on it," he said.

"Why you?" she asked.

"Are you trying to make me feel unimportant?" he said. "I made a lot of enemies in Iraq. One of the pictures on my particular I4NI Web page was a wanted poster of me that was circulating in Balad. And elsewhere. That was probably already on the Web somewhere. What struck me was the amount of work it would have taken to put it together."

"We agree. Either it's a few people who really know what they're doing, or a lot of people who don't."

"Or they outsourced it. To Pakistan"

"Perhaps," she said. "Where are you staying?"

"I'm at the Cooper," he said. "If I was Halliburton, I would've picked the Four Seasons. You think I4NI is Eastern European? Not European, or American?"

"That's possible, but the linguistics say Slavic, for now. Not Asian, and not Arab."

"I was told there's chatter about some major attack," DeLuca said. "WTC level or higher?" He knew the answer to his question, but he wanted to hear how much of it she was willing to give him.

"Higher," she said. "The talk is of something big that will be in all the newspapers and talked about for years to come."

"Boston, New York, San Francisco, or Chicago?" DeLuca said.

"We've partially eliminated San Francisco and Chicago," she said. "It looks more like northeast America, coastal town."

"What's wrong with Portland?" DeLuca asked. "Nobody ever picks on Portland."

"Part of the fatwa on the site talks about creating maximum collateral damage," Dawn Massey said. "We're taking that to mean a suitcase nuke or a dirty bomb, anywhere downtown will do, as long as it takes out Joe Quinn, along with the rest of Boston."

"So how do we work together without stepping on each other's toes?" he asked. "Do we pair up or go our separate ways in peace?"

"We keep each other informed," she said. "You give us what you get from your resources, and we'll share what we have. I had a long talk with legal before you came in. They tell me the Posse Comitatus Act of 1878 still prohibits the government's use of active-duty military personnel in civilian or domestic law enforcement. I know DOD keeps talking about 'active layered' defenses and the president has special signing authority to deploy combat forces on U.S. territory to 'intercept and defeat threats,' quote unquote. It sounds to me like they want it both ways. I'd rather not get caught in the middle."

"If it makes you feel any better," DeLuca said, "comitatus exempts National Guard troops under the control of state governors. I'm Massachusetts National Guard, active duty. Technically."

"Joint-tasked to INSCOM," Massey said. "Not under the control of the governor."

"Special assignment, but not federalized," DeLuca said. "CI was at Waco. We interdict drug flights all the time—look, we could probably go back and forth on this, but what's your point?"

"My point is that as I read it, gathering and coordinating intelligence is permitted. Taking direct actions against terrorists isn't. You have a support role. The law prohibits action only when civilian resources are 'overwhelmed by multiple simultaneous attacks resulting in multiple casualties,' again, quote unquote. We're a law enforcement agency, and that's the law. We're busy, I'll grant you, but we're not overwhelmed. Not yet. We're chartered to form interagency centers for counterterrorism teaming, 'modular reaction forces,' they're calling them, but that still restricts you to intelligence gathering only."

"So this morning," DeLuca said, "instead of chasing the guy who shot up my house, I should have just sat on my steps and waited for the FBI to come? Seriously?" He wasn't interested in getting into a chest-thumping contest with her as to whose authority overrode whose— his came from the White House by executive order, and it was not restricted by posse comitatus or accountable to civilian law enforcement. He held the ultimate trump card. That didn't mean he needed to play it. Not just now, anyway. What politician was it who said, "To get along, go along"?

"I think you know what I'm saying," Dawn Massey said.

"I hear what you're saying," he told her. "As long as you hear what I'm saying."

"Let's look at it this way," she said. "I'll give you what-ever background you need, but let's keep it simple. Have you ever done any cave exploration?"

"Some," he said.

"Then think of this as a big cave with two entrances. You go in your entrance, we'll go in ours. You investigate the murder of Katie Quinn. Let us go after I4NI. You take it on, the same way you would have if you were still working with BPD, and if we meet in the middle and if the Quinn murder leads back to I4NI, so be it. Personally, if I'm to be frank, I'm inclined to agree with Wexler."

"Care to rephrase that?" he offered. "Let's let Frank be frank."

"Why go after Joe Quinn's daughter," she said, "when Joe Quinn himself is asleep in his bed, alone, less than a mile away? Why not hit his house? It's just not like the other four homicides."

"It was premeditated."

"That doesn't make it terrorist."

"Are you giving me Katie because it's low on your list of priorities?" he asked her. "You can be honest."

"If it ties in, it's important," Massey said. "But until it does, I have to go in a different direction."

"I understand," he said. "Katie Quinn was my original assignment anyway."

"What are you doing next?" she asked.

"Next, I'm meeting with my team to figure out how to use them," DeLuca said. "After that, I'm talking to Downtown Danny Rhodes about Katie Quinn. Gathering intel. I'll call you if I need to blow my nose or something."

*   *   *

He stopped down the hall to knock on the door of his old friend Mike O'Leary. They'd worked the organized crime task force together, back in the day. He'd been partnered with O'Brien when DeLuca took O'Brien down—"The Two Micks," they'd been dubbed—but O'Leary had never been even remotely tainted by his partner's activities, and he never bore a grudge against DeLuca for doing what he had to do.

"David DeLuca," O'Leary said, surprised. "What brings you here? I thought you'd be wearing a uniform or something."

"CI doesn't wear uniforms," he said. "I'm working with Massey's office. I thought it was going to be a guy."

"Yeah?" O'Leary said. "Work with her for a few weeks. You might still change your mind."

"Fortunately, I believe she's madly attracted to me," DeLuca said.

"Right," O'Leary said. "Now if you'll excuse me, I need to go let a few hundred monkeys fly out my butt."

At the Cooper, DeLuca found Walter waiting in the lobby. His hair was grayer than it used to be, and in retirement he'd added a few pounds to his six-foot-four-inch frame, but other than that, Walter looked good. He was talking to MacKenzie, who was wearing jeans, sandals, and a black sweater over a white tank top. The hoop earrings added a distinctive nonmilitary touch. A California surfer girl who'd joined the military mostly to piss off her parents, she seemed to have recovered her equanimity after their previous mission in Liger, West Africa, where she'd lost a friend. DeLuca had told her time would help, but he doubted she'd had enough time yet. Vasquez appeared shortly thereafter, a twenty-nine-year-old CI agent who'd joined the team in Iraq and a streetwise Angeleno who'd been educated in the East, though he rarely spoke of it, out of humility more than anything else, though he was cocky and high-spirited most of the time. Dan Sykes was ten minutes late, arriving with a five-day beard and the excuse that he'd been visiting his parents in Washington, D.C., where his father represented California in Congress. Sykes was quick-witted, charming, held a sixth-degree black belt in karate, was fond of extreme sports in his off hours and cutting to the chase when he was working. He apologized for getting stuck in traffic.

"I had to pahhhck my cahh in the Hahhr-vahhd Yahhd," he said.

"That's the worst Boston accent I've ever heard," Vasquez told him. "You sound like Cliff Clavin after five glasses of plum wine."

"Did you guys know there's a bar on Beacon Street that looks just like the bar from the TV show *Cheers?*" Sykes said. "I think that's where they filmed it. Anybody want to go?"

"That's so weird," MacKenzie said. "There was one at the airport in Chicago too."

In his room, DeLuca brought his team up to speed. He briefed them on the murders of Wagner, Masland, McNulty, and O'Hara, adding that their task was restricted to solving the murder of Katie Quinn, and at the same time protecting General Joe Quinn. Sami Jambazian, his irascible former partner on the force, now retired and a fishing-boat captain, when he wasn't working on CI cases as part of the Ready Reserve, was baby-sitting the general, DeLuca explained.

He told them what he knew of Katie Quinn's murder. He showed them the Web site, and the pages that referred to him and to the other members of his team.

"So far it's just a bunch of fuzzy candids taken of us in Iraq and no last names on you guys," he said. "I was easy to find. I'm kicking myself for this morning, and for not recognizing the threat sooner. Lesson: it can happen here. Stay armed, stay alert, stay connected, check your rear-view mirrors, and be ready to back each other up. ROEs allow for deadly force if you have to, backed by executive order, but remember where we are. We have support from the White House, but I'm sure they'd rather not hear from us if they don't have to. We've been all over the world to-gether, so if anybody gets hurt in my backyard, I'll never get past the irony. Okay?"

"How are we going to divide this up?" Sykes said. "I got hopelessly lost just coming from the airport. I'm going to need my own personal NAVSAT if you expect me to find anybody in Boston."

"Take a cab if you have to," DeLuca said. "Tell the driver you can get him courtside seats at the FleetCenter for a Celtics game if you need him to go fast."

"We can do that?" Ford said. "Sheesh. I had no idea."

"Dan, Colleen, I'm putting you on I4NI," DeLuca said. "You're going to need to liaison with the FBI on this. You'll work with Dawn Massey, D-a-w-n, head of the Intel Analysis Unit at Center Plaza. She is, as they say in Massachusetts, 'wicked smaht,' but she will also bust your balls, or your ovaries, respectively, if you fuck up. Tech-nically, she told me we take the Quinn case and they'll handle I4NI, so tread lightly. You're only asking insofar as it connects to the case. FBI thinks they're team leader on this, and we might as well let them go on thinking that, as long as it makes 'em happy. The bottom line is, if you need something and you can wait, go through them. If you need it right now, do it yourself. The site is in Arabic but the working sense is, we're looking at Eastern Europeans posing as Arabs. Or Arabs living in Eastern Europe, but more likely the former. Who's going to tell me how Joe Quinn connects to Eastern Europe?"

"Oh, man," Vasquez said. "I didn't know there was going to be a quiz."

"Allied Force," Sykes said. "Kosovo was my cherry mission. I was assigned to the OSCE verification team. They pulled us out on March 20 when Milosevic refused to sign the Rambouillet accords. I think I was in country for three weeks."

"What was OSCE?" Mack asked.

"Oh God, I don't even remember," Sykes said. "Organization for Security and Cooperation in Europe. Something like that. Joe Quinn was NATO Supreme Allied Commander Europe. I was gathering intel for the ground invasion that didn't happen."

"I was at DLI, cramming to learn Serbian," Mack said. "Unsuccessfully. They think I4NI is Serbian?"

"*They* don't think that," DeLuca said. "I'm only guessing. I'm focusing strictly on Joe Quinn and whoever might have a beef against him. It's called 'eye for an eye.' Call me literal, but if somebody killed Joe Quinn's daughter, I'm going to look at people who lost their own daughters in Allied Force. Somebody with a sense of poetic justice. We bombed for seventy-seven days and came out more or less unscratched. The Serbs shot down one F-16, and that was a complete fluke."

"Scott O'Grady," Walter Ford said. DeLuca nodded.

"Basically, from March until June of 1999, we beat the Serbs like a redheaded stepchild and sent them home with their tails between their legs," DeLuca continued. "We took down all their triple A, all four hundred of their tanks, all their aircraft in the first two days, somewhere between half and two-thirds of their troops, maybe thirty thousand Serb casualties, and more or less gave them an atomic wedgie in front of the whole class. I wouldn't be surprised to learn that somebody over there is carrying a grudge against us, given that the whole ethnic cleansing thing in Kosovo, and we're talking about one and a half million displaced and a quarter million killed or missing, started from a grudge that went back to 1389 and the Battle of Kosovo."

"The Turks had occupied Serbia," Vasquez said. "Sultan Murad the First defeated Prince Lazar on the plains of Polje. I remember it like it was yesterday."

"So do they. I thought you weren't prepared for a quiz," Mack said.

"And now they're posing as Muslims?" Vasquez said. "They probably think that's pretty clever."

"I'm not saying that's what's happening," DeLuca said. "There were other military leaders on the I4NI Web site, from other conflicts, but that may be to cover up their true intentions. Masland made enemies in the Philippines. I just don't know how to connect Eastern Europe any better than that, so look for those connections—Walter, where are there neighborhoods of Serbs or Eastern Europeans?"

"Lemme think," he said. "Dorchester. Quincy. A few in Brookline. Somerville, I think. Don't forget—Katie had checked out a Serbian phrase book. I thought maybe it was to help interview that Serbian basketball player the Celtics just signed, but it could be more than that."

"We can rule out the Boston Celtics—they can't hit anything anymore. Look for displaced people, refugees working for cash under the table, war criminals, Albanian or Serbian or Croatian social clubs, Eastern Orthodox churches," DeLuca said. "Find out where the biggest threats are in Boston and look for correlations. Pretend Boston is a foreign country and you've parachuted in to find the black-listers."

"We're from California," Sykes said, gesturing to Mackenzie. "It shouldn't be hard to pretend we're in a foreign country."

"Walter and I will start from Katie Quinn and work backwards," DeLuca said. "We know the town pretty well, plus I need Walter to run interference with me on the force. Apparently I'm a Fed now, and Frank Wexler has me on his shit list."

"Where any of us would be proud to find ourselves," Ford said. "I can talk to Frank for you."

"Hoolie," DeLuca said, "I have a special assignment for you. You went to Harvard, right?"

"I was there during Allied Force," Vasquez said.

"You went to Harvard?" Sykes said.

"Why so surprised, cabrone?" Vasquez said. It was, of course, true that he cultivated an aura of Los Angeles street-smart. No one doubted how bright he was, but he'd asked DeLuca specifically not to mention his education.

"You never said anything," Sykes said.

"Not everybody goes around for the rest of their life talking about where they went to college," Vasquez told the Stanford graduate. "Some people actually move on.

Though I've noticed that I've been in Boston for a little over two hours and already three people have asked me where I went to school."

"You still know people at Harvard?"

"A few," Vasquez said. "I was going to stay with some friends in Cambridge until I learned about the Web site. Now I think I won't, if snipers are going to be shooting through the window at me."

"Elizabeth LeDoux is a sophomore," DeLuca said. "General LeDoux's daughter. She's on the I4NI Web site, though I don't know if Phil has told her. I want you to look after her. LeDoux didn't ask me to do this, but I want to make sure she's safe. I would have been her godfather if the army hadn't sent me on assignment when she was baptized. I'll leave it up to you as to how, but get close and stay close. I haven't seen her since she was fifteen, but she's a sweet kid. I'll let you know when your mission is up."

Vasquez nodded.

"We'll HQ here, with Scottie at INSCOM/JTIOC via CIM and SAT phone if you need tech," DeLuca said. "Scottie will liaison with IWD. These hand-helds are slightly different from the ones we used in Africa, so get to know them."

"Are they waterproof?" Sykes asked.

"These are," DeLuca said. "These have real-time video streaming, but I don't want anybody watching Leno when they should be working. Sami is looking for a secure location to move the general to. Walter and I have an errand to run, so we'll brief again in the morning. Any questions?"

"What's a frappe?" Sykes asked. "I was trying to get a chocolate malt and they said all they had was frappes."

"Any *serious* questions?" DeLuca asked.

* * *

The crowd at Murphy's Irish Steakhouse was thin, in part due to the late hour and in part due to the rain that had begun to fall earlier, a heavy summer rain that left large puddles on Boylston and Tremont and emptied the Common. Murphy's was one of a handful of venerable Irish pubs in Boston, a traditional watering hole, like Doyle's or Locke-Ober or Anthony's Pier 4 where people revered a business establishment the same way they revered the Old North Church or the African Meeting House, a place where you went because your father took you there when you were a kid, because his father took him there when he was a kid. DeLuca had a photograph of Danny Rhodes on his CIM taken from the WSPO *Sports Nation* Web site where, as he'd expected, there'd been no photographs of Katie Quinn. He found Rhodes sitting in a corner booth, the sports pages spread out in front of him, staring into space, smoking a cigarette.

"Danny Rhodes?" DeLuca asked.

Rhodes broke his stare and looked at him. It was clear from the glassiness of his gaze that he was half in the tank. More than half.

"Yeah?" he said.

"I'm Special Agent DeLuca and this is Detective Ford," he said. "Mind if we sit down and ask you a couple questions?"

He was slow to answer, and seemed oddly passive. According to the Web site, Dan the Man was "one of the most aggressive voices in interactive radio," whatever that meant.

"Sure," Rhodes said. "I've been up since noon, answering questions. I don't think I have anything new to say."

"That's all right," DeLuca said. "I apologize for making you repeat yourself. Can I get you a cup of coffee? Aren't you supposed to be on the air in an hour?"

Rhodes looked at his watch, squinting to see the digital numbers on it. "Yeah, I guess I am," he said.

DeLuca summoned the waitress and ordered three coffees with milk.

"You really going to go on the air tonight?" DeLuca said. "After what happened?"

"Yeah," Rhodes said. "I thought maybe if I worked through it . . . But now I think maybe that's a bad idea."

"Numbing yourself isn't a good idea either," DeLuca said. "I know the temptation, don't get me wrong. Sox win tonight?"

Rhodes looked at him. "Who gives a shit?" he said.

DeLuca looked at Ford as the waitress set the coffee cups down in front of them. Rhodes had a glass of whiskey in front of him and sipped from it, ignoring the coffee.

"I mean, really," he continued. "Who gives a flying fuck about the Red Sox? What difference would it make if they were wiped from the face of the earth? Zero."

He finished his whiskey, staring at his shot glass.

"You might want to think about an attitude adjustment before you punch in tonight," DeLuca said. "I know how tough it is."

Rhodes looked at him again. "You know what I was doing in 2001, summer of 2001?" he slurred. "I'll tell you. I was writing a book. I'd been doing eight hours a day solo at a sports station in Newark and I took a leave of absence to write a book about the Atlantic League. Loser League—you know what the Atlantic League is, Agent . . . what did you say you name was?"

"DeLuca."

"It's a Loser League," Rhodes spat. "I was in New Jersey, writing about the Somerset Patriots. Sweet little team. Sparky Lyle was the manager and John Montefusco was the pitching coach. His first job after getting out of prison for stalking his ex-wife. Purportedly. But that was the Atlantic League. Place where veterans and has-beens who couldn't catch on with the pros in spring training or Rule 5 guys who got bounced out of double A ball came to show the scouts they could still play and maybe get a call-up in September. Guys ducking paternity suits in the Dominican. Guys who played in Mexico where the umpires offered to shave the plate for them to get their batting averages up for twenty bucks a game, or guys who went to Taiwan hoping to make a couple hundred thousand throwing games for the gamblers there who bet on baseball and make one last score before they admitted their careers were over. Loser League. Chokers and jokers. Great guys. I loved those guys. A lot of good stories. I was writing a book. I spent the whole summer with the team. Then guess what happened? In September."

"The World Trade Center happened," DeLuca said.

"Exactly!" Rhodes said. "And after that, who really gave a shit about minor-league baseball anymore? Who gave a shit about *major*-league baseball anymore? People used to have athletes as heroes, and then they watched the firefighters going into the towers, and afterwards everybody realized, holy shit, my athlete heroes are just a bunch of illiterate motherfuckers who can't talk, except in clichés, and don't know anything, and play little-kid games for a living because they can't do anything else. We realized who the real heroes are, and what it really means to lose something you love, or someone. And there went my fucking book, because sports is just a metaphor. I know that. You know why people listen to my show?"

"Why?"

"Because they're half asleep and they don't want to listen to something that's actually important, because if they do, they'll have to get involved and it'll keep 'em up. All the emotions in sports are totally fake. And you know what's really pathetic? What's really pathetic is that all these dumbass moron motherfuckers who call in all riled up about some coach or some umpire who did this or that, they don't even know it's fake. They think it matters. That's how stupid they are."

"Maybe you've got a topic for your show tonight," DeLuca said. "Tell me about Katie."

"Katie," Danny Rhodes said. "I think Katie was maybe my best friend. Did you know Katie?"

"I never met her," DeLuca said. "I knew her father."

"Too bad they didn't get along," Rhodes said. "I think he was maybe the only person in the world she didn't get along with. Katie was a fantastic woman. Really special. You never heard her?"

DeLuca shook his head.

"I heard her once in a while," Ford said. "I got a bad prostate. Sometimes when it wakes me up, I listen to your show."

"She had the sexiest voice," Rhodes said. "I swear to God. You wouldn't believe the number of e-mails and calls and letters we'd get from guys who wanted to hook up with her. It was constant. But if you knew her, she was like your instant best friend. Like one of the guys."

"But she wasn't a guy," DeLuca said.

"No, she wasn't," Rhodes said, tearing open a sugar pack and dumping it in his coffee before stirring it with his spoon. "You ever hear the phrase, 'face for radio'? It's a cliché, but that was Katie. She could have made so much money in endorsements if she was just a little prettier. She actually—listen to this, she actually had an offer from some shoe company, just from talking to them on the phone, but when she had some head shots taken, she sent them in and they took back the offer. It was a done deal and they backed out. She had the negatives destroyed and never tried again, apart from voice work. But if you knew her, you knew how tough she was."

"Tough?"

"Tough," Rhodes said admiringly. "That's a big part of the show, callers calling in to tell the on-airs they're full of shit or whatever, so you give it right back to 'em, and Katie could give it back as good as anybody. That's 'interactive' radio. The last thing you want is somebody calling in without an opinion, saying, 'What do you think of the Patriots' chances this year?' You *want* assholes, and we're totally free to call them any name in the book and hang up, except that if you really hate somebody, the more you hang up on them, the more they call back. They'll sit there like morons on hold for an hour and a half, just to get hung up on again. It's crazy. It's absolutely fucking crazy. We get the same guys, and sometimes they think they can disguise their voices and call back, like we don't have caller ID."

"How about Katie's last night?" DeLuca asked. "How was that?"

"That was a good night," Rhodes said. "A good night to listen, anyway. It was kind of weird, actually, because

most nights, guys would call in asking her what she looked like or making jokes about her boobs or something, but last night, for a while, they were all turning on her. It was weird."

"What do you mean, turning on her?" DeLuca asked.

"Calling her a suck-up," Rhodes said. "Telling her she was a worse toadie than Ed McMahon was to Johnny Carson. That she didn't have any opinions of her own and always agreed with everything I said, which was ridiculous if you actually listened to the show and heard all the disagreements we'd have, almost every night. About players she liked or hated, and I didn't. Who was the best scrambling quarterback of all time."

"Fran Tarkenton," Walter Ford said.

"John Elway," Rhodes countered. "But she liked Tarkenton too. Anyway, for about an hour, or maybe the first half of the show, it was like there was this groundswell of hostility towards her. Vicious really personal stuff, some of it. But then, the last half of the show, most of the callers were calling in to support her and say what a fantastic woman she was. Which was true. I asked her halfway through if she was okay and she said she was fine. Like I said, she was tough. I think men admired that about her as much as anything. She could give shit as well as she could take it. Most guys thought she was perfect. Guys wanted to meet her all the time."

"That was why she cut through the Emerson building to get to her car?" DeLuca asked. Rhodes nodded. "Did women ever call in?"

"One out of a thousand calls," Rhodes aid. "I tell my engineer to put through every call we ever get from a woman. Women don't like sports, generally. Maybe you heard."

"Women play all kinds of sports," DeLuca said.

"Name one sport that women invented," Rhodes said. "One."

DeLuca couldn't.

"Did you hear the rumors that Katie Quinn was a lesbian?" DeLuca asked. Rhodes nodded. "Well?"

"How would I know?" Rhodes said. "None of my business."

"Was she dating anybody? She ever talk about anybody she was seeing?"

"I don't know," Downtown Danny Rhodes said. "She never really talked about personal stuff."

"I'm going to take a wild guess here," DeLuca said, "but if you thought of her as your best friend, but she never talked about personal stuff with you, then I'm betting the friendship was pretty much a one-way street. I might be the last guy to give out informed opinions about women, but I do know that if you don't talk about personal things with a woman, they don't think you're talking about anything. And men think they've just had a great conversation when all the woman does is nod and smile while the guy talks."

"We talked about sports," Rhodes said.

"My point exactly," DeLuca said. "How about her business? She tell you anything about that?"

"Her phone service?" Rhodes said.

"Yeah," DeLuca said. "What was that?" He briefly wondered if Katie Quinn had moonlighted as a phone-sex provider. It would have made sense, in a way.

"Ex-Communications," Rhodes said.

"Which was?"

"She'd call your ex for you if your ex had a restraining order against you," Rhodes said. "For a fee. She called my ex for me for free."

"About what?"

"About why I was late with my alimony, and when my ex could expect a check," Rhodes said. "The station was almost bankrupt. My ex was hurting, but legally, I couldn't pick up a phone and tell her. And it was too embarrassing to ask anybody else to call her. Katie said she had rules—she wasn't going to pass along threats or help people fight, but if she could smooth things over, she would. Especially with that voice of hers."

"Did you know her partner Freddy?"

Rhodes shook his head. "I didn't know she had a partner. You're talking about a business partner?"

"Yeah," DeLuca said. "I'm going to talk to him tomorrow."

DeLuca told Walter to go home, telling his friend he had a few things left to do before going back to his hotel. From the WSPO building he found the back door and crossed through the alley, retracing the steps that Katie Quinn would have taken the night she was killed. An Emerson College security guard let him in the back door of the Emerson College building where the writing, literature, and publishing departments were housed. In the front foyer, DeLuca turned his collar up to the rain and crossed Tremont. He paused in the doorway at Boylston station, where a homeless girl was asleep, curled up in a ball by the stairs. He crossed the park, walking past the cemetery and the tennis courts and the baseball fields, until he arrived at the kiosk that led down into the parking garage. Had she been afraid? Had she checked over her shoulder? Had she suspected anything at all was amiss? Was she hurrying, or taking her time? Singing a song to herself? Thinking of what? Of how the show went? Of her father, who lived so close by but who was so far from her now?

The Boston Common was, as city parks go, one of the safer ones, and certainly better than Central Park, but it still would have been a scary place for a single woman, walking alone at 4:30 in the dark of night. Why did she park there? Did she carry anything to protect herself? Pepper spray? A gun, perhaps? A .50 caliber Smith & Wesson? Not exactly a ladies' gun, but she was, after all, a general's daughter.

Before walking back to his hotel, he paused beneath the shelter to check his e-mail. On his CIM, he read the autopsy report that Mitch Pasternak had compiled. It told him mostly what he already knew or suspected, that Katie Quinn died instantly from massive trauma due to a gunshot wound to the head, that her stomach was empty, that she was drug and alcohol free and had no extraneous DNA on her to implicate anybody else. None of this was surprising.

What was surprising was the last item Pasternak noted.

Katie Quinn, at the time of her death, was two months pregnant.

DeLuca turned his radio to 690 AM as he fell asleep. The show was a taped repeat. Dan the Man had been too drunk, DeLuca surmised, or too sad, to carry on, so someone had pulled the plug for the night and run a repeat, even though none of the scores were therefore current or correct. He heard Katie Quinn's voice, saying how the Braves tomahawked the Astros, 6–2, and the Rockies rocked the

Dodgers' world, 9–1, and the Bronx Bombers marooned the Mariners in extra innings, 8–6. He could hear the sun shining in her voice, and he could picture the twinkle in her eye, the voice somehow both light and smoky, polite, respectful, animated, wise, and self-deprecating. Very briefly, he fell in love.

Chapter Four

DELUCA CALLED BONNIE WHEN HE WOKE UP to see how she was settling in. He tried the number for her cell phone first, but there was no answer, so he went through the switchboard. She told him the army had given her a small cottage on the base, two bedrooms, one for her and one for the wife of a colonel stationed in Bahrain, due to a housing shortage that was forcing families to double up, an arrangement the army assured her was only temporary. She told him they were not allowed to speak to anybody about the reasons why they were staying at Fort Bragg, such that the detainees were only able to really socialize with each other.

"I don't know if 'detainee' is actually the best way to describe it," he said. "You're at Bragg, not Guantanamo."

"'Detainee' is exactly the word," she told him. "'Detainee' is how I would describe my entire life, David. Waiting waiting waiting. Waiting for things to change. Waiting for things to get better. Waiting for this to end. I don't want to wait anymore."

"What do you mean, 'Waiting for this to end'?" he asked her. "Waiting for what to end?"

"Oh, David," she said. "If you don't know . . . What's going on? How's my house? Why can't I live in my house? Why are people shooting at my house? Why do I have to be so afraid all the time? Why do I have to be so lonely all the time?"

In a way, he wished she sounded angrier, because if she did, he knew she'd calm down eventually. As it was, she sounded cold. Resolved. Like she'd already made up her mind.

"I just can't really talk about this right now," he said. He wondered if going through the switchboard meant that someone was listening in on the call.

"You never can," Bonnie said. "You never can. I know what you do is secret. Maybe some women could live with that. I can't. I don't want to live with someone who has to keep so many secrets. I want to live with someone who's open. I want to live with someone I can talk to. I don't deserve this. I told you before. You said it would get better, once you got home from Iraq. It hasn't gotten better."

"I know," he said. He didn't know what he could say. She was right about everything, and she was wrong. He let the silence go on, hoping she would say she was sorry, that she missed him, that when this was all over maybe they could go away somewhere, just the two of them.

"Look," she said. "Here's the deal. I was talking this over last night with Caroline . . ."

"Oh, great," he said. "Caroline's been trying to split us up for years."

"Caroline knows how unhappy I've been," Bonnie said. "For years. Apparently you don't. Or you know, but you don't care, which is worse. Either way, David, here's the thing—I suppose I'll stay here for as long as I have to. When I get home, you have to either quit the army, or I'm going to get a lawyer and file for divorce. I won't do this anymore. If you quit, I'm willing to give it another chance. If you don't, I'm not, because it's just going to be more of the same."

"Bonnie . . ."

"No, David," she said. "There has to be a deadline. Otherwise it's going to be one more mission, one more 'Bonnie, Phil just called . . .' That's what I mean by 'detainee,' David. There's no end in sight. I'm permanently suspended. That's over. Tell you what—I'll make it easy on you. At some point, I'm going to walk through the front door of our house again. When I do, I'm going to look on the dining room table. If I see a piece of paper there, telling me you've quit, I'll unpack my bags. If I don't see that piece of paper, I'm going to leave. Is that clear enough for you? Until then, let's not talk."

He was about to mutter something stupid and ineffective when she hung up.

Vasquez had decided to recon a bit before approaching the subject directly, picking up the trail as Elizabeth LeDoux left her class in Thayer Hall. He'd downloaded her schedule using the CIM and Scottie's help. Even though it had been seven years since he'd graduated, the campus hadn't changed, and he still knew his way around well enough not to require Scottie's help with falcon views or mapping. She spent an hour studying in the Widener Library, had lunch at Finagle-a-Bagel on JFK Street, where she talked on her cell phone the entire time. She had another class at the science center, after which he followed her down Mass Ave, crossing through heavy traffic at Church

Street and proceeding down Church past the Loews Theaters until she turned left on Palmer, a narrow cobblestone street where Vasquez feared at first that he'd lost her.

Then a hand grabbed him at the shoulder, and two more by the arms, four men in all, he estimated, dragging him down off the street into a kind of open basement well where he could look into the windows of Club Passim, a folk music club he'd attended a few times as an undergraduate. The men threw him up against the wall, banging his head. Two, both blond-haired boys, wore T-shirts that said "Crew" on them, and they were well muscled enough to tell him they were on the rowing team and not part of the audiovisual crew. A third boy was African-American and large, probably a tackle on the football team, Hoolie guessed, though he didn't mean to stereotype. The fourth boy looked like a surfer, with sun-streaked hair and a puka shell necklace, in a Hawaiian shirt and khaki shorts.

"Why are you following our friend?" Puka Shells said menacingly.

"Who are you?" Large Young Black Man said.

"Shut the fuck up," Crew Boy #1 commanded.

"Do you want me to talk or do you want me to shut the fuck up?" Hoolie asked.

"What are you doing here?" Crew Boy #2 said.

"Listen, guys," Vasquez said. "I think there's been a misunderstanding."

"Why were you following me?" he heard a woman's voice say. He looked up to see Elizabeth LeDoux, standing on the sidewalk above him. She was livid. "I saw you at Thayer. I saw you at Widener, and I saw you at lunch. I don't like being followed by old guys. The last man who tried to stalk me was arrested. Just because you saw me at work does not give you the right to follow me. Give me one reason why I shouldn't call the police right now."

"He's got a gun," Puka Shells said, reaching inside Hoolie's jacket. Prior to this, Vasquez had refrained from turning the window well off Palmer Street into a six-inch-deep puddle of preppie, much as he'd indulged in the fantasy as an undergraduate, when he was a young Latino Angeleno having a hard time fitting in. He couldn't allow any of his assailants to touch his weapon. He took Puka's hand in a thumb lock and bent it back, dropping the boy to his knees, gave Crew Boy #1 a shot to the throat with his elbow, and swept Crew Boy #2's feet from under him while pushing him down to the brick. He stopped Large Young Black Man from approaching simply by staring him down. Another rush and he was prepared to draw his Beretta, with the safety on, just to save them all the exertion.

"Tell the Beagle Boys to sit down," Hoolie said to the woman above him. "I work for David DeLuca, Elizabeth. He asked me to keep an eye on you."

"You're fucking army?" she said. "Jesus, I should have known."

"What do you want us to do, Biz?" Crew Boy #2 asked.

She thought a moment.

"You can go," she said. "Thanks so much for coming to help me. I really appreciate you guys."

"You sure?" Puka said.

"Yeah, I'm sure," Elizabeth said.

"You guys are good," Hoolie said. "Really. Here, give me your hand."

He helped Puka Shells up and pulled on his thumb, popping the dislocated digit back in place. "Put some ice on that for about an hour and take some Advil. If you need to, go to Student Health and send me the bill and I'll pay for it, but I think it'll be okay."

When they were alone, she regarded him for a moment and then turned and walked away. He ran to catch up to her, but given the view from behind, he wasn't in any great hurry. She was wearing red pumps, tight low-rider jeans (Sevens—why did he know that?) and a black belly shirt that showed more skin than he could recall from his days at Harvard, but that was how girls looked these days. She had a full head of curly brown hair that fell to her shoulders, her forelocks pulled back and fastened behind her head with a red barrette that matched her shoes. She wore red lipstick, semi-chandelier earrings, makeup that couldn't be described as modest, and she had a faint spray of freckles across the bridge of her nose that made her seem younger than she was. She was quite beautiful, in short, the kind of girl Hoolie would have fantasized about in college while feeling too intimidated to ask her out.

"Can you hold up a second?" he called after her.

"I'm late," she told him. "I'm meeting a girlfriend for dinner to study Spanish and then tonight I have to write a paper."

"Si necesitos ayuda con tu español, solo pregúntame," he told her. *"(C)reci hablándo."*

"No thank you," she told him. "I would much rather have dinner with my girlfriend. Why are you here? I specifically told my father I didn't want anybody watching over me. I'm perfectly capable of taking care of myself."

"I'm sure you are," Hoolie said. "Don't blame your father—I don't think he knows I'm here. DeLuca's the one who sent me, as a favor to your dad."

"Are you regular army?" she asked.

"CI," Hoolie told her.

"Of course," she said. "You want somebody spied on, send a spy."

"I'm not here to spy on you," Hoolie said. "I take it your old man told you about the Web site. There've already been some . . . incidents."

She stopped, looking at him.

"And they think Boston might be particularly at risk," he said. "I'm not here to interfere. And I can see you have good friends who can come to your rescue. We just think that for the next week or so, it would be a good idea to err on the side of caution."

"What's your name?" she asked.

"Julio," he told her. "Vasquez. My friends call me Hoolie."

"Okay, Mr. Vasquez," she said. "This is just a thousand percent annoying, but I suppose there's nothing I can say to make you go away, is there?"

"Call me Hoolie," he said. "And I'm not an old guy. I'm twenty-nine."

"It's important for you to know something," she said. "This is the first time I've ever had a chance to establish a life of my own, okay? I don't know if you can understand what that means, but it's really important to me. I'm twenty-one years old and I've lived in twenty-four different houses. I've been taking orders since I was born and I don't want to anymore. Nobody here knows my father is a general and I don't want anybody to know. This is the first place where I feel like I'm really me and not just an extension of my father. I don't care if you think that's a cliché—that's how I feel, here. I have my own life, and my own apartment, and my own friends, and I go where I want to go, when I want to go there, and I'm just not going to change any of that. It would mean giving up too much. All my life, I was told, 'What you do reflects on us.' I don't want to reflect on anybody anymore. I'm just me."

"I'm not here to change any of that," Vasquez said. "I'm here to make sure you can keep doing all of that."

"Can you promise me that?" she said. "I really don't want my friends saying, 'Who's that guy who keeps following you?' I just want to live a normal life."

"Okay," Hoolie said.

She stopped walking in front of the Café of India restaurant, on the corner of Brattle and Story streets. Inside the restaurant, half the tables were occupied by single diners, reading books or tapping away on their laptops.

"This is where I'm meeting my friend," she said. "I live down the street. What do you want me to do?"

"Here's my mobile number," he said, writing it down on a slip of paper he tore from the corner of a discarded alternative weekly paper that featured a story on all the massage places near Harvard Square: "Rub You the Right Way—How to Get a Happy Ending in Cambridge," the headline read. "Give me yours, and I'll stay out of your way, as much as is humanly possible. Call me when you're going somewhere. Or if you'd rather, I could pretend we know each other . . ."

"No," she said. "I'll call you. I promise."

"Good enough," he said. "And let me know if anything strange or unusual happens, any hang-up calls, weirdos, that sort of thing. One more thing—I need to take your picture."

He raised the CIM and pointed the lens at her.

"What for?" she asked.

"In case I need to send your picture to somebody," he said. "Smile. Remember—it takes more muscles to frown than it does to smile."

"That's true," she said, scowling. "And it took more muscles to point that out than it would have to leave me alone."

She flashed him a brief, sarcastic smile.

"And I'm sorry I called you an old guy," she said. "You're not an old guy."

"I feel like one, walking around campus," he said. "When I went here, everybody was older."

"You went here?" she asked.

"I did indeed," he said. "You seem surprised."

"I guess I didn't think there were a lot of Harvard grads in the army," she said.

"Subvert the dominant paradigm," he told her. "Isn't that what the bumper stickers tell you to do?"

He waited across the street until her friend joined her, an overweight redheaded girl who talked with her hands. Once it appeared that everything was all right, he moved down the street until he found Elizabeth LeDoux's house, a triple-decker, second house from the corner of Mt. Auburn and Nutting. Hers was the only name on the mailbox for the ground-floor apartment—it couldn't be cheap, living alone in a large apartment off Harvard Square. He wondered how much support she was getting from her daddy. As an undergrad, he'd always been amused by the people striving so hard to be independent of their parents who nevertheless depended on them for every nickel they ever spent. On the mailbox, someone (Elizabeth?) had attached a red-and-white sticker that had originally read

"No War in Iraq," but whoever had put it there had taken a scissors, clipped the 'W,' and inverted it, such that the sticker now read, "NoMar in Iraq," a reference to the Red Sox' former all-star shortstop, Nomar Garciaparra.

Using the lock picks he'd been trained to use at counter-intelligence school at Fort Huachuca in Arizona, he moved to the back porch and let himself into her apartment. The idea wasn't to invade her privacy, only to make sure there was no one lurking under the bed or hiding in the closet. She had more clothes than any woman he'd ever known, and a plasma TV big enough to use at a drive-in movie, and jewelry on her dresser that she really shouldn't be leaving out in the open, but no bad guys under the bed. When he was satisfied, he exited the apartment and paused on the sidewalk to use his SAT phone, placing a call to the operations officer at INSCOM/JTIOC. Captain Scott DeLuca was about to go off duty after a long day, he told Vasquez.

"You're working too much. Go home," Hoolie said. "But watch yourself."

"Home is the Bachelor Officers Quarters at McNair," Scott said. "I think I'd rather sleep under my desk. What can I do for you?"

"We have birds over Boston?" Vasquez said. "Orange alert."

"We have birds over Boston," Scott confirmed. "Butterflies too. UAVs etcetera. And a lot of civilian-looking guys walking very large German shepherds, if you notice. What's up?"

"How about video surveillance?" Hoolie asked.

"I'll send you a map of camera sites," Scott said. "Not ours, but we have access to them. Homeland pretty much covered the place prior to the 2004 Democratic National

Convention to watch the protesters. And they've added a few since then."

"What's in Harvard Square?" Hoolie asked.

"One second," Scott said. "Okay, we have a 360 camera on top of the news kiosk, another on the corner of Mt. Auburn and JFK, one in Porter Square, Davis, Center Square. We have them in all the MBTA stations and on all the trains. I can send live feeds to your CIM whenever you want. What do you need?"

"I'm sending you a picture of a very pretty girl," Hoolie said, tapping the keys on his CIM. "Can you plug it into the VACE system and keep me posted as to where she shows up?" VACE, as Hoolie understood it, stood for Video Analysis and Content Exploitation, an automated pattern recognition program that followed on from the NORA, or Non-Obvious Relationship Awareness, software first developed by the Pentagon after 9/11 to assist in face recognition and human intentions prediction. "I'm supposed to keep an eye on this girl but she doesn't want me hanging too close. To be honest, she totally made me today. I wasn't exactly being careful, but still."

"I can do better than VACE," Scott said. "DARPA just sent us a new Combat Pattern Visualization program that uses multiple data feeds to track vehicles in urban environments. It's pretty cool. Tracking a person is a little harder. We have programs that could probably track Shaquille O'Neal in a crowd at Tiananmen Square or find Elle McPherson on the midway at the Indiana State Fair—"

"No offense to the women of Indiana," Hoolie interjected.

"It's tougher when you get a big crowd of people who look somewhat alike. There's a company in California called Pixilogic that added the human component to the CPV program. It also looks for anomalies, like people carrying guns or people with six-foot-long tubes on their shoulders. Wow. This girl is cute."

"She is," Hoolie agreed. "She'd probably have a hard time hiding in Indiana too."

"Wait a minute," Scott said, pausing. "I know this girl. Who is she? I know this face."

"You're a human pattern recognition program," Hoolie said. "That's Elizabeth LeDoux. General LeDoux's daughter."

"That's Bizza?" Scott said. "Jesus, Julio—I used to play with her when I was a kid. I was five years older, but—I think she had braces on her teeth, the last time I saw her. Holy shit."

"She growed up good," Hoolie said. "In all the right places. My GPS is her house. Can you watch it for me and let me know if anything happens?"

"I'll draw a tripwire around it," Scott said, describing a digital device similar to the yellow first-down lines they were artificially imposing on football fields these days. Tripwires could digitally box a video feed from a satellite or UAV. Anything crossing the tripwire, in or out, sent an alert. "Tell her Scooter says hello. She'll know who you mean."

"Okay," Hoolie said. "Except that I don't think she necessarily needs to know we're watching her. She's a very independent person."

"She always was," Scott said.

Sykes and MacKenzie met briefly at 2 Center Plaza, room 734, with Dawn Massey, who then introduced them to a young agent named Neal Hartshorn who would, she said, assist them in any research they needed to do. Hartshorn was about thirty, slender, in a black suit that he seemed to have outgrown, his white socks showing beneath his pant cuffs. They began by downloading batches of files pertaining to all known Eastern Europeans in the Boston area with any possible links to terrorism, people who'd had contact with the Al Qaeda bombers who'd left from Boston the morning of 9/11, people who'd visited terrorist Web sites, people who'd blogged on political Web sites, people who'd been seen protesting during the 2004 Democratic Party convention, students studying political science or nuclear engineering, people who'd sent e-mails to the convicted Oklahoma City Murrah Federal Building bomber Timothy McVeigh in prison, people who'd rented *Black Hawk Down* more than twice, people who'd converted to Islam, people who'd sent money to Serbian relief funds, or Bosnian relief funds, or Croatian relief funds, or Kosovo-Albanian relief funds, even people of Eastern European descent who'd given money to Democratic Party candidates during the 2004 elections, back when the Republicans in general and the vice president in particular had tried to suggest that a vote for the Democrats would weaken America's antiterrorism defenses.

"I wouldn't say we believed that," Hartshorn said. "But we were certainly interested in finding people who did. Deputy Director Massey thinks I4NI might be one of the independent Al Qaeda–style groups popping up in Europe, not taking orders directly from Osama bin Laden in his cave but creating themselves in his image and spirit. They've ID'd the pilot of the plane that hit General Masland and found downloads from the I4NI site in his apartment."

"Arab?" Sykes asked.

"Yemeni," Hartshorn nodded. "Not much more than that, so far."

"It still doesn't mean the site is Arab," Sykes said. "What about locally?"

"Locally, we've been looking particularly hard at the airports and at the container ships coming into Boston Harbor for fissile materials, biological or chemical weapons, and that sort of thing—we've tripled the manpower in both areas."

The list of people to investigate came to a total, finally, of over fifteen hundred names.

Hartshorn brought them to a list the FBI had drawn up as well of possible targets in the Boston area, including the airport, the subways, the John Hancock Building, the Prudential Center, the JFK Federal Building, the Tip O'Neill Federal Building, City Hall, the State House on Beacon Street, Fenway Park, the Boston Garden, Faneuil Hall, Quincy Market, and a number of other places, with diagrams marking where each place was thought to be most vulnerable. It was Sykes who noticed that the target at the top of the list had been blacked out.

"What's this one?" he asked.

"That one is classified," Hartshorn said.

"We have top security clearances," Sykes said. "We'd like to know."

"And this is related to Katie Quinn how?" Hartshorn wondered.

"Her killer might belong to a terrorist organization also targeting local assets," Mack said. "He could show up in surveillance imagery. We need to know where to look."

"Wait here," Hartshorn said. "I'll ask Director Massey."

He returned a moment later saying she needed to speak on the phone with somebody at the Joint Task Force on Counter-Terrorism and/or INSCOM and/or NORTHCOM who could verify their clearances. Sykes gave Hartshorn the number they needed to call. Even so, they waited for nearly an hour before Hartshorn returned and told them he'd received permission to let them view the number one target in the Boston area, including Suffolk and Middlesex counties—a liquid natural gas facility in Everett called Unigas, on the shores of the Mystic River between the Tobin and Malden bridges.

"This is what you made us wait an hour for?" MacKenzie said. "I was reading about this in my in-flight magazine. This isn't classified."

"Parts of it are," Hartshorn said.

"What parts?" Sykes said. "We were reading about threats to LNG facilities back in November of 2001. For a while every LNG tanker making a delivery had a full Coast Guard and navy escort with helicopters and divers and SEAL teams until Homeland Security decided the risk was so great they shut the whole thing down. They don't even store LNG there anymore."

Agent Hartshorn looked like the proverbial cat that swallowed the canary.

"They do?" MacKenzie asked.

"They do," he said. "That's the part that's classified. On the record, they made a big public statement about how the Unigas facilities no longer stored flammable liquids, other than propane, which has been stored there safely for years. Publicly, those tanks are now full of nonflammable helium and other inert gases. We don't want any terrorist with a rocket-propelled grenade or a shoulder-fired missile or a car bomb to think they can still start trouble at Unigas. Even if they knew, we believe our security measures are adequate to withstand a direct attack."

"How so?" Sykes said.

"Would you like me to show you?" Hartshorn offered. "They said it would be okay. It's only about a mile and a half from here. I have a car downstairs."

He drove them on Causeway to Washington Street and then took Chelsea across Charlestown all the way to the foot of the Tobin Bridge, spanning the Mystic River bearing cars north and south on the Northeast Expressway. Hartshorn used a telephone at the base of the bridge's southern tower, and then they took an elevator to the top, where two men in National Guard uniforms watched the scene below through binoculars, one of the men armed with a .50 caliber sniper rifle mounted on a tripod.

"That's it?" Sykes said. "One guy with a scope? No offense, but I think you need more."

"We have more," Hartshorn said, leading them up one more flight of stairs to the roof of the elevator house where they saw, topping the tower, what looked like a miniature observatory, a canister the size of a very large garbage can or a small porta-potty, sitting above a small shed, and atop the canister a dome with a slot in it, inside of which they saw a glass lens, about three inches across, at the end of a black tube. Inside the shed, two men manned the device, one looking over his shoulder at the visitors, the other remaining fixed on his computer screen.

"I'll bet you don't know what that is," Hartshorn said.

"Well," Sykes said, "I could be wrong, but I'm pretty sure that's a megawatt-class MTHEL mobile tactical high-energy laser developed at the Helstaff facility in Albuquerque. The Russians had their own lab in Dushanbe, Tajikistan. MTHEL is three generations from the MIRACL mid infra-red advanced chemical laser they put on the ground at White Sands in 1996. It has a continuous wavelength of between 3.8 and 4.2 microns and burns C_2H_4 ethylene and NF_3 nitrogen fluoride, mixing the excited fluorine atoms with deuterium in the exhaust cavity to make deuterium fluoride. The resounder mirrors extract energy in the exhaust cavity and reroute it into an eighty-millimeter beam. Hughes Aircraft builds the tracking system and the rest is Lockheed-Martin/Boeing/TRW. The gun turret has 360 degrees of motion and can acquire targets as close as 450 meters, all computerized. Five years ago, the MTHEL took down twenty-three out of twenty-four Katyusha rockets at White Sands, and more recently these things were knocking mortar rounds out of the sky about 97 percent of the time. The hope is that they will replace all the old Patriot batteries. Did I forget anything?"

Agent Hartshorn looked crestfallen.

"We're sorry, Neal," Mack said. "We didn't mean to spoil the surprise. Why don't you tell us what it is? We'll pretend we don't know."

"Never mind," Hartshorn said.

"Please tell us," she repeated.

"I don't want to," he said. "Anyway, that's what we've got. There's another one on the Northern Avenue Bridge at the southern approach to the harbor. These will take out any threats from the air. They can be fired manually too if the computer target acquisition system fails. We also have round-the-clock video surveillance, razor wire, millimeter-wave heat denial systems, patrols, dogs, you name it. We think the facility itself is secure."

Sykes surveyed the cityscape below, the Charlestown rail yard on the south side of the river and the tank farm on the north.

"Which ones have LNG?" he asked.

"Those four big ones there," Hartshorn said, pointing. "Each one holds twelve million gallons. The gas is cooled to minus 260 degrees to keep it liquid. It boils at minus 258 degrees, so the fear is that a leak or intentional breach could release enough gas to form a cloud over the city. There are facilities like this in Maryland, Georgia, and Louisiana, but this is the only one in the heart of an urban environment."

"And it's loaded onto railroad tank cars here?" Mack asked, pointing to the trains below, resembling a massive model railroad set from this height. Sykes had picked up a pair of binoculars to scan the cityscape.

"No," Hartshorn said. "The propane goes out by rail because it only boils at forty-four below zero. The LNG gets loaded onto the ships in Algeria, mostly, and a few other countries, comes in here, gets stored in these tanks, and then it's piped out to where it's needed. You store it in liquid form and then to pipe it out, you let it warm to vaporize and then you push it with compressors. You need a mix of twenty-five parts air to one part gas to get the maximum explosion. The estimate is that a cloud a mile across would create an explosion equal to a medium-yield nuclear device."

"And how much gas would you need to form a cloud that size?" Sykes asked.

"If I had my calculator, I could tell you exactly," Hartshorn said. "A couple thousand gallons."

"And we're looking at forty-eight million gallons?"

Hartshorn nodded.

"At full capacity. Unigas supplies the Northeast and New York City. Montreal and Quebec too. South of New York, they get their supply from Maryland."

"What are those two tanks next to the LNG tanks?" MacKenzie asked.

"Those are propane," Hartshorn said.

"And LNG is more dangerous than propane?"

"Actually, propane is two and a half times more volatile," Hartshorn said. "One cubic foot of liquid can produce two hundred cubic feet of vapor. If you ignite it, you get pressures as high as eighty pounds per square inch. Most walls can only take two or three. LNG just gets more publicity. I guess because the ships go right past downtown Boston and the airport."

"And propane goes out by rail, you said?"

"By rail and by truck, mostly," Hartshorn said. "It's been targeted before. I was with the Elk Grove task force in 2000. I think that's why they brought me into the East Coast unit."

"What was Elk Grove?" Sykes asked.

"Elk Grove, California," Hartshorn said. "Near Sacramento. We stopped three guys from blowing up a pair of twelve-million-gallon Suburban Propane storage tanks. Not Al Qaeda at all—Timothy McVeigh types. White survivalist/supremacist guys from a San Joaquin County militia with stockpiles of guns, trying to take advantage of the Y2K frenzy to get some attention. Everybody's already forgotten how crazy that time was. The facility was right off Highway 99. SP had dug these big trenches around the facility and built berms, and they tried to tell the public the liquid propane would have just poured out and stayed inside the berms to contain the fire."

"They *tried* to tell them that, or they *did* tell them that?" Sykes asked.

"They *did* tell them that," Hartshorn said. "I don't know how they got away with it, to tell you the truth. Propane boils at minus forty-four, and it vaporizes virtually instantaneously. It would have stayed within the berms if it was forty-four degrees below zero out, but central California usually doesn't get that cold."

"I have a question," Mack said. "They mounted the MTHEL up here to get the maximum amount of coverage, I presume."

"I think that's right," Hartshorn said. "We can cover the airport too, you might have noticed."

"So suppose some terrorist on the bridge below fires an RPG at one of the tanks, and the laser misses but the beam hits a tank instead. What happens?"

"There's been some concern about that," Hartshorn admitted.

"Some concern?" Mack said.

"We have a lot of faith in the technology," Hartshorn said.

"I appreciate that you're giving me the party line because you want to be loyal," MacKenzie told the young FBI agent. "The whole reason we exist, Dan and I and the team we're part of, is because the army realized we've been putting too much faith in technology. Let me ask you—what's your feeling? Your sense, about all this? Off the record."

"My sense," Hartshorn said, "is that we're in more trouble than we know. We think we've taken every precaution, but we thought that before 9/11 too. Every time I come up here, I look down at those tanks and it scares the shit out of me. But then I think, maybe we'll get lucky and it'll just be anthrax in the T or something."

"That's true," Mack said with mock cheerfulness. "We could always get lucky."

"Who's Tony and why do you think he loves Angie?" Sykes asked the agent.

"I beg your pardon?" Hartshorn said.

Sykes handed him the binoculars. "The tank on the right, about six feet from the ground," Sykes said, pointing. "Spray paint. 'Tony Loves Angie.' That new, or was that there before?"

Agent Hartshorn examined the graffiti on the tank, in large red letters.

"No, I think that might be new," Hartshorn said. "I'll have to report that."

"I'll sleep better tonight," Sykes said. "At least you didn't try to zap the paint can out of Tony's hand."

"How do you know Tony did it?" Mack asked." Maybe Angie wanted the world to know."

DeLuca left three messages on Freddy King's voice mail without hearing back. Finally, he and Walter Ford located the offices of Hard Moves after one of Ford's contacts at the telephone company tracked down the address using a number from Katie Quinn's call log. The sign on the door was a white notecard, held in place with duct tape, upon which someone had written "Hard Moves/Ex-Communications" with a black Sharpie. Below that, fastened to the door with a thumbtack, was a piece of paper upon which someone had written, "Rehearsal is canceled due to toothache—rescheduled for next

Saturday. The gig is the 28th, not the 18th, so there's time," in pencil. The door was on the third floor of an old mill building in Malden, converted to accommodate smaller businesses, mostly potters and photographers and artists of one kind or another, a piano repair shop on the ground floor, next to a coffin maker, which seemed to be the building's anchor tenant. A neighbor in the building, an acupuncturist named Star, told them she hadn't seen anybody in there lately, and that Hard Moves and Ex-Communications had the entire north end of the top floor, mostly for storage and a space where bands could practice, with a freight elevator off the back loading dock to bring their equipment up and down.

DeLuca and Ford went back to their car and were contemplating letting themselves into the Hard Moves offices via the fire escape when DeLuca's phone chortled. It was Freddy King, calling him back. When DeLuca told King they were at the warehouse, King said he'd prefer to meet somewhere else, because the place was such a mess. They met instead at a Subway sandwich shop in Arlington. Freddy King was fifteen minutes late. He appeared to be about forty, thin, dressed in black jeans, black Converse sneakers, a black T-shirt, and a green Red Sox cap, his long hair pulled back into a ponytail. He had a weak handshake, and first thing he said was to ask if they minded sitting at one of the tables outside so that he could smoke a cigarette.

"I got your message," Freddy said. "Sorry I didn't call you back right away, but it took me a second to realize you're Jackie's cousin."

"Are you screening your calls?" DeLuca asked him.

"No, no, not at all," Freddy said. "I'm just bad about calling people. I'm always, like, people say, 'Freddy, I thought you died or something.' I'm bad."

"How do you do business?" DeLuca asked. "You're not in the white pages or the Yellow Pages. How do people find you?"

"Strictly word of mouth," Freddy said. "So thanks for keeping me in the loop with Katie. Jackie said you were the guy to talk to. He said if anybody knew what was going on, you would."

"Have you talked to the police?" Walter asked him.

"Not yet, not yet," Freddy said. "I got a call from them. This has really been rough, I gotta tell you."

"How did you know Katie Quinn?" DeLuca asked. "Where did you meet?"

"We met at AA, believe it or not," Freddy said. "I just knew her as Katie. We used to go to a meeting in Somerville. That's where we met."

"You still sober?" DeLuca asked him.

"Oh yeah," Freddy said. "Three years. It was tough for me, because I was playing in a band, and bands play in bars, so to stay sober, I had to quit the band. I'm not as tempted now."

"What do you play?"

"I play harmonica," Freddy said. "The other guys hate me because I can load out in five minutes and carry all my stuff in a backpack. I mean, they don't really hate me . . ."

As he spoke, Freddy kept glancing over their shoulders, looking nervously up and down the street, ashing his cigarette on the sidewalk more frequently than he needed to.

"Blues?" Ford asked.

"Yeah," Freddy said. "We've been putting together a Beatles cover band too, just to get gigs. Not much harmonica playing needed."

"So you and Katie are talking in AA and you just decided to go into business?" DeLuca asked.

"Not exactly," Freddy said. "It was sort of serendipitous, actually. When I bottomed out, before I quit drinking, I screamed at my ex-wife—she wasn't my ex yet. So she got a restraining order or whatever, and one night her father, my ex-father-in-law, had a heart attack, and they knew where I was living but not where she was living, so they called me and left a message to tell Sarah. My ex, except she had caller ID and wouldn't answer my calls, plus it was illegal for me to contact her, so Katie said she'd call her for me, except that that same night, her landlord was evicting her so she needed somebody to get her stuff, so I said I'd get some guys together and get her stuff if she'd call Sarah."

"Why was she getting evicted?" DeLuca said.

Freddy shrugged. "Landlord was renovating," he said. "Something like that."

"Did she talk much at meetings?" Walter asked.

"Never," Freddy said. "You can tell people you're just there to listen. She didn't want anybody to recognize her voice."

"Did she work out of your office or from home?" Ford asked.

"She did it mostly on her cell," Freddy said.

"She keep a list of her clients?" DeLuca asked. "Invoices. Billing. Call logs, stuff like that?"

"I don't know," Freddy said.

"Did she have a computer?" DeLuca asked.

"Yeah, I think she did," Freddy said.

"You're not sure?" DeLuca asked. "You never saw her working at a computer?"

"Yeah, I saw her," Freddy said. "She had a computer."

"Where?"

"It was a laptop," Freddy said.

"Is it at your office?"

"It might be," Freddy said. "I haven't been in in a while."

"Would you mind taking us there so we could look at it?" DeLuca asked.

"I'd love to, but I think the band is practicing there today, so it'd be pretty loud . . ."

"Rehearsal's canceled," DeLuca said. "Somebody has a toothache. Let's go."

"Now?"

"Yeah, now," DeLuca said.

"Okay," Freddy said. "You guys are coming with me, right?"

"Yeah, we're coming with," DeLuca said.

"Maybe you should drive," Freddy said, smiling apologetically. "My car at the moment is a step van. It's only got one passenger seat.

"Is that your truck?" DeLuca said when they rounded the corner. Across the street, he saw what appeared to be an old bread truck, and even from a distance, he could tell that the sides had recently been painted white, and not by a body shop but rather by someone using a brush and roller.

"That's it," Freddy admitted.

"No sign on the side?" Ford said, reading DeLuca's mind. "No phone number? Wouldn't that be good for business?"

"Yeah, we were talking about doing that," Freddy said. "That's probably a good idea."

At the warehouse, Freddy suggested they go in the back door, via the loading dock. The headquarters of Hard Moves/Ex-Communications was indeed a mess, for the most part, a huge space with eight-foot-tall multipaned glass windows, light from the clerestory streaming in overhead, band equipment set up on one side of the room, empty beer cases, mike stands, cords and wires on the floor, instrument cases, a drum kit, Styrofoam coffee cups, ashtrays overflowing with cigarette butts, and two desks along the opposite wall, one stacked with paperwork, the other tidy, with a flowering plant in front of the window. DeLuca could guess which desk belonged to Katie and which belonged to Freddy. On the other side of the far wall was another large space where Freddy said they stored the belongings of people who wanted their things moved but didn't have a place to put them. Most of their customers were women, he explained, leaving relationships and often taking advantage of evenings when their significant others were temporarily out of town. They'd worked for a woman who wanted, for example, to take possession of the record and CD collection she and her husband had built together, at least until the courts decided who really deserved them. Another job they'd done was for an old man whose wife collected driftwood her whole life.

"Sometimes I think we don't ask enough questions. When she died, he wanted us to go to his garage and pick up all these pieces of driftwood and put 'em back on the beaches in Rhode Island, so we did, and guess what— the cop on beach patrol gave us a ticket for littering."

"Cops," DeLuca said. "Go figure. This would be the computer you couldn't remember if she had?" He pointed to a laptop on her desk.

"That looks like it," Freddy said. "I'm not saying that's it, but that looks like it."

DeLuca and Freddy watched over Walter's shoulder as Ford turned the computer on. They saw the Windows XP welcome screen come up, then a desktop containing all the usual icons plus a number of work folders. When Ford opened the work folders, they were empty.

"It looks like somebody deleted all the work files," Ford said.

"Deleted?" DeLuca said.

"Looks like," Ford said.

"Who could have done that?" Freddy wondered.

"How long will it take you to recover the deleted files?" DeLuca asked his old friend.

"About five minutes," Ford said. "Slightly longer if she has dial-up instead of DSL. I didn't bring my disks but I can download the software I need online."

"Do it," DeLuca said. "It's all right, right?" he asked Freddy. "We're not in any hurry, are we?"

"I guess not," Freddy said nervously. "How can you find deleted files? I thought that meant they're gone."

"When you delete a file, the computer doesn't go in and remove anything," Ford explained, tapping away on the keyboard. "All you're doing is marking that space as available to be written over, but unless somebody's been doing tons of work on this thing since the files were deleted, they probably haven't been written over yet. You'd have to completely fill the hard drive with new data to really make the old stuff go away." He addressed DeLuca. "I'd say whoever tried to delete the files didn't know what he was doing. Definitely not a professional. Even amateurs know about data recovery software by now."

Freddy sat down at his desk. He glanced around the room. He drummed his fingers on his desk. He touched his nose about seven or eight times, by DeLuca's count.

"I wonder if the files have been deleted on your computer too?" DeLuca said to Freddy while Walter worked. "Maybe you should turn it on and see. Walter might have to restore the data on your hard drive next." Freddy smiled weakly. "Or maybe you could just tell us what it was you deleted, and why you recently painted your van, and who you're hiding from? Are you living in your van? You smell like you haven't had a shower in days."

"I don't know what you're talking about," Freddy said.

"Freddy, come on," DeLuca said. "You're my cousin's buddy. Jackie asked me to help you. How can I help you if you don't trust me? Seems to me you're in trouble. Tell me what's going on. Maybe I can help."

Freddy looked like he was about to cry. "Okay, but Jesus, you gotta know we didn't know," he said. "We thought she was a nurse. She said she was a nurse."

"Who did?"

"Ashley," Freddy said. "Ashley Olsen."

DeLuca and Ford exchanged a puzzled glance.

"You mean like Mary Kate and Ashley?" DeLuca said. "Like the Olsen twins from TV?"

"Oh man," Freddy said. "I knew that sounded familiar. That wasn't her name, was it?"

"Five foot tall, forty pounds, blonde, haunting blue eyes, mouth big enough to swallow a beach ball?"

Freddy shook his head.

"That wasn't Ashley Olsen. What'd she look like?"

"Dark brown hair with highlights," Freddy said. "Medium height. Really . . ."

"Chesty? Curvy?"

"Yeah, I suppose so," Freddy said. "We thought she was too good-looking to be a nurse."

"What's that supposed to mean?" Ford said. "My niece is a nurse. You think all nurses are ugly?"

"No, no," Freddy backtracked. "That's not what I mean. I just mean, you know, you look at some girls and think, 'Jesus, she'll never have to work a day in her life if she doesn't want to.' You know?"

"So what happened?" DeLuca said.

"She said she was a nurse," Freddy said. "And that she worked the late shift and didn't get off until midnight, so could we come at midnight and help her get her stuff out of the apartment because she was going home to visit her mother the next morning and didn't have any other time. But because it was so late, we had to be quiet, and we had to work quickly, which is what we advertise, that we'll get anybody out in an hour. So I put on maybe twenty guys to help."

"When was this?"

"Four days ago," Freddy said.

"What guys?"

"Musicians," Freddy said. "Guys who didn't have gigs that night. She said she'd pay a hundred bucks a guy. That's more than you usually get, playing. She hadn't even packed. We threw everything loose into steel-sack garbage bags and took the rest by hand truck."

"Where was this?"

"Number two, Harbor Towers," Freddy said. "Apartment 18B. Really nice place. So we go in and get her stuff and she pays us. We're taking computers, a real high-end stereo system, a big-screen high-def plasma TV off the wall, a wine collection."

"A nurse has a wine collection?" Ford observed.

"What do I know? Next thing I know," Freddy said, "we find out some Mafia guy has put out an open contract on whoever burglarized his apartment, number 18B, two Harbor Towers. She said it was her stuff. It was her clothes in the closet. Really fancy dresses and sparkly things. I packed them myself."

"Nurses' uniforms?" DeLuca asked.

Freddy shook his head.

"How'd you find out?" DeLuca asked. "Who told you?"

"Jackie told me," Freddy said. "He said, 'You didn't take some stuff from number two Harbor Towers last night, did you? You fucking moron . . .' Like that."

"Did he say who was after you?" DeLuca ask

"He didn't say," Freddy said. "I don't think he knew. He said he just heard this rumor that they were offering ten thousand dollars for the head of whoever hit two Harbor Towers. Jesus, I got twenty guys in trouble. Twenty friends of mine. I don't know who saw what. I don't know what neighbors are peeking out their doorways. I'm so screwed."

"Did you tell 'em?" Ford asked. "Your friends?"

Freddy shook his head.

"You might wanna do that."

"How'd this girl find you?" DeLuca said, having a hunch as to the answer he was going to get.

"Katie gave her my number," Freddy said. "It worked that way a lot. She'd refer people. My sense was that she'd been dealing with Ashley . . . with whoever."

"And maybe her number, this girl's, was in Katie's computer," DeLuca said. "But you deleted it."

"Yeah, but you can get it back, right?" Freddy said.

"Walter?" DeLuca asked. He was shaking his head.

"I don't know," Ford said. "I'm looking with the data recovery program I use and there's nothing. Zilcho."

"I swear," Freddy said, "I just put everything in the trash bin. When you first sat down, I'm asking myself, Jesus, did I forget to empty the trash bin?"

"Well," Ford said. "Then somebody who knew what they were doing came in after you and wiped the drive, 'cause there's nothing there."

"Why?" DeLuca asked. "It's a laptop, not a safe. Why not just take it and throw it in the incinerator?"

"Maybe destroying it raises more suspicion than just wiping it," Ford said. "I don't know the answer to that."

"So you're thinking whoever's stuff you took killed Katie?" DeLuca asked Freddy. Freddy nodded.

"Where's the stuff now?"

"It's still in the truck."

"Your truck?"

"The other truck," Freddy said. "We got two trucks. It's parked in back of a Radio Shack at a strip mall in Newton. Look, I don't give a shit about the stuff—I'll give it all back today if I knew who to. I just don't want whoever it is to think we stole it."

"Well, you sort of did," DeLuca said, turning to Ford. "The call log you had was from her home phone, right? We need her cell phone. The numbers for both the girl and her boyfriend could be on her contact list. I want to see the videotapes from the garage, and I want to hear the audiotapes of her last show. I also want to have a look at her apartment. I think we're going to have to talk to Wexler, as much as I'd prefer not to. You think I should call Halliday to smooth things first?"

"You want to piss Frank off?"

"Yeah, I do."

"Then call Halliday," Ford advised. "Ask the commissioner to tell Frank he has to cooperate with us. Tell him to tell Frank he has to salute."

"One last question, Freddy," DeLuca said. "Was Katie Quinn seeing anybody? Dating anybody? She have a boyfriend? Or a girlfriend, maybe?"

Freddy shook his head.

"How about Dan Rhodes?" DeLuca asked. "You think maybe they ever hooked up?"

"I doubt it," Freddy said. "She told me she thought he was gay. I think they were just friends."

"She ever talk about anybody? Maybe somebody she wished she was dating?"

"I don't think so," Freddy said. "Why?"

"We think maybe she was seeing somebody," DeLuca said. "We have reasons to believe she was."

"What reasons?" Freddy asked, but DeLuca didn't feel comfortable divulging the news that Katie Quinn had been pregnant. Perhaps she hadn't wanted anyone to know. Maybe she hadn't cared. For now, it was a secret he thought best to keep.

"I can't say, at the moment," DeLuca said. "We think maybe she knew her killer, and nine times out of ten, if the victim knows the killer, it's going to be somebody they're involved with. Or used to be involved with."

"I know her parents thought she was a lesbian because she had a gay roommate, in Northampton," Freddy said. "She wasn't one, but they thought that. I met her once. The roommate. I think her name was Claire. McGowan or McGovern or something like that. She owns a candy store."

"How do you remember that?" Walter asked.

"She brought us a huge bag of jelly beans," Freddy said. "So do you think Katie's murder was work-related? I really gotta know if it was something I did."

"Honestly, I can't say," DeLuca told him. "It sounds to me like she stepped into a lot of domestic situations where there were probably a lot of crazy angry people. Keep your cell phone on and don't screen my calls. I might have other questions I'll need your help with. And just so you know my level of commitment, these guys shot at my house this morning. Call me old-fashioned, but I take that personal."

"Should I go talk to the cops?" Freddy said. "I was thinking of doing that. I mean, I'd rather not, if I didn't have to."

"It's going to depend on what cop," DeLuca said. "Let me handle that. You don't want the kind that gives you a ticket for putting driftwood on the beach. If it looks necessary, I'll set you up with the right people."

Chapter Five

POLICE COMMISSIONER PAUL HALLIDAY WAS
delighted to hear DeLuca's voice on the other end of the
line. DeLuca knew he'd hurt the older man's feelings when
he'd reenlisted, even though Halliday understood his reasons. He'd been part of Halliday's team, early on, when De-
Luca was a young cop fresh out of the army, beginning with
the Anguillo investigation, one of the biggest Mafia family
takedowns in the history of law enforcement. He'd worked
hard under Halliday, proved himself, rose through the ranks,
and had ultimately been offered a promotion to deputy commissioner, in the summer of 2001. He was contemplating
taking the job when, in September of that year, two airplanes
hijacked by Arab terrorists hit the World Trade Center towers, where his sister Eileen worked. From that point on,
there was never a doubt as to what he needed to do to make
himself the most useful—he needed to reenlist in the same
army he'd left fifteen years earlier, for good reasons, a service filled with some of the best men he'd ever met, soldiers
who were courageous and self-sacrificing and who truly believed in the ideals that some people thought were clichés,
service to country, honor, sacrifice, loyalty to their fellow
soldiers, but also an army staffed in the higher echelons by

the biggest horses' asses he'd ever met, forming a bureau-cracy he'd come to see as insufferable. Halliday had said, "Well, I guess if we're going to be the world police, we're going to need world-class policemen."

He'd confessed that he'd always considered DeLuca as one of the top candidates for commissioner one day. De-Luca's detractors, mainly Frank Wexler and a few of his cronies, said DeLuca had ridden to the top on Halliday's coattails, and that he was a suck-up who'd been given preferential treatment his entire career.

"What can I do for you, David?" Halliday said. "I guess this isn't a social call. Wish it was."

"I'd love to catch up," DeLuca said. "Some other day. Right now, I was hoping you could call Frank for me. I'm working the Katie Quinn case for the army, but Frank's got everybody treating me like a Fed. I don't care if Frank likes me or not, but if he's going to make this personal, it's going to interfere with what I have to do. It sounds like he's doing pretty good for himself."

"He's got friends in the mayor's office," Halliday said. "His wife's brother is Speaker of the House. Did you know that?"

"I didn't," DeLuca said.

"I don't know if I told you, but I'm retiring in six months. They're talking like Frank's the next guy," Hal-liday said. "He gets results. I may not always agree with the way he gets them."

"Does he get results, or does he get the credit for the results his people produce?" DeLuca asked.

"It's a fine line, isn't it?" Halliday agreed. "I'll call Frank for you and tell him to help you. You see the evening news? Channel Six?"

"I missed it," DeLuca said.

"They did a story about how tomorrow, the *Boston Voice* is doing a story about the I4NI Web site. They listed the Web site address."

"On TV or in the *Boston Voice*?"

"Both," Halliday said. "Six at Six says they got the story from the paper."

"They connect it to Katie Quinn?"

"The paper called to ask," Halliday said. "So far, we're officially 'on another line.' Everybody's working late because of the orange alert. My FBI contacts say they've tied the Web site to the thing in South Carolina. With the golf cart. You hear about that?"

"I heard something, but it's not my beat."

"Fertilizer bomb. The got the instructions off the Web site, apparently."

"Directed, or inspired by?" DeLuca asked.

"They don't know."

"Where'd the paper get the story about the Web site?" DeLuca asked. "I doubt they were just surfing the Net and came across it."

"What do you mean?"

"Nothing," DeLuca said. "I'm just thinking that if I'm trying to spread the word about my kill-all-the-generals Web site, I might want to call in the media directly."

He called Sami on Sami's SAT phone, reaching him where Sami had taken transient slippage in the town of Vinalhaven, on the island of the same name, six miles off the coast of Maine, east of Rockland. After shots were fired at DeLuca's house, General LeDoux finally convinced General Quinn that it was no longer safe for him to stay in his home. Jambazian knew of a circle of cottages on Vinalhaven with its own small cove and dock. After retiring from the force, Sami had run a party boat, the *Lady J,* taking fishing groups out from a marina in Gloucester, a business he committed himself to when his marriage to his wife Caroline fell apart. Caroline was Bonnie's best friend, and DeLuca knew Bonnie had told Caroline at the time that she could do better. DeLuca had kept his mouth shut. In his opinion, there weren't too many men better than Sami Jambazian, a sawed-off, crabby man who'd lay down his life for his friends in a heartbeat. They'd sailed the boat two hundred miles north up the coast, but De-Luca hadn't had a chance until now to check in.

"How's he doing?" he asked Sami.

"Not good," Sami said. "He's not used to sitting out the wars."

"Is he keeping busy?"

"I thought he was reading, until I noticed he hadn't turned the page. This stuff is hitting him pretty hard."

"Can I talk to him?"

When General Quinn came on the line, DeLuca felt himself automatically straighten, a subconscious reflex but one of genuine respect.

"What can you tell me, Agent DeLuca?" Quinn asked.

"Making progress," DeLuca said. "I'm headed over to the police department now. We met with the FBI and I have two of my people working with them. They're getting indications that I4NI is Eastern European, maybe an Al Qaeda splinter or wannabe or maybe not. It's going to hit the papers tomorrow. We're also looking into Katie's businesses, in case there's a connection there. When was it you last spoke?"

"I'm truly ashamed to admit this," Quinn said. "I think it was almost a year ago. She'd called and asked me if I wanted company, decorating her mother's grave. It was the first anniversary. I'd already been that morning, so I told her that, but apparently that wasn't what she was asking. I realized that as soon as we hung up."

"Did she ever talk about her work?" DeLuca asked.

"No," General Quinn said. "But I was aware of it. I mean, I listened to her, almost every night. I haven't been sleeping all that well. When I'd lie in bed, it gave me some comfort to hear her voice. She sounded a bit like her mother, to my ear. Though I'm probably the only one who thought so."

"Did she ever talk to you about her other business?"

"I wasn't aware she had another business," General Quinn said. "What was it?"

"Kind of domestic mediation service, I suppose you'd call it," DeLuca said. "I have another question. This might seem obvious, but can you think of any specific Serbian groups who might be acting vindictively towards you? Anybody who ever threatened you directly?"

"How about all of them?" Quinn said. "I can't think of anybody specific. I know that at one time, there was a million-dollar reward placed on my head."

"By whom?"

"Well, I thought it was Milosevic," Quinn said. "Or the goverment. Some nationalist group. We were never sure."

"Do you think that reward might still be in place?"

"I don't know," the general said. "I haven't really thought about it. I suppose it could be. I'm sorry I can't be of more help."

"That's all right," DeLuca said. "Could I talk to Sami again?"

When Sami came on the line, he asked him what was going on in the department, since Sami had stayed in closer contact with his former colleagues than Walter had. Sami said Wexler was the guy everybody assumed was going to be the next commissioner, though nothing was carved in stone. There was talk of a major department shake-up in the near future, budget cuts, personnel layoffs, restructuring, and everyone knew the shake-up would commence once Paul Halliday stepped down. Everybody wanted to be on Wexler's good side when it happened, if he was going to be the new commissioner, and nobody wanted to be on his bad side. Wexler was expected to settle a few old scores once he took over. Even guys who were mere weeks short of retirement were afraid of him, where getting canned could affect their pensions or make them have to pay for their own health insurance once they retired.

"Easier to appease than oppose," Sami said. "People wonder why assholes rise to power. By the way, I've been following your reports on the Chim you gave me—"

" 'Sim,' " DeLuca said, correcting his friend's pronunciation.

"CIM," Sami said. "Anyway, the general and I were talking about the reward earlier, and it reminded me of something, so I called some CI friends in Balad—you remember that wanted poster of you that they had in Iraq? The one on the Web site now? And you thought the reward was funded by Mohammed Al-Tariq?"

"Yeah?" DeLuca said, Sami referring to the former head of Saddam Hussein's Mukhabarat, or secret police. Al-Tariq had been killed by an allied bombing raid. De-Luca was quite sure he didn't have to worry about him.

"It's back," Sami said. "I guess they don't know you left. It's up to $50,000 now too. That's a record, for a guardsman."

"Whoo-wee," DeLuca said. "I feel so honored. Who's putting up the money? They know?"

"They think Al-Durri," Sami said. "Maybe Zarqawi, or bin Laden himself. You think that's got anything to do with anything?"

"Maybe," DeLuca said. "Sounds like they miss me."

"As long as they keep missing you," Sami said.

Vasquez was playing solitaire on his handheld when his phone rang.

It was Elizabeth.

"Agent Vasquez?" she said.

"Call me Julio," he said. "Or Hoolie."

"How about Hools?" she asked.

"Works for me," he said.

"Where are you?" she asked.

"I'm in the camper van across the street," he told her. "It's a rental. I figured if I was going to be spending the night in my vehicle, I might as well be comfortable."

He saw her silhouette appear in the window where she pulled the curtains aside, her curves obvious even from that distance.

"Nice ride. Watch out for the meter maids," she said. "They're pretty nasty around here."

"I already got a ticket," Hoolie said. He looked at the house. She moved away from her bedroom window and closed the curtains. He'd already determined that the other two floors of the house were unoccupied.

"I just wanted to apologize for before," she said. "I'm sorry if my friends hurt you."

"They roughed me up pretty good," Hoolie said facetiously. "I thought I was a goner there for a minute."

"For a minute?" she said.

"Maybe not a minute," he said.

"Anyway, I want to thank you for looking out for me," she said. "I'm home now. I guess you knew that. I have to work on my paper but I'm so wiped. I might just go to bed. Anyway, thanks. I'll see you tomorrow. Hools."

"See you tomorrow," he said.

"Call me Biz."

"Biz."

He'd returned to his game and had played through six times, winning twice, when the alarm sounded, indicating someone had breached the digital tripwire Scott had drawn around Elizabeth's house using satellite imagery.

Vasquez quickly found his sidearm and exited the van on the passenger side, peering cautiously around the rear of the vehicle. The house looked dark and undisturbed, the light off in Elizabeth's window. Yet when he checked his CIM again, he saw that though he'd feared someone entering the house, in fact, someone had exited it.

He ran to the back of the house, which was separated from the yard and the house behind it by a gated fence and a row of lilacs. He pushed through the gate and ran to University Road in time to see Elizabeth turning the corner onto Mt. Auburn. He followed her past the Harvard Square Hotel and Ben and Jerry's, more careful now, knowing she'd spotted him before, and watched as she turned left on Dunster. She had a cloth bag over her shoulder, and she walked quickly, as if she were late for something. As he followed, he called INSCOM/JTIOC and asked for Captain DeLuca, only to be told Scott was off shift. He ID'd himself to the officer on duty, a lieutenant named Boyd, and asked to be patched through to the Harvard Square surveillance system, setting the pattern recognition program to watch for Elizabeth LeDoux, whose biometrics Hoolie had transmitted earlier. It took Boyd a moment to call up the appropriate files. While he waited, Vasquez followed Elizabeth down into the Harvard Square T station, still crowded with people, and used the camera on his CIM to watch from around the corner where she waited on the Red Line's inbound platform, the music from her iPod blasting in her earphones.

When she got on the train, Vasquez boarded two cars behind her and watched the surveillance feed from the camera at the front of her car. He was prepared to move in when two men appeared to loom closer to her in a menacing manner, but then they walked to the end of the car and sat down. She got off at Downtown Crossing and switched to the Orange Line, taking it one stop to Chinatown. He followed her past the sushi shops and the noodle shops and the Asian markets, past the florists and the funeral parlors, the bars, and down Harrison Avenue toward what was once called the Combat Zone, a collection of seedy bars and strip joints that had mostly closed in the last ten years, replaced by more lucrative office buildings and parking garages. Half a block short of Tyler Street, she turned down an alley where Vasquez caught up just in time to see her enter the back door to a building, where a pair of beefy-looking bouncer types were smoking cigarettes.

When he went around to the front of the building, things became a bit clearer. The building was home to the

Gold Club, the last strip joint in downtown Boston, formerly the Glass Slipper until the management had tried to upgrade their decor and clientele to keep up with the changing times, now that naked women and hardcore porn were everywhere on the Internet and in the video stores, and live clubs had to try harder.

Vasquez paid the cover charge and found a dark booth in the back, asking for a Diet Coke when the half-naked waitress came to take his order. The doormen had decided not to frisk him—he'd been prepared to flash his B's and C's and hope for the best, had they tried. As with most strip joints he'd ever been in, the crowd was sullen, drunk, and silent, mostly single men, a large number of them Asians in food-stained white chef's smocks, none of the men seated closer than ten feet from each other, save the few at the stage rail who'd come armed with ones and fives to buy as much artificial intimacy as they could from the girls whose real names they didn't know and never would.

When Elizabeth LeDoux appeared onstage, the DJ announced her as "Kitten," full name "Kitten Kaboodle." Her entrance song was "Why Can't We Be Friends?" by the band War, which, given that she was a general's daughter, had to be an inside joke that only Vasquez got. "I seen you walkin' down in Chinatown," the lyrics went, "I called you but you could not look around . . ." Her body was incredible, it did not take Vasquez, or anybody else in the room, long to discover, though as an occasional visitor to strip clubs the world over, Vasquez had to say her pole work was only average. Her face, even behind the heavy eye shadow and lipstick, remained sweet and youthful, her smile genuine and smirkish, as if she were thinking something dirty, and maybe she was. Eventually she was one of three dancers on the stage, squatting by the Plexiglas sneeze guard to pay attention to her regulars, and in particular a middle-aged Chinese man who appeared to be tucking twenty-dollar bills in her garter belt at a rapid clip. She chatted with him, leaned in, talked to him from between her legs, smiled, licked her lips, and, on three separate occasions, adjourned to a private room for a personal lap dance.

She took a cab home at around two in the morning, Vasquez following from a distance in a second cab. She got out on University and cut between buildings to enter her apartment through the back door. Vasquez noticed, as they drove, that a third cab had followed them both, but by the time his own vehicle stopped, the third cab had turned away and was gone. By the time he thought to call Lieutenant Boyd back at JTIOC to track it via satellite, it was too late.

"David DeLuca," Frank Wexler said. "It's Sergeant, right? I heard you were a sergeant in the National Guard."

"You got it wrong, Frank. It's Special Agent," DeLuca said. "You remember Walter."

Heads had turned in the squad room as they made their way to Wexler's office, a lot of faces DeLuca remembered and a number of friends, including Billy Morrissey and Kaz Takata, but few of the detectives on duty dared to say hello or shake hands. Wexler was eating sushi from the black plastic take-out tray, a can of caffeine-free Diet Coke on his desk.

"I remember Walter," Wexler said. "So you're like below lieutenant now, in the army, right? I got a nephew who's a lieutenant. I think he's twenty-five years old. That must suck, being outranked by so many kids."

"Rank doesn't matter in counterintelligence," DeLuca said. "We can arrest generals. We don't even wear our rank on our uniforms. Half the time we wear suits. Personally, I'm happy as long as the suits I wear are nicer than yours, Frank."

"Well that didn't take long," Ford said, rolling his eyes. He'd politely suggested that David mind his manners. DeLuca had promised he'd try.

"I'm not going to let you get to me, DeLuca," Wexler said. "I don't have to. You're a civilian, as far as I'm concerned. You're not a part of this, and if I want Feds, I already got the FBI. I'm only talking to you because your sugar daddy called and said I had to work with you. As far as I'm concerned, I don't need the Fucking Bureau of Investigation and I definitely don't need the army. Particularly considering how you fucked up in Iraq."

Maybe that was the problem, DeLuca thought. Wexler's efforts to bait him had always been so transparent and obvious that DeLuca often took the bait, just to show him how easy it was to throw the hook. Their styles could not have been more opposite. DeLuca liked to enter into a line of inquiry by establishing a rapport and building trust, bit by bit, with the people involved, creating a web of support where individuals within the network felt safe or at least realized it was in their best interest to help, a style and technique that was sometimes at odds with how the rest of the military worked, he granted, but really the only way to get the results you wanted when operating in a foreign combat environment under asymmetrical conditions. Frank, on the other hand, liked to needle and annoy,

threaten and intimidate, bully and berate, and that was just
the people who worked for him, in the belief that his employees worked best when they were scared of losing their
jobs. He treated suspects and witnesses worse, though he
could turn on a kind of unctuous charm when the politicians were present. Halliday had tried to pair them once
in an interrogation, a good-cop/bad-cop experiment that
ended badly when DeLuca took Wexler out in the hall and
punched him in the nose for the way he was treating their
guest.

"Can we have a look in the evidence room, Frank?"
DeLuca said. "Then we'll be out of your way."

Wexler resisted a moment longer, then snapped his fingers to summon a young detective named Jones, who he
instructed to take DeLuca and Ford to evidence.

"You can see what we've got," Wexler said dismis-
sively. "Anybody wants to talk to you, that's their business. Greg, make sure they don't accidentally remove
anything."

In the evidence room on the third floor, the clerk examined their credentials and made them sign in, then left
to return with a pair of cardboard boxes, which he set on
a large silver table. They set aside the labeled plastic bag
containing the clothes Katie Quinn had been wearing the
night she was killed. In a large bag marked "purse contents," DeLuca found a can of pepper spray, about the size
of a small banana.

"Can you talk to us, Jones?" he asked. "We'll understand if you'd rather not."

"I guess I've been given permission," Jones said.

"It's Greg, right?" DeLuca asked. The man nodded.
"This says 'purse contents'—the pepper spray was inside

the purse when they found the body? I thought I looked in her purse at the crime scene. She wasn't holding it in her hand?"

"It was in the purse," Jones said. "That's what it says here."

"I must have missed it. How fresh were the fingerprints on it?"

"I'm not sure," Jones said.

"What I'm wondering was, did she have the spray in her hand, crossing the park or entering the garage, and then she put it back in her purse when she got her car keys, or did she just leave it in her purse? I took some pictures of the scene but I didn't see it."

"I'm not sure what the answer to that is," Jones said. DeLuca came close to telling him to get the answer, then remembered that he couldn't give the young detective orders.

"Might be a good thing to know," DeLuca said. "It might tell us whether or not she knew the killer. Or what her state of mind was. Maybe the pepper spray was under the body."

"Is there a list somewhere of the numbers on her contact list or her recent calls?" Ford said, holding up the bag that contained Katie Quinn's cell phone.

"I don't think so," Jones said. "I'm not sure anyone's gotten to that yet. We've been pretty tied up with the orange alert."

"You mind if I make a list?" Ford said. "I won't open the bag."

"Okay," Jones said. "I guess that's good."

"Can I use this?" Ford asked the clerk, pointing at one of the desktops in the evidence room. The clerk shrugged.

While Ford worked, DeLuca examined two items that caught his eye, taken from Katie Quinn's apartment. One was a lavender negligee, made of lace-trimmed satin, the garment cheap and trashy-looking. The second was a necklace made from rather exquisite glass beads. According to the evidence registration tags, the negligee came from TJ Maxx, a discount bargain store near Downtown Crossing, eighty dollars originally, marked down to twenty. The necklace was a one-of-a-kind item that had been sold at a jewelry store on Newbury Street called Le Bling, with a price tag of just under three hundred dollars.

"What can you tell me about this?" DeLuca asked Jones, holding up the negligee.

"That was in her laundry," Jones said. "There's a semen stain on it."

"I can see that," DeLuca said. "The DNA report not back yet?"

"Not yet," Jones said. "I know they put a rush on it. I think they expect it in the morning."

"No idea who purchased it?"

"They're looking through the store credit card records," Jones said. "But if she paid cash for it, that's not going to help."

"You think *she* bought this?" DeLuca said. "This feels like a gift to me. This isn't the sort of thing you buy yourself. Or maybe it is. Maybe she wanted to cheer herself up."

"Or cheer somebody else," Ford said. "Apparently somebody became quite cheerful."

"How about the necklace?" DeLuca asked. "Somebody talk to the clerk who sold it?"

"We did," Jones said. "The clerk remembered how the guy was bragging about how he had an American Express

Black Card and how only a few Hollywood celebrities had them because they carried a hundred-thousand-dollar credit line. That was purchased by a man named Vincent Pastorelli."

"Vinnie P?" DeLuca said. "Vinnie Potatoes? Really?"

Jones nodded, asking, "You know who he is?"

"Vinnie P. and I go way back," DeLuca said. "I just figured he would have been twenty feet under a gravel pile somewhere by now. What's he up to these days?"

"I heard he did a year at Walpole," Ford said. "He's running a crew out of Brookline and Newton, mostly sports book. That was his big thing."

"Remind me to talk to my cousin," DeLuca said. "So how did a necklace purchased by Vincent Pastorelli end up on Katie Quinn's dresser?"

"Wexler thinks Pastorelli was trying to influence the victim, to get her to work with him," Detective Greg Jones said. "The guys who bet on sports all listen to her show. If she said David Ortiz was hurting or Tom Brady had a hangover, that could swing a lot of money one way or the other."

"So Wexler thinks this was a bribe?" DeLuca asked. "A payoff of some kind?"

"Something like that," Jones said. "Maybe just a gift."

"We got two gifts then," DeLuca said. "From two different people. Because I'll tell you one thing, Vinnie Potatoes is not going to be caught dead waving his American Express Black Card around in TJ Maxx."

"That makes sense," Jones agreed.

"What are you guys making of the Web site?" DeLuca said. "The I4NI Web site?"

Jones shrugged. "Not a whole lot," he said. "That's more FBI than us."

"So Frank's just looking at Vinnie P. and nobody else?" DeLuca asked.

"We think Vinnie owns a Smith and Wesson fifty," Jones said. "We don't have purchase records but we got someone who said they saw him with one."

"How many fifties like it were sold in Massachusetts in the last year?" DeLuca asked.

"Thirty-seven," Jones said.

"And they're all accounted for?" DeLuca asked. "Sounds like the kind of gun that would be hot on the streets. I'm guessing every gangbanger from here to L.A. wants one. You talk to the New Hampshire gun show guys and the illegal dealers too?"

"We're talking to them," Jones said. "We haven't talked to all of them yet."

"What are these?" DeLuca said, holding up a pair of CDs in plastic bags.

"One's the transcript of the radio show from the night she was killed," Jones said. "The other is the video from the parking garage security cameras. We digitize everything now."

"These are backups?" DeLuca asked. "You have this on your hard drive?"

Jones nodded.

"Mind if we download to our handhelds?" DeLuca asked.

"Frank said you weren't supposed to remove anything," Jones said.

"We're not removing anything," DeLuca said. "We're making copies. I'll listen to them later. Okay? These'll be right here, safe and sound."

"I guess it's okay," Jones said.

While Walter performed the data transfer, synching files wirelessly and burning CDs as well, DeLuca looked through the rest of the evidence. He saw credit card charges at modestly priced restaurants where the tabs totaled to between thirty and forty dollars for two entrees—she was buying somebody dinner. He saw purchases made at men's stores, something at Yale Genton for five hundred dollars, something else at Cole Haan for three hundred. She'd been buying someone, someone male, expensive gifts. On the list of items found in her bathroom, he saw both women's and men's deodorants. He hoped somebody had been taking DNA samples from her pillows and hairbrushes and bathtub drains, but he didn't see anything in the reports to suggest anyone had.

He thanked Detective Jones for his assistance and said he hoped Wexler wouldn't hold it against him, even though it was exactly the sort of thing Wexler did.

"I'll tell him you were a useless piece of shit," DeLuca offered.

"Thanks," Jones said. "I'd appreciate it."

They boarded the elevator to the ground floor. Before the doors closed, Kaz Takata got in. DeLuca thought to say something, but Takata stood silent with his hands clasped behind his back, staring at the numbers near the ceiling and at, DeLuca saw, the surveillance camera in the elevator, which DeLuca took to mean Takata wanted to talk, but not here.

Outside the building, they went separate ways, though when DeLuca reached his car, he saw Takata waiting down the street. When he pulled over, Takata got in the back.

"Hey, Walter," the detective said. "David."

"What's up, Kaz?" Walter said. "We're sorry about Frank."

"We're all sorry about Frank," Kaz Takata said. "Part of me doesn't care what he does to me, but part of me does."

"I thought you said you were bulletproof," DeLuca said over his shoulder.

"I am, but I have friends he could screw, just because he knows he can't screw me," Takata said. "Let me give you my cell if you need anything. I'll screen my calls if I can't talk, but if I can, I'll be glad to help. Morrissey told me to tell you the same thing. I wrote his cell down too." He handed DeLuca a slip of paper with two phone numbers on it.

"I appreciate it, Kaz," DeLuca said. "What do you think—you think Pastorelli is in the picture?"

"He's connected," Takata said. "I couldn't say how. He had the gun, a possible motive, he's already killed people. We got six calls to his cell phone, including one the night she was killed. Plus we can't find him anywhere. Why would he be hiding?"

"Why do people hide?" DeLuca said. "They're scared."

"You can let me out on the corner," Takata said. "I'll let you know if I hear anything."

They drove the seven blocks from police headquarters and pulled up in front of the Harbor Towers apartment building, a high-rise off Pier 4 and one of the priciest pieces of real estate in Boston, overlooking the harbor and a short walk from the Aquarium. Walter was still talking to his wife on the cell phone from the passenger seat when they arrived, explaining why he was going to be late. DeLuca told him he'd have a look inside for himself.

He approached the doorman and showed his badge. The doorman was dressed in a red coat festooned with gold braids and epaulets, a bellman's hat rising from his head. He looked like he'd seen a ghost. His nametag said his name was Mohammed.

"Please," he said, his hands folded in front of him as if in prayer. "Please, I beg you, I have a family. I've been in this country for fifteen years. Please sir. I am Shiite, not Sunni. Please."

"Mohammed—" DeLuca said.

"Please, there is no need. I will tell you anything you need to know. You must listen. I have three boys. Ramzi is only four years old—"

"Brother," DeLuca said in Arabic. *"Abu Ramzi. I did not come to arrest you. I only want to ask you some questions. If you help me, perhaps I could help you."*

How many times had he said the exact same thing in Iraq?

"What can I do?" Mohammed said. *"Please. There's no reason to arrest me. I cannot go to Guantanamo. I have a family."*

"Nobody's going to Guantanamo," DeLuca said. *"You can relax, friend. You'll be home with your family tonight and for many nights to come. I just need to know who's living in apartment 18B."*

"Apartment 18B?" Mohammed said.

"Yeah," DeLuca said.

"That is Gina," the doorman said.

"Blonde, sort of . . . shapely?"

"Gina," Mohammed repeated.

"Last name?"

"I don't know her last name," Mohammed said. *"Please, I would like to help you."*

"Can you give me a key?" DeLuca asked.

The doorman said he would.

When DeLuca used the key to let himself in, he saw that the apartment, a spacious single-bedroom, was empty of all furniture, the plush tan carpet in need of a good vacuuming, but apart from the stray ponytail holders and bobby pins and a toothpick he found in the kitchen, there was nothing. He put the pony tail holder in one of the plastic bags he'd carried in his coat pocket and the toothpick in the second, for possible testing. The carpet directly in front of the door was dirty, indicating that a number of people had come in and out without wiping their feet. It had rained the night Freddy's crew of twenty unemployed musicians had emptied the apartment, if DeLuca recalled correctly. They would have tracked mud in. He spoke with the doorman again on his way out.

"Did she pay the rent or did someone pay it for her?" he asked.

"I don't think she paid it," Mohammed said. "It's not her apartment."

"I thought you said it was."

"You asked who lived there," Mohammed said. "Not whose apartment it is. I try to be honest for you."

"Whose apartment is it, then?"

"She called him Vinnie," Mohammed said.

"Tall guy?" DeLuca said, holding his hand over his own head. "About this tall, black hair, big nose, wears a lot of leather jackets?"

"That's him," Mohammed said. "It was his apartment. He paid the rent. I don't know his last name but you can ask the management. But it would be better if you didn't tell them I told you."

"That's all right, Mohammed," DeLuca said. "I already know his last name."

He paused at the car before getting in, opening the door and telling Walter he'd be just another second. He'd spotted a brown sedan across the street and crossed to it, knocking on the tinted window. When he did, the window slowly rolled down. He stared at the man for a moment, trying to remember his name.

"Is it Peters?" DeLuca asked.

"Peterson," the man said. "Detective."

"Detective Peterson—I'm Special Agent David DeLuca with army counterintelligence."

"I know who you are," Peterson said, embarrassed.

"I was just wondering—have you guys been watching the apartment for a long time, or just since the shooting?"

Peterson looked at his partner, whom DeLuca didn't recognize. The partner shrugged to say he didn't know what to do, or if it was okay to answer the question.

"We've been here about a month," Peterson said.

"What for? You were taking down the sports thing?"

Peterson nodded.

"You were here the night Gina moved out?"

"I wasn't, personally," Peterson said.

"So you're looking for Vinnie Potatoes?" DeLuca said. "You think he might come back here?"

"He might," Peterson said.

"Yeah, he might," DeLuca said. "Tell Wexler if he's still looking for Freddy, I might be able to help him."

DeLuca returned to the car, where Ford loaded the disk containing the recording of her last radio show into the

car's CD player. They listened while DeLuca drove
Walter to his home in Sudbury, one of Boston's western
suburbs. The show was, to DeLuca's ear, a kind of roller-
coaster ride, mixing layer after layer of clips, quotes, and
samples, song fragments, promotions, plugs, and sound
effects in a sonic jumble that was hard to deconstruct as
it raced by, a sort of aural chaos that mimicked an offensive line colliding with a defensive line, perhaps, or a fast
break down a basketball court, and then the chaos would
abate after a minute or two, and Dan Rhodes would break
in in a singsongy voice, speaking rapidly, almost shouting, "You got Dan the Man the sports fan of *SPORTS NA-
TION* gone crazy *SPORTS NATION*'S in the third hour,
we're the night shift, I'm Downtown Danny Rhodes with
Katie Q and Simon on the board as my Little Engineer
That Could, Simon just took a break to go down to the gay
bar on the corner for a mochaccino latte—"

"Gotta have those mochaccino lattes," Simon cut in,
to the sound of obviously canned laughter, cut short after
only a second.

"Katie Q with the scores on the fifteen, callers; the
lines are open but people, please, when you call, I beg
of you—have something to say. Is that asking too much?
Preferably something intelligent. Have an opinion. Don't
call in and say, 'Uh, Dan, um, uh, I was, um, wondering, um, what do you think the Patriots' chances are this
year, um . . .' because you know what? First, I don't care.
Actually, I don't know what their chances are. I'm not a
fortune-teller. And that's not good interactive radio. Second, we have a two 'um' rule. I know at ESPN or Fox
sports radio they let the callers 'um' all night. We don't.
So get to the point. Give me your bang, and I'll bang you

back. Call 1-880-SPO-NATN, that's 1-880-776-6286, and if you're a complete idiot, I mean, a total moron, like our last caller, call 1-880-222-ESPN or 1-880-FOX-1212, because those are the other shows."

"Can we do that?" Katie asked.

"Sure, why not?" Dan said. "What are they gonna do—sue us?"

"Now that's interactive radio," Simon said.

"E-mails at www.danmansports.com, hello, Tony from Dallas, you're on the air . . ."

Most of the calls, in the early part of the show, had to do with the pennant races and what trades the various baseball teams needed to make to shore up their rosters for the final run in September. The middle of the show turned personal, beginning with a series of callers professing their love for Katie Q.

"I just think you're great," one typical caller said. "I think you're like the best thing on the radio. I know you're a bit of a Yankees fan—"

"I'm not a Yankees fan," Katie corrected him. "I'm just saying you don't have to hate the Yankees to love the Sox. I'm not big on George Steinbrenner, but who's not going to love Derek? Or Bernie? Or even A-Rod?"

"Yeah, I know," the caller said, "and I think the best thing about you is two things. You're not afraid to speak your mind, but you're not afraid to change your mind."

"Maybe you two should get a room?" Dan suggested.

"I'm just saying," the caller went on . . .

But then, for the last hour of the show, the calls turned viciously personal. Walter fast-forwarded through the positive callers, but the negative ones quickly outnumbered them.

"I don't know what these guys are talking about," Ron from Las Vegas said. "I mean, really, I think Katie is just a toadie. She never disagrees with you, Dan, she just smiles and laughs at all your jokes—"

"She *smiles*?" Dan said, cutting Ron from Las Vegas off. "THIS IS RADIO! YOU CAN'T TELL WHEN SOMEONE IS SMILING! Rick from Missoula, you're on the air."

"I think that last caller had a point . . ."

"I just don't think Katie's opinions are all that well-informed," Russell from Charlotte said. "I find myself sort of tuning out while she's talking or taking the opportunity to go to the bathroom and waiting until Dan comes back on . . ."

"I just don't know why all these callers think Katie is so hot," Mike from Nashville said. "First of all, there's no pictures of her on the Internet, so I think that has to mean something, and second, everybody's got this idea because you guys joke about her boobs so much that she has a big chest, and I've seen her—"

"You've seen me?" Katie asked him. "You've seen my chest?"

"Yeah, I was in Boston at a Celtics game last year, and I saw you with my binoculars in the press box—"

"That's funny," Katie said, "because I was looking for your penis with a microscope and I couldn't find anything."

Dan the Man came to Katie's defense time and time again, though he was right when he'd said Katie could give as well as she got. All the same, it was ugly. It was hate radio, rampant misogyny, a series of frustrated, lonely men listening to their radios in the middle of the night and taking out their frustrations on the one woman willing, or forced, to listen to them. It was cruel, DeLuca thought, for the amount of time Dan Rhodes and his engineer let it go on. Surely there were other callers with other things to say. He felt embarrassed for Katie as she took shot after shot, forced to respond, and she sounded like she was rolling with the punches, but you could only roll so far. Why hadn't Rhodes cut it off? Did it make good radio? Did it help the ratings?

DeLuca paid closer attention when, toward the end, a caller with a deep voice, identifying himself as Robert from Baltimore, phoned in and said, "Katie Q, I think you are good girl. You should not listen to these people. You know who you are in your heart. Okay? That's all."

"Did you hear that?" DeLuca said, stopping the CD.

"What about it?"

"What was that accent?" DeLuca asked. "Was it Slavic?"

"I don't know," Walter said. "I guess it could have been."

"Can you copy that section?" DeLuca said. "I want you to send it to a guy at the Defense Language Institute in Monterey to identify the accent. And run it through voice recognition too, while we're at it. Who knows? Maybe Robert from Baltimore is our guy."

"I can do that," Walter said. "I'll work on this when I get home."

"Get some sleep too," DeLuca said. "Poor Katie. What a bad night to have as your last night."

"It probably explains this," Walter said, handing De-Luca back his CIM. "I put it on your handheld so that you could look at it. I was watching it while you were upstairs in the apartment. This is the only footage from the parking garage surveillance cameras that Katie is in. It's a bit hard to watch."

"Why?"

"You'll see," Walter said. They'd reached his house, DeLuca's car idling at the end of Walter's cul-de-sac. "Just tap 'play.'"

The image was from the parking garage elevator. According to the digital clock signature in the corner, the time was 4:51 a.m., the footage taken a few minutes before Katie Quinn was murdered. DeLuca watched as the elevator doors opened and Katie Quinn got in. She pressed the buttons, turned, slumped against the back wall of the elevator, looked up at the numbers and toward the camera, and then she burst into tears. She cried for a moment, then dried her eyes on her sleeve and sniffed, but she didn't move when the elevator doors opened on her floor. Instead, she stayed in the elevator and sobbed, lowering her head and covering her eyes with her hands, her shoulders shaking. There was no sound accompanying the footage. At one point, she turned her back to the camera, facing into the corner of the elevator, her anguish complete. He saw her struggle to regain her composure, straightening up and taking deep breaths through her nose, trying to still herself. She turned, tilted her head up again, eyes closed, hugging herself, and then DeLuca read her lips as she said, "Please, God . . ."

"I guess she wasn't as tough as everybody thought she was," Walter said.

"Guess not," DeLuca said.

As he drove home, DeLuca thought about loneliness. Katie had been lonely, probably for a long time. She'd been buying expensive gifts for someone. Who? She wasn't wealthy. Buying expensive gifts made her seem desperate.

She was two months pregnant. When he checked the inventory of her apartment that he'd downloaded to his CIM at police headquarters, there weren't any home pregnancy tests in her medicine cabinet or bathroom wastebasket. There were two large bottles of women's multivitamins on the list, one still unopened, suggesting she knew she was pregnant. She would have missed her period for two menstrual cycles. She would have tested herself. Yet the thought that she would give birth gave her no comfort, there in the elevator. Maybe she wasn't feeling good. Bonnie had been sick as a dog for the first trimester that she was pregnant with Scottie.

Thinking of Bonnie, and of loneliness, made him want to drive past his house, just to have a look at it, an impulse he resisted. Bonnie had said she felt lonely, living in the same house with him, and he understood what she meant because he'd felt it too, a massive gulf between them, too wide to bridge. They were cordial, friendly, but she hadn't acted like she was in love with him for a long time. He remembered when the yard was full of Scottie's toys, his Big Wheel always left in the middle of the driveway, his T-ball tee loaded and ready for action beneath the maple tree— the house had once been filled to the brim with joy, or so it had seemed. Perhaps it didn't take much joy to fill a house. The house was empty now. He considered calling Bonnie, but it was too late, plus he could imagine what she'd say. "Oh, you're at the Cooper, and I'm at Fort Bragg . . ."

He parked his car in the hotel parking garage.

The hotel lobby was empty. He looked to see if he could find a copy of the next day's *Boston Voice* in the newsstands out front, but they hadn't been delivered yet, a stack of *USA Today*s and yesterday's *Globe*s on a table by the elevator.

In the elevator to his floor, he finally allowed himself to realize how tired he was. He'd been at it all day. He paused at the vending machine off the elevator lobby on his floor and considered his snack options. The six-pack of Oreo cookies appealed to him, but without a carton of milk to wash it down, what was the point?

At his door, he put his key card in the slot, watched the light on the door lock turn from red to green, but then he changed his mind about the Oreos—Oreos and a Diet Coke wasn't as good as Oreos and cold milk, but it was still better than no Oreos at all.

He pulled his key card out of the slot and turned to head for the snack machine. He'd walked three steps when the blast hit, a tremendous explosion that blew out the door, filling the corridor with smoke and debris, the percussion knocking DeLuca to the ground and leaving a loud ringing in his ears that persisted for over an hour, but other than that, he was unharmed. A quick inventory revealed no broken bones or major lacerations. He struggled to clear his thoughts. People ran in the hall, in all directions, some of them in bathrobes and pajamas, frightened. Security guards appeared. Firefighters too.

Someone asked him if he was all right.

He said he was, struggling to his feet. He felt dizzy.

Someone asked him if he knew what day it was.

He said it was night, not day.

Someone asked him his name.

He said he'd rather not say.

Slowly, the smoke cleared, inside his head and out. The explosion, he saw, had not been so large after all, just enough C4 (he suspected) to kill one man—him—wired to the lock on the door with a brief delay.

It meant two things. Somebody who knew what they were doing, probably with military experience, was still trying to kill him. It also meant they knew how to find him. Perhaps he'd felt safe in his own hometown, his guard down, but for whatever reason, he'd made the mistake of registering under his own name when he'd signed in. It wasn't a mistake he would have made in a combat arena, but he'd forgotten that that definition now included the United States.

Chapter Six

WALTER CALLED HIM THE FOLLOWING MORNING on his mobile.

"Good morning, chief," Walter said. "You sleep okay?"

"Not really," DeLuca said. "I had a problem with my hotel room."

"Somebody blow it up or something?"

"Something like that."

"What happened?"

"Somebody blew it up."

"Really? Geez. I was kidding. How'd they blow it up?"

"IED," DeLuca said. "They're getting better and better at it. In Iraq, they were wiring them to garage door openers and motion detectors. This one was wired to the door lock."

"You okay?"

" 'Okay' wouldn't be the first word I'd choose," he said. " 'Uninjured,' I suppose."

"How about 'angry'?"

" 'Angry' works too," DeLuca said. "At myself. I didn't register under a fake name. You can check your reservation online just by going to the hotel Web site and typing in your name and social."

"They have your social?"

"Apparently," DeLuca said.

"It takes some technological sophistication to access stuff like that," Ford said. "You never did one of those on-line family tree things, did you?"

"Bonnie was into that," DeLuca said.

"It's not hard to get somebody's mother's maiden name through a genealogy Web site," Ford said. "You're not supposed to post information any newer than a hundred years old."

"Now you tell me," DeLuca said. "It still doesn't explain how they knew to look for me. Did we search the names Dan and Colleen gave us for people with advanced computer engineering degrees or people who've worked in tech support, stuff like that?"

"We started," Ford said. "I can get on that. There were a lot of names."

"Take the day," DeLuca said. "I have some errands to run that I can do myself."

"I went over the tape of Katie's last show and the call logs," Ford said. "I sent that clip you wanted me to send to DLI, by the way. I think I found something interesting."

"What's that?"

"Well," Ford said, "I made a time line to run beside the transcripts of the show. So get this. Between the hours of midnight and five in the morning, she made four calls on her cell phone. One to a number in Northampton at 12:36, one at 2:01 a.m. to a cell belonging to one Joey D'Angelo—"

"Who takes bets for Vinnie Pastorelli."

"Correct, for Vinnie P., who she called at 2:45, and one from her own cell phone to the station from 3:50 to 4:12," Ford said.

"So she called Vinnie's boy and then she called Vinnie," DeLuca said. "What about?"

"That's just it," Ford said. "She couldn't have called Joey or Vinnie. According to the chronology, she was on the air at 2:01 and 2:45. She couldn't have been talking on her phone and on the radio at the same time."

"Meaning the show was taped?" DeLuca said.

"The show's live," Ford said. "Interactive radio. The only thing they tape and rerun is her final scoreboard of who beat who, which she records at 4:15, and then they run it again at 4:30 and 4:45."

"She loaned her phone to somebody else," DeLuca concluded. "Somebody else made the calls."

"Uh-huh."

"Who?"

"Well," Ford said, "I'm not sure, but Robert from Baltimore with the foreign accent was on the air from 4:10 to 4:12. If you figure he was on hold for twenty minutes or so, the timing works. I'll bet his name isn't Robert."

"I'll bet he's not from Baltimore either," DeLuca said. "She gave her phone to somebody. To the guy she was buying suits and briefcases for."

"Could be."

"Suppose it's Robert. The boyfriend, or whatever we call him. He listens for a while, then calls in to support his sweetheart."

"Why's he calling Vinnie Potatoes?"

"I don't know, but stay with me here. So Bobby from Baltimore is Serbian. Serbs hate Joe Quinn for humiliating them in Kosovo as head of NATO. The Serbians fight a war over a battle that ended six hundred years ago, so why wouldn't they carry a grudge about a war that ended six years ago? Or maybe they want the reward. They want to hurt him, so they have someone get close to his daughter. She's lonely, vulnerable. I mean, what are the odds she just bumps into someone Serbian?"

"Maybe they think they can take her hostage and ransom her back to him," Ford said. "Then they kill him too when he delivers the money. Is that a plan?"

"Not a very good one, but it's a plan," DeLuca agreed.

"She had her phone on her when she died," Ford said. "So she meets him, he gives the phone back, then he pops her. Why?"

"That sounds like less of a plan," DeLuca said. "You know who I'm thinking is going to help us with Bobby Baltimore?"

"Who?"

"The first person she called, before she loaned him the phone. In Northampton. Claire McGovern."

"McGowan," Ford said. "She owns a candy store called Sweet Somethings. Where'd you sleep last night, by the way?"

"I'm staying away from hotels," DeLuca said. "I called Sami and asked him where he kept his spare key."

"How was that?" Ford asked.

"Premonitory," DeLuca said. "His place is a mess. He's living like a UMass freshman. I slept on the couch, but I remembered what a nice house he used to have when he and Caroline were together."

"I know what you mean," Ford said. "It's a bit depressing. So you and Bonnie . . . ?"

"Don't ask," DeLuca said.

"You gonna be okay?" Ford said. "Maybe you should talk to somebody."

"I am talking to somebody," DeLuca said. "I'm talking to you. Besides, you know what they say about how exhilarating it is to be shot at and missed? Think how much fun it is to be IED'd and missed."

"But only the first time," Ford said. "The second time, you start to think somebody is out to get you."

"Why would I think that?" DeLuca said.

He listened to the news on NPR as he drove to Walpole State Prison the first of the errands he'd told Ford he had to run. In Oxford, England, the announcer said, Sean Denby, the son of General David Denby, commander of British forces in Iraq, had been found dead from gunshot wounds in an alley off High Street. DeLuca waited for the reporter to put it together, but no connection was drawn between the killing and the I4NI Web site.

In the visitors' area, Mickey O'Brien looked surprised to see him. He'd been behind bars for four and a half years but he looked twenty years older, in part because he'd stopped dying his hair black. He had the florid loose face of an Irishman who'd been drinking since he was a teenager, his gray hair falling in front of his eyes despite his efforts to push it back with his fingers. He was wearing a gray jumpsuit and tennis shoes, and looked something like a grade school janitor. When he saw DeLuca, his face registered surprise, but not pleasure.

"Mickey," DeLuca said, sitting down across the table from the inmate. DeLuca dismissed the guard with a nod. Mickey didn't say anything. When the guard was gone, DeLuca took a bag of gourmet licorice, Dutch and lightly salted, from his pocket and threw them across the table to

O'Brien. "That's what you like, right?" He'd remembered D'Brien had a sweet tooth.

O'Brien looked at the licorice but didn't touch them, glancing in the direction of the guard.

"Why are you here?" he said. "I didn't think I was going to see you again."

"I didn't think so either," DeLuca said.

"I heard you quit the job," O'Brien said.

"I did."

"Why? I heard Halliday wanted you to head up his an-titerrorism commission."

"I joined the army," DeLuca said. "I went back into counterintelligence. After 9/11."

"Why?"

"Personal reasons."

"Okay," O'Brien said. "You gave up a lot."

"So did you. How you doing?" DeLuca asked.

"I'm all right," O'Brien said with a shrug. "You can get used to anything. They keep ex-Feds pretty separate from the general population. Don't tell me you're here to say you're sorry."

"You *want* me to say I'm sorry?" DeLuca replied.

"No," O'Brien said. "I wouldn't, if I was in your place. But you must want something."

"I want to talk," DeLuca said.

"So you thought you could bribe me with a bag of licorice?"

"I thought I'd start with a bag of licorice," he said. "If I have to, I'm prepared to go as high as a Whitman Sampler."

O'Brien smiled, opening the bag and putting a piece in his mouth, savoring it.

"Jimmy Keenan used to say you were a dumb Wop fuck," O'Brien said. "I told him you were a Wop fuck, but you weren't half as stupid as you looked. By the way, if you want to ask me where he is, I have no idea."

"Right now, I could care less about Jimmy Keenan," DeLuca said. "How's Buttercup, by the way?"

"He's not good," O'Brien said. "He's living with my mother, but she's eighty-five. She told me his cancer is back. The vet says they can't operate this time."

"So he's gotta be put down?"

O'Brien nodded.

"I'm looking for Vinnie P.," DeLuca said. "But I need your help. You hear about the Katie Quinn murder?"

"I mighta heard something," O'Brien said.

"Wexler thinks Vinnie Potatoes did it. I don't think so," DeLuca said, "but he might know who did. My problem is, I got nobody on the streets anymore, and nobody in the department will talk to me because they're afraid of what'll happen when Frank becomes commissioner. So we're mostly working the Fed side—you know Dawn Massey?"

"Yeah, sure," O'Brien said. "I knew her husband better. He was a prick. She's a terrific agent."

"She's heading up an intel unit under the Joint Task Force on Counter-Terrorism," DeLuca said. "Something big may be going on. It's going to be in the papers. Probably tomorrow. I think the Katie Quinn murder is connected to terrorism. Officially, they're telling me anything other than her murder is beyond my mission, but I've always had a hard time sticking to parameters. I just can't figure out how Pastorelli fits in. I think the killer called him, just before he did it, but I can't see it as a work for hire. I was hoping you could arrange a meeting with Vinnie. Talking to the people you know in here, or outside. Today."

"Today?" O'Brien said. "Jesus. You don't ask for much."

"You still know some Italians, don't you?"

"Yeah, but it's all going to the Albanians these days."

"I heard that," DeLuca said.

"What's in it for me?" O'Brien asked. "You know I gotta think that way, right?"

"You help me, I'll get you a day pass so you can go take care of your dog," DeLuca said. O'Brien appeared to be thinking, but DeLuca knew already that he had a deal. He'd known, coming in, that he probably wasn't Mickey O'Brien's favorite person in the world, but also guessed, accurately, that deep down, Mickey O'Brien was a good guy who screwed up and probably felt like any retired cop—useless.

"You could do that?"

"I could and I would. And if everything works out, maybe we can talk about moving you to a nicer hotel."

"How 'bout an ankle bracelet on Martha's Vineyard?" O'Brien said, rolling the licorice over on his tongue. "No harm in asking."

"I'll leave you my number and I'll tell the warden to let you make as many calls as you have to," DeLuca said.

"I can't promise anything," O'Brien said.

"I know," DeLuca said. "But I can."

At the offices of the *Boston Voice* on Massachusetts Avenue off Central Square, in a suite of rooms above a place called the Cantab Lounge, Sykes and MacKenzie asked to speak to Gordon Lipski, the editor in chief. The receptionist was a young gum-chewing woman with rings in her ears, eyebrows, and lips, and tattoos that began at her neck and ended somewhere beyond where they should have. Behind her, on the wall, was a large poster from the movie *The Motorcycle Diaries,* featuring a picture of the actor playing the young Che Guevara, indicating, if any indication were needed, the newspaper's political leanings. In the large room behind her, Sykes and Mack saw a chaotic array of desks and cubicles, laptops and desktop flat-screen monitors, bulletin boards and whiteboards, copy machines, faxes, and stacks of books, magazines, and newspapers. The girl told them Lipski was in an editorial meeting and couldn't be disturbed.

"Could you tell him agents from U.S. Army counterintelligence would like a minute," Sykes said.

"Counterintelligence?" Tattoo Girl said, blowing a small bubble and snapping it. "You here for the whistle-blower thing?"

"Yeah," Sykes said, exchanging a glance with MacKenzie to tell her to play along. He lowered his voice conspiratorially. "We have information. About—"

"Something," Mack said, cutting him off. "We can only talk to the editor in chief. In person. That's why we're here, instead of calling."

"He's downstairs, at the Cantab," Tattoo Girl told them. "He'll be the only one there under fifty."

"I thought you said he was in an editorial meeting," Sykes said.

"I lied," she said.

Gordon Lipski was sitting in a booth by the front door, smoking a cigar and nursing a beer while he read the *Boston Globe.* He was a slender man, dressed in a white-striped shirt with the sleeves rolled up and a brown-and-red-striped bow tie, horn-rimmed glasses, and long brown hair that fell to his shoulders, parted in the middle. Sykes had the impression, though it was only an impression, that having a beer in a working-class bar at ten in the morning made Lipski, by his own estimation, both a hard-drinking man of the world and a hard-drinking man of the people, a Jimmy Breslin–style intellectual. Two large women in nurses' smocks sat at the bar, unwinding after working the night shift, doing beers and shots to wash down their Cheetos and beef jerky breakfasts. In a booth at the back, an old man sat staring intently at absolutely nothing. The bartender was a middle-aged Latina who asked them if she could get them anything. Sykes ordered a coffee, Mack a cranberry juice. They took their drinks to the booth where Gordon Lipski sat reading the paper by the light of the morning sun that showed through a square of glass bricks behind him.

"Gordon Lipski?" Sykes said. "Mind if we join you? Your receptionist told us we could find you here."

Lipski looked up. "You can join me if you want, but don't expect me to say anything intelligent this early in the morning."

"Don't worry," Sykes said. "We never expect journalists to say anything intelligent."

MacKenzie rolled her eyes. They'd just sat down and they were already off on the wrong foot. She'd hoped to establish a rapport. Her partner had apparently abandoned the idea before giving it a try.

"You guys look very governmental," Lipski said. "Am I under arrest or something?"

"Not by us," Sykes said. "We're just here to ask a few questions, if you don't mind."

"You have some sort of credentials?" Lipski asked.

They showed him what he needed to see. He looked at them carefully before handing them back.

"Counterintelligence," he said. "Aren't you the people responsible for Abu Ghraib?"

"No," Sykes said. "That's the MPs. We're the ones who busted the MPs responsible."

"So you're the police policing the police," he said. "Good job. Well done."

"I'm going to guess you don't have a 'Support Our Troops' sticker on your car," Sykes said.

"Oh, I support the troops," Lipski said. "I just don't support an irresponsible government that goes to war on a premise of lies, killing hundreds of thousands of innocents in order to change the regime of a dictator we put into power and supported for years, without any plan to repair the damage we've done or rebuild the society we destroyed."

"I had no idea," Sykes said.

"Neither did I," MacKenzie said. "Why hasn't anybody said anything?"

"Do you have any idea what's really going on in Iraq?" Gordon Lipski said.

"Do you have any idea what's really going on in my ass?" Sykes replied. "Can we just make this simple? All we need to know is how you heard about the I4NI Web site. You tell us that and we'll be on our way, because I'm sure you're not enjoying this conversation any more than we are."

"As a journalist, I can't reveal my sources," Lipski said.

"So it was a source," Sykes said. "A person. Somebody you personally know."

"I didn't say that."

"Yes you did," Mack said. "You said 'sources.' And you said 'I,' not 'we.'"

"Do you know the person who told you about the Web site?" Sykes said. "Because I should warn you, at this point, that we are in fact talking about a matter of national security. The threat is to American citizens on American soil, both to the people listed on the Web site and to a major American city, quite probably Boston. We're required by law to take these threats seriously."

"This administration issues orange alerts every time they need to draw attention away from their own misdeeds," Lipski said.

"Now that's just dumb," MacKenzie said. "If the president wanted to change the subject or draw attention away from something, all he has to do is say something stupid. Didn't you know that?"

"I just heard one yesterday," Sykes said. "Quote: 'The problem with the French is that they don't have a word for 'entrepreneur.'"

"He said that?" Lipski said.

"See what I mean?" Mack said. "He's been doing it for years and it works every time. His father did it too."

"Judith Miller at the *New York Times* refused to reveal her sources and went to jail for her principles," Lipski said. "I'm prepared to do no less. I don't care if you send me to Guantanamo and make me sit in the sun with a bag over my head."

"Well, you could use a tan," Sykes said. "The bag might be an improvement too. Listen—tell you what—I'll give you a hundred bucks if you tell me?"

"You think you can buy my integrity?" Lipski said.

"Okay, a hundred and fifty," Sykes said. "But that's the best I can do."

"A guy called and told us about the site," Lipski said. "He didn't give a name and he'd put a block on caller ID. He had an accent. Sort of like my Russian grandfather. Eastern European."

"And what'd he say exactly?"

"Just 'go to,' and then the URL, and then, 'You'll find something interesting there.'"

"Did he leave a message on voice mail or did you speak to him personally?"

"I talked to him, but really, he talked to me and then hung up. I asked who it was but he'd already cut me off. But it checked out, once we went to the site."

"Thanks," Sykes said, rising from his seat. MacKenzie drained the last of her cranberry juice and stood as well.

"Where's my money?" Gordon Lipski said.

"I'm not going to give you any money, you moron," Sykes said. "Next time, get the money first. Don't you watch TV?"

DeLuca took the Mass Pike west, the traffic flowing at eighty-five miles an hour. Northampton was a college town fifteen miles north of Springfield on I-91, six miles west of Amherst and the University of Massachusetts, part of the Five College area that included Amherst College, Hampshire, Mount Holyoke, and Smith. Northampton was an "arts town," filled with painters and writers and bookstores and art galleries, a wide Main Street lined with great restaurants and boutiques, sushi shops and ice cream parlors, vintage clothing and gay apparel to don-we-now. Bonnie had wanted to move to Northampton, the first time they'd come when Scott wanted to look at colleges as a junior in high school. DeLuca had looked into possible employment with the local police department, but other than taking the job as chief, were it to become available, he couldn't see taking both a pay cut and a demotion just to move to a lovely but sleepy little college town on the Connecticut River.

It surprised him to see how many panhandlers were on the street, kids and older people, male and female, squatting on the sidewalk beside filthy dogs and cardboard signs in black Magic Marker advertising their various plights, "homeless, disabled, veteran, recently unemployed, need money for food, anything helps . . ." One kid sported a sign DeLuca rather admired for its creativity, reading, "PARENTS SLAIN BY NINJA'S—NEED MONEY FOR KUNG FU LESSONS!" Spaced between the panhandlers were street musicians strumming guitars with open guitar cases in front of them to catch the quarters and dollars tossed by passersby. It looked like a good town to panhandle in, lots of liberals willing to part with their spare change, and if you weren't making any money, at least you had live entertainment just down the sidewalk. It was also a town known far and wide for its large lesbian population, having been written up as such in numerous magazines and publications, in part because of the two women's colleges in the area, Mount Holyoke and Smith, which gay women traditionally chose for their college educations, sticking around afterwards for the tolerant social climate.

Sweet Somethings aspired to be an authentic antique penny-candy shop, with row after row of glass jars with broad wooden lids and tin scoops nearby, jars filled with sweets of all sorts, jelly beans, gummy bears, stick licorice and rope licorice and button licorice, chocolates, mints, pastilles, rock candy, wax lips, wax syrup bottles, paper sugar tabs, Walnettos, Slo Pokes, Black Cows, Sugar Babies, gumballs, jawbreakers, and so on. There were Norman Rockwell prints on the walls and a four-stool fountain counter, currently unoccupied, where you could get ice cream cones or malts or sodas. He asked an attractive young woman with a nice smile if he could speak with the owner.

"I'm the owner," she said cheerfully. "How can I help you?"

She was petite, soft, feminine, pretty, well dressed, unpierced and untattooed, as far as he could tell, not strident, not angry, not remotely weird, and nothing like the stereotyped image he'd had in mind.

"You're Claire McGowan?" he asked.

"You got me," she said. "Who are you?"

"My name is David DeLuca," he said. "I was hoping to ask you a few questions about Katie Quinn?"

"Why?" Claire said. "Is everything okay?" She read the expression on his face. He didn't have to tell her, though the next thing she said surprised him. "Oh my God—did Marko do something?"

An interesting comment.

"Katie was killed," he said. "Two days ago. I'm sorry. I'm trying to find the person who did it."

It took Claire McGowan a few minutes to recover to where she could speak with him. She put a "Closed" sign on the door and locked it. She took him to her office, where she broke down again and cried. She asked him how it happened. He told her, as gently as he could, only that Katie had been shot in the Boston Common parking garage, after her radio show.

"God damn it," she said. "Just God damn it. Jesus. It's . . . God damn it. She was one of the sweetest people you could ever meet. She wouldn't hurt a fly."

"I know," DeLuca said. "I'm a friend of her father's. I never met Katie but I've heard him talk about her."

"You know General Joe?" Claire asked. "Did he mention how much he hurt her?"

"He told me they'd had a falling-out," DeLuca said.

"Did he tell you why?"

"He said they'd had words about some lifestyle choices she made."

Claire almost laughed. "Choices," she said. "My God. If they only knew how few choices Kate ever had. Because of how she looked, and because of who her father was. I'm not dissing General Joe, by the way—she really loved him, despite the things he said and did. I respect her opinions. The problems between them were all his, if you ask me."

"I think he knows that," DeLuca said. "For what it's worth. I worked with him in the Middle East and I think he's one of the most courageous men I've ever met. I think that applies to facing up to some things he said or did that he probably doesn't want to face up to. Too little too late, for sure."

"You're with the army?"

"I am," DeLuca said. "Why did you say, 'Did Marko do something?' Who's Marko?"

"Marko Simic," Claire said. "A man she'd been seeing. I don't have an address, but he worked at Massachusetts Senior Services, doing private care."

"I know MSS," DeLuca said. "Also under its previous name, Bay State Elder Care. I used to work with

Boston PD. We busted Bay State Elder Care for twenty-some cases of elder abuse. They were famous for hiring criminals and illegals to take care of disabled people. I haven't been following what the new company has been up to."

"That fits," Claire said. "Katie saw Marko as some sort of rescuing angel, taking care of old people. I thought he was a terrible man from the first moment I met him."

"You met him?"

"She wanted to introduce him to me," Claire said. "She couldn't wait, she was so excited. She told me he was the first boyfriend she ever had. She said she was in love."

"And you thought?"

"What do you think I thought?" Claire McGowan said. "He was sullen and hardly said a word all during lunch. I think he was homophobic. She apologized all over the place for him and said he'd had a brain injury that made it hard for him to remember things. I couldn't see what she saw in him, but of course, you don't say anything. You just smile and wish 'em luck. And then when—"

"When she found out she was pregnant?"

"You knew?"

"We know," DeLuca said. "How did she feel about that?"

"Happy and scared. She never thought it would happen, but by then, Marko was being such an asshole to her that she wasn't sure she was going to tell him. She said she thought she'd go somewhere and have the baby and raise it by herself. She was thinking of moving back here, if she could swing the childcare and the commute to the show in Boston. It was pretty impractical. There's no such thing as overnight childcare."

"And you thought Marko was capable of violence?" DeLuca said.

"I did," she said. "There was something about him. Just so you know, I'm not some Andrea Dworkin all-men-are-rapists feminist. I had a number of wonderful boyfriends, back in high school and the first part of college."

"And Katie wasn't gay?"

"Not even remotely," Claire said. "We tried a kiss once, just to test, and all she did was laugh. She was only interested in men, which almost made no sense, given the way they treated her. She actually had a date once with a guy who fell in love with her voice, over the phone, and when she showed up, dressed so pretty, he pretended he was someone else, even though she'd seen his picture on Match. com and knew exactly who he was. I kept telling her if she really wanted a kid, use the NWSC and do it by herself."

"What's the NWSC?" DeLuca asked.

"Northampton Women's Sperm Cooperative," she said.

"Which is?"

"What it sounds like. It's an association of sperm donors who've been screened and approved for use by the area's lesbian population. Mostly gay men, but not entirely. We formed an association because women here had been using the same donors for so long that our sons and daughters were starting to date each other. There was an increasing chance that siblings might start hooking up, unless we kept track."

"And this was only for gay women?"

"This is only for gay women."

"But Katie wasn't gay."

Claire hesitated before replying. "I was going to pose as her girlfriend," she said. "Or she was going to pose as mine. I think that's what the private detective her father hired found out."

"I wasn't aware that he'd hired anybody," DeLuca said. "You don't think the cooperative would have made an exception?"

"NWSC doesn't use frozen sperm or artificial insemination, Mr. DeLuca," Claire said. "The most effective way to get pregnant is actually the old-fashioned method of insemination. The woman having an orgasm at the moment of injection actually assists in the uptake of sperm into the cervical cavity. Lesbian couples usually participate together. With the man. That's why it doesn't work if the people creating the embryo are heterosexual. Maybe I shouldn't say it doesn't work. It can work, but it gets more complicated. And it's complicated enough between gay men and women, with custody suits and visitation rights. Litigiousness is part of what the NWSC is supposed to screen for. Anyway, this has nothing to do with Katie, because ultimately she decided she'd find someone to get pregnant by on her own."

"That was what she'd set out to do?" DeLuca asked. "How'd they meet? Katie and Marko?"

"They met online," Claire said. "He e-mailed the show and then he started to Instant Message her. When he told her he wanted to talk to her online at home, she said she didn't have a home computer so he bought her one."

"And she used it," DeLuca said. "Without checking to see what sort of spyware programs might have been hidden on the hard drive. We're thinking the people we're looking for have a fairly high level of technological savvy."

"People?" Claire said. "You're looking for more than one person?"

"We think Marko might have been part of a group," DeLuca said. "You're probably going to start seeing some stories in the newspapers about a Web site listing the names and addresses of retired or active-duty American military people and their families, called I4NI. Or a logo resembling a hydra. We think Katie might have been targeted as a result of that."

" 'Targeted'?" Claire said. "You make her sound like some village in Afghanistan."

"At any rate, the concern is that a group of Eastern Europeans, posing as Arabs, has set up the Web site to get even revenge for American military actions abroad. I think Marko sought her out to get to her father."

"Oh my God," Claire said. "This is so horrible. It doesn't seen real."

"Can I ask you one more question?" DeLuca said.

"All right," she said.

"Why did Katie call you two nights ago?" he asked. "The night she died."

"She had a moral issue she wanted to discuss," Claire said.

"Can you tell me what it was?"

"She'd been thinking about tricking some other guy into thinking he was the father," Claire said. "So Marko wouldn't think it was his, and maybe so that she could get some support. I told her it was wrong."

"It wasn't a man named Vincent Pastorelli, was it?" DeLuca asked.

"She didn't say what his name was," Claire McGowan said. "I had the impression it was somebody she knew. Would you like a picture of Marko Simic?"

"You have one?"

"She sent it to me as an e-mail attachment, before I met him in person" Claire said. "I'll print you a copy. I was almost going to Photo shop it and crop him out. I'm glad I didn't."

The picture she found on her computer screen was of the two of them, Katie and a man who appeared to be in his late forties, stubbled, with hard, sunken cheeks, a pit-bull-like jaw, thick eyebrows, small ears that stuck out from the sides of his head, hair clipped short on the sides but longer on top, a smile with a hard cruel quality to it, and eyes that were black and did not twinkle. The picture had been taken in the dunes at Cape Cod, the sun setting in the background, Katie wearing a sweatshirt and appearing to be cold, but happy all the same. DeLuca guessed it had been taken around Memorial Day, when people started heading to the Cape, even though it was still cool at night. Katie had labeled the file "Isn't he handsome?"

Claire cropped the picture and blew up the head of Simic, the image maintaining its integrity without too much pixilation. When she was finished, DeLuca downloaded the file to his CIM and sent it to image analysis at INSCOM/JTIOC, with a note to Scott asking him to load the image into his CPV program and search for it in as many ways as he could think of, on SIPERNET, on the Web, and in the streets and subways of Boston. He sent a copy to Dawn Massey's office as well, with a paragraph on how he'd found the image and what it might mean.

"Call me," he texted.

"Something might turn up," he told Claire McGowan. "It's a little like searching for a needle in a haystack, but that's not quite as hard as it used to be. I'll try to keep you informed."

He could tell that she wanted to say something but wasn't sure if she should.

"Is there something else?" he asked.

"No," she said. "I mean, it really has nothing to do with this. When Katie and I were talking about using the sperm cooperative, she decided she didn't want to do that, but what she did do was have some of her eggs frozen, at a clinic here in town. She said she knew she was getting older, but maybe if she met someone in a few years, and he wanted to have kids, she could use the frozen eggs for in vitro. I don't know exactly why I'm telling you this. I just think, you know, Katie's dead, but they're not."

DeLuca thought of all the men he'd known who'd told him they'd had their sperm frozen before deploying to Iraq, a procedure that was actually covered by army medical benefits, men hedging their bets against mortality. He understood the concept, and the impulse, but it seemed to make the grieving process more difficult.

"You've been very helpful," he said. "Call me if you think of anything else."

The mystery of who Katie was trying to hang the pregnancy on was solved when DeLuca reached Walter Ford, who'd spent the morning running all the credit card numbers used in Filene's Basement in the previous month to purchase items costing $19.95 and sorting the results against the list of names Sykes and Mack had given him, and then against the list of names newly entered into the case file, which turned up the name of one Freddy King, Katie's business partner.

"I pulled his credit report, such as it is—this guy is not buying a house anytime soon. He bought Katie all sorts of things. We got a Coach wallet, a silk scarf—who else is he buying this stuff for? His mother? I'm guessing he gave them to Katie. I'm going to check 'em against the inventory from her apartment to be sure. Did you get the impression he had a crush on her? I did."

"I did," DeLuca said. "I'm gonna go out on a limb and say maybe we know whose spooge was on the negligee. It didn't match the DNA of the fetus, did it?"

"No match. I found something else Freddy bought," Ford said. "A Smith and Wesson fifty-caliber Magnum, from a dealer in Wrentham. The guy said after the paperwork cleared, he shipped the piece to arrive the day Katie was shot."

"That's interesting. I have two more things for you," DeLuca said. "Search everywhere for the name Marko Simic. Employee of Massachusetts Senior Services. Search MSS for any employees they might have hired recently of Eastern European extraction. Over or under the table. Any name comes up, run that against the International War Crimes Tribunal database with Interpol. And cross-check with tech jobs or computer know-how. I think we might be getting closer."

Chapter Seven

ELIZABETH KNOCKED ON THE WINDOW OF Hoolie's van in the morning and asked him if he wanted to walk with her to Starbucks, where she ordered a venti soy vanilla latte and a scone, adding that she was going to have to go for a run that afternoon to work off the calories, but she couldn't live without her soy vanilla lattes. When he asked her how her paper was coming along, she said she had to go to the library to do some more work.

"Most people just do research online from their rooms," she told him. "Not that you can't do that, but there's still so much more you can do at the library."

"What's the topic?"

"It's for my Modern African History and Neo-Colonialism class," she said. "I'm writing about the revolution in Liger and the populist movement that led to the co-presidency of Paul Asabo and John Dari."

"Really?" Vasquez said. "I might be able to help you with that."

"Thanks, but no thanks," she said. "Between the scholarly papers and the stuff I'm pulling off the Internet, I think I have plenty. My professor's a real expert. He thinks the CIA made a deal with the Muslim imams to split the country in two in exchange for oil rights."

"Did you talk to your dad?" he asked.

"What—about his work?" She laughed. "You can't be serious."

Vasquez knew for a fact, because he'd been deployed to Liger with DeLuca and the others, that the only CIA agent remaining in Liger had spent the revolution drunk in a hotel bar in Baku Da'al. The White House had been trying to kill Dari and failed only because they couldn't find him. He also knew that the Muslim imams in the northern towns of the Sahel region were of only minimal influence in a country where tribal loyalties and polytheism mitigated the effects of religious affiliations. In fact, the president of Liger and his cabinet had only fled the country because DeLuca put them on a helicopter in the courtyard of the Castle of St. James, where they'd taken refuge from rebel troops, telling them it wasn't safe to stay and that the United States would provide sanctuary, when in fact DeLuca had known the United States was neither prepared, equipped, nor inclined to do anything of the sort. Dari and Asabo had assumed power in the vacuum that was created by the president's departure. Vasquez knew because he was there in the courtyard, the night it happened.

"Sounds like a good theory," he told Elizabeth. "So why isn't the country in fact split in two, according to your professor?"

"He thinks the CIA botched it," Elizabeth said.

"Always a possibility," Vasquez said. "You mind if I come to the library with you? I have some research to do myself."

Until he learned who'd been in the third cab the previous night, he wasn't going to let Elizabeth out of his sight.

A check with all the regular cab companies hadn't turned up any fares from the Gold Club in Chinatown to the corner of Nutting and Mt. Auburn in Cambridge at two in the morning, but there were gypsy cabs he could look into.

Elizabeth found a vacant computer station at the Widener, near the periodicals collection. Vasquez found a station he could use across from her. The library seemed emptier than it had been when he was an undergraduate. He resisted the urge to wax nostalgic, though he did remember a carrel on the top floor, in the corner, where he'd had a romp with a girl who later informed him she'd always wanted to join the Friends of the Widener, which was the code name for students who'd had sex in the library.

His alumni status gave him access to the library system, but he needed to go further than that. Occasionally, Elizabeth looked his way, smiling (was she flirting, he wondered?), though from where she sat, she was unable to see what he was up to. Using his CIM, Scottie and a tech sergeant walked him through the protocols and passwords he needed to breach the university computer's firewalls. Out of curiosity, he clicked briefly on his own transcript, where he had the opportunity to change any of his grades, had he so desired. There was a B he hadn't deserved that he'd gotten in a Latin American Studies course from a professor who'd hated him because he spoke Spanish better than the professor did and kept questioning his translations. A look at the professor's file showed he was one of the lowest-paid teachers in the department, and also that the decision had been made to deny him tenure—Vasquez was satisfied and let it go.

Elizabeth had gotten straight A's the first semester of her freshman year, but her grades had dropped spring semester, as was common, if his memory served, among nervous students afraid of failing who usually learned by second semester how to relax and party.

> **JulioVasquez:** It looks like she discovered her independence, spring of freshman year.
> **CaptScottDeluca:** I wasn't sure if I should send you this, but I took the photograph you sent of Bizza and CPVed it on the net.
> **JulioVasquez:** Explain?
> **CaptScottDeluca:** Combat Picture Visualization. It's a pattern recognition program. You can use it to search the net for photographic images, the same way Google searches for text. So if you arrest a guy or take a prisoner or find a body without any ID, you can run the photograph, and if his face is in a digital mug book in Istanbul, or if his high school yearbook is online, or he got his picture in a newspaper with a website, you can find out who he is. I ran the picture of Bizza, just because I was curious. I found the below link. FYI.

The link was to a Web site at www.girlsgonecrazy. com, where, under SpringBreak/PanamaCity/8475k.html/, Vasquez saw a picture of Elizabeth LeDoux in a bar, lifting her shirt and flashing her breasts at the camera. She appeared to be quite drunk, and quite enjoying herself. The two Budweiser-swilling frat boys next to her were having a good time as well, though Hoolie realized it probably hurt to have your eyes pop out of your head like that.

> **JulioVasquez:** Yikes. What do you think?
> **CaptScottDeluca:** I think my spring breaks were pretty tame. I went to South Carolina with some buddies and played golf.

JulioVasquez: Are you surprised?
CaptScottDeluca: Yes and no.
JulioVasquez: Pleasantly?
CaptScottDeluca: Yes and no.
JulioVasquez: Yes and no?
CaptScottDeluca: I can't exactly say I hadn't given some thought to the prospect of seeing such an image before.
JulioVasquez: Oh.

Her credit history was admirable, Vasquez thought, logging into the AmeriCred records to learn that she had four credit cards that she used frequently and paid off in full and on time each month, while putting up some pretty big numbers. He'd seen how much money she made in a night, dancing at the Gold Club. He wondered how many nights a week she danced, and how much she was able to pull in, so he looked at her bank records, again following the instructions Scott sent him to breach the firewalls protecting her online banking files. He was shocked to discover that she had more than two hundred thousand dollars in her checking account.

CaptScottDeluca: Finding anything?
JulioVasquez: Maybe.

More interesting, Vasquez thought, were the electronic cash transfers into her bank account from another account, registered to a user named jcchen, full name James Chiang Chen, a name Vasquez then asked Scott to run. He watched Elizabeth while he waited. She was reading a scholarly journal and taking notes, curling her hair absentmindedly between her fingers and chewing on the end of her pen. She was wearing large gold hoop earrings and a tight belly shirt. Vasquez wondered if she was a Friend of the Widener. When he looked at the bank records for James Chiang Chen, he saw that Chen had transferred funds into his account a few minutes before transferring similar sums into Elizabeth's. The source of those funds was an account at the Massachusetts Institute of Technology. The funds transferred electronically into Elizabeth LeDoux's account accounted for two-thirds of her total.

> **CaptScottDeluca:** James Chiang Chen, 52. Professor of Advanced Physics at MIT. Tenured, there for twenty years. Single (divorced), doing classified government research.
> **JulioVasquez:** On what?
> **CaptScottDeluca:** Can't say. Don't know. Right now.
> **JulioVasquez:** Can you find out?
> **CaptScottDeluca:** Eventually.
> **JulioVasquez:** While you're at it, find out where the funds in Fleet acct. #374-85475-37 come from.
> **CaptScottDeluca:** Relative to?
> **JulioVasquez:** Probably nothing.
> **CaptScottDeluca:** Want a picture of Chen?
> **JulioVasquez:** Sure.

By the time the photograph Scott found on the MIT Web site downloaded, Vasquez had already figured out who it was of—the Asian gentleman he'd seen at the Gold Club, tucking twenty-dollar bills into Elizabeth's G-string.

When Vasquez looked up Elizabeth's most recent tax return, the only income she'd declared, and the only 1099 form attached, was for a waitressing job she'd had in Washington, D.C., during the summer.

"You wanna get some lunch?" she asked. Vasquez looked up from his computer screen, unaware that she'd approached. He shrank the window before she could look over his shoulder and logged off. "What were you doing?"

"My taxes," he told her.

"Now? In the summer?"

"I try not to wait until the last minute," he said.

"I know a great sushi place," she told him. "My treat."

"So how'd you end up going from Harvard to the army?" she asked, using her fingers to raise a piece of yellowtail to her mouth. The restaurant was a place called Osaka, off Massachusetts Avenue.

"Have I ended up?" he said. "I thought I was still at the beginning."

"Beginning of what?" she asked.

"Not sure. Maybe that's what I like about it," he told her. "I'm like the guy who's lost on the freeway who says, 'I don't know where I'm going, but at least I'm making good time.'"

"You're lost?"

"Nope," Vasquez said. "Bad analogy. Basically, I told the army I'd give them four years, and then right when that was up and they were asking me for four more, Iraq came along. I couldn't exactly cut and run."

"Why not?"

"I could answer that," he said, "but it seems a little odd that someone from a military family would ask. I stayed because my country needed me. The job I had to do became more important. It's pretty simple, but I guess that could sound corny to you."

"Not to me," she said. "Maybe to someone else. Where were you?"

"Afghanistan," he said. "Sorting warlords. It was interesting."

"How so?"

"Well," he said. "Let's just say the distinctions between who we wanted in and who we wanted out were not exactly black and white. We didn't have a whole lot of boots on the ground before we went in, but in a place like that, it's the only way to gather the intelligence you need. Not much use having a satellite that can monitor telephone conversations positioned over a country that only has six telephones, and four of those don't work. Or the most sophisticated technology in the history of warfare when you don't know where the targets are."

"Not exactly a modern country?"

"They play polo with dead goats instead of polo balls."

"You still haven't answered my question," she said. "Why the military? Didn't you want to do something where you could apply the education you got at Harvard?"

"What makes you think I'm not?" he said.

"Are you?"

"My father's a lawyer in Los Angeles," Vasquez said. "He offered me a job. I was pre-law here with a concentration in international relations, but my uncle Tito, who was CI in Vietnam, told me if I wanted a hands-on education in international relations, I couldn't do any better than counterintelligence."

"Was he right?"

"He was."

"So are you going to work for your father when your tour is up?" she asked.

"Maybe," he said.

"You'd have to go to law school, though."

"Yup."

"So this must be a big disappointment for you, after all that international intrigue," she said. "Being a bodyguard for a general's daughter."

"I'm eating sushi with you," he said. "How could that be bad?"

"Are you flirting with me?" she asked him, smiling.

"Was I?" he said.

"Weren't you?"

"You're the one asking all the questions," he said.

"You think *I'm* flirting?" she said.

"Aren't you?"

"Maybe a little," she said, smiling again. "I'll stop if it makes you feel uncomfortable."

"I didn't say I felt uncomfortable," Vasquez said, though in fact he felt like he was being given a verbal lap dance, in the way she was showing interest in him, pressing forward, pulling back, accompanied by a body language that was speaking volumes, in the way she leaned in, looked him in the eyes while lowering her head, or arched her back to yawn.

"Well, good," she said. "I'm just trying to make this easier on the both of us. I know you're just doing what you're told."

He took that to have been intended as a mild rebuke or insult, a way to set him back on his heels a bit, and get him to respond, which was, he knew, also a part of the flirtation process, something he needed to stop. It was obviously a power she'd discovered, and one she deployed with formidable skill. He'd been playing it by ear, whether or not to confront her about his discoveries, and if so, when to do it, and how, but he saw an opening. He wasn't concerned about the lifestyle choices she'd made, but he was concerned about James Chen and what his intentions were. DeLuca had warned the team to be alert to the possibility that I4NI might resort to abductions as well as killings. They'd been told to watch for anomalies, and this was an anomaly of significant proportions.

"If you really want to make it easier," he said, "you could start by telling me the truth. That would help."

"How am I not telling you the truth?" she asked.

"Last night," he said. "You told me you were staying home to write a paper. But instead, you went out."

"I went out to see some friends," she said. "You weren't invited."

"Elizabeth," he said. "I know where you went."

"You followed me?"

"Did you think I wouldn't?" he asked.

She looked at him. The friendliness she'd shown before was gone.

"I suppose you think this is where I say, 'Please, please, don't tell my daddy.' Go ahead if you want. I don't care."

"Neither do I," Vasquez said. "I've been in strip joints before. That's not the point."

"I can make my own decisions," she said. "I've been making my own decisions for a long time. And earning my own money, by the way. You have no idea how hard it is to go to school here when everyone you meet comes from a wealthy family and you have no money."

"Elizabeth," Vasquez said. "I'm not your enemy. And for your information, in the last twenty-four hours, we've passed four restaurants where I worked washing dishes while I was a student here, so don't tell me about economic inequalities at Harvard. My father gave me nothing. Your father puts a thousand dollars in your bank account every month."

"How the hell do you know my father puts money in my bank account?" she said.

"He told me," Hoolie lied. "I told you—I don't care about where you work. I'm not passing any moral judgments, and I don't care if you buy plasma-screen TVs or fancy stereos—"

"You've been in my apartment," she said. "You were in my goddamn apartment."

"My assignment is to protect you," he said. "I wouldn't be doing my job if I didn't look to make sure there weren't six guys in ski masks with Kalashnikovs waiting for you to come home."

"You could have asked," she said, still outraged. "I would have let you in. What business is my personal life to you? My life is *my* life. My life is private."

"It didn't look all that private last night," Hoolie said. "Elizabeth, I know you're smart, so it surprises me to have to say this, but you do know what this is about, right? There are people trying to harm the families of American military personnel. Your picture was on the Web site, along with the fact that you go to Harvard. That's all it said, but God only knows what else they know. They're looking to exploit vulnerabilities, and this, frankly, is a vulnerability."

"Bullshit."

"It's not bullshit," Vasquez said. "For the record, somebody followed you home last night."

"I know," she said. "You did."

"Not me," he said. "There was another cab. I haven't been able to track it down yet but I will. Somebody may be stalking you. We have reason to believe they may be planning a kidnapping."

"I'm not worried about it," she said.

"I know you're not, and that's what worries me," he told her. "Who's James Chiang Chen?"

She paused, then rolled her eyes, tilting her head back and drawing a sharp angry breath.

"That," she said, "is who followed me. Followed us."

"Why?"

"He does it every night," she said. "Jimmy wants to make sure I get home safely. He's like my oldest regular. I mean, he's been my regular the longest."

"And he knows where you live?" Hoolie asked. "Does he know your real name isn't Kitten Kaboodle?"

"Everybody knows that," she said. "What kind of mother would name her daughter 'Kitten Kaboodle'? And for the record, I told him he can't come any farther than the corner, and he never does. He's very respectful."

"Does he know your real name?" Hoolie asked.

She appeared to be deciding whether or not to lie.

"Yes. He knows my real name," she said. "He's just a friend."

"Have you told any of your other regulars what your real name is or where you live?"

"No," she said. "I wouldn't do that."

"So why Jimmy?" Hoolie asked. Elizabeth didn't answer. "Because he's so respectful and well-mannered? Because he's in love with you? Or thinks he is? Or because he's given you so much money?"

"What he does with his money is his business," Elizabeth said, her anger rising visibly. "If he wants to give me a twenty instead of a one, or pay for a private dance, he can do that. It's legal."

"I'm not talking about twenties," Hoolie said. "I'm more concerned with the hundred thousand dollars-plus that's he's transferred into your bank account. Largely because actually, guess what? It's not his money. From the looks of it, he's borrowing—to use the most polite word I can think of—money from MIT. I'm going to go out on a limb and guess MIT doesn't have funds set aside for professors to pay strippers. Or did you think a fifty-two-year-old professor of advanced physics makes that kind of money?"

He realized he'd made a mistake, revealing the extent to which he'd investigated her. It was customarily his style to lay all his cards on the table and let the chips fall where they may, trusting in his ability to dance between the chips as they fell.

She bolted from the table, saying "Goddammit" before leaving the restaurant as Hoolie dropped a pair of twenty-dollar bills on the table and went after her. She ran with abandon, faster that he thought she could move, and disappeared down the T station stairs before he could catch her.

The timing was bad, a train already waiting on the platform with its doors about to close. He reached the bottom of the stairs in time to see her board the third car, but the doors slammed shut before he had a chance to get on. They made eye contact once as the train pulled away. She hated him. That much was clear. A lot.

Then she was gone.

DeLuca stopped at the Natick/Framingham rest area, just beyond the state police headquarters, on turnpike property where, in a large bunker fifty feet underground, the Federal Emergency Management Agency offices were housed, an operations and disaster response center where the governor and his staff would relocate in case of a nuclear attack or red alert, managed 24/7/365 by a skeleton crew. Today there were twice as many cars as usual in the parking lot, indicating that some sort of preparation was under way, perhaps just a readiness drill, but he doubted it.

At the rest area opposite the turnpike, he grabbed a sandwich and a Coke and paused to collect his e-mail, taking a booth at the McDonald's next to an old couple who were studying a map of Boston's Freedom Trail in anticipation of their day's adventure. He found a message from Walter Ford, the text accompanied by a series of photographs, each with an explanation:

David,

Luck. Been working on those names and the Jpeg you sent me, with Scott and some of his people at Image Analysis. Also referenced are SIPERNET, Interpol, plus DoD's "Blackbird" database of all Balkans theater/ national and open-source CI/HUMINT. Here are the files we think are relevant, so far, sorted for the parameters you gave me. Analysis continues. It appears, in brief, that a Serbian "death squad" may be wholly or partially reconstituted and operating in the U.S., and elsewhere, as follows:

1. **Marko Simic,** 43. This photograph comes Interpol, as do the others. From 1995–1999, member of a group, I would call it a death squad, called Jelan's Wolves, operating in Serbia/Croatia/Bosnia under

the overall command of President Radovan
Karadzic and General Ratko Mladic. Jelan is Jelan
Dvoradjic (next picture), commander of aforemen-
tioned team, officially a special operations unit
of Serbian army. Dvoradjic is Montenegran, as is
Simic. Wolves believed to be responsible for atroci-
ties/mass murders/rapes in villages of Foca (January 12, 1996), Obijic (May 5–6, 1997), Dakovica
(August 24, 1997), Pristina (June, 1998), Pljevjila
(July 4, 1998), and Prizren (December 12, 1998),
and were, according to witnesses/SIGINT/Black-
bird, among the leadership at Srebrenica during
the massacre there in 1995. Simic was the number
two guy. No wife/kids, criminal in Beograd before
the war, mostly drugs, also rape. Simic is wanted by
Interpol (murder, rape, genocide), to stand trial at
War Crimes Tribunal at The Hague. **Believed to be
in United States.**

2. **Jelan Dvoradjic,** 54. Leader of Jelan's Wolves,
   promoted during the war by Mladic himself to rank
   of major. Before the war, Dvoradjic **ran a software
   company** in Novi Sad. **Wife and children** (other
   than son, Ivan, next photo) killed by NATO bombing
   during the war—**INCLUDING ELDEST DAUGH-
   TER HELENA—he was holding her in his arms
   when she died, according to NY Times story on
   him at the time.** Charged with genocide, murder,
   rape, made himself rich by essentially stealing
   everything he and his men could get their hands
   on from Croats/Bosnian Muslims/Albanians, also
   bank robbery and kidnapping for ransom. **Cousin
   to Slobodan Milosevic with strong government
   connections.** Dvoradjic is wanted by Interpol, to

stand trial at War Crimes Tribunal at The Hague. Last seen in Dublin (Sept. 2002)—#4 on Interpol most wanted list. Whereabouts unknown.

3. **Ivan Dvoradjic,** 29, son of Jelan, member of Wolves. Charged with genocide, murder, rape, wanted by Interpol to stand trial at War Crimes Tribunal at The Hague. Worked for father before the war as **software engineer.** Degree University of Beograd in mechanical engineering. **Lost wife** to NATO bombing. Third in command. **Speaks Arabic.** W/u.

4. **Arkady Stipanich,** 28. Member of Wolves. Charged with genocide, murder, rape, wanted by Interpol to stand trial at War Crimes Tribunal at The Hague. From village of Breca, Kosovo, site of early "ethnic cleansing." **Construction / Ironworker experience.** Believed to be in Canada, last seen 2001.

5. **Milos Stipanich,** 31. Arkady's older brother. Member of Wolves. Charged with murder, rape, wanted by Interpol to stand trial at War Crimes Tribunal at The Hague. **Truck driver.** Believed to be in Canada, last seen 2001.

6. **Jotso Sinhavsky,** 33. Member of Wolves. Charged with genocide, murder, wanted by Interpol to stand trial at War Crimes Tribunal at The Hague. Arrested in London, 2000, for Y2K bomb plot, skipped. Accomplished **sniper.** Believed responsible for **bombing** of mosque in Vrbana. W/u.

7. **Radislav Divac,** 26. Member of Wolves. **Nursing degree.** Charged with genocide, murder, wanted by Interpol to stand trial at War Crimes Tribunal at The Hague. Arrested in Madrid, April 2001, released

by mistake. Wanted for questioning in Madrid
bombing.

8. **Mihielo Arpanov,** 37. Member of Wolves. Experience as **plumber's assistant.** Charged with murder, rape, wanted by Interpol to stand trial at War
Crimes Tribunal at The Hague. W/u.

Simic, Divac, Arpanov, and Sinhavsky listed, under
aliases (below), as part-time employees of Massachusetts Senior Services, caregivers or personal
aides to disabled. MSS is owned by Anthony Simeone
and David Simeone, same scumbags we busted
before. David Simeone currently under investigation
for illegally obtaining power of attorney/undue influence for clients. MSS employees required by law to
have photo IDs—CPV program located them at MSS
site. Simic is on file as **Mark Kenny,** Divac as **David
Green,** Arpanov as **Michael Adnusian,** Sinhavsky as
John Samples, each with what are evidently phony
green cards also on file—I suspect/assume Dvoradjics
have some skill with Photoshop etc. to manufacture
documents. All addresses/contact info in employment
records are false. Payments probably cash under table.

Attached are links to sites on Jelan's Wolves, news
stories/open sources. These are very bad people. Two
others currently in jail in Amsterdam, awaiting trial. Another killed in shootout at Schiphol airport. Unlike many,
they have resisted/refused all attempts to plea bargain.
Loyalty fear-based, most likely—Dvoradjic once shot
one of his lieutenants in drunken dispute. I personally
find it significant that all left Serbia to avoid tribunal.
Dvoradjic offered immunity in exchange for testimony

against Milosevic, declined just prior to disappearance. Ideologue espousing theories of ethnic purity etc., claims to be direct blood descendant of Prince Lazar, loser/hero of Battle of Kosovo on plains of Polje. May feel some sense of higher calling (I'm just guessing here).

Question: have we now identified I4NI? If so, where are they?

Walter.

P.S. Simic's DNA is on file from a prior arrest. It matches fetal DNA taken from autopsy. That confirms.

P.P.S. If Jelan Dvoradjic is I4NI, using Al Qaeda rhetoric/etc. to conceal his presence/actions, exposure would enervate efficacy of site. He killed 400+ Muslims in Breca. Etc. No friends in the Arab world. Arabs would not hit on his site or show support if they knew. Preliminary investigations indicate Al Qaeda involvement with murders Wagner, Masland, and O'Hara. IRA remnants may be involved with McNulty. Not that you asked, but someone should look for connections.

P.P.P.S—here's a link you might be interested in: <www.I4NI/dailynews/updates/targets/78#94/html/>

When DeLuca clicked on the link, he saw a story he didn't have to read, because he knew the details as well as anyone:

Daily News
American counterintelligence agent targeted in Boston hotel. U.S. Army counterintelligence special agent David De-Luca was attacked in his hotel room in downtown Boston last night *More* ⇨

DeLuca forwarded the information to Dawn Massey and got back on the road, after asking Walter to see if he could learn where Jelan Dvoradjic or his son might have been employed—if Dvoradjic had owned a tech company, it was possible, perhaps even likely, that he'd sought employment, under an alias, in the tech sector, a thriving part of the Massachusetts economy comprising businesses connected to Harvard and MIT along the 128 corridor, the region second only to Silicon Valley in California. Or maybe he was selling women's shoes, but DeLuca doubted it. When he reached the tollbooths where 128 intersected the Pike, he waited in line and paid cash rather than use his EZ-Pass, concerned now that whoever was looking for him may have gained access to the MTA computers to monitor who passed through which turnpike tollbooths and when. Maybe it was silly, but he couldn't afford to drop his guard again. He might have been on his home turf, but it was no longer the comfort zone it had once been.

While he waited to pay his $3.60, he dialed a number on his SAT phone. When his aunt Eva answered, he spent the requisite first five minutes apologizing for not calling more often and for not stopping by. His own mother had been the opposite of the stereotypical Italian housewife, a sullen, joyless woman who didn't like to cook. Aunt Eva was more traditional.

"Why don't you come over for dinner tonight, Davy?" she said. "You bring Bonnie and I'll make you pasta fagioli. I'm already making it, Davy, so it's no trouble."

"Thanks, Aunt Eva, but I don't think so," he said. "Bonnie's out of town—"

"Your wife is out of town?" she interrupted. "You're taking separate vacations now? I don't think I like the sound of that."

"It's not exactly a vacation," DeLuca said.

"It's a business? She has a business? I thought she volunteered at the hospital."

"It's not business," DeLuca said. "She's visiting a friend. Who's sick. In South Carolina. Anyway, I was actually looking for Jackie."

"You want to see Giacomo, come to dinner," she said. "He's going to be here in twenty minutes. But he's always late. You know him. He just called me on his cell phone. What are you going to do—cook for yourself? You can't cook for yourself with your wife out of town."

"Okay," DeLuca said, "I'll come to dinner, but listen, I want to surprise him, so don't tell him I'm coming, okay?"

"Oh, that'll be fun," his aunt Eva said. "He'll love it."

Half an hour later, it appeared that she was wrong. By the way he fidgeted and touched his nose, Jackie seemed extremely uncomfortable when he saw his cousin David sitting on the couch.

"Hey man," Jackie said. "I wasn't sure when I was going to see you again."

"Didn't you get the messages I left you?" DeLuca said. "I've been calling you all day."

"I been having trouble with my phone," Jackie said.

"You used it to call your mother to say you'd be late for dinner."

"I been going in and out of coverage," Jackie said. "Stop busting my balls."

"You boys come and eat now," Aunt Eva said. *"Giacomo—vieni a lavarti le mani prima del pranzo. E' un bravo ragazzo.*

"David, can I get you something to drink? You want a Capri Sun? I just went to Costco. How about a nice box wine? Maybe some Chianti?"

"One glass," DeLuca said.

Eva served the meal after Jackie returned from washing his hands in the bathroom. The food was delicious and came in large servings, beginning with rolled-up prosciutto with capers and anchovies and cream cheese in the middle, ending with cannolis she'd made herself.

"So Jackie tells me when you were in Iraq, you got hit by a grenade," Eva said. "I thought, oh my goodness. That's terrible. How are you then? Where did it hit you?"

"I'm okay," DeLuca said. "I had an operation on my neck, but other than that."

"You got hit in the neck by a grenade!"

"No, I wasn't hit by a grenade. My Humvee hit something and I went through the windshield."

"It hit something?" she said. "What'd it hit? They should be more careful. They don't have signs? I thought those windshields were bulletproof."

"Davy's head is harder than titanium," Jackie said.

"Well, I think you and all your army friends have done a wonderful job and I don't care what anybody says," Eva said. "I think that Saddam Hussein is going to think twice before he sends airplanes full of terrorists to attack the World Trade Center again. That's the important thing. When I think of poor Eileen—"

"Ma," Jackie said. "How is he going to attack the World Trade Center again? The World Trade Center isn't there anymore."

"You know what I mean," she said.

They made small talk during dinner, and then Eva took the dishes into the kitchen to clean up, turning the TV on the kitchen counter to the baseball game.

"We need to talk, Jackie," DeLuca said, once they were alone.

"Let's go sit on the porch," Jackie said, keeping his voice down and glancing toward the kitchen. "Ma doesn't like it when I smoke inside."

From the second floor of the triple-decker where Eva lived, on Princeton Street in East Boston, they looked down on a Spanish market across the street where two men in "wife-beater" T-shirts were playing dominos on a card table on the sidewalk. Jackie sat on the railing, knocking his ashes from his cigarette over the side as he smoked. Between the houses, DeLuca could see the sunlight reflecting off the Chelsea River.

"You mad at me?" Jackie asked his cousin.

"What do you think?" DeLuca said.

"I think you're mad at me," Jackie said. "Come on, David—this is me. I'm not going to fuck with you."

"You already did," DeLuca said. "You haven't told me the truth. I'm not blaming you, Jackie, but I got my house shot at and my hotel room blown up since I saw you last. I need to start shedding some light on this fast."

"What?" Jackie said. "David, that makes no fucking sense. I had no fucking idea. Why would they hit you?"

"Who's 'they'?" DeLuca asked.

"You don't know?"

"I have an idea, but I want to hear yours."

"You know," Jackie said. "The people who have an interest in the thing. The Katie Quinn thing."

"Stop talking about 'the people' and start naming names," DeLuca insisted. "I don't think you know how big this is."

"Oh, I know," Jackie said. "Why you think I've been so hard to find?"

"What do you know about Jelan Dvoradjic?" DeLuca asked.

"Who?"

"You don't know the name?"

"Jello Dvorak?" Jackie said. "Wasn't he a composer or something?"

"Who are you talking about then?" DeLuca asked.

"Vinnie P. Vinnie Potatoes," Jackie said. "Why? Who are *you* talking about?"

"Tell me about Vinnie Potatoes," DeLuca said. "Are you in trouble?"

"Maybe a little," Jackie said.

"Why? What happened?"

"He thinks I've been doing his girlfriend," Jackie said.

"Have you?"

"Maybe a little," Jackie said. "Look, I told her I would hook up with her *if* and *only* if she and Vinnie were through. And not before that. And I didn't. I would never—I respect relationships, David. I do. Jesus, she was the one who asked me if I wanted to have a drink. I told her I was in AA and she said, 'Well then, what's a girl gotta do to take advantage of you?' She said that."

"She said that?"

"Yeah. Can you believe it?"

"What'd you say?"

"I said, 'Not a whole lot,'" Jackie said, laughing. "Breathe in and out. But like I said, I was kidding, because she was Vinnie's girl. Jesus, I only met her doing him a favor when there was a party and he was with Gina—"

"That's his girlfriend?"

"Yeah, Gina," Jackie said, "and Vinnie's with her, and then his wife walks in, so before I know what's happening, he introduces me to his wife, Lisa, and says Gina is *my* girlfriend, so I play along and put my arm around Gina even though Vinnie is giving me a look."

"So you hooked up with Gina, and now Vinnie wants to kill you?"

"Something like that," Jackie said. "It's all a big misunderstanding, because he thinks I took his stuff and I didn't."

"You put Gina in touch with Freddy," DeLuca said. "With your friend."

"Yeah," Jackie said. "He needed the work. That's what he does. I didn't know she was going to steal Vinnie's stuff. I thought she just needed help with her own stuff. But she and Vinnie weren't exactly talking because he refused to leave Lisa when he promised he would, so Gina felt totally screwed. She felt like she had to get something out of it. It's not like she could hire a lawyer to get half."

"You connected Gina with Katie?" DeLuca said. "With her business, Ex-Communications?"

"Yeah," Jackie said.

"But you didn't tell Freddy Vinnie was after him because if he knew, he might go to Vinnie and sell you out," DeLuca said. "Was that what you were afraid of?"

Jackie shrugged.

"You knew Katie how?"

"Through AA," Jackie said. "Me and Freddy and her all went to the same meeting."

"How about Marko?" DeLuca asked.

"Katie's ex," Jackie said.

"Did you know him?"

"I met him once," Jackie said. "Talk about creeps. This guy took it to a whole new level, know what I mean? He was like, 'Dude, call me when the mother ship comes to take you back to your planet.'"

"Scary?"

"You could say that," Jackie said. "Put it this way— nobody at Walpole would have dreamt of fucking with him, just from the vibe he gave off."

"Where'd you meet him?"

"I ran into him and Katie at Piccolo Venicia, on Hanover," Jackie said. "I guess they were on a date."

"And you knew Freddy had a crush on Katie?"

"Big time," Jackie said. "He was like a kindergartner. He was so happy when she started to notice him."

"When was that?" DeLuca asked.

"About a month ago," Jackie said. "Out of the blue. He'd had a crush on her for a long time and then one night she says, 'I want you to make love to me.'"

"Does he?"

"Of course he does," Jackie said. "What do you mean, 'Does he?' Jesus, I told you, he'd been dreaming of it for a year. Which, frankly, I didn't get because she wasn't exactly Kate Mosh, if you know what I mean."

"Moss."

"What?"

"Kate *Moss,* not Kate *Mosh,*" DeLuca said. "Did you know Katie Quinn was two months pregnant?"

"What?" Jackie said.

"She was pregnant."

"Well that explains it," Jackie said.

"Explains what?"

"Why she was so emotional," Jackie said. "By Freddy?"

"I said two months," DeLuca said. "You just told me she and Freddy only hooked up a month ago."

"So it wasn't his," Jackie said. "What are you looking at me like that for? Do I look like a fucking mathematician? Come to think of it, though, Freddy's not exactly Einstein in the math department. I bet he wouldn't have counted back nine months."

"Actually, it's ten," DeLuca said.

"What are you talking about?"

"Ten. Ten months."

"It's nine. Everybody knows women are pregnant for nine months," Jackie insisted.

"Women are pregnant for ten months," DeLuca said. "They're usually one month pregnant when they find out, and then nine months later, they give birth."

"Bullshit."

"Jackie—I have a kid. I think I know how long the human gestation period is."

"Don't be such a know-it-all," Jackie said. "You were always a know-it-all. I'm doing my best. So it must have been Marko's baby."

"It was," DeLuca said. "But Freddy didn't know about Marko?"

"I don't think so," Jackie said.

"Why did Katie and Marko break up?"

"You're asking me?" Jackie said. "Like I said, it was kind of surprising they were together at all. Maybe she wised up. Did he know Katie was pregnant?"

"I doubt it," DeLuca said. "My guess is, she hooked up with Freddy so that she could tell people the kid was his, instead of Marko's. Now I want to know why Marko would call Vinnie Potatoes twice on the night Katie was killed. First he calls Joey D'Angelo and then Vinnie."

"He'd call Joey to get to Vinnie," Jackie said. "Nobody just calls Vinnie. You gotta get Joey to give you the number."

"Katie had the number," DeLuca said. "She'd already called it. For Gina."

"Oh, right," Jackie said. "I don't see how you keep all this stuff straight. Maybe he wanted Joey to soften Vinnie up a little."

"So why would he call Vinnie?"

Jackie touched his nose again. "I might have an idea about that," he said.

"What?"

"Well, actually, she called me from the radio station an hour before her show and asked me if I'd have a word with Vinnie about his stuff," Jackie said. "Katie was trying to help Freddy arrange with Vinnie to get his stuff back, because it was still all in the truck. Vinnie was so pissed he put a job on whoever did it."

"But you didn't make the call?"

"No."

"Why not?" DeLuca asked. "You were still trying to figure out how to help Gina keep it."

"No," Jackie said.

"You were," DeLuca said.

"I mean, Jesus, David, have you ever seen a football game in high def? It's incredible," Jackie said. "Anyway, even if I wanted to make the call, I couldn't."

"Katie didn't know you'd hooked up with Gina?"

"No."

"But Vinnie did."

"Yeah."

"How?"

"I think Gina might have mentioned something to him about how I could satisfy her in bed because I'm better equipped than he is," Jackie said. "Hey, it's a biological fact. I can't help it if God was generous to me in the schlong department."

"Or stingy in the brains department," DeLuca added.

"Exactly," Jackie said. "I never claimed to be a rocket scientist about this shit. Sometimes I let 'Little Jackie' do the thinking. So what? Who doesn't? Katie must have called Marko to ask Marko to ask Vinnie to back off. Marko wouldn't have backed down from Vinnie P. That's for sure. So who shot Katie?"

"Marko," DeLuca said.

"Not Vinnie?"

"I don't think so."

"Why Marko?"

"Because of Katie's father," DeLuca said. "Or maybe because Katie found out about Marko's friends. Or their plans."

"What plans?"

"Did Vinnie give Gina a glass necklace?" DeLuca said. "One he bought at a place on Newbury Street called Le Bling?"

"I couldn't tell you where he bought it," Jackie said. "But yeah, she had a necklace like that."

"Does she still have it?"

"No," Jackie said. "She was looking for it. She thinks maybe it's on the truck."

"It's not," DeLuca said. "It's in the evidence room at Boston police headquarters. Freddy pocketed it during the move and gave it to Katie. They found it in Katie's apartment."

"Oh," Jackie said. "Freddy copped it? Well. Shit happens. I can see how that might occur. Don't tell Gina."

"Where's Gina now?" DeLuca asked.

"I got her at a Motel 6 in Natick," Jackie said. "She wants me to make a deal with Vinnie. She's not exactly a Motel 6 kind of girl, if you know what I mean. He gets his stuff back on condition he leaves her alone. And me. And Freddy."

"You think Vincent Pastorelli is going to like you giving him ultimatums like that?"

"It's all how you put it," Jackie said. "You need to use finesse."

"Where's Vinnie now?"

"Beats me," Jackie said.

"I'm sure he will if he catches you," DeLuca said.

Aunt Eva appeared on the porch, carrying a tray bearing two root beer floats in tall glasses, the frothy heads rising high above the rims, with a straw and a spoon in each glass. It was a tradition, at Eva's house on hot summer nights, to have root beer floats on the porch.

"How are my kids doing?" she said, distributing the drinks. "It's good to see you, David. I wish you'd come by more often."

DeLuca was half finished with his drink when his SAT phone rang. On the other end was Mickey O'Brien, who asked him what he was doing.

"Having a root beer float on my aunt's porch," DeLuca said.

"Don't rub it in," O'Brien said. "It's all set up. Vinnie will meet you in an hour at Galiano's. You know where that is?"

"I know where that is."

"You gotta come alone," O'Brien said. "Vinnie's keeping his head down—Wexler's got him for the Katie Quinn murder."

"Wexler's wrong."

"I told him that's what you'd say," O'Brien said. "Can you set it straight?"

"I doubt it," DeLuca said.

"I told Vinnie you'd talk to Frank."

"I can try," DeLuca said.

"I kept my end of the deal," O'Brien said. "My dog is really sick."

"I'll make some calls," DeLuca said. "I don't know if they'll let you go home without an escort."

"I don't care about that," O'Brien said.

"I'll make some calls."

"I appreciate it."

He called Paul Halliday and explained the situation. He called Phil LeDoux, and he called Congressman Danforth Sykes, Dan's father and a member of the committee that oversaw the activities of Team Red at INSCOM special ops. The congressman called the governor, who had been hoping for Congressman Sykes's support for his forthcoming presidential bid. The governor called the warden at Walpole, who'd hoped to be appointed state corrections superintendent and was eager to curry favor. From

DeLuca's perspective, it wasn't all that different from how he played the various politicians, sheiks, and tribal leaders off against each other in Iraq—it was how he found people who didn't want to be found. You asked the people who knew the people who knew the people who knew the answers, and you made it in everybody's self-interest to help you.

He checked in with Sami, who told him General Quinn was finally sleeping. He conferenced in Sykes and MacKenzie, who said they were working on a project for Walter, tracking Marko Simic/Mark Kenny, Radislav Divac/David Green, Mihielo Arpanov/Michael Adnusian, and Jotso Sinhavsky/John Samples, "All of whom," Sykes said, "quit their jobs three days ago. The guys at Mass Senior Services won't talk to us anymore without their lawyers because of what happened last time. They're swearing they're only hiring people with green cards, but apparently these guys had 'em. Are we certain they've got the know-how to forge documents?"

" 'Certain' might be too strong a word," DeLuca said. " 'Confident.' "

"Good enough for me," Sykes said. "Things have been cooking around here since you e-mailed the files. Simeone brothers won't open their books without a warrant. Massey is trying to get one—*we* can't. I doubt it will do any good. I'm wondering why they worked at all. Walter says they made a lot of money in Croatia."

"Made a lot or spent a lot?" DeLuca said. "Joe Quinn has a million-dollar bounty on his head. They seem interested. Why not mix politics and profit, if you can? I'm a little worried that they've quit their jobs. It confirms something could happen. Soon."

"That's the feeling here too," MacKenzie said. "Milos Stipanich was a truck driver, so we're looking into hazmat licenses and traffic violations and things like that. They've been on it here but they're going over it again. The FBI's had a strong history of profiling for Al Qaeda types lately, but Serbs are going to look like just another white guy. Arkady Stipanich did construction—we're thinking if they're going to get jobs as covers, they're going to take the path of least resistance and go with their expertise, just like anybody else."

"What about communications?" DeLuca asked. "Having SIGINT is too much to ask, I suppose, but they've got to be able to talk to each other."

"Massey says they're probably using clone phones or prepaid calling cards or leaving signal ads in the newspapers to meet in person," Sykes said. "She's looking at identity theft as well. They're flagging credit cards used simultaneously thousands of miles apart, anomalous purchases like a guy who buys diabetes supplies and candy bars, and of course gun buys, explosives, and IED components and all that, garage door openers, baby monitors."

"Any luck finding buyers of fifty-caliber Smith and Wessons?" DeLuca asked.

"Nothing too promising," MacKenzie said. "Everything so far is legitimate. But as you said, if they could forge documents, how are we going to find illegitimate buyers? Background checks just look for troubled history. There's not going to be a history for a fake identity, troubled or otherwise."

"Check against employment," DeLuca said. "These guys are stalkers. They had Simic get close to Katie Quinn but they waited. They gave out the information about

Wagner and O'Hara and the others well in advance of operations. Let's assume I4NI is going to be at least as careful as the 9/11 guys, if they're planning something on that scale. See if you can find somebody who got a job at some high-risk target like the Government Center or the Federal Building who bought a fifty. Let's also assume they're not going to be in it for the seventy black-eyed virgins that await them in paradise—these aren't suicide bombers. They might find some idiot suicide bomber and use him, but they're not going to do it themselves. Check air travel out of Logan, Green, Bradley, Portland, Worcester, and Manchester. Check for eight males buying tickets at the same time on the same flight, or one credit card buying tickets for all eight. Flights out of the country, not domestic, I'm thinking. Even if they're feeling clever, they're still going to leave U.S. jurisdiction. Obviously, one-way flights, though I'm thinking they can't be that stupid. Narrow it down to something in the next day or two."

"You think that soon?"

"Yeah," DeLuca said. "I'm not sure why I think that. It's just a feeling."

Galiano's was an Italian restaurant in the North End, off Hanover Street, and not a particularly smart place to meet, if you were trying to remain inconspicuous. Even in DeLuca's day, the police had known to keep an eye on Galiano's, owned by a mob guy named Galiano Ricci who'd loaned the money to the talented chef who started the restaurant and then had taken over when the chef had trouble paying back the loan. Word was that Galiano had held a gun on the chef for three days while he taught his replacement everything he knew. Vinnie Pastorelli was sitting in a booth toward the back of the restaurant, near the kitchen. It was nine o'clock, and there were no other customers, due to the two men at the door who told DeLuca when he arrived that there was a private party going on inside, parting only when DeLuca told them he had an appointment. He handed them his gun when they moved to frisk him and received a quick patting down anyway. Vinnie had gained twenty pounds since DeLuca saw him last. He was sitting with a platinum blonde in a red dress who was delicately picking at a piece of cheesecake with a fork. Vinnie was wearing black pants, a black shirt, and a gold chain on his neck to tell him where to stop shaving. He had reading glasses on the end of his nose and was poring over the *Boston Globe* sports pages when DeLuca approached the table. Pastorelli looked up.

"Detective David DeLuca," he said. "I thought you'd quit."

"I'm not with the department anymore," DeLuca said, "but I've still got friends there."

"I got friends there too," Vinnie said. "I have friends everywhere."

"That's great, Vinnie," DeLuca said. "It's nice to be loved."

"So why do you want to see me? They told me maybe you could straighten this thing out. Who are you working for?"

"I'm with the army," DeLuca said, sitting down without waiting for Pastorelli to invite him. "Katie Quinn was a general's daughter. I'm looking at her murder as a terrorist action."

"Well that's the first fucking thing I've heard that makes fucking sense," Pastorelli said. "Wexler thinks I did it. I even got an alibi. I was with my girlfriend."

"Gina?" DeLuca said, looking at the blonde.

"Who's Gina?" the blonde said.

"This is Donna," Vinnie said. "Donna is my girlfriend. Not Gina. Tell this man that I was with you."

"He was with me," Donna said. "All night. At my apartment. Swear to God. We did it three times."

"Donna, thank you, but that's not the point," Vinnie said. DeLuca would have bet his paycheck that Vinnie told her to say that. "Why don't you go wait in the car? Detective DeLuca and I have to talk a little business now."

"I don't want to wait in the car," she said.

"Well then go fucking shopping," he told her. "Go to Newbury Street. Just get the fuck out of here for a few minutes. Jesus. Tell Joey to drive you."

"Can I have your black card?"

"No," he said. He reached into his wallet and took out five one-hundred-dollar bills, laying the money on the table in front of her. She scooped up the cash greedily. "Take that. Just a little spree. Nothing extravagant tonight, all right, sweetheart?"

"Okay," she said. "I don't know what's open at this hour. Can I get you anything?"

"Yeah," he said. "If you're near the record store, get me the new Fountains of Wayne CD. I don't know what it's called."

"Okay," she said, turning to DeLuca. "It was nice to meet you."

When she was gone, Vinnie held up his empty wineglass to the waiter and asked DeLuca if he wanted a glass. DeLuca shook his head.

"This shit is killing me," Pastorelli said. "Do you have any idea how expensive it is to have two mistresses?"

"I don't think I do," DeLuca said.

"One is much better," Vinnie said. "I don't know what I was thinking. I was getting no rest whatsoever. Plus we have a three-year-old at home who sleeps in the bed with Lisa and me who likes to kick me in the head all night, swear to fucking God—he snuggles up next to Mommy and then he pushes me away with his feet. Like, off the bed. So I tell my wife I'm getting a hotel room just to get some sleep, and then Donna keeps me up all night. I'm not complaining, but I'm complaining, you know what I mean? I'm biting the fucking candle off at both ends."

"Donna doesn't know about Gina?"

"No, and she doesn't have to," Vinnie said. "But you see my problem. I'm a family man now—you got kids, DeLuca?"

"One," he said.

"Then you know what I mean," Vinnie said. "I live for my kids, and for my wife—Lisa is the best fucking mother in the world. But if I get popped for the parking garage thing and Donna has to testify that I was with her that night, then my wife finds out and I'm fucked, because she's the mother of my kids, so what am I gonna do? I can't shoot her."

"Plus you love her."

"Plus that," Vinnie said. "So I need you to straighten this out with Wexler. Maybe if Gina talks to him in person, one-on-one, maybe that'll be enough."

"You mean Donna."

"Right, Donna," Vinnie said. "That's another reason to cut back to one—I can't keep this shit straight. It's hard enough to remember not to call them by the wrong name when you're in bed. I called Lisa 'Gina' once and I thought I was going to lose it."

"She didn't mind?"

"She wasn't listening," Vinnie said. "That's one thing I really like about her."

"Are you paying for Donna's apartment too?" DeLuca asked. "That must bother you, paying for two apartments when one is empty."

"No shit," Vinnie said.

"So you want to move Donna into Harbor Towers," DeLuca said. "And you want your stuff back to furnish the apartment, the way it was before."

"You're fucking right I do," Vinnie said. "That shit is mine. I could care less about the bitch. She thinks she's going to fuck me over and then take my shit? Can she really be fucking serious? She thinks I'd sit still for that?"

"I'll tell you what," DeLuca said. "I'll talk to Wexler, and I'll get your stuff back. But I need you to do something for me."

"I'm already doing something for you," Vinnie said. "I'm meeting with you."

"You're doing this for Mickey O'Brien," DeLuca said. "What I need from you is something more important. I want you to help me find somebody."

"Find somebody?" Vinnie said. "Why?"

"Love of country," DeLuca said. "You gotta admit it, Vinnie—where else can a man have a wife and three kids and two mistresses? Look what you've done for yourself. The first time I met you, you were Angelo Anguillo's errand boy, and now you've got your own crew."

"Only in America," Vinnie said.

"Right," DeLuca said. "And parts of Sicily. I want you to help your country."

"Like Lucky Luciano," Vinnie said. "Or like Kennedy asking Sam Giancana to hit Castro."

"Like that," DeLuca said. "A guy named Marko Simic, a.k.a. Mark Kenny, called you the night Katie died. I think he clipped her. I think he's hooked up with some people who are going to do something in Boston. Something big. We don't know what. I know you got people on the docks—I imagine with the FBI and BPD and Homeland people all over the place, looking into every container, you're having problems. You probably want the orange alert to be over as much as we do."

"Suppose I did," Vinnie said. "What do you need from me?"

"Why did Simic call you?" DeLuca asked.

"He wanted me to leave Katie alone," Vinnie said. "He told me he was going to hurt me if I fucked with her. He's going to hurt me? I fucking laughed. I told him to go fuck himself."

"Had you spoken with him before?"

"No," Vinnie said. "I never heard of him. Who is he? He's fucking nothing. *He's* busting *my* balls? It's fucking shit."

"You'd spoken to Katie, though."

"Gina hired her to negotiate," Vinnie said. "Like she needed a go-between."

"To say what?"

"To break up with me," Vinnie said. " 'Gina wants to be friends. It's not you, it's her. Gina has to learn how to love herself.' I mean, Jesus Christ, I bought her three fucking vibrators. I think she was okay in the loving herself department. If anything, she was maybe a little bit too okay. If you know what I mean."

"She ever talk about seeing other people?" DeLuca asked.

"She wouldn't be that stupid," Vinnie said. "She was stupid, but not that stupid."

As DeLuca had suspected, Gina had only told Jackie that she'd mentioned him to Vinnie, probably to keep Jackie in line.

"You didn't have a problem with Katie Quinn?"

"Nothing," Vinnie said. "That's what I keep saying. Why would I want to kill Katie Quinn?"

"They think it has something to do with the sports book," DeLuca said.

"Why?"

"Because what she said on the radio could influence the action you get."

"So the fuck what?" Vinnie said. "What she said on the radio was smart. I don't make money on people who bet smart. I make money on people who bet stupid. People who bet their hearts. This town is a fucking gold mine for finding people who bet stupid. Believe me, there's no shortage. And they're not going to get any smarter, listening to the radio. I was getting action on the Sox when they were down three games to nothing to the Yankees."

"I thought you took a beating on that."

"Yeah, sure, but I'd take one again if I had to. One beating every eighty-six years is good business. General Motors should be so fucking lucky."

"You put out a contract on the people who took your stuff," DeLuca said.

"I wouldn't call it a contract," Vinnie said. "More like an open-ended reward."

"Whatever," DeLuca said. "Ten thousand dollars, right?"

"What does Katie Quinn have to do with the people who took my stuff?" Vinnie Potatoes asked. "The guys who took my stuff were fifteen or twenty guys. Musicians, somebody said."

"Katie referred them."

"She did?" Vinnie said. "This is the first time I heard that."

"Cancel the reward," DeLuca said. "They didn't know they were stealing anything. Gina told them the stuff was hers. What's your e-mail address?"

"Why?"

"I'm going to e-mail you a file," DeLuca said, showing Pastorelli his CIM. "It's going to have eight photographs of eight guys. These guys. Eight names, and their aliases. I want you to find these guys. Four of them worked for the Simeones, but they're not talking to us. You tell the Simeone brothers we don't want them—we want the guys they were paying under the table. I want you to find them, but if you do, don't do anything—just call me. We got two guys working construction, or one construction and one driving trucks, we think. I want you to show the pictures around and use all the contacts you have. This guy is Marko Simic. This is a guy named Jelan Dvoradjic. He's the boss. Is your crew on e-mail?"

"My crew?" Vinnie said, laughing. "On e-mail? Half my guys can't fucking read. You think I'm going to do all this for you?"

"If you want your stuff back," DeLuca said. "If you don't want Donna's picture on the front page of the *Globe*. Or, for that matter, Gina's, because I know where she is too. Look at it this way—how did you feel when 9/11 happened? You remember—how did you feel?"

"I felt like shit," Vinnie said.

"You wanted to do something, right?"

"I did do something," Vinnie said. "I gave blood."

"And you felt like you wanted to kick somebody's ass too, right?" DeLuca said. "We all did. So this is your chance to do something. Because if we don't find these guys, I gotta tell you, something just as bad as 9/11 is going to happen. Anything from blowing up the Pru to God knows what. We need these guys, like, yesterday. It's your country too, Vinnie."

"You're fucking right it is," Vinnie said. "Maybe more so."

"Okay," DeLuca said, not certain exactly how Vinnie figured that. "So you help me and I'll help you. I'll keep you posted and you tell me what you know, as soon as you know it. I'll give you my mobile phone number too so you can call me."

"All right," Vinnie said.

"So what's your e-mail?" DeLuca asked.

"Mrpotatohead@crime.org." Vinnie said.

"Crime dot org?" DeLuca said. "Is that a joke?"

"No," Vinnie said. "It's a chat room. For people who want to meet real mobsters. My real name was already taken."

"I'll send you the files," DeLuca said.

As he drove away, DeLuca realized he had a problem. He believed Vinnie. Vinnie was telling him the truth, at least about Marko. Katie was afraid for Freddy, once they realized whose stuff they'd stolen. She asked Jackie to help, maybe figuring Jackie knew the right people, but Jackie couldn't, so she asked Marko. Marko obliged. He used her phone and called Vinnie. But Katie had her cell phone on her when she died, or at least they'd found it near her body. That put Marko at the scene. So why would Marko Simic be warning Vinnie to leave Katie alone, if he knew he was going to kill her in the next hour or so. Why bother?

And Katie was crying in the elevator. She'd had a bad night, and she was pregnant, but she had Freddy to turn to. She was at the beginning of a plan she'd cooked up to fool Freddy into thinking he was the father of her child—then Marko came back into her life. He was still willing to help her. He'd called Vinnie? Why help her? Maybe because she told him about the baby.

He was at the crime scene, but he wasn't the killer.

That meant he knew who the killer was.

That meant either the killer let him walk, because he knew him, and the killer wasn't worried, or else the killer killed Marko too, because he couldn't trust him and didn't want to leave a witness.

DeLuca called his friend Billy Morrissey and told him to meet him at the Boston Common parking garage. He told him to bring with him a corpse-sniffing dog. When he got to the garage, DeLuca met Morrissey and took him to the corner of the second level where they'd found Katie's body. He asked Morrissey if any of the cars in the garage were there the night Katie was killed, but Morrissey couldn't remember. The dog handler turned the dog loose. The dog, a yellow Labrador named Martha, made a bee-line for a two-year-old Saab parked against the wall, about a hundred feet from where they'd found Katie Quinn. In truth, they probably didn't really need the dog—DeLuca thought he would have been able to smell the body himself if he'd given himself a few more minutes. They popped the trunk, where they found the necroticized but still recognizable body of Marko Simic, his head bloated and discolored, a piece of braided picture-hanging wire still drawn taut around his neck.

Chapter Eight

VASQUEZ HAILED A CAB ON THE STREET. HE dialed Scott at the ops center at the Pentagon and asked him to use his CPV program to find Elizabeth LeDoux, looking specifically on the surveillance video imagery from the inbound Red Line train that had just left Harvard station. It took a moment. When he had a picture of Elizabeth on his handheld, he asked Scottie to superimpose a Boston subway map over a Boston city street map. Clicking back and forth between windows, he followed the train as best he could, instructing the driver to take Mass Ave and the Harvard Bridge to Storrow Drive and then I-93 south when it appeared that Elizabeth was staying on the Red Line past downtown. He counted the stops she made. When she got off the train at the University of Massachusetts/JFK Library station, he was less than a mile away.

A surveillance camera at the JFK Library, a building long thought to be a potential terrorist target, picked her up as she walked toward it. She was speaking into her cell phone as she walked. He considered asking Scott to check with NSA to see if they could intercept the call, but he changed his mind about it when he decided she'd probably had quite enough of that sort of thing, and more invaded privacy wouldn't necessarily help him. The library, a beautiful white building on a point overlooking Boston Harbor, evoked the sensation of sailing, wind blowing against white canvas, a theme that was echoed in the small sailboat mounted on a stand outside, one of the late president's personal boats. When Elizabeth took a seat on a bench by the harbor, Vasquez stepped inside the atrium and watched her through the tinted windows. Maintaining a completely covert surveillance on her was not going to be possible for much longer, but for now he stayed back—something told him she'd used her phone to make an appointment, and that she was meeting someone.

Sure enough, after a wait of perhaps twenty minutes, a man approached.

Vasquez recognized him as James Chen, the MIT professor.

Chen stood at first, then sat down when Elizabeth patted the marble bench she was sitting on. The first thing he did, once he sat down, was reach into his pocket and produce something that he wanted to give her. Vasquez couldn't see what it was, something small, a ring or maybe some earrings. Elizabeth smiled and shook her head. When he held the gift up to her, she smiled again and put both her hands on his and pushed them gently away.

She spoke, and Chen listened, occasionally nodding without reply. Her manner and her body language were apologetic, filled with sighs and shrugs and a slight turning away. He seemed to feel awkward, as if he didn't know what to do with his hands, unable to look her in the eye, in broad daylight, though perhaps her eyes were never where he looked. Occasionally she'd reach across the gap between them and pat him on the hand. He seemed to nod in agreement. He wiped his eyes with his sleeve.

He was crying.

Then he began to resist the things she was saying. Vasquez watched. Elizabeth's manner became more vehement, more insistent, her gesticulations more emphatic. When she shook her head no, Chen nodded his head to say yes, and when she nodded, he shook his head; they were obviously having an argument. She stood.

He stood.

When she tried to walk away, he blocked her path. She stopped but raised a finger to his face, pointing at him, then pointing downtown, then pointing far away. Vasquez imagined she was saying something like, "Go home, you miserable twerp." When Chen stepped toward her, she put both her hands up, palms toward him, to tell him to stop. He stopped, but when she tried to walk away, he grabbed her arm. She spun, twisting to break his grip, lashing out at him with her arm. She held up her cell phone, as if to say she was ready and willing to call the police.

He slapped the phone out of her hand.

Vasquez stepped up behind him and took him down with a choke hold. Chen was slight and not strong and went down easily, his glasses skidding across the sidewalk. When he struggled, Hoolie pushed his face against the concrete and pulled his jacket halfway down to bind his arms, kneeling hard on the small of the man's back.

"Don't move or I'll break your arms!" Hoolie commanded. "Elizabeth, call the police."

"What are you doing here?"

"Call the police," Vasquez repeated.

"Stop it," she said. "You're hurting him."

"You're right, I'm hurting him," he said, and as he spoke, he felt something hard in the pocket of James Chiang Chen's jacket. When he reached in, he found a small automatic .22 caliber with a pearly white handle, a girly gun, but enough gun to kill somebody. He held it in front of Chen's eyes, and if he accidentally banged the man's face against the concrete, he'd apologize later.

"What is this?" Vasquez said. "Why did you bring this? Talk to me."

"I keep her safe," Chen said. "I keep her safe. I would not hurt her."

"*I* keep her safe!" Vasquez said. "That's *my* job from now on."

"Let him go," Elizabeth said. "Please."

"Call the police," Vasquez said.

"No," she said. "Please. Let him up."

"He had this," Vasquez insisted, showing her the gun. "I don't think—"

"Just please," she said. "Get off of him."

Vasquez grabbed Chen by the collar and assisted him to a sitting position, ordering him to sit on his jacket with his feet out in front of him.

"It's all right," Elizabeth said to Chen. "Don't worry. It's all right."

"We're still a little far from all right," Vasquez said. "Are you okay?"

She had a bruise on her cheek. She touched it.

"I'm fine," she said. "It was an accident."

"Elizabeth," Vasquez said, "you—"

"It's okay," she said. "Let him up. It's all right."

The Asian man struggled to his feet, flapping his arms until his jacket was over his shoulders again. He hung his head, looking from Elizabeth to Vasquez.

"Who are you?" he asked Vasquez.

"He's my husband," Elizabeth said. "I told you, James. You don't know me. You think you do but you don't."

"He's your husband?" he said.

Elizabeth nodded. "Why don't you go home now, James?" she said. "Go home and grade papers."

Chen looked at her, then at Vasquez, who exchanged glances with Elizabeth, her eyes pleading with him. Hoolie understood the reasons why neither Elizabeth nor Chen wanted this to go any further, and why they wouldn't want their relationship written up or described in the newspapers.

"Look at my face," he told Chen, "and remember what I look like. I'm your personal restraining order. If I see you at the club, or if you come within a hundred yards of Elizabeth again, I'm going to hurt you, much worse than you're hurting now, and I'm going to have you arrested. You'll lose everything. Do you understand?"

Chen nodded.

"I'm sure the police would love to know about the money you've been transferring into your bank account too," Vasquez said. He drew back and then threw the small pistol as far as he could into the bay. "I've been a lot of places and I've dealt with guys who were a lot scarier than you. I know your life is pretty fucked up right now, but I want you to think about how much more fucked up it's going to get if you don't leave Elizabeth alone. Make the right choice, James. Make the right choice."

He picked up Chen's briefcase and handed it to him.

Chen walked away, pausing once to look over his shoulder, then walking as fast as he could on uncertain legs toward the UMass-Boston T station in the distance, his baggy pants flapping as he moved.

"He wouldn't have used his gun," Elizabeth said.

Vasquez stopped her with a look. "He would have," he told her. "I'm sorry, Elizabeth, but there are things you don't know about violence. I'm glad you don't know them, but you don't. And I don't care what books you've read. He would have."

The message on DeLuca's voice mail was identical to the one on his e-mail when he opened it.

"Agent DeLuca," the woman's voice said. "Dawn Massey. I'd like to speak to you, tonight. Call my cell and don't worry if it's late."

When he called, she told him she hadn't eaten all day and suggested, when he told her he could use a bite himself, that they meet at Anthony's Orotto, one of Boston's more famous restaurants on the waterfront, near Fan Pier. The owner, Anthony Anakis, was an Albanian, though everyone assumed he was Italian, and there were black-and-white photographs of him on the wall shaking hands with or hugging virtually every famous person who ever came through Boston, from Ted Kennedy to Ted Williams to Ted Nugent. Dawn Massey was sitting at the bar, nursing a Long Island iced tea. She was wearing a white blouse over a dark skirt, a pair of small silver earrings decorating her ears. A bag that was halfway between a purse and a briefcase hung from a strap on the back of her barstool. She smiled when he sat on the stool next to her.

"I'm absolutely positive you've heard this before," he told her, "but you don't look like an FBI agent."

"What makes you so sure?" she asked. "You've just never seen the pictures of J. Edgar Hoover wearing a dress."

"Oh come on," DeLuca said. "Everybody's seen pictures of J. Edgar Hoover in a dress."

"I have a friend who thinks Director Hoover and Pat Nixon were the same person," she said. "He says you never saw them in the same room at the same time."

"I never thought of that. But now it seems so obvious."

"How you doing?" she said.

"Why do you ask?"

"Your hotel room," she said. "I have some good people on it. They found traces of Semtex."

"The poor man's C4. They're going to have to do better than Semtex if they want to blow me up," DeLuca joked.

"They said you were tough," she told him.

"They don't know what they're talking about," DeLuca said. "I just seem to have this weird ability to not think about things that ought to scare the shit out of me."

"Some people might call that courage."

"I don't," he said. "I think of it as a sort of selective stupidity. When we were in Balad at Camp Anaconda, we took mortar rounds every night. They never came close, but if you really gave it any thought, it would probably bother you."

They were interrupted when the maitre d' approached to say their table was ready, leading them to a two-top against the wall, beneath a picture of Anthony Anakis with his arm around early TV comedian Milton Berle, who'd autographed the photograph with a black pen, writing,

"What's this fly doing in my soup! Love, Uncle Miltie," and if you looked at the picture long enough, you could hear the rim shot that followed.

Massey ordered the filet mignon. DeLuca ordered an appetizer and a glass of Dönnhoff '89 Riesling. Massey asked him if he was an oenophile.

"I like a good Fenway Frank every now and then," he said.

"Not a wiener-lover," she said. "A wine connoisseur."

"I know what 'oenophile' means," he said. "And hardly. I know what I like. I got into Rhine wines when I was serving in Germany. A long time ago."

"It takes a real man to order white wine," she said. "So are you the sort of person who orders the same thing every time you go to a particular restaurant?"

"How'd you know?" DeLuca said. "It used to drive my wife crazy, because every time we'd go to, like, Locke-Ober or something, I'd read the whole menu, because I'd really want to try something new, but in the end, I always had the veal. And I'm always satisfied."

"Why do you say, 'used to'?" she asked.

"You're right," he said. "I'm sure it would drive her crazy if we ever went there again."

"And you'd still get the veal? Knowing it would drive your wife crazy?"

He shrugged. "Let's not overthink it. It's just a plate of veal."

"I have to tell you," she said, "I think I underestimated you. I have to admit that when we first met, they'd sent me a file on you but I only skimmed it. I read about the things you accomplished in Iraq. I don't think I quite fully appreciated what you do. It's a lot like police work."

"With some notable exceptions," he said.

"Chiefly?"

"Well," he said. "Here, people do things because the law tells them to. There, there aren't any laws to tell people what to do. I try to use common sense, but in a war zone, common sense isn't always the first tool in the kit."

"How's your neck?"

"It's fine," he said. "Couldn't be better."

"MacKenzie told me you have a bounty on your head," Massey said. "Fifty thousand dollars."

"A lot of people over there had them."

"That may be," she said, "but yours has gone up since you left."

"I'm not sure they know I left," he said.

"Somebody apparently does," she said. "Do you think that's why you've been targeted?"

"I think they got my name somewhere and found out I was looking into the murder," DeLuca said. "I don't know where they got it, but once they had it, all they had to do was search their database to perceive me as a threat and then do something about it."

"Any idea where the leak might have come from?" she asked. "I hope not my office."

"BPD, would be my guess," DeLuca said. "It might not be a leak. At least not from a person. They obviously have the technological savvy to hack into secure systems. I'd be willing to guess the FBI firewall is a whole lot stronger than BPD's. For me, what's more interesting is that there's an ongoing component to the site. They didn't just stick it on some ISP and then run away like kids on Halloween lighting a bag of dog shit on somebody's front steps and ringing the doorbell. They're right there, on top of it, updating and managing it. Information warfare is a lot quieter than the other kind, but to me it means they're fully engaged and firing back at us. MacKenzie was the one who pointed that out to me."

"I think she has a crush on you, by the way," Massey said.

"Mack?" DeLuca said. "I don't think so."

"She's very respectful of you," Massey said.

"That's not the same thing," he said. "I gather you've seen the headlines?"

The story of the murders of Wagner, Masland, McNulty, and O'Hara had been on all the front pages, as well as the nightly news, with graphic captions that read "Homeland Attack" and "Murder in Our Backyard." Public reaction, as best DeLuca could gauge, was an overall feeling of, "That's too bad, but what's it to me? I'm not a retired general." The newspapers and news programs were not mentioning any larger threats, beyond referring to the I4NI Web site and the map where visitors could vote on what cities they wanted to blow up, treating the threat as if it were a joke, with broadcasters making quips like, "So, Yankee haters—here's your chance." Terror fatigue, someone had described it—too many orange alerts that turned out to be false alarms.

"Saw them, yes," Massey said. "Have I had a chance to sit down and read the papers? No."

"The *Globe* said there's evidence linking Wagner and Masland to Al Qaeda," he said. "Do you know what evidence?"

"DNA," Massey said. "The golf cart and the Cessna were both packed with enough explosives to obliterate the bodies of the terrorists, but we've been able to extract tissue smears and run DNA tests. The two men in the golf cart were brothers. Their genetic father is a man named Abdullah bin Rajan. He's been held at Guantanamo for the last two years. There's not much he can tell us about recent contacts. The Cessna pilot was a man named Hamid Jubal whose brother Omar gave us a DNA sample at Camp Barracuda in Iraq. He's still being held there, and he's being interrogated, but he isn't giving us anything. He says he's never heard of I4NI. Omar Jubal and bin Rajan are both Al Qaeda. Omar's Egyptian with ties to al-Zawahiri. Of course, the fact that the suspected terrorists were related by blood doesn't mean anything in and of itself."

"And I4NI?" he asked. "Where'd Jubal and bin Rajan's boys get their information?"

"Still looking."

"I can't help thinking," DeLuca said, "that this thing isn't Arab. They're using Arabs to do their dirty work, because it's so easy, but I can't shake the feeling somebody else is puppet-mastering the whole thing."

"I have something for you," she said, taking a file from her bag.

"Is this that cave you were talking about?" he asked. "The one where we use separate entrances and meet in the middle?"

"Could be," she said. "I put half my team on the names you sent me. Jelan's Wolves. Did you read the history of the things they did in Croatia and Kosovo?"

"Not the details," he said. "Enough to know they're shitty humans."

"Shitty as humans get," she said. "In Dvoradjic's case, it goes beyond mere brutality. Did you ever read about the Odessa program during World War II, towards the end?"

"Sure," DeLuca said. "Odessa was a pipeline to supply Nazi war criminals with false papers and get them to Argentina. And elsewhere."

"Dvoradjic put together the same sort of project in Serbia for Serbian war criminals," Massey said, "except with a whole lot more technology than the Germans ever had. Jelan's businesses, before the war, included software and desktop publishing companies. His contribution to 'ethnic cleansing' was wiping out Muslim/Albanian property records and forging new deeds and titles to grant ownership to ethnic Serbs. It helps when you have the government behind you. That's how he got rich, stealing Muslim properties."

"He had access to everything."

"Exactly. Imagine what they could do if your own government was trying to steal or erase your identity. And then, when they finally realized NATO was coming, he had the know-how to create false documents and false histories for whoever needed them. Including himself and his men. Straightening it out and finding the people responsible for the atrocities over there has been a complete nightmare. Most of them have slipped away and 're-digitized,' as my superior likes to say."

"Dvoradjic sounds like the kind of guy who'd be capable of compiling the I4NI site," DeLuca said.

"He does," Massey said. "I have people at Interpol who're scrambling to find relatives or acquaintances. We're also hoping the Senior Services leads will take us somewhere, but the Simeone brothers won't talk to us. They came in with a lawyer—"

"Mark Ciccone?"

"Yup," she said. "You know him?"

"Had dealings," DeLuca said. "He does a lot of the family work."

"He was going to broker the immunity deal," she said, "but now he's saying he can't contact his clients, and we can't find them either."

"If it helps," DeLuca said, "I talked to someone who might get through to them. We busted them ten years ago for using illegals and ex-cons as CNAs—"

"As what?"

"Certified nursing assistants," DeLuca said, "so they're not going to help us unless it's to their advantage." He explained to her how he'd managed to meet with Vincent Pastorelli, and how Pastorelli had gotten involved with Katie Quinn and Freddy, and with his cousin Jackie. She listened, slightly amused and slightly appalled, occasionally stopping him to ask intelligent questions or make astute observations. She was impressive, and she seemed to have the mysterious ability to get better-looking with each passing moment.

"Simic was trying to help her?" Massey asked, when DeLuca had finished. "You think he was going to kill her and had second thoughts?"

"I'm not sure," DeLuca said. "I think that was why he was getting friendly with her in the first place, but I think something shifted."

"He felt sorry for her?"

"He felt something," DeLuca said. "We'll probably never know what. The ME found evidence of a brain injury, years prior to his demise—he was fairly messed up, cognitively. Katie told a friend of hers that she was considering tricking somebody into thinking he was the father—"

"Freddy."

"Freddy," DeLuca said. "Her friend told her that would be wrong. Most people hate to lie. I think Katie tried to do the right thing. I think she told Marko she was carrying his baby. No idea how he might have reacted to that."

"He was helping her," Massey said. "Protecting his offspring."

"Maybe," DeLuca said. "He was strangled from behind. He doesn't sound like the sort of person who'd let someone he didn't know sneak up behind him. Brain damage or no brain damage."

"He was killed by someone he knew."

"I think so," DeLuca said. "Someone he arrived with. Or someone who met him there."

"They shot her," Massey said. "Why didn't they shoot him?"

"To avoid warning her? Who knows?" DeLuca said. "I've been trying to sequence the whole thing. The way they rigged the mirror means it wasn't spur of the moment. Suppose Simic and the others in the crew were all in on planning it. But only Simic knows Katie is pregnant with his kid. The others don't. Jelsn wants to kill her. Eye for an eye, Joe Quinn's daughter for his own. Maybe Simic goes to the garage, thinking it's a snatch. The killers, I'm thinking at least two, have orders Marko doesn't know about. Maybe Dvoradjic doesn't trust Marko anymore and wants him taken out before he screws the whole thing up. Marke gets an inkling of what's really going on and tries to stop it."

"They kill Marko and put him in the trunk," Massey says. "When Katie shows up, the killer—"

"Who Katie recognizes," DeLuca interrupted. "She's met him before. One of Marko's Serbian buddies. She's not alarmed."

"Says, 'Marko asked me to bring you your cell phone,' gives it to her, walks her to her car, and shoots her," Massey said.

"Did you know both Jelan and Ivan Dvoradjic were in Boston?" she said. "They came over in 1990 to look at colleges. Ivan spent two years at MIT studying computer engineering. We've talked to two people he went to school with, but they haven't heard from him since then. They described him as quiet. And religious. Orthodox."

"He dropped out?"

"He went home to serve his country," Massey said. "I'm not sure if they were calling it 'ethnic cleansing' yet."

DeLuca thought for a moment.

"Did he stay here, the summer between terms?"

"He did."

"Where'd he work?"

"He worked on the Big Dig," Massey said. "The Ted Williams Tunnel, I believe. Early stages."

"Have you got somebody on that?" DeLuca asked.

"It came up, obviously. I'm not sure how far along my people are," she said. "Why?"

"Suppose he comes here after the war, either with his father and the others or separate, and he needs work," DeLuca said. "Maybe he goes back to his old boss. Especially if he's working off the books and needs someone who trusts him."

"Maybe," Massey said. "We think they changed their names. Wouldn't his old boss wonder why he changed his name?"

"Emigrants change their names all the time, to sound more American," DeLuca said. "My grandfather's name was Delluchiesa but he threw his suitcase in the bay before the ship landed because he didn't want to look like a foreigner. Would you mind if I put my people on it?" She shook her head. "Maybe he changed the name but kept the initials 'I.D.'"

"Or 'J.D.,'" Massey said. "'Ivan,' in English, is 'John.' You feel pretty certain that these guys are involved?" Massey asked.

"I don't have any other leads," DeLuca said. "I'm sure you do."

"Nothing that converges like this does," Dawn Massey said.

"We don't even know when these guys entered the country," DeLuca said. "I don't know about you, but sometimes I worry we're too centered on the twin towers. For all we know, these guys were here before 9/11, setting this up. If we've searched a building a hundred times since 2001, that doesn't mean they weren't there in 1999, hiding things before we ever thought to look."

"I agree," Massey said.

"Any sense as to what their next move might be?" he asked. "Or when?"

"We've got people who've been working the anti-American chat rooms who say they've been told they're going to be given special passwords tomorrow to go to some other room. We won't know until then."

"It's already tomorrow somewhere," DeLuca said. "Did I just sound like Scarlett O'Hara in *Gone with the Wind*?"

"And as God is my witness, I'll never be hungry again," Dawn Massey said, pushing her plate away. "I think I'm about at my sixteenth hour of work today. Can I ask you a question?"

"Sure," he said. "Can I order you another drink?"

"Absolutely," she said. "Then I have a question."

He got the waiter's attention and gestured for another round.

"What's the question?"

"How was Mickey O'Brien?" she asked. "How'd he seem?"

"He lost weight," DeLuca said. "He's doing all right, considering. I'm looking into getting him a change of accommodations."

"Good," Massey said. "You can. I can't go there."

"He speaks very highly of you, by the way. He said he worked with your husband," DeLuca said.

"Ex-husband," Massey corrected. "Mickey was the one who told me my husband was having affairs. He didn't volunteer the information, I understand that, but he told me the truth when I asked him. I thought Mickey was a stand-up guy."

"Your ex was in the bureau?"

"Still is," she said. "New York office. We worked together side by side for six years."

"Are you in touch?"

"Were we ever?" she said, noting the expression on DeLuca's face. "Why the smile?"

"It's just interesting," he said. "You and your ex worked together and you lost each other. Fair characterization?"

She rolled her eyes.

"I can't tell my wife anything about what I do," he told her. "Not while I'm doing it, and not after I've done it. Our telephone conversations are full of these big pauses where we don't know what to say. She's down at Fort Bragg right now, talking to her lawyers about the divorce, and I can't do a thing about it. I never could."

"Really?"

"I suppose that's not really true," he said. "I could always quit and get a job in an office, doing security for somebody."

"But that never really seemed like an option?"

"No. Sometimes I've thought, if she knew what I do, there wouldn't be this gulf between us. We've been like roommates since—I can't even remember when we weren't. Even when I was a cop . . . When I got back from Iraq, we tried to put it back together, but it wasn't working. Since then . . ."

"You live in the same house but you can't even look each other in the eye?"

"Yeah," DeLuca said. "Something like that. The odd thing was, when she told me she'd called her lawyer, instead of feeling shocked, all I thought was how overdue it was. Right now I couldn't say if the marriage ended two years ago or two months ago. All I know is that it's been over for a long time. There must be better things to talk about than this."

"There must be," she said. "Where are you staying?"

"I have the keys to a friend's apartment," DeLuca said.

"My apartment's not far from here," she said, looking him in the eye, and then he understood, more by her look than by her words, that she was thinking the same thing he was. His attraction to her had been growing from the moment he sat down next to her at the bar. He'd sensed the same thing happening in her, but now he was sure. He felt his pulse quicken. "Why don't you stay with me tonight?" she said. "If you want to."

"I do," he said, looking her in the eye. "But I want you to know something—I don't want to sleep with you."

"No?"

"No," he said, shaking his head. "I want to keep you up all night."

She was a vigorous and a clever lover, a marvelous kisser, and when he took the clothes from her, he saw the body of a girl half her age, fit and athletic but soft too, warm and giving. They made love first on her couch and again in the shower before collapsing into sleep on the bed. As he drifted off, he thought of all the reasons why people made love, and he supposed he ought to have felt guilty, but he didn't.

He'd begun to kiss her again in the early-morning light when his phone rang. He threw the pillow on top of it rather than answer it, but then her phone rang as well. She sat up to take the call while he answered his.

They both received the same news at the same time, from different sources. DeLuca found Phil LeDoux on the other end of the line. He explained that a terrorist cell had been arrested in Amsterdam, and in their possession was a nuclear device, small enough to fit into a backpack. All of them Arabs. Also in their possession was a list of cities.

"Amsterdam, London, Paris, Bucharest, and Ankara. And Boston. There's your multiheaded attack."

"Those weren't the cities getting the most votes on the Web site," DeLuca said. "Those are NATO capitals. U.S. allies in Kosovo. If this was Al Qaeda–sponsored, there'd be other names on the list. Tel Aviv, for one. Or Jerusalem. No Arab group is going to leave Israel off the list. I4NI is Serb."

"Noted," LeDoux said.

"When was it supposed to happen?" DeLuca said.

"Tonight," LeDoux said. "They're meeting right now at the White House to discuss declaring a red alert."

"This is hard intel?" DeLuca asked.

"It's pretty firm," LeDoux said. "The Amsterdam cell has no idea who any of the other cells are. It looks like I4NI is coordinating everything. We're still questioning them, but they don't know any more about who I4NI is than we do. We only got the guy because his girlfriend turned him in. She was angry because he broke up with her because she said they weren't allowed to have girlfriends."

"He had the bomb on him?"

"Negative," LeDoux said. "The thing was in place for almost two years, hidden in a building during construction, inside a wall, on a timer set for midnight tonight. We're tearing the thing apart, but by the looks of it, the timer and the detonating device were manufactured somewhere else and added on once the bomb was built locally. The Amsterdam cell didn't know until yesterday when the thing was set to go off."

"So we have seven devices, timed for midnight?" DeLuca asked. "Zulu? Local time?"

"We don't know," LeDoux said. "The bombs in the London subways and Madrid trains were rigged for simultaneous detonation. We might be looking at the same thing on a global scale, or maybe they staggered it for maximum effect. There are also signs of an information attack coming. I'll keep you updated, but you're going to need to step up the mission. I'm sure you're already pedaling as fast as you can, but do your best. Can I ask you a personal favor?"

"Anything," DeLuca said.

"Can you find my daughter and tell her Vermont is lovely this time of year? I mean really, really lovely. I tried her phones but she's not answering."

"I'm on it," DeLuca said.

"Thanks."

By the time he hung up the phone, Dawn Massey was already dressed. She took two mugs out of the microwave and handed him a cup of instant coffee.

"You heard?" she asked, tucking her blouse into her skirt.

"I heard," he said. "Mind if I ride with you while I call my people? I seem to be between office spaces right now."

"Sure, but you drive," she told him. "If I don't do my makeup in the car, I really will look like J. Edgar Hoover in a dress."

Chapter Nine

VASQUEZ WAS AWAKE AND CHECKING HIS
e-mail when his phone rang. He answered it quickly before it
woke Elizabeth, who was still asleep in the back of the van,
curled up on top of the sleeping bag he'd opened to accommodate the two of them. After leaving the JFK Building,
he'd spent the afternoon giving her as complete a debriefing
as he could, within the limits of what was classified and what
wasn't. He showed her the I4NI Web site, and led her to the
page that described her daily activities, which stopped short,
they noted, of where she worked. She'd decided it wasn't safe
to stay in her house, nor would she feel right staying with
friends and putting them in jeopardy. She'd accepted Hoolie's offer to stay in the van. He'd taken Storrow Drive up the
Charles to Route 2 and found a campsite in the Leominster
State Forest in Westminster, where they spent the night. He'd
stopped at a convenience store and bought graham crackers,
marshmallows, and Hershey bars to make s'mores, but Elizabeth was in no mood to eat, or for that matter talk.

"Agent Vasquez," DeLuca said on the other end of the
line. "Rise and shine. We've got problems. Where are you?"

"Somewhere near Leominster," Vasquez said. "At a
campground."

"Why?" DeLuca said. "Where's Elizabeth?"

"It's in the e-mail I sent you," Vasquez said. "Her house wasn't safe, so she stayed in the van. She's with me."

"Why wasn't her house safe?" DeLuca asked.

"Hang on a second," Hoolie said, stepping outside the van so that he could speak freely without waking Elizabeth. The morning air was cool and fresh. He would have killed for a cup of coffee.

He told DeLuca what he'd found out, where Elizabeth worked and how James Chiang Chen was involved.

"It would have been in my final report," Vasquez said, "but she really doesn't want her father to find out. I'm not sure what we're going to do about the money, but I checked Chen out. He's harmless, except for the part about transferring funds. He has access to a couple of grants, but so far, nobody seems to know he's been drawing off 'em. I've got nothing to connect him to I4NI. I think he's just a basic lovesick doofus. Little bit psycho, maybe, but everybody at MIT is a little psycho."

"Wake her up," DeLuca said. "I need to talk to her. They've busted a cell in Amsterdam with a pocket nuke and a list of cities that are next, including Boston. We're all hoping they're not going in alphabetical order."

Vasquez slid the side panel open, woke Elizabeth up, and handed her the phone. She was still groggy.

"Hullo?" she said.

"Good morning, Elizabeth," DeLuca said. "This is David. How are you?"

"Uncle David?" she said, sitting up suddenly and running her hand through her hair as if she needed to look more presentable to talk to him. "What's up?"

"We need your help," DeLuca said. "I'm working on a project for your father. We're trying to figure out who killed Katie Quinn."

"The all-night sports talk show woman?" Elizabeth said.

"That's her," DeLuca said. "Did agent Vasquez brief you regarding I4NI?"

"Uh huh," Elizabeth said.

"We think the men who killed her did it to keep her quiet," DeLuca said. "They also had a rule that no one was allowed to have girlfriends. We caught some people this morning in Amsterdam because one of the terrorists' girlfriends turned him in."

"Okay," Bizza said. "What's this got to do with me?"

"Agent Vasquez tells me you've been dancing at the Gold Club . . ."

She cupped her hand over the phone, turning to Vasquez.

"You told him?" she said in an urgent whisper. "You told my Uncle David?"

"He's my team leader," Vasquez said. "I have to tell him."

"Elizabeth?" DeLuca said. "Listen, I don't care, all right? I just want you to be safe. I'm not going to tell your dad. I do think you should tell him but that's up to you. Agent Vasquez has told me about Mr. Chen. He says he's harmless. Can you vouch for that?"

"He's a big puppy," she said.

"Glad to hear it," DeLuca said. "I want to ask you about the Gold Club. The men we're looking for were not the type to go entirely without girlfriends or sex for the time that they were here under whatever names they were using. I'm thinking they probably visited your club, since it's the last one left in downtown Boston. If I showed you some pictures of their faces, would you mind having a look at them?"

"I wouldn't mind," she said.

"Would you put Agent Vasquez back on?" he asked.

He asked Hoolie to download the file of jpegs and show Elizabeth the faces of the members of Jelan's Wolves. She looked at them slowly and deliberately, flagging four. One was Marko Simic. The others were the brothers, Milos and Arkady Stipanich, and last, Ivan Dvoradjic.

"You're certain?" DeLuca asked her.

"I'm positive," she said. "Especially the guy with the monobrow. He used to scare the shit out of me."

"Do you know what names they were using?"

"I don't," Elizabeth said, pausing. "But I'll bet my friend Holly does. She dances at the club."

"They were her regulars?"

"They were more than regulars," Elizabeth said. "Holly does happy endings. And private parties."

"And that's how she knows these guys?"

"I'm pretty sure," Elizabeth said.

"How do we find Holly?"

"Her real name is Sarah," Elizabeth told him. "Sarah Rubin, I think. She works during the day at the Dunkin' Donuts on Tremont and Boylston. I think she's taking a class at Emerson in creative writing. I don't want her to get in trouble."

"She's not in trouble, Elizabeth," DeLuca said. "Can I talk to Agent Vasquez again, please?"

Vasquez listened a moment longer, then started the van and backed out of the camping space.

"Where are we going?" Elizabeth asked him.

"A place called the Wind River Inn, outside of Bellows Falls, Vermont," Vasquez said. "Boss says it's run by an ex-Navy SEAL. You'll be safe there. Safer than me, anyway."

"Why safer than you?"

"Because I'm going to be the only Latino in Vermont," Hoolie said.

"I'm hungry," she said. "What do we have for breakfast?"

"I've got MREs," Hoolie said, handing her his bag. She picked through the selections.

"What do you recommend?"

"I don't," he said. "But if you're really hungry, you can eat the box it comes in."

By the time DeLuca and Massey got to FBI headquarters at Center Plaza, the regional director, James Lilly, had already begun his briefing in a large conference room. DeLuca recognized Commissioner Halliday and Frank Wexler with Billy Morrissey and Kaz Takata in tow. He was introduced to the heads of FEMA, Massport, the MBTA, FUSION, the Boston office for Homeland Security, the State Police, a colonel from National Guard headquarters named Egan, the mayor's deputy assistant, and a team from the governor's office, though not the governor himself, who was bunkered up at the underground FEMA ops center in Framingham. There were a number of people DeLuca didn't know as well.

So far, Lilly seemed to be going over much of the same information DeLuca had already learned on the phone. He saw MacKenzie and Sykes in the corner of the room, by the coffee urn, and made his way to them.

"You're up early," he whispered.

"Up late is more like it," Sykes said. "We never left after we got your message about Ivan Dvoradjic last night. You pull an all-nighter too?"

DeLuca had messaged them on his CIM while Dawn was in the bathroom the night before.

"I got some sleep," he said.

"This isn't a drill," Director Lilly continued. "This is what all those drills prepared us for. When the White House issues the red alert, and it's not guaranteed that they will, but if they do, we need to be ready to go. Area hospitals have been notified. We've initiated an evacuation of nonessential government personnel to Framingham and Hanscom and elsewhere according to level two procedures. Commissioner Halliday tells me he's called in all shifts and has over two thousand men on the ground, and Colonel Egan has put almost two thousand National Guard troops on alert to assist, though obviously the police know the city better than the Guard does. Ms. Peters from the governor's office is here to handle any chain-of-command conflicts and report to the governor. Mr. McCulski—is the Transit Authority going to shut down the Central Artery?"

"We are," McCulski said. "Once the red is issued. That puts an additional 200,000 cars on the streets of Boston, so there will be traffic problems, even for emergency vehicles. Hopefully with the Guard to handle traffic control, it won't be too bad."

"Questions, at this point?"

DeLuca raised his hand. Lilly nodded toward him.

"Special Agent David DeLuca, army counterintelligence," he began.

"With General LeDoux's office?" Lilly asked.

"That's right," DeLuca said.

"He's flying in, by the way."

"Good."

"What's your question?"

"Do we want the terrorists to know we're on them?" DeLuca said. "It's been my experience that they scatter when they know you're coming. Their preference is to watch their bombs go off and stay close until the last minute, but with the obvious exception of suicide bombers, they'll want to fight another day if they can. They know it's asymmetrical as well as we do."

Director Lilly looked at him. "And your experience is in Iraq, is that right?" he asked.

"Yes sir," DeLuca said. "Most recently. And elsewhere, worldwide. I was also a cop in Boston for over ten years."

"This isn't Iraq," Lilly said. "The pattern from Amsterdam says these things have been embedded for a long time. For all we know, the people who put them in place are halfway around the world, watching their televisions."

"With due respect," DeLuca said, "we have a single incident. You need at least three to suggest a pattern. Using a suitcase nuke in Amsterdam doesn't mean they're going to use one here."

"Well, let's not rule that out, shall we?" Lilly said with enough sarcasm in his voice to suggest he wasn't going to listen to anything else DeLuca had to say. DeLuca caught the eye of Dawn Massey, who was standing next to the director. Her eyes were saying, "Sorry about that." DeLuca crossed his own briefly in reply.

He felt MacKenzie tapping on his arm.

"Can we have a word with you?" she whispered in his ear. "We might have found Ivan."

"Sure," he said. "Mind if I bring a friend in on this?"

He wasn't quite sure what the look Mack sent him meant—she seemed to be questioning his use of the word "friend"—but he tugged on Dawn Massey's sleeve and nodded toward the door.

They left the briefing together and followed MacKenzie and Sykes down the hall to a conference room, where a thin, nervous-looking young man in black pants, blue shirt, and black tie, loosened at the neck, was staring at a computer monitor, one of the old-fashioned cathode-ray-tube monitors and not the flat screens that everybody else seemed to have.

"This is FBI agent Neal Hartshorn," Sykes said. Hartshorn stood, appearing uncertain whether or not he was supposed to shake hands or salute. DeLuca shook his hand. "Neal was assigned to us. I think we've been keeping him pretty busy."

"Pleased to meet you," Hartshorn said. "Dan and Colleen speak very highly of you." He looked somewhat nervously at Massey. "I didn't know you were going to be here."

"It's all right, Neal," she said. "We're all on the same page today."

"What have we got?" DeLuca said.

"Ivan Dvoradjic," Mack said. "Neal really helped us pull this together, by the way." She put the Interpol photograph of Ivan on the screen, then clicked on a different image of a man who'd died his hair and shaved his beard but was otherwise the same. The second image came from an Actel-Simmons employee identification card, for a man named John Divine Sr.

"Middle name 'The'?" DeLuca asked.

"No, but he is a junior. He's got all the documents and credentials anybody could possibly need," Sykes said. "Including two years in computer engineering at MIT, the same years as Ivan Dvoradjic. What a coincidence. When we looked for Ivan's academic records, there weren't any."

"They switched the names," Massey said.

"Evidently," Mack said. "Ivan Dvoradjic was born in 1968. A child named John Andrew Divine Jr. was born at Brigham and Women's on April 9, 1968, and died a month later from SIDS. There was a request made for a copy of his birth certificate in August of 1999. That's on file. We were looking for names with the initials 'I.D.' or 'J.D.' Divine has the 'V' in it as well. According to Actel-Simmons's records, John Divine Jr. ran a ceiling panel machine and later worked as a ceiling panel inspector. Ivan Dvoradjic had been more of a basic laborer, years before when he worked on the Ted Williams Tunnel. The man who hired him back then retired in 1993, but he remembers getting a call asking for a recommendation in early 2000."

"Modest credit history," Sykes added. "Two cards, barely used them, paid them off in full at the end of every month."

"Nothing to raise suspicions," DeLuca said. "What about John Divine Sr.? Is there one?"

"Believe it or not, there is," Mack said. "The real John Divine Sr. died of cancer in 2001, in January. He applied for a Visa card last May and a MasterCard in June. Same story, modest purchases, paid in full."

"They remained father and son, even in their aliases," DeLuca said. "That strikes me as a bit reckless."

"Or cocky. What else do we know about John Divine Sr.?" Massey asked.

"Neal?" Mack said.

Hartshorn turned his monitor so that DeLuca could see it.

"Here's Jelan Dvoradjic," he said, showing the Interpol photograph, "and here's John Divine Sr." Again, DeLuca saw two pictures of the same man. In the second instance, he'd shaved his head, wore glasses, and appeared to have sustained a broken nose.

"Poor man's plastic surgery," Sykes said.

"He wasn't poor," DeLuca said.

"Maybe he didn't want any doctor's records," Massey said. "Where'd he work?"

"This is the problem," Hartshorn said. "John Divine Sr. was a 1099 subcontractor with Bay State Data Services."

"Which was? Is?"

"A subcontractor for the NGIC in Charlottesville," Mack said. "Joint-tasked to FUSION. The state task force."

Dawn Massey looked puzzled.

"National Ground Intelligence Center," DeLuca said. NGIC was tasked to keep track of and assess all enemy troop strengths and assets. Scottie's reports at IMINT and most SIGINT analyses eventually went through NGIC. "Part of DOD."

"Why joint-tasked?"

"Massachusetts was one of the worst states," Hartshorn said, "as far as security-related databanks were concerned, prior to the election of the current governor, who made it his priority when he was elected to get the state up to speed."

"Because he's running for president," DeLuca said. "He needs to look tough on terrorists."

"I don't know about the politics," Hartshorn said. "I'd just as soon leave that to others. Are you aware of the FIRES program?"

"I am," DeLuca said.

"I'm not," Massey said.

"Facilities, Infrastructure and Engineering Systems," Hartshorn said. "The original idea was for NGIC to compile a global database of blueprints and building specs for potential targets in combat theaters. It was a huge job that they started after Gulf One. After 9/11, DOD and Homeland Security decided we needed to have a database of U.S. structures, meaning airports and subways and transportation systems, but also office buildings, like the World Trade Center, government buildings, corporate headquarters, bridges, and really anything that might present a target. DOD gave the work to the states. The states contracted out the manual labor, the data entry. The contractors hired 1099 subcontractors to do the actual work. There were security clearances required, but nothing terribly rigorous."

"And James Divine Sr. cleared to work as a subcontractor?" DeLuca said.

"He did," Hartshorn said. "He worked in a building just down the street, nine to five, every day. He had all the software and CAD experience called for by the job requirements, and he seemed like a model employee."

"Until he quit three days ago?"

"Right."

"Paychecks?" Massey asked. "Bank records? Phone bills? Addresses?"

"They both picked their checks up in person," Sykes said. "Mail went to P.O. boxes. The addresses they gave were to an empty parking lot near Fenway."

"So in other words," DeLuca said, "Jelan Dvoradjic, under the name John Divine Sr., worked for the FUSION project inputting data about various buildings and blueprints and designs in Massachusetts and the Boston area. For how long?"

"A little more than four years," Hartshorn said.

"And if he wanted to, he could have modified any of the files he inputted?" DeLuca asked. Hartshorn nodded. "Do we know which files he worked on?"

"We might be able to find that out," Hartshorn said. "Unless he concealed it or signed someone else's name to the work he was doing. We'd have to go over each report he filed or all the reports filed, during the times he worked at Bay State Data Services for FUSION, and compare his work to the originals to find the modifications. Assuming he didn't modify the originals too."

"So what you're saying is, they could have put a bomb in a building, hidden in room number 34, for example, and then modified the blueprints so there is no room 34?" DeLuca asked. Hartshorn nodded grimly. "How long would it take to go over the reports filed by Bay State Data Services?"

"Two or three weeks," Hartshorn said. "If we had a staff of a hundred people or so."

"And we don't," DeLuca said.

"Tell Agent DeLuca what you told us, Neal," MacKenzie said. "Tell him your theory."

"Well," Hartshorn said, "it's just . . . my little bailiwick here at intel has been gas and chemicals. Liquid natural gas and propane, nitrogen, how they're stored and transported."

"They have MTHELs guarding the tank farms in Everett," Sykes said. "n-Wave generators too, like DOE uses to keep people away from nuclear facilities."

"We've been trying to convey the sense that the threat from gas has been taken care of," Hartshorn said, looking nervously at his boss, "but I don't think it has. When we learned that the Amsterdam bomb had been implanted in new construction, a sort of light went off."

"This is good, Neal," Dawn Massey said, to reassure him.

"What's the biggest construction project in the history of Massachusetts?" Sykes asked.

"Ted Kennedy's head," DeLuca replied. "The Big Dig. Central Artery. John Divine Jr. worked there. Put it together—you think they'd plant a bomb in the Big Dig?"

"Not plant a bomb in it," Sykes said. "Turn it into a bomb."

"The Central Artery tunnel is three and a half miles long," Hartshorn said, calling up a map of downtown Boston, with a blue line curving through it from north to south, "with a brief gap here"—he put his finger on the screen— "but other than that, it runs directly beneath the heart of the city. Three hundred feet from Quincy Market, eight hundred feet from Faneuil Hall, nine hundred thirty feet from City Hall and the JFK Building, twelve hundred feet from where we are now, and half a mile from the State House."

"You take out the Big Dig, you take out essentially every vital building in Boston," Mack said. "You get the Hancock, the Pru, Fenway . . ."

"What do you mean, take it out?" DeLuca said. "Show me how."

Hartshorn clicked on the map to show an overlay of green lines.

"The liquid natural gas is distributed from Everett on pipelines that run north and west to routing centers," he said. "We've been looking at securing the ships that bring it in for a long time, and the tanks that store it. We haven't been looking as closely at propane, for some reason. It's more volatile than LNG, but I guess we're just more used to it. Just one of those little tanks people have attached to their backyard barbecues is enough to destroy a house. Most of the propane gets piped across the Charles to railcars at the Charlestown yards. But not all of it. There's a surplus line converted from the old pipelines that used to deliver propane directly into people's homes that runs south to the rail yards in Dorchester with distribution pipes to Fish Pier and Commonwealth Pier and the Naval Reservation, and that runs right here."

He clicked on the map again, and a yellow line appeared, atop the Central Artery, between the northbound and southbound lanes.

"That's propane?" Massey asked.

"It is," Hartshorn said. "Running right down the center of the artery, inside the access tunnel."

"What's the worst-case scenario?" DeLuca asked.

"Worst-case?" Hartshorn said. "They rig a device of some kind, just a small charge, would do it to breach the pipeline. Propane boils at negative forty-four degrees, so it vaporizes instantly. If the breach is sizable enough, the artery tunnels fill with gas in about twenty seconds. Any sort of source of ignition could set it off."

"And what happens?"

"The best estimates are, you'd get an explosion equal to or in excess of a low-yield nuclear device," Hartshorn said. "I think 'in excess' is more like it."

"What about the ventilation?" Massey asked.

"A good-sized leak would overwhelm the ventilation," Hartshorn said. "Particularly if they close the tunnel. Without traffic, the sensors and motion detectors shut down the fans. They increase and decrease ventilation according to need. I'm not even sure we want the fans venting gas into downtown Boston. It could blow up there too, though it's more dangerous when it's confined. Something like this could shoot the Prudential Center into the sky like a bottle rocket."

"Can we shut down the pipeline?" DeLuca asked.

"There's already enough gas in the pipeline to do the job."

"Pump it back into the facilities at Unigas?"

"The valves only go in one direction to prevent backflow."

"Pump it out the other end then."

"Into what?"

"Trucks."

"Too small. It would take too long."

"An empty LNG ship."

"Wrong apparatus. Plus where do you get one? Plus if they could, then the ship becomes a sitting duck."

"So in other words," DeLuca said, "the bomb is already in place and there's nothing we can do about it."

"Not in the next twenty-four hours," Hartshorn said. "We'd have to find the device they left to breach the line. And there could be more than one. The line is three and a half miles long."

"Did you mention this to Director Lilly?" Massey asked. The younger FBI agent nodded.

"He apparently thinks the problem has been dealt with adequately," Hartshorn said. "I just had a quick word with his assistant, but they tell me he's focusing more on nuclear devices similar to the one they found in Amsterdam."

"Stay on it," Massey said. "Get the schematics for every inch of the pipeline and every inch of the service tunnel. Look for any anomalies. And compare what's in the FIRE files with what's in the Actel-Simmons files."

"Hold on," DeLuca said. Something had stuck in his memory. He could see it, some sort of diploma or document. Then he remembered. "General Quinn. He's on the board at Actel-Simmons. If you have any trouble getting access to their files, call him. Mack has the number. Dan, why don't you come with me?"

"Where are we going?"

"A little old-fashioned footwork. I used to be a cop in Boston," DeLuca said. "We're going to get a doughnut. It's a tradition."

It was faster to walk the nine blocks down Tremont Street than it would have been to drive or take a cab. They passed the Suffolk County district attorney's office, the U.S. Immigration office, the Justice Department Bank Fraud Task Force office, the Beantown Pub, and, where Tremont picked up the Freedom Trail, the Granary Burying Ground where Thomas Paine, John Hancock, Samuel Adams, and Paul Revere were all buried.

"That whirring sound you hear is them spinning in their graves over what's happening in this country," De-Luca told Sykes.

The Dunkin' Donuts on the corner of Tremont and Boylston hadn't changed and, as far as DeLuca could tell, hadn't even been cleaned since he'd left the force. He recognized the homeless woman who wrapped her legs in

Ace bandages sitting in the corner, having an animated conversation with invisible aliens. Business was slow, the usual clamor of passersby and Emerson College students down to a manageable buzz. He asked Sykes if he wanted anything. Sykes said he'd have a decaf. DeLuca ordered two coffees and a cruller for old times' sake, then asked the girl with the nametag that said "Holly" if her real name was Sarah Rubin.

"Holly" looked momentarily startled.

"My name is Holly," she said. "I don't know any Sarah Rubin."

"Elizabeth LeDoux said we could find you here," De-Luca said. He showed Holly his badge. She looked at it, but not closely.

"If you're the police, I really can't talk to you," she said, glancing nervously over her shoulder. "Look, my probation officer told me if I kept this job—"

"We're not the police," DeLuca said. "And you're not in trouble. We're just looking for some people you might know. From the Gold Club. It should only take a few minutes."

She glanced nervously at her boss again, then at a clock on the wall.

"I get my break in five minutes," she said. "I could talk to you then."

They waited in a booth. When she was done, Holly took her apron off and gestured for them to follow her outside, and they crossed the street to the opposite corner, where there was a Starbucks. She ordered a latte and joined them at a table.

"I'm sorry," she said, "but I don't want my boss to know where my other job is. It's bad enough to have him hitting on me here, but there, I'd have to let him."

It seemed like something of a contradiction, but De-Luca let it go.

"Do you know these men?" DeLuca said, showing her the pictures on his handheld. "We're looking for them."

"Oh God," she said, clicking from one to the next. "Oh my God. Yes, I know them. Why? What did they do? Did they kill somebody?"

"Why do you say that?" Sykes asked her.

She didn't answer, fearful.

"We know these are rough people," DeLuca said. "That's why we want to find them."

"They said . . ." she began.

"That they'd hurt you?" DeLuca said. "If you told anybody what they'd done to you?"

"They said they'd hurt my kid," Holly said.

"Are you okay?" DeLuca asked.

"I'm okay," she said. "It's part of the business. I told Benny at the door not to let them in again. I haven't seen them around lately."

"Do you know their names?"

She looked at the pictures again. "This one is Arthur," she said, pointing to Arkady Stipanich. "And this one is Mike. And Marko. He's . . . scary. And this is John."

"John Divine?"

"That's right," she said. "I thought it was sort of a weird name. Given his tastes."

"Do you know where they live?" DeLuca asked.

"I know where he lives," she said, pointing at Ivan Dvoradjic. "He has an apartment on Atlantic and State. I thought it was a pretty high-priced neighborhood for such a lowlife. That's where . . ."

"Where you went for a private . . . show?"

"Uh-huh," she said. "Number 17D. I don't know the address of the building, but it's on the corner."

They took the T from Park Street to Aquarium station. DeLuca called Dawn Massey on the way. DeLuca found a team of FBI agents waiting for them in the lobby and was forced to defer to them when the decision was made as to who got to break down the door.

The apartment was, as he suspected it would be, empty. The furniture was from Filene's. There were scraps of paper on the floor, but nothing of any significance, and enough stray hairs left behind on the bathroom linoleum to get a DNA sample without too much trouble. A forensics team was called in to collect fingerprints. The rent, at a hefty $5,400 a month, had been paid automatically each month via bank transfer, the superintendent said. To his knowledge, the place was still occupied—nobody had turned in any keys or asked for the security deposit back. The neighbors said John Divine never said anything in the hall or elevator and generally kept to himself and was quiet, though one night, one neighbor said, they heard a girl who sounded like she was having a very good time. No one could recall seeing John Divine in the last three days.

DeLuca noticed, near the glass doors that opened onto the balcony, sets of depressions in the carpeting, small circles in a triangular array. He showed them to Sykes and asked him what he thought.

"It's a tripod of some kind," he said. "For something heavy. Not a camera. Maybe a sniper rifle?"

"Or a telescope," DeLuca said. "Moved in and out from the balcony."

They opened the glass doors and stepped out onto the balcony.

"Great view of the harbor," Sykes said. DeLuca saw the skyline and the Tobin Bridge in the distance. "Pretty much anything moving in or out."

"Great view of the Big Dig too," DeLuca said, leaning out over the railing and looking down at the construction below. The elevated highway that the Big Dig replaced had been chopped up and hauled away. Where it had stood was now the Rose Kennedy Greenway, where landscaping and light construction was still in early progress. "I think we're looking right at it."

At that moment, Dan Sykes's phone rang. He took the call and spoke for a few minutes before holding his hand over the phone.

"You're not going to believe this," he said. "The police department got an anonymous tip. They found a nuke at the airport."

"At the airport?" DeLuca said. "Where?"

"An abandoned bag in one of the bars at terminal E. International flights. They're questioning an Arab kid they think may have left it."

"Terminal E?" DeLuca said. "And this is Wexler, calling to tell us out of the goodness of his heart?"

"No," Sykes said. "This is Gordon Lipski. Asking for a comment. I gave him my number."

"Who?"

"Gordon Lipski," Sykes said. "The editor of the *Boston Voice*. He wants a comment."

"This is a monumental crock of shit," DeLuca said.

"Is that our comment?" Sykes asked. DeLuca shook his head.

"Tell him 'no comment,'" DeLuca said. "Tell him you'll call him later—ask him how he found out."

"No comment, at this time," Sykes said into the phone, "but I'd like to help you later. But you have to tell me how you found out if you want me to help you later. Uh-huh. Uh-huh. Okay, thanks."

He pressed the button to hang up and turned to DeLuca. "BPD," he said. "They called him."

"They call the alternative weekly, but they don't tell us?" DeLuca said. "We only find out when the editor calls us for comments?"

"That ain't right," Sykes said.

"You realize this is a crock, right? How big a bomb?"

"He said half an ounce of material," Sykes said. "More like a dirty bomb, I guess."

"In the fucking airport?" DeLuca said. "In the bar? The only reason anybody would leave a bag in an airport was if they wanted somebody to find it. This is a decoy. They have somebody under interrogation?"

"I guess," Sykes said. "You wanna go talk to him?"

"What would be the point?" DeLuca said. "It's as red as herrings get."

"Wexler's not going to think so," Sykes said.

"Of course he's not," DeLuca said. "Wexler is going to spend the next seventy-two hours going from TV studio to TV studio, giving interviews about how he stopped the attack."

DeLuca was about to dial Halliday when his phone chirped in his hand. When he answered, his cousin Jackie was on the other end.

"Davy-boy," Jackie said. "Where are you? Jesus, traffic is really fucked up. I heard they closed the tunnel. Why'd they do that?"

"Leaks," DeLuca said.

"Jesus," Jackie said. "What else is new? Listen, I was going to tell you in person but I can't get to you. Freddy wants to talk to you. He says it's important."

"I got a lot on my plate today, Jackie," DeLuca said. "Tell Freddy I'll talk to him tomorrow."

"He says he knows where Marko is," Jackie said. "I'm just trying to help, David. I'm sorry about before, man—I should have been completely honest with you."

"We know where Marko is," DeLuca said. "He's in a freezer in Mitch Pasternak's morgue. We found him in the trunk of a Saab."

"Typical Saab story, huh?" Jackie said. "Freddy said he knows where Marko lived."

"He does?" DeLuca said. "Where's Freddy now?"

"He said he's on the Esplanade, off Storrow," Jackie said. "Near the Mass Ave bridge. He's pretty nervous. Apparently Vinnie Potatoes has been asking a lot of questions around town."

"Is Freddy on his cell?" DeLuca said.

"He threw it in the Charles," Jackie said. "Like I said, he's pretty nervous. He was saying the CIA could track him with satellites if he keeps his cell on. I told him he was crazy. The CIA can't do that, can they?"

"Not to my knowledge," DeLuca said. "DOD, DHS, NORTHCOM, NSA, and INSCOM can, but I don't think the CIA can. Is he waiting for me?

"He said he'd wait until one o'clock, and if he didn't hear from you, he'd have to leave," Jackie said. "I just want you to know I'm trying to make it up to you for lying, Davy—I'm on your team, you know."

"That's great, Jackie," DeLuca said.

"I was thinking, just kind of having a thought, that maybe I'd join the National Guard and be in counterintelligence like you—what do you think? You think they'd let me?"

"I don't think they want people with criminal records," DeLuca said.

"Yeah, but I read they were having trouble recruiting," Jackie said. "Maybe if I slip the guy a Franklin or two, he looks the other way."

"I'm not sure you can bribe the army, Jackie," DeLuca said. "But it's worth a try."

"Would you write me a letter?"

"Let's talk about it later, okay?"

A pair of uniformed cops standing at the top of the stairs at the Aquarium Blue Line T station stopped and told them the MBTA was temporarily closed due to the orange alert. DeLuca was tempted to argue that the T was only supposed to shut down during red alerts, but he knew arguing would only make him look like an asshole. This was, no doubt, more of the governor wanting to appear tough on terrorism.

They made their way quickly through the crowds of angry people at a half trot to Quincy Market, where De-Luca knew a place that rented motor scooters for tourists who wanted to do the Freedom Trail the easy way. Unfortunately, they only had one scooter left, a small red Honda. DeLuca gave the vendor his credit card, rented the scooter, and told Sykes to get on.

"That's okay," Sykes said, eyeing the Honda. "I'll run."

"Get on," DeLuca said. "It's almost three miles."

"I'll run."

"Dan . . ."

"I own a Harley," Sykes said. "If anybody sees me on a scooter . . ."

"Get on!" DeLuca said. "That's an order."

The machine would have been drastically underpowered, had there been only a single passenger. Carrying two full-grown men, there were times, going up hills, when it might have been better to run. It was still the best way to navigate the congested streets. DeLuca wove through stalled traffic, taking State to Tremont to Park and then hopping the curb to cut across the Common, where a mounted policeman rode up next to him and ordered him to stop, in a place where motorized vehicles weren't allowed. DeLuca slowed long enough to hold his badge up for the officer on horseback to see, at which point the officer waved him through and turned his horse. They passed to the right of Frog Pond and caught Beacon where it intersected with Charles, winding their way past shirtless hippie boys playing guitar and girls throwing Frisbees.

They found Freddy on a bench by the river, watching the sailboats on the Charles and the joggers running past in either direction. DeLuca introduced Sykes and asked Freddy what it was he wanted to tell them.

"I talked to Jackie," Freddy said. "He told me I needed to tell you everything. I don't know if you know this, but Katie and I were sort of seeing each other."

"We know," DeLuca said. "You bought her the negligee at Filene's. And you stole the glass necklace from Gina Ruggieri when you moved the stuff out of her apartment."

"I didn't steal it," Freddy said. "She'd thrown it in the wastebasket. I rescued it."

"Whatever," DeLuca said. "Lots of people shop for their girlfriends in wastebaskets. Jackie said you know where Marko lived. How?"

"Katie told me about him," Freddy said. "She said he was trouble and she didn't want to see him again, but then she did."

"When?'

"About two weeks before she died," Freddy said. "She said she needed to have a talk with him. I offered to go with her and wait in the car, but she said she wanted to go alone."

"So you followed her," DeLuca said. "You were jealous. You were afraid she was going to get back together with him. Were you stalking her?"

"I wasn't stalking her. I was keeping my eye on her."

"Did she know you were keeping your eye on her?"

Freddy shook his head. "I really did love her," he said. "Everybody else loved her for her voice, but I loved the real person. I know people said things about . . . how she looked, but I just didn't get that at all. People are crazy. I thought she was the most beautiful person I'd ever met, inside and out."

"Where did Marko live?" DeLuca asked.

"If I tell you, you have to make sure he doesn't find out I'm the one who told you," Freddy said.

"You don't have to worry about it," DeLuca said. "The same people who killed Katie killed Marko."

"In that case, I could show you," Freddy said. "I don't remember the exact address, but I could take you there. It's in Somerville."

DeLuca was trying to figure out the logistics of getting three men on the scooter when a pair of motorcycle cops approached. When he showed them his credentials and explained to them why they needed transport, they quickly agreed to help. Freddy sat behind the lead motor-cycle cop, blue flasher flashing as they sped between the cars on Mass Ave, gaining speed as they passed the build-ings of Massachusetts Institute of Technology, with De-Luca on the second big white Harley-Davidson and Sykes bringing up the rear on the scooter.

They stopped around the corner on Hawley Street. When Freddy pointed out the house, Sykes rode past it on the scooter, turned around, and rode past it again. He re-ported that the house appeared to be empty, but there was no way to be certain. It was a two-family, and Marko lived on the first floor, Freddy said.

"I'll call for backup," one of the officers said, a cop named Bailey.

"Hold on," DeLuca said. "Let me call somebody first."

When he reached Scottie at INSCOM/JTIOC, his son told him that in the last twenty-four hours, two more sat-ellites had been brought online and positioned in geosyn-chronous orbit, 18,000 miles above Boston. DeLuca gave Scott the GPS coordinates for the house, third from the corner on Franklin, and asked for a thermal read. Scott came back a minute later and confirmed that the house appeared to be empty. There was a heat signature coming from what was probably a television, but that was the only heat source in the building.

"Confidence?"

"High," Scottie said. "With a caveat. We've been hav-ing some minor computer problems."

"Meaning?"

"We're not sure what it means," Scottie said. "IWD is looking into it. Just be careful."

"Aren't I always?" DeLuca said. He'd been hoping to find Jelan Dvoradjic, Ivan, and the others, sitting around a bong or something, but that was wishful thinking. He asked one of the motorcycle cops to cover the back of the house and the other the front. They complied without questioning him, even though he was an army officer. They were good men.

He drew his weapon as he approached the door. Sykes did the same.

When DeLuca tried the knob, he found the door unlocked.

He pushed it open.

The window shades were drawn, casting a funereal pall over the front sitting room. The place was a mess. He saw unemptied ashtrays, a plate with a half-eaten sandwich on it, covered in mold, a loose pile of newspapers in Cyrillic, soccer magazines, *Guns and Ammo*, *Penthouse* magazines, comic books, dirty clothes, food wrappers, empty slivovitz bottles, and on the coffee table, a *Fodor's Guide to Colombia*.

The living room was in equal disarray. There was an easy chair, and beside it a stack of books that included books to teach yourself Spanish, an English–Serbo-Croatian dictionary, an English-Spanish dictionary, a World War II history, a biography of Sam Adams, and copies of *Harry Potter*, *The Da Vinci Code*, and *The Sisterhood of the Traveling Pants*. There was no television, but there was a boombox-style stereo/CD player, and on the table next to it, an assortment of CDs that included rap, rock, polka, classical symphonies, Green Day, Josh Groban, and Frank Sinatra, loose CDs far from their original jewel cases.

The kitchen was filthy as well, something stinking to high heaven from the garbage, a sink full of dirty dishes, a table where a large bowl of half-eaten cereal sat atop a *Boston Globe* sports section from the day before Katie Quinn was murdered.

"Looks like he gave the cleaning lady the day off," Sykes said.

"Don't fix it if it ain't broke," DeLuca said.

There was a dish of cat food on the floor, though no sign of a cat anywhere.

"That reminds me," Sykes said. "Hoolie called. I promised him I'd go to Elizabeth's house and put her cat in the basement."

"If we don't find this guy's friends," DeLuca said, "I'm betting it's not going to do much good to hide in the basement."

In the back bedroom, the bed was unmade, the floor covered with dirty laundry. The television atop the dresser was hooked up to a DVD player, and a DVD of porn star Jenna Jameson had been paused, in medias res. DeLuca turned the television off and looked around the room. The radio played softly, tuned to WSPO sports radio 690 AM, the station Marko had been listening to while watching his DVD.

"You need to see this," Sykes said, holding a piece of paper he'd found on the bedstand. DeLuca crossed to him, and Sykes handed him the paper. It was a letter, handwritten from Katie. Sykes reread it over DeLuca's shoulder.

Dear Marko,
    After our last conversation, I thought I should take a little time to write you, just to put this down on paper.

I just want you to know that I agree with you,
after thinking over the things you said, that this baby
wasn't meant to be, so I have had an abortion, as of
this morning. By the time you get this letter, it will
have been taken care of. It all went well, actually—the
nurse told me to count backwards from one hundred,
and I think I got to ninety-eight, and the next thing I
knew, she was patting me on the hand and telling me
to wake up, I could go home.

So there you have it. I'm going to need to be alone
for a while, so please don't call me—I'll call you if I
need anything.
Kate

"I thought you said she was two months pregnant," Sykes said.

"She was," DeLuca said. "Apparently she gave Marko a different story."

"Apparently," Sykes said.

"Go get Officer Bailey and his friend," DeLuca said. "Get Freddy too—we need to toss this place, and quickly."

"What for?"

"Claire McGowan told me Katie made an excuse for Marko having some sort of brain injury that made it hard for him to remember things," DeLuca said. "Pasternak found head scars. I've been trying to think of why he's the only one of these guys using his real name. The others all have cover IDs. Rather elaborate ones too. It would make sense if Marko had memory problems. He'd never keep his cover straight."

"I thought MSS had him as 'Mark Kenny,'" Sykes said.

"Yeah, but Katie knew him as Marko," DeLuca said. "Claire knew him as Marko Simic. Freddy knew him as Marko. He told Vinnie P. his name was Marko. It's like he kept forgetting his fake name."

"Could be," Sykes said. "If that's true, you gotta think the others saw it as a liability. One more reason to take him out. What are we looking for?"

"My uncle Tony had a stroke," DeLuca said. "He had memory problems. He used to write everything down. Marko's body didn't have anything on it when we found him, but I'll bet you he made notes. What's with all the Spanish dictionaries?"

While Sykes went to get the troopers, DeLuca began his search. It seemed reasonable as well that if Marko had problems remembering things, he wasn't going to hide something in a place he'd have trouble finding again. De-Luca looked in all the most obvious places first, between the mattresses, under the sofa cushions, behind the water tank to the toilet. He found what he was looking for in the freezer, a plain envelope that had been slipped between a pair of TV dinners. When he'd worked investigating cases of elder abuse, he often found old people, some afflicted with Alzheimer's or simple senility, keeping documents in the refrigerator, which they believed, erroneously, would keep them safe in case of fire.

He dumped the contents of the envelope onto the kitchen table.

He found a passport and a driver's license, both containing photographs of Marko Simic, under the name Mark Kenny, as well as an airline ticket, round trip on Varig flight number 3298 from Bradley International, an hour and a half west of Boston between Hartford and

Springfield, to Bogotá, Colombia. The flight was scheduled to leave at 3:15 p.m. He looked at his watch.

It was 3:10.

Inside the airline ticket folder was a slip of paper. On the paper was a list of names, handwritten in pencil, which read:

Jelan = John Divine Sr./Stefan Gregory
Ivan = John Divine Jr./Paul Sheridan
Ark = Richard Staples/Peter Sayles
Milos = Brent Tauber/Charles Reid
Jotso = John Samples/Joshua Arnold
Rad = David Green/Philip Cooke
Mih = Michael Adnusian/Nathan Platt

He called Dawn Massey's office and conferenced Walter Ford in as well.

"What's the situation?" he asked first.

"Nothing much, globally," Massey said. "Intensified chatter. A good number of interviews going on. The airport bomb checks out. It's real. The kid we stopped says he was following directions he got in his e-mail from someone calling himself Allah's Messenger. He's a total head case—I think he thinks he was taking directions from Allah himself. We're trying to suppress the news for as long as we can. Wexler looks like his head's going to blow up. He's dying to give a press conference. He keeps asking us when he can call one."

"He's already leaked the story, at least to the *Boston Voice*," DeLuca said. "Where are we with the alert? Orange or red?"

"Red is on standby," Massey said. "We're still at orange."

"Dawn, I need you to ground Varig flight number 3298. Marko was booked on it," DeLuca said. " 'Allah's Messenger' is Dvoradjic. He's the puppet master. He finds Arab kids and martyr wannabes and tells then what they want to hear. I'm going to give you some names to write down: Stefan Gregory, Paul Sheridan, Peter Sayles, Charles Reid, Joshua Arnold, Philip Cooke, and Nathan Platt. Search the passenger list for those names and hold them. Marko left a list of his friends' new identities. If they're not on that flight, search other flights, international first and domestic second. Destinations in Spanish-language countries. What's the rule on red alerts—all flights are grounded, right?"

"Right."

"What about international flights? Planes that are already in the air?"

"Flights in U.S. airspace are brought down. Flights that have left U.S. airspace are reviewed," Massey said. "Some are called back, some are allowed to continue. Anything refusing to return to U.S. airspace is going to have a pair of F-15s on its wings, but it gets handled on a case-by-case basis, depending on the flight profile."

"Profile?"

"Different factors," Massey said. "Passenger list, destination. Flights to the Middle East might get looked at more closely than flights to Bermuda, for example."

"I'm thinking Dvoradjic and his people wanted to be out of the country before it happens. So Varig 3298 leaves U.S. airspace when? Maybe six?"

"I could find out exact," Ford said.

"Do that," DeLuca said. "That's going to be H-hour. Dawn, can you get Lilly on board with this? Tell him what Hartshorn told us? Again."

"I can try," she said. "It's going to be hard to get him to give up a bird in the hand for another theoretical bird in the bush. He thinks he's already got the bomb."

"That's what they want him to think," DeLuca said. "We're coming back in. We should be there in about fifteen minutes."

Outside, DeLuca told the motorcycle cops he needed them to stay on the scene to secure it—an FBI team was on the way. Meanwhile, he apologized, they were going to need to borrow their motorcycles.

"You're Jim Bailey's kid, aren't you?" he said to Officer Bailey, finally placing him. "I used to work with your dad. I'll take good care of your bike, and I'll make Dan do the same. You'll get 'em back without a scratch."

Bailey and his partner handed over their helmets.

"Better?" DeLuca asked Sykes.

"Better," Sykes said, revving his engine. "You want me to skip Elizabeth's cat?"

"Cat?" DeLuca said. "Did we promise?"

"We promised," Sykes said. "It's on the way."

DeLuca reached for his phone. "Take one minute and meet me at the FBI. I'm going to call Hoolie and send him to Bradley—he's already close. You know the way?"

"I know the way," he said. "If I get lost, I'll ask Scottie for directions."

Before he left, Freddy approached him. DeLuca thanked Freddy for his help and said he'd be in touch.

"What about me?" Freddy said. "Who's going to give me a ride?"

DeLuca tossed him the keys to the scooter.

"Return this to the rental place outside of Quincy Market," DeLuca said. "If you steal it, we'll find you. And

Freddy—I know you have that fifty-caliber cannon you bought on you, but if you know what's good for you, you'll throw it in the Charles. You're gonna blow your head off with it. Vinnie isn't after you anymore—you don't need it."

DeLuca had parked the motorcycle in front of the FBI building on Center Plaza when his phone rang. It was Walter, who said he had good news and bad news.

"You'd better start with the good news," DeLuca said. "I could use some."

"It's not that good, actually," Ford said. "We stopped the flight. All eight guys were booked on it. Director Massey thinks they were prepared to hijack the flight—otherwise they probably would have taken different flights. So that's the good news."

"And the bad news is?"

"None of them were actually on it," Ford said. "Homeland Security had already flagged it for that reason. Any international flight with that many sudden cancellations is going to draw attention."

"Did they confirm their reservations?"

"They had," Ford said.

"What made them change their plans?"

"Excellent question," Ford said. "We're looking for other flights. Trains, rental cars, credit cards in the new names."

"If they missed their flights, where'd they go?" DeLuca asked. "Did they book backup flights somewhere? Hoolie's headed for Bradley, just in case."

"The DHS program would have flagged that as well," Ford said. "One guy booking two flights at the same time isn't going to clear the parameters. Maybe they had a second set of fake passports. Or a third, I guess it would be."

"If they did, they would have been on Simic's list," DeLuca said. "They missed their flight. I don't think they wanted to. Something happened. Something went wrong."

"Maybe they decided to stay behind," Ford said. "Just to see things through. Maybe they're ready to die for the cause."

"I don't think so," DeLuca said. "They don't fit the profile. These aren't jihadis. Something went wrong."

On the seventh floor, Dawn Massey was in a heated conference with Director Lilly. General LeDoux was there as well, dressed in his green Class A uniform with ten rows of ribbons ranging from Vietnam to Iraq. DeLuca stood in the doorway.

"Agent DeLuca," Massey said. "We were just talking about you."

"Sorry it took me a while to get here," DeLuca said. "I had to find some shortcuts."

"You're the one who thinks we still have an H-hour of six, is that right?" Lilly asked.

"The flight we're looking at would have cleared U.S. airspace at 6:12 p.m., according to a member of my team," he said. Ford had calculated the time according to average airspeeds. It was only an approximation. "Dvoradjic and his team were all booked on the same flight, so it looks like they might have been prepared to act in concert to take over the flight, but I think they would have preferred to step off the plane unobserved if they could. I'm sure they know nobody really gets away with taking over an airplane."

"The 9/11 bombers did," Lilly countered, as DeLuca had expected he would.

"They weren't trying to live happily ever after," De-Luca said. "These guys are."

"And you seem to know, for a fact, that these people, 'Jelan's Wolves,' are the I4NI people, because they're foreigners who hate America and have computer skills—is that right? Do you want to see my list of foreigners who hate America and have computer skills, Agent DeLuca? We have a bomb, at the airport, and it practically has Al Qaeda written all over it. We have a kid in custody who's going to lead us to the others."

"I wouldn't be surprised if it literally did have 'Al Qaeda' written on it in big block letters," DeLuca said. "Maybe with an arrow pointing towards Mecca. I'm also guessing that some time in the last hour, you received a credible communication from some Al Qaeda splinter group, claming responsibility for the device at Logan. They have information only the person who left the bomb could possibly know. Correct?"

Lilly turned to Massey. "I believe I instructed you not to brief anybody on that," he said sternly.

"As I said, I'm guessing," DeLuca said. "Assistant Director Massey didn't brief me about anything. I just walked in. The kid's not going to tell you anything. He doesn't know anything. He's a pawn."

"Some of what we include in the field of human intelligence gathering is subcognitive," LeDoux began. "I believe Agent DeLuca is seeing this in terms of military strategy, since Dvoradjic's people are military and this has the appearance of a classic feint. Feint attacks are designed to draw enemy defenses away from the actual targets. I think some of the problem with the WMD intel was relying too much on signals intelligence and imagery and not enough—"

"Oh please," Lilly said. "If you're going to tell me about your hunches and gut feelings, you can keep it to yourselves. Not only is it possibly the biggest cliché in the world, but I believe your people's gut feelings about weapons of mass destruction in Iraq were somewhat off base, weren't they?"

DeLuca looked at LeDoux. It was clear not only that Lilly had his facts wrong but that he'd made up his mind about them. Talking with him further was only going to be a waste of time.

"I must be wrong," DeLuca apologized. "I'll tell my people to stand down, then. If you don't mind."

"I'm not here to tell the army what to do," Director Lilly said. "But I would say domestic surveillance may not be your long suit. We've been doing it for quite a while at the FBI and I think we've gotten pretty good results."

"Who could argue with that?" DeLuca said.

When Director Lilly turned his attention to other business, moving down the hallway, Dawn Massey could only smile weakly.

"I'm sorry," she said. "I was hoping he'd be more receptive."

"You briefed him with Hartshorn's theory?"

"I did," she said. "I thought maybe if it came from me. Frankly, I expected better treatment from him. It's not about me, but . . ."

"We're all new at this," DeLuca said. "It's not you. He doesn't want to take directions from the army. We'll figure out how to get along. General LeDoux, I see you've met Assistant Director Massey. What resources can we bring in, at this point?"

"I've got three thousand guardsmen on call but I can't move them without the governor's office," LeDoux said. "I can't bring in regular army troops without permission from both the governor and the Pentagon."

"In other words, nothing," DeLuca said.

"You've got the technical support," LeDoux said. "Just not the people."

DeLuca looked at his watch. It was just after four o'clock in the afternoon.

He was about to suggest they all take a walk down to FBI agent Hartshorn's desk to see what he and MacKenzie had discovered when his phone rang. When he picked it up, his cousin Jackie was on the other end.

"Davy-boy," Jackie said.

"I have to cut you off, Jackie," DeLuca said. "Now's not a good time."

"This is important," Jackie said. "Not for me—for you. You know how sorry I am about lying to you . . ."

"It's all right, Jackie," DeLuca said. "I gotta hang up."

"Vinnie P. called me," Jackie said. "He wants to meet with you. He said he couldn't call you because he was afraid the FBI had satellites that could track down his cell phone. I told him that was only DOD, DHS, NORTH-COM, NSA, and INSCOM. Anyway, he said he has some information about some people you're looking for. He wants to tell you in person."

"Where is he?"

"Do you know Calcagnino's Auto Body on Charter and Commercial, North End?" Jackie said. "Next to the funeral home?"

"The chop shop," DeLuca said. "We busted it three times in the nineties for parting out Beemers."

"Look, I don't know what they might have done in the past," Jackie said. "That's really none of my business. Anyway, Vinnie said he wanted to meet you there and to come alone. He's been trying to do you a favor, but it's been hard with Wexler on his ass every step of the way. That's why he wanted me to call you."

"I'll be there in ten minutes," DeLuca said.

When he found MacKenzie, he expected to find Sykes as well, but Sykes hadn't arrived yet. He told Mack to call Scott and find Sykes, and to stand by. He had an errand to run. He'd be right back.

His CIM vibrated in his pocket.

He found a text message from Scottie waiting for him.

Massive IW attack underway on all systems. VACE down. NORA down. CPV down. Comlinks compromised. Zombie herd ≥ 2,000,000 bots and counting—years in planning. Tracesource ineffective. Virus spreading. Global. Coms/TS may be out for the immediate——▫✱✪✱✱▫⊠✱✱ ▫◆ ✱✪■ ✱✱✱◆▫✱ ▫◆▼ ▶✱◇▼ ▼✱✱▲ ▲✪▲▲⊠ ✱▫■✱▫♥▼◆✪✪▼✱▫■▲✥ ✱▫◆ ▫◇✱✱▫◆▲✪▮ ✱✪✱✱ ▼▫▫◯◆✱✱ ▼✱✪✱ ▫■▮▫◆▫▲ ✱✪■✱▲ ✱✱▼ ✪ ✪✱✱✱✪

When he tried calling, a recorded message told him the number was temporarily out of service.

There wasn't time to solve the problem. His task was to find Dvoradjic. Vinnie P. knew where he was. The North End was close enough to walk to, if he had to. With an information war under way, he found himself reduced to using police tactics from a hundred years ago. It would have to do.

* * *

Sykes had run into a small bit of difficulty. He'd found Elizabeth LeDoux's house without any problem, parking the police Harley in front and running quickly up the front steps. Vasquez had told him where he could find the key to let himself in. He was surprised when he discovered that the front door was unlocked.

Inside, all the lights were off. The cat's name was Max. He called out the name twice, "Max—come on Max . . ." and walked into the living room, where he saw a man, sitting in the easy chair opposite the television. The man had a large gun in his hand, and he was pointing it directly at Sykes.

Chapter Ten

DELUCA HAD TO MANEUVER THE MOTORCYCLE through the crowds on New Sudbury Street who were protesting the traffic conditions in the city, an angry mob that was shouting and throwing things toward the building. He took Cross to North Washington, moving between the cars and ignoring the honking horns he left in his wake. Every intersection was gridlocked, the traffic lights gone haywire, either changing every five seconds or not changing at all. The Charlestown Bridge was bumper to bumper with cars trying to get out of the city. Through the open door of a bar as he passed, he saw a man standing on a ladder trying to adjust a television that wasn't getting a signal. In an office window, he saw a man tapping in frustration at his computer, then throwing his hands up in the air. He couldn't get through to anybody on his phone. Across the harbor, he saw airplanes rising into the sky from Logan Airport, indicating that air traffic control computers were apparently unaffected. He turned right on Commercial and stopped when he saw his cousin sitting beneath a sign for Calcagnino's Auto Body.

Jackie jumped to his feet and crushed a cigarette beneath the toe of his boot when he saw his cousin.

"Nice wheels," he said. "Bring that inside, I'll bet they'll give it a paint job so good no one will know you stole it."

"Where's Vinnie?" DeLuca said. He looked at his watch. It was 4:32.

"He's inside," Jackie said. "I thought I'd wait for you before I knocked."

"I thought he said he wanted me to come alone," De-Luca said.

"You're going to need me to facilitate," Jackie said. "These guys can be a little difficult sometimes."

"Jackie, I've been handling guys like this all my life," DeLuca said.

"I know, I know, hands off, just a thought," Jackie said. "Maybe you'd need some backup, that's all I thought. Me and Vinnie are cool, by the way. I mean, you know, as far as Gina goes, I wouldn't go bringing it up maybe, but . . ."

"Wait here," DeLuca said. "Guard the bike. You never know, in this neighborhood, right? With all these fucking Eye-talians around."

"You never know," Jackie said. "I'll stay here and guard the bike. I can do that."

DeLuca knocked on the door, where a "Closed" sign had been hung. There were no lights on inside, the view blocked by a set of vertical Venetian blinds. He saw a finger pull the blinds aside, and then the door opened. He recognized Joey D'Angelo on the other side.

"You're DeLuca, right?"

"That's right," DeLuca said. "I believe Vinnie wants to see me."

D'Angelo let him in the office and told him to wait. He heard muffled voices down the hall. The radio on the desk was tuned to a news station, where a special report said banks and shops were closing due to a crash in bank, ATM, and credit card company computers. Something smelled, but he wasn't sure what it was, as if something were burning, but more of a cooking smell than something one might ordinarily associate with a garage.

"Agent DeLuca," Vinnie said when he entered the room, a big smile on his face. "Thanks for coming so quickly. I think you're going to like what I got for you, but first off, we gotta get something straight—I got immunity, right? Me and my people too—we got that, right?"

"I'm not a cop anymore, Vinnie," DeLuca said. "I can't make any deals. I'm not part of the system."

"No, but you're army, right? So that's even better than the fucking cops, right?"

"I suppose you could say that," DeLuca said,

"My point is, we got immunity, because we're working for the government, right? And you're the government. Good enough for me. I just want to make sure we understand each other—you scratch my back and I scratch yours, right? Quid pro fucking quo."

"That depends on what you have," DeLuca said.

"Depends on what I have," Vinnie said, smiling again. "You're not going to believe what I have. I'm going to get a fucking medal for this. Follow me."

He strode down the hall, turning right into the garage area, the source of the burning smell.

"Welcome to Guantanamo North," Vinnie said, chuckling to himself.

In the garage area, DeLuca saw a total of fifteen men. Six of them had bags over their heads and were hanging from the hydraulic lifts, their arms bound at the wrists by duct tape, pulled high above them. Four of the six men were spattered with blood, and five of the six had wet themselves, the blood and urine running down into a large drain in the middle of the floor meant to catch oil and transmission fluids.

"Who are these guys?" DeLuca asked, though he believed he knew the answer.

"These are them," Vinnie said. "The guys you asked me to find. The terrorists. One got away, but these are the others. It's taken a while to establish that we all speak English here, don't we, pal?" Vinnie said, whirling and punching the nearest body in the solar plexus with his fist, causing the man to groan. "I've been getting names too. Jotso is the one who got away, but we're still looking. This is Radislav, Arkady, Milos, Miheilo, and this is Ivan. We don't know this guy's name yet, but it's either Jelan or Marko, according to the list you gave me."

"It's Jelan," DeLuca said.

"Jesus, DeLuca—don't you know anything?" Vinnie said, shaking his head in disbelief. "I know it's fucking Jelan—I saw his fucking picture. I was just *pretending* we didn't know his name. Jesus Christ."

"Sorry," DeLuca said. "I'm new at this."

An oxyacetylene welder's rig had been wheeled into place next to the victims, as had a variety of other tools more commonly deployed to fix cars: crowbars and vises, C-clamps and drills, saws and bolt cutters. DeLuca realized where the burning smell had come from. As gruesome as the scene was, DeLuca had the sense that Vinnie hadn't been at his work all that long.

"I talked to the Simeone brothers, who told me where I could find our friend Radislav here," Vinnie said. "We found him yesterday, but he told us they were all meeting up today for a ride to the airport, so we got these other motherfuckers. Marko wasn't with 'em. We waited but he fucking never showed. Neither did Jotso."

"These men killed Marko," DeLuca said. "We found him in the trunk of a car in the parking garage."

"You see, Joey?" Vinnie said. "I told you these were not nice people. Agent DeLuca, I want you to meet a couple guys. This is Gregor and this is Luka. They're Albanian, but they speak the same language as these guys, so they've been working as my interpreters."

Two men stepped forward, both of them wearing bibbed welder's aprons that were soaked in blood. Each man extended a hand for DeLuca to shake.

"Gregor and Luka knew all about Jelan's Wolves in Serbia. I mean, in Kosovo. Wherever—who gives a fuck? My point is, they know all about these guys. These guys killed a bunch of people in Gregor's hometown. Mass graves, et-fucking-cetera. Anyway, Gregor and Luka have been particularly helpful, and I dare say, inventive in a physio-persuasilogical sense, but I mean that in the best possible way. I would suggest that when you start thinking about medals, that they be included, even though technically they're not U.S. citizens, so that may not work out. But I'll leave that shit to you."

He pulled on the hood of one man whose head had fallen forward. The head remained erect for a moment, then fell forward again.

"I guess this guy is taking a nap," Vinnie said. He slapped the head. "That's for the World Trade Center, you fucking fuck fuck. I had a cousin who was going to steal millions from that place." He punched the man again before turning to DeLuca. "Anyway, I thought maybe you'd want to ask them some questions, so we've been softening them up, right, Luka?"

"Soft, yes," Luka said, comprehending and grinning.

DeLuca moved to the one identified as Jelan Dvoradjic and asked Vinnie's man to remove the hood. Dvoradjic's eyes were swollen but open, a large bruise welling up on the right side of his face, where his ear was lacerated. His lip was cut as well, the bottom lip swollen and blue. The man managed to lift his head and looked DeLuca in the eyes.

"Your name is Jelan Dvoradjic?" DeLuca asked, moving in close.

The other man didn't speak.

"If you tell me what I want to know, I can take you and your friends out of here," DeLuca said. "I need to know where it is, and I need to know when it's set to go off. Where and when. I know you speak English, so I know you understand me."

"Fuck you," Dvoradjic said. One of Vinnie's men moved to strike the prisoner, but DeLuca stayed the blow.

"Where is it," DeLuca repeated, "and when is it set to go off?"

"I said fuck you," the man repeated. *"Jebêmte udupe!"*

"Stop!" DeLuca said when Gregor moved forward to assist in his efforts to negotiate. Ordinarily, DeLuca would have spent as long as it took, hours or days or weeks, learning what it was that Dvoradjic wanted and how to make it in his best self-interest to cooperate. In all the interrogations DeLuca had conducted in Iraq, he'd never resorted to the use of physical force. It simply wasn't the most effective way to get the job done. Positive reinforcement was better, combined with allowing the imaginations of the people he was interrogating to go in whatever directions they chose to go. That, however, required time, and patience, and he didn't have time, and there was too much at stake.

He looked at his watch. It was 4:47.

When he tried calling General LeDoux, his phone once again failed to connect.

He was on his own.

The decision was his.

He leaned in close and spoke directly into Jelan Dvoradjic's ear.

"I'm the only friend you have in this room right now," DeLuca said calmly. "I can stop this. If you help me, we might even be able to negotiate a reduced sentence for your son. He might not have to spend the rest of his life behind bars. He might get out in time to give you grandchildren. Do you want grandchildren, Jelan? Nobody else is going to help you. Nobody is going to come step in and make this better except me. No one else can. This is your one chance, so think about it. I'm all you've got. Do you want to help me, Jelan? Tell me where it is, and when it's set to go off. You tell me those two things and I'll stop this and get you to a hospital."

He waited.

"Fuck you," Dvoradjic muttered. "Go to hell."

"If I do," DeLuca said, "I hope I can find the restroom where your mother is cleaning toilets."

He turned to Vincent P.

"I guarantee you, I can get this guy singing like Pavarotti in five minutes," Pastorelli said. "Ten, tops. Gregor and Luka have got some pretty creative ideas about this one."

DeLuca considered his options.

He had none.

"Ask him where it is, and when it's set to go off," De-Luca said. "If he wants to tell us more than that, he is, of course, free to do so. I'll wait outside."

Jackie was sitting on the motorcycle when DeLuca came outside. He jumped off, nervously, and wiped the gas tank clean with his sleeve.

"That's a nice bike," Jackie said. "So how'd everything go inside? May I ask?"

"We're almost finished," DeLuca said. "I'm referring, of course, to my career."

"Does Vinnie know I'm the one who brought you here?" Jackie asked. "I think Joey D' saw me. Just so they know I'm still on the team, you know? Not that I'm on the team. So did you get what you were looking for?"

"Not yet," DeLuca said.

"It's pretty crazy in this town with the traffic, isn't it? You hear about all the computers? You're lucky you got this bike. There'd be no other way to get around. They gonna open the tunnel up again?"

"I don't know," DeLuca said. "Eventually."

"I heard they found a bomb on the T and that's why they shut it down," Jackie said. "Did you hear that? Anything like that?"

"I didn't hear anything about a bomb on the T," DeLuca said.

They heard a high-pitched but muffled scream coming from behind the closed garage doors.

Then silence.

Then they heard loud music coming from inside the garage, somebody turning on the stereo to mask the sounds.

"Jesus," Jackie said. "What are they doing in there?"

"They're working on a Yugo," DeLuca said.

"You go fuck yourself," Jackie said nervously. "Remember that old joke?"

"How's Wesley?" DeLuca said.

"He's good," Jackie said. "He's at home. Probably sleeping on the bed. Laziest fucking dog I ever met."

"You talk to Gina?"

"A little bit," Jackie said. He took a pack of cigarettes and tamped it against the back of his hand, then opened it. "I didn't tell her what was going on or anything. I told her you were helping me straighten things out with Vinnie. I told her how my cousin David has always looked out for me. And how much I've always appreciated that you do. I know I'm sort of the fuck-up in the family—"

"*Sort* of?" DeLuca interrupted.

"I mean, I am," Jackie said, opening the cigarette pack and taking out two. "But I always knew I could count on you, David. I hope you know you can count on me too. I've really changed." He offered DeLuca a cigarette. DeLuca didn't smoke, but he'd always said if a nuclear bomb were coming, in the air, on the way, and nothing could stop it, then maybe he'd try one. All things considered, he decided to tuck the cigarette into his shirt pocket.

"Everybody fucks up," DeLuca said. "I'm fucking up right now."

"How so?"

"Can't tell you," DeLuca said.

"You mean, you could tell me, but then you'd have to kill me?" Jackie joked. "So how's Bonnie, by the way?"

They were interrupted when Joey and Vinnie P. came out. Vinnie was holding a brown shopping bag. He looked scornfully at Jackie for a moment, then turned his full attention to DeLuca.

"Any luck?"

"Yeah," Vinnie said, laughing. "All bad, for him. It's between ventilation houses three and four, in the utility tunnel, pipe three. He couldn't be any more specific than that. It's set for six."

DeLuca looked at his watch. It was 5:08.

Vinnie handed him the bag. Inside, DeLuca found a .50 caliber Smith & Wesson, as well as a handheld computer.

"The password to the computer is 'Polje.' 'P-o-l-j-e.' He had these on him. He admitted killing the girl, by the way."

"I'll talk to you later," DeLuca said, pocketing the gun and giving the handheld PC to Jackie as Vinnie went back inside.

"Listen, Jackie," DeLuca said. "I need you to do something. Maybe nothing you've ever done is more important than this. You know where the FBI building is, at Center Plaza? Seventh floor. You said you've been running a couple miles a day . . ."

"Maybe not *every* day," Jackie admitted.

"You remember high school, right? When you were all-state? I need you to find that Jackie again. I want you to take this and run it over to the FBI building, just like when you were on the track team in high school. It's about a mile from here, maybe a mile and a half. You put this in the hands of Dawn Massey. That's a woman, D-a-w-n, not D-o-n. Tall and blonde. Seventh floor. I'd call ahead but the phones are out. Tell her it's from me. Tell her the password is 'Polje.' 'P-o-l-j-e.' "

"Polje," Jackie repeated. "Polje."

DeLuca found a pen and wrote the password on a scrap of paper.

"Then find Sergeant Colleen MacKenzie and tell her to meet me in the Big Dig utility tunnel, between ventilation houses three and four, as fast as she can, and to bring everybody they can spare. I'm writing that down too. And don't start hitting on her because we don't have time."

"Davy . . ."

"Shut up, Jackie. Just do this for me and you don't have to pay me the thousand bucks I loaned you," DeLuca said.

"I was going to pay that back," Jackie said.

"I know you were," DeLuca said.

"Maybe if I took the bike . . ."

"I need the bike. Go now. Run as fast as you can. Dawn Massey, FBI, seventh floor, Center Plaza. Colleen MacKenzie. She's at the FBI building too. You know the way, right?"

"Sure I know the way," Jackie said.

"You do this, this is like a get-out-of-jail-free card for the rest of your life from the FBI. Think of it that way. Go!"

He fired up the Harley and roared off. A patrol car had been parked to block access to the Central Artery tunnel at the Exit 12 off-ramp. DeLuca flashed his badge and told the car to follow him. One officer stayed behind to man the ramp, but the other turned the car and pulled in behind him. They rode south in the northbound tunnel, DeLuca traveling as fast as he could while trying to read the signs on the doors to his right, accessed via a raised walkway about five feet above road level, with a thin railing to keep anyone on foot from falling into traffic. The fluorescent lights flashed overhead as he sped, the sound of his engine echoing off the walls. The doors leading up to the ventilation buildings were clearly marked, each building (there were seven in all) a five-story tower above the surface filled with massive fans to pull the exhaust fumes from the tunnels below, scrub the gases for pollutants, and blow what remained up into the sky. Ventilation capacity could be reduced to zero, to choke off any fires in the tunnel, or raised in an instance where hazardous materials somehow found their way in, despite the signs at the entrances rerouting any tankers or trucks carrying hazmats. He recalled wondering, back when the Central Artery Project was being built, what they thought was going to stop someone from intentionally driving a tanker filled with gasoline or ammonia from barreling into the tunnel at high speed and crashing the vehicle on purpose—a few yellow signs or flashing lights weren't going to deter anybody intent on doing harm.

He shut the motorcycle off at the door to building three. The officer behind him parked the cruiser and approached.

"You wanna tell me what we're doing here?" the officer said. "Can I see that badge again, by the way? I'm afraid I didn't quite catch your name."

"Special Agent David DeLuca, army counterintelligence," DeLuca said, showing his badge and credentials again. "Can you get us a couple of flashlights please, Officer . . . ?"

"Sienciewicz," the cop replied. "No relation to *NYPD Blue*."

"Sienciewicz," DeLuca said. "Is your radio working?"

"It's about all that is," the cop said. "They reinforced the system after all the radios failed in the WTC. There's some kind of nasty computer virus. I guess it's all over the world or something."

"Outer space too. My satellite phone is out," DeLuca said. "Do you mind?"

The policeman removed his radio and handed it to De-Luca, who clipped it onto his shirt.

"Dispatch can still put you through to federal frequencies, right?"

"Oh yeah," Sienciewicz said. "After 9/11, they made sure all our radios talk to each other. What are we looking for, exactly?"

"A bomb," DeLuca said. "We don't know what it looks like."

He glanced at his watch. It was 5:32.

BPD connected him to the FBI radio dispatcher, who put him through to Agent Hartshorn, who said he was with MacKenzie.

"Mack—where are you?"

"Coming down the stairs at building four," she said. "Where are you?"

"Building three. I have a uniform with me—who'd you bring?"

"Just Agent Hartshorn," Mack said. "Turnpike Authority said they were sending people but they couldn't say when they'd get here."

"We don't have time to wait for them," DeLuca said. "Start at your end in the service tunnel and work towards me. Remember that this thing was installed during construction. Look for anomalies, wires, anything that looks out of place."

He tried the handle to the access door. It was locked.

"We're locked out," DeLuca said.

There was no time to try to reach anyone with a key. DeLuca took the .50 caliber from his pocket, aimed it at the door lock, and fired. The gun had a kick like a mule, leaving a twelve-inch hole in the metal door where the knob lock used to be.

The door swung open.

"I'm in," he said.

He heard four shots ring out from farther down the tunnel.

"We're in," Mack said.

The central utility tunnel was designed to provide access to all the electronics employed to keep the state-of-the-art traffic tunnels open and running efficiently, including lights, cameras, monitors, pressure sensors, motion detectors, and programmable electronic signs to tell motorists of lane closures or conditions. It was also designed to provide access for road crews and to evacuate motorists in the case of an emergency. It was about ten feet wide, with an array of pipes, tubes, wires, and conduits overhead, as well as a large exhaust duct, five feet across and four feet high. Hartshorn explained that the utility tunnel itself was the intake duct, bringing fresh air into the tunnel at the same rate that the fouled air was drawn out.

"So the gas has to leak into the tunnel we're in," DeLuca said. "It goes from here into the main tunnel and then kaboom. Is that right?"

"I believe so," Hartshorn said.

Officer Sienciewicz took one side of the access tunnel and DeLuca the other. They shone their flashlights on the ceiling, the way otherwise dimly lit by a sequence of battery-powered emergency lights spaced every hundred feet, but as with everything else about the Big Dig, many had malfunctioned.

"Which one is pipe number three?" DeLuca asked.

"The big yellow one," Hartshorn replied. "The one that's cool to the touch. The gas inside is at about sixty pounds of pressure. It was eighty, but we had Unigas shut it down at their end. It's not enough, but it's something."

DeLuca looked at his watch.

It was 5:41.

"Do we know how they might have intended to breach the line?" DeLuca asked. "They can't blow up the pipe itself. That would ignite the gas. They want to fill the tunnel first, right?"

"Correct," Hartshorn said. "The engineer at Unigas thought I was crazy when I asked him, but he thought they might try to sever the supports. The pipeline itself is suspended from the ceiling by steel cable stanchions. They did that so that people could walk under it. He said it's heavy, so he thought if they could fire small charges to blow the cables, maybe four or five of them, gravity would be enough to pull the pipe down and crack it open. The tunnel will fill in maybe twenty to thirty seconds."

"I'm looking at the supports," DeLuca said into his radio. "I'm seeing ceiling brackets. Four bolts. Four bolts. A sprinkler system. Brackets. Braces. Four bolts. Cables. Where are you?"

"We can see your lights," MacKenzie said. "We're about a hundred yards down."

"Braces," DeLuca narrated. "Ceiling brackets, four bolts, four—hold it. I have a bracket that has three bolts and a rivet. What do you have?"

"Bolts," Mack said. "Wait—now I'm getting three hex bolts and a rivet."

DeLuca looked down the tunnel and saw Mack approaching. The support brackets to the yellow gas supply pipe were spaced every ten feet. Mack was about forty yards away.

"Sienciewicz—what are you seeing?"

"Same as you," the officer said. "It was four bolts in each anchor point and now it's three bolts and a rivet."

"This is the section," DeLuca said.

He looked at his watch.

It was 5:45.

MacKenzie and Hartshorn met him in the middle.

"I'm gonna guess the rivets are exploding bolts," DeLuca said, shining his flashlight on one of the anchor plates in the ceiling. "It looks like maybe a dozen have been set to go."

"Redundancy," Hartshorn said. "If one or two don't blow, they'll still pull out of the ceiling when the others go. They were already having trouble with the epoxy."

DeLuca ran his flashlight from one bracket to the other.

"The wiring is inside the ceiling," he said. "We'd have to either pull the rivets or crack the ceiling to cut the wires."

"In other words," MacKenzie said, "we can't get to the exploding bolts. Not in time."

"There has to be a controller somewhere," Hartshorn said. "Something accessible. This was planted when?"

"Three to four years ago," DeLuca said. "It's unclear."

It was 5:48.

"They had to have some way to change their minds," Hartshorn said. "Wouldn't they?"

"They didn't seem like the kind of people who change their minds," DeLuca said. "But I think you're right. Even if they planted the bomb four years ago, they'd want to check on it to make sure it was still working. If something is that important, you'd want to keep an eye on it. Nobody trusts technology that much."

"Check how?" Mack said. "Somebody climbing around in here would have been suspicious."

"Ivan Dvoradjic worked as an inspector," Hartshorn said. "He would have had access."

"It still seems like a lot of trouble," Mack said. "Coming in here. Somebody would have seen him."

DeLuca saw a stairway leading to the surface.

"It's on the roof," he said, the setup suddenly appearing to him in an intuitive leap. He flashed on the triangular pattern of dents in Ivan Dvoradjic's shag carpeting. "Everybody else lived in dumps, but Ivan had a luxury apartment with a telescope on the balcony. He used the telescope to check on the bomb. He could have seen building three from there but not building four. It's on the roof of building three."

"I'll stay here in case there's something you want me to do," Hartshorn said.

DeLuca, MacKenzie, and Officer Sienciewicz ran up the stairs, passing the door to the street and continuing until they reached the top of the stairs and another locked door.

"Stand back and cover your ears," he told Mack, drawing the .50 caliber gun again. He fired at the lock, blowing a four-inch hole, but the door held.

It was 5:51.

He fired at the hinges. The top hinge fell away but the middle and bottom hinges held. He fired twice more at the lock, his ammunition now spent, and then Sienciewicz slammed into the door with his shoulder.

The door flew open, sunlight pouring into the opening.

On the roof were a pair of ventilation cowlings, large round structures about fifteen feet across and ten feet high.

He looked at his watch.

It was 5:52.

They surveyed the rooftop but found nothing.

"It has to be on top," DeLuca said, finding a set of steel rungs forming an access ladder on the side of one of the cowlings. He pointed to a nearby apartment building.

"That's where Ivan lived. He was looking down from there."

He looked up, trying to locate the apartment.

He saw someone on the balcony.

He saw a muzzle flash.

Sienciewicz went down, falling hard, screaming in pain. MacKenzie pulled back into the doorway, while DeLuca scrambled for cover behind a rooftop air-conditioning unit, two more shells ricocheting off the metal as he dived for safety. The report from the rifle itself was lost in the distance and the roar of the ventilation fans.

"I'm hit!" Sienciewicz said. "Oh Jesus.!"

"Officer down!" DeLuca shouted into his police radio. "Officer down on the rooftop of Central Artery ventilation building three." He called out. "Sienciewicz, can you hear me?"

"It's my leg," Sienciewicz said, trying to pull himself across the roof. "Oh Jesus. I can't move. I can't move!"

Sienciewicz's position was entirely exposed—another shot from the man on the balcony would have finished him off, and yet the man was holding fire. DeLuca had drawn his .38 Smith & Wesson, MacKenzie her service Beretta. The distance between them and the balcony was well over two thousand yards and a hopeless shot for a sidearm.

DeLuca flashed again on what he'd read in the file for Jotso Sinhavsky, the one terrorist who'd escaped capture when Vincent Pastorelli and his men took the others. His file said he'd been a sniper.

"Mack—are you okay?"

"I'm fine," she called back. "How did he know we were here?"

"My guess is, he's monitoring police frequencies."

"Do we have UAVs?"

"They're deployed, but I can't get through to Scottie," DeLuca said. "Computers are down. Sienciewicz—you're going to be all right. Can you hear me? He's not going to shoot you. He's using you as bait. He wants us to come get you. It's a standard sniper tactic."

He recalled how, during the war in Yugoslavia, the bodies of a young couple had sat for days on the Banja Bridge in Sarajevo while snipers on both sides of the river killed anybody trying to get to them.

Sienciewicz's leg was a bloody mess. DeLuca had lied about him being all right—he was bleeding from the femoral artery, one of the larger blood vessels in the body, and would bleed out in a few more minutes unless somebody got to him.

When he peeked over the top of the air-conditioning unit to see if the sniper was still there, another shot zipped past his head, burying into the tar of the roof behind him as he ducked again.

It was 5:55.

"I can't get to the ladder," DeLuca called out. "He's got a clear shot of it."

"Hartshorn is here," MacKenzie called back from the doorway.

"I came when I heard your call," Hartshorn said. "I think I have a clear shot at the balcony."

"It's too far," DeLuca said. "Save it."

DeLuca tried to think of a strategy. Waiting for assistance was off the table, but they were pinned down.

"Neal has an idea," Mack called out. "It's worth a try, I think."

"I am extremely open to suggestions," DeLuca said, his back to the air-conditioning unit.

"We have a laser on top of the Tobin Bridge," Hartshorn said. "It can be hand-fired if the computers fail. I just don't know if he has a clear shot."

"He does," DeLuca called back. "I remember seeing the bridge when I was standing on the balcony. That's over a mile away."

"Not a problem," Hartshorn said. "You don't have to allow for elevation or windage with a laser."

"Do it," DeLuca said. "But switch your radio to a secure frequency. Tell me when and I'll draw his fire to get him to stand up."

Hartshorn called on his radio to be put through to the security station atop the bridge tower. DeLuca looked at his watch.

It was 5:57.

"They've got the building in sight but they don't see anybody on the balconies," Hartshorn said.

"Number 17D," DeLuca called back.

"I told them that," Hartshorn said. "They don't see anybody. They're saying he's firing from somewhere inside the apartment."

DeLuca knew a trained sniper would do that.

"I'll have to get him to come out then," DeLuca said. "Tell them to get ready."

"What are you going to do?" Mack asked him.

"The only thing I can do," DeLuca said. "I'm going to surrender."

He quickly took off his shirt, then his white T-shirt, which he waved in the air overhead. He threw his gun out onto the roof, where the sniper could see it, then stood up with his hands over his head.

He looked up to see the man in the apartment, Jotso Sinhavsky, walking out onto the balcony, still aiming the rifle at him.

Jotso waved, as if to say, "So long, sucker," then reaimed the rifle.

And then, in an instant, DeLuca saw a flash of light, and then a spray of blood, and then Sinhavsky was no longer there, blown apart like a cat in a microwave.

He threw his shirt back on as he ran to the ladder. MacKenzie was right behind him. Hartshorn went to attend to the fallen policeman.

When he reached the top or the cowling, peering over the edge, he looked down through a wire cage at the fan blades spinning below him, a strong wind blowing in his face now. Was that gas he smelled?

It was 5:58.

Then DeLuca saw it, a small black box, about the size of a pound of butter, mounted beneath the grate at the point where the two cowlings abutted, with a digital read-out visible. The only way to get to it would be to crawl across the wire grate atop the cowling.

He moved to the side, to make room for MacKenzie. When she got to the top, he pointed toward the middle.

He began to cross on the wire grate. The fan blades spun below him. The grate, a mesh of quarter-inch-gauge steel webbing with about three inches or so between interstices, gave slightly beneath his weight, bowing in. Were the grate to collapse entirely, he'd be diced into a thousand pieces.

MacKenzie crawled along the grate next to him, staying closer to the edge, her hair blowing straight up in the wind created by the fans.

The digits on the clock's face counted down in red numerals and read in years, months, days, hours, minutes, and seconds, showing the numbers 0:00:00:00:00:36. On the left-hand side, he saw a pair of wires, one blue and one white.

"Oh my God," Mack shouted above the wind that roared in her ears.

"My watch must be slow," DeLuca shouted back, shining his flashlight down into the cowling.

"You have twenty-eight seconds," MacKenzie said.

"Give me a count," DeLuca asked. "Can I borrow your Swiss army knife?"

"Twenty seconds," Mack said, handing it to him. "Nineteen. Eighteen."

DeLuca opened the knife blade.

"Sixteen, fifteen . . ."

He couldn't tell how close to the surface the fan blades were because they were spinning too fast to see, the wind blowing directly into his face, making it difficult to keep his eyes open. There was a chance that if he reached in, he'd slice his arm like a large bologna.

"Eleven, ten . . ."

Satisfied that he had enough room, he rolled up his sleeve and reached his arm through the grate, his watch momentarily catching on the wire mesh. He put the blade first to the blue wire, then the white one.

"Any hunches?" he asked MacKenzie.

"Do something! Seven, six, five, four . . ."

He had a better idea, upon further inspection, reaching around behind the clock.

"It stopped," Mack said. The face of the clock was blank. "What did you do?"

When he drew his arm from the grate again, he showed MacKenzie the plug at the end of an electric cord connecting the timer to an electrical socket inside the cowling. He'd unplugged the clock.

"What would you have done if you couldn't unplug it?" MacKenzie asked.

"I don't know," DeLuca said, drawing a deep breath. "I was hoping you'd think of something."

He called Dawn Massey on the radio from the rooftop.

"All clear," he said. "For now."

"Good to hear your voice," Massey said. "Are you all right?"

"I'm fine. We're going to need an ambulance for Officer Sienciewicz. I'd say medevac, but there's no place up here for a chopper to land. Did you get what you needed from the handheld? My cousin Jackie show up?"

"He did. Out of breath. We think we might be okay," Massey said. "We have locations for all seven bombs. They were set to go off one every hour. Boston was first. That gives us an hour to disarm the next one, in London."

"You have communications?"

"Spotty," she said. "Land lines work better than mobile."

"What about the Internet?"

"It's a mess," she said. "Fortunately, according to your friend General LeDoux, your information warfare people found the antiviral software they need on Dvoradjic's handheld. It's going to take a few days to disinfect everything, but they have a list of all the zombie bots I4NI was herding, so that's a head start. They'd been putting together the attack for years. They had something like seven million computers, lined up against us. IWD thinks they can send to antivirus to all seven million and disseminate it from there."

"Would I be wrong to guess that IWD and the U.S. government has been sending out secret spyware and making bots of their own from the computers of private citizens, without telling them, for the last several years, on the chance that someday we'd need a zombie herd of our own to fight off an invasion? Am I right?" he asked.

"I can't confirm or deny," she said. "But I think I'm going to stop leaving my computer on overnight. Needless to say, I can't talk right now."

"Needless to say," DeLuca said. "Any sign of Sykes?"

"Nothing here," Massey said.

"That's odd," DeLuca said. "Are you saying land lines are still working?"

"Most of them," she said.

"Thanks," he said. "See you soon."

He called Scott from a pay phone. His son asked him if he was okay.

"I'm good," DeLuca said. "We can't find Dan. He's not answering his phone. Have you got a GPS from his CIM?"

"Our systems are still soup," Scottie said. "I had him, before the shitstorm hit."

"Where is he?"

"He was in the house off Harvard Square," Scott said. "The one Hoolie had me draw the tripwire around. Where Bizza lives."

"Was the tripwire program still running when Dan got there?"

"It was," Scott said. "Let me back up the events logo. I can't get any new information, but I think I can search the recent archives. Just a second . . ."

"Just the last eight hours," DeLuca said.

"One second . . ." Scott said. "This computer is slow as molasses. Hang on. Okay. I have two events. Somebody entered about three hours ago . . ."

"That's too long ago to be Dan," DeLuca said.

"Okay," Scott said. "And then, at 1640 hours, somebody else. Would that be Dan?"

"Probably," DeLuca said. "The timing is about right. Some somebody was in the house before he got there?"

"Maybe Bizza came home. They're probably sitting in front of the television, watching the news."

"Elizabeth is in Vermont," DeLuca said. "Have you got thermals?"

"Just a minute," Scott said. "Nothing. Sorry."

"Keep calling him," DeLuca said. "Try the home phone."

DeLuca told Mack to keep up with him and ran to the Harley. At tunnel level, he saw a number of people, including some men DeLuca recognized from the bomb squad and from the Turnpike Authority, as well as a crew from

Unigas and an ambulance pulling up. He told the bomb squad quickly where they would find the timer, told the EMTs where they would find Officer Sienciewicz, then jumped on the bike, with Mack behind him.

He raced south in the northbound tunnel. At the tunnel entrance, he saw a sea of stalled cars where the interstate had become a parking lot full of angry people who gave him the finger and shouted obscenities. He turned the bike around and took the next exit, gunning the throttle at the top of the ramp and turning left against the one-way traffic. He shot across the Common, across Beacon and across Storrow, taking the Mass Avenue Bridge, skidded through a left turn in Central Square, skidding left again onto Mt. Auburn at Harvard Square.

He stopped the bike in front of Elizabeth's house. The front door to the house was wide open.

He took the steps two at a time, his weapon drawn, with MacKenzie right behind him.

They found Dan lying in a large pool of blood in the middle of the living room floor, curled up on his side, his mobile phone less than a foot from his hand but beyond reach. Dan's Beretta lay just beyond the phone. Seated in the leather easy chair opposite, they found the body of James Chiang Chen, who held a .32 caliber revolver in his hand. Chen had died from a bullet from Dan's gun, taking the round in the middle of his forehead. Dan had been shot in the neck, the bullet severing his carotid artery.

When Mack rolled him over, cradling his head in her lap, she saw his eyes flicker open. DeLuca was already on the phone, summoning help.

"What the fuck?" Dan managed to say, but when he spoke, blood gurgled from his wound, forming a trickle of foam.

"Don't try to talk," DeLuca said. "Help is coming. They'll be here soon." But DeLuca had a feeling, or more than a feeling. He had a conclusion to draw, based on too much personal experience. He'd seen men lose blood before, in Iraq and elsewhere. He had a rough idea of how much blood a man could lose and still survive. Dan had lost too much.

"What the fuck?" Dan said again, confused, his eyes moving to the body in the chair across the room. "Who . . ."

"That's one of the guys," DeLuca lied. "You got him. You did good."

"I did?"

"You got him," DeLuca said. Mack was pressing a pillow against Dan's neck, but there was too much blood.

"I got him," Dan said.

"One of the terrorists," DeLuca said, laying his hand on Sykes's chest. MacKenzie held Dan's head, smoothing his hair from his forehead. "The I4NI guys. It's okay now. We took care of 'em."

"That's good," Dan said. "Will you tell my dad . . ."

"I'll talk to your father," DeLuca said, but he wasn't sure Sykes heard him.

An ambulance arrived a moment later. DeLuca pulled MacKenzie aside while the EMTs took over, but it was only a matter of a few seconds before one of them shook his head to indicate that Dan had passed.

DeLuca took MacKenzie and led her to the front porch, where he held her as she cried. There was little to say. There was no call to second-guess. There was no need to bring meaning, because he knew MacKenzie understood, as well as he did, that in the line of duty, in this war that they were in, against terrorism, against chaos, against disorder,

that death more often than not had a random quality to it.
Men died because they stopped to tie their shoe, or paused
to help someone, or for no apparent reason at all. Men died
doing their duty, and the precise details of how and when
and where varied, but seldom mattered. Dan died for his
country. It didn't make it any easier to stand there on the
porch, watching the EMTs moving at a slow deliberate
pace now, bringing stretchers up the steps.

Mack dried her tears on her sleeve and pulled herself
together, staring off for a moment before managing to
look DeLuca in the eye again. She said she'd stay to talk
to the police, who'd just arrived and were going to need
an explanation.

DeLuca got back on the motorcycle, riding until he'd
reached Calcagnino's Auto Body. He was surprised to
see, from a distance, that the garage doors were raised,
and that the garage itself appeared to be open and ready
for business, with a black Jaguar up on one of the lifts and
a mechanic beneath it, working on the brakes. The floor
was wet, where it had recently been washed. Vincent Pastorelli was in the waiting room, reading the paper.

"Agent DeLuca," Pastorelli said. "I was assuming you
were coming back. You see, Joey? I told you he was a man
of his word. I believe you know where some of my belongings are."

"Your stuff is in a panel truck, parked behind a Radio
Shack in Newton, off Route 9. There's only one Radio Shack
in Newton, so you shouldn't have any trouble finding it,"
DeLuca said.

Pastorelli gestured to Joey D'Angelo, who took a man
with him and drove off in a gray sedan.

"I'd tell him to take my car," Pastorelli said, "but I'm having trouble with my brakes. That's why I'm here. I brought my car in because I was having trouble with my brakes."

"Where are our friends?" DeLuca asked.

"What friends do you mean?" Vinnie said. "I have lots of friends. I know people from all walks of life. What friends are you referring to?"

"Vinnie," DeLuca said.

"You know the thing about friends?" Vinnie interrupted. "Some of them can be fucking fickle. One minute they're your friends, and then you never see them again. They're just gone, and you can't find them again, no matter how hard you try."

"That's true," DeLuca said.

"Make new friends but keep the old. One is silver and the other is fucking gold," Vinnie said. "That's what I always say. And now you're my buddy—what was the line Humphrey Bogart said? This could be the start of a beautiful fucking friendship, right, DeLuca?"

"I don't think so, Vinnie," DeLuca said.

"Well, that's entirely up to you," Vinnie said. "As far as anyone has to be concerned, the only reason I came here today was to have my brakes done. Anything else that might have happened is pure speculation, even if somebody somehow accidentally made a videotape. But you know how they can fake anything, these days. Right? We all have things we gotta do. It's your call, smart guy. Friends?"

Epilogue

WHEN DAWN MASSEY ANSWERED HER DOOR
that evening, she was wearing navy blue sweatpants and a
pink hooded sweatshirt. It seemed odd, to see her wearing
pink. She was barefoot, her hair tied up in a bun. DeLuca
was wearing the same thing he'd worn for the last forty-
eight hours. When he buzzed her apartment number from
the lobby, she'd said only, "Who's there?" He'd said only,
"David."

She smiled to see him, but it was a smile more of sym-
pathy than joy. The news was on the television behind her.

"Before you let me in," he told her, "there's two ways
we can handle this. One is, I come in and tell you everything, and then you're involved. The other is that you
close the door without saying anything. I wouldn't hold
it against you."

She stood a moment, looking at him, then smoothed
her hair back with her hand and asked him if he wanted
a drink.

"What have you got?" he said, stepping inside.

"What do you need?" she asked him.

"I would like a nice glass of bourbon, on the rocks," he
said.

"Have you eaten?" she asked him.

He sat at the dining room table while she got the drink. He glanced at the television. Two of the major networks were back on the air, but one was still down with computer problems. CNN was fine, though a scroll at the bottom of the screen apologized for technical difficulties. World financial markets had shut down but were expected to reopen tomorrow. Schools would reopen as well.

When she set the drink before him, he took a long swallow, letting the whiskey burn its way down his throat. She turned the TV off. The silence was welcome. He drank whiskey once or twice a year, but tonight seemed like a good night to make it twice.

"I'm not hungry, to answer your question, but thanks," he told her as she sat at the table across from him. "What have you been doing?"

"You're going to need food. Reading," she told him. "Reports. We didn't get the bomb in Paris in time, but luckily, it malfunctioned. Otherwise, we seem to have gotten them all."

"I heard," he said.

"Is your phone working?" she asked. "I tried to call you."

"Not yet," he said, "but I'm in no hurry to fix it."

"Ballistics on the gun you gave us matches the bullet that killed Katie Quinn, by the way. That lets Vinnie off. We're going over Marko's apartment for whatever else we can find. Where've you been?" she asked. "I got involved with Lilly and I didn't see you again."

"I've been debriefing with LeDoux," DeLuca said. "Writing up my report. I have to fly to Washington tomorrow for a fact-finding. The meeting before the meeting."

"Who's going to be there?"

"I'm not sure," DeLuca said. "The whole crew, I think. All my bosses. John Maitland from INSCOM. Jose Canales from DIA. Warren Benjamin from DHS. Schlessinger from CIA. Carla White from the White House. And Dan's father."

"The senator?" she asked. DeLuca nodded.

"And Phil LeDoux," DeLuca said. "Who may be in as much trouble as I am, thanks to me. How much did you hear?"

"I read the report you filed. Your general forwarded me a copy. Unofficially. He said he thought I'd be interested. It's still special access."

"I figured it would be."

"What are you going to say?" she asked him.

"I'm going to tell them whatever they need to know," DeLuca said. "You want to know the funny thing about me? I'm really good at bullshitting, but I'm no good at lying. I can convince an Eskimo I'm a polar bear, but I can't cover up drinking the last of the milk when there's still Oreos left."

"I know," she said. "Somehow, I knew that about you."

"If they're going to bury this, they're going to need to know exactly what they're burying," DeLuca said. "They might try. They're not going to find any bodies. Unless Vinnie wants them to, but they're not going to let him hold that over them. He could do some damage, but he has no idea who he's dealing with. He is so out of his league."

"You didn't do anything," she said. "Systems were out. You made the best decision you could, under the circumstances."

He shook his head.

"I fired under a white flag," he said. "That's one charge Phil says they're going to bring against me. Or I ordered fire under a white flag. Same thing."

"Sinhavsky *was* going to shoot *you* under a white flag," Massey said. "You fired in self-defense."

"The Code of Military Justice is pretty clear on the matter," DeLuca said. "We got off the shot first."

"This is such crap," she said. "You didn't have a choice."

"This isn't even where the crap begins. I also sanctioned the torture and murder of six people," he said. "On U.S. soil. People who hadn't been tried or proven guilty. I made a judgment, and that was the result. And they can't say it's okay, and they can't risk getting caught burying it. The McCain bill against that sort of thing passed the Senate ninety to nine. The buck stops here, as they say. And let me tell you something—nobody, and I do mean nobody, is better at making sure the buck doesn't go any further than it has to than the military. Scapegoat is almost an official pay grade. Philip is going to stand up for me and I have to make sure he doesn't. He had nothing to do with it. It was my call."

"A call that saved an untold number of lives," Dawn Massey said. "Millions. Is that somehow not going to matter?"

He shrugged. On the television, the pundits and news analysts were only beginning to piece it together. They were discussing the significance of the bomb found in Amsterdam, and the rumors that other bombs had been suspected. In another twenty-four hours, the full story would emerge. The White House had called a press conference. The wheels were turning.

"It won't change anything," he said. "I'm not going to

have too many friends on the committee. Senator Sykes is going to want to screw me any way he can, and I don't blame him. I got his kid killed."

"I'll testify on your behalf, if you think—"

"No. You have to stay out of it," DeLuca said. "Jesus, Dawn, I shouldn't even be here. I shouldn't have come. You want to hear something funny?"

"Funny ha-ha, or funny peculiar?" she asked.

"Neither," DeLuca said. "Halliday asked me if I'd be interested in the job as commissioner. Frank Wexler is out. Halliday has no idea what happened. Yet. You hear how I4NI found out I was involved in the Quinn case?"

"Wexler had a blog," Massey said. "We found it pasted into Dvoradjic's handheld."

"CopStory.com," DeLuca said. "Everything you could possibly want to know about the great Frank Wexler, in his own words. All about his old enemy, Dave DeLuca. He didn't even disguise my name. I think he thought somebody was going to make a movie of his life someday."

"Maybe somebody will," Massey said.

"Maybe," DeLuca admitted.

"What'd you tell Halliday?"

"I said he should ask me again in six months," DeLuca said.

"How are your people?" she asked.

"They're okay," DeLuca said. "I was with them before coming here. I think it's still hitting us. Vasquez was blaming himself. I told him not to. Mack is pretending not to feel anything. Elizabeth LeDoux is having a long talk with her father. Hoolie already helped her put the money back in the MIT accounts."

"I'm not following," Massey said.

"I didn't have time to get into the details before," De-Luca said. "Chen was giving her money. A lot of it, mostly stolen from grants he'd written. He had a whole shrine built to Elizabeth in his house. He was in love with her, or so he believed, and he was out of his mind with jealousy. Literally out of his mind. I think he would have shot the first person to walk through the door."

"I'm so sorry."

"That's my fault too," DeLuca said. "Phil never asked me to put someone on her. I did that because he's my friend. That was bad judgment on my part."

Dawn Massey shook her head.

"Have you got anybody in your corner?" she asked. "Besides LeDoux? My God, David, you did everything right. This is ridiculous. So what if you used Vinnie to get results? I read your file. Correct me if I'm wrong, but isn't that what you do? Play people against each other? In Iraq, you dealt with people worse than Vincent Pastorelli every day. That's the world you live in."

"I don't live in it," DeLuca said. "I just work there."

"My point exactly," she said. "We've all made deals with the devil. There's nothing new about that—"

"Dawn, stop," DeLuca said, reaching across the table and gently laying his finger on her lips to shush her. He spoke softly. "It doesn't matter. I know you get it."

"But you had no way of knowing," she said. "You never authorized anything."

"It doesn't matter," he repeated. "It really doesn't. Even if I agreed with you. If they need somebody to take the fall to make this right, I'm it. It's my turn."

"David . . ."

"Mickey O'Brien's in prison for letting a couple of goombahs pay for his dog's kidney operation," DeLuca said. "If they can do that to him, think what they can do to me. It doesn't matter. That's the bottom line. I'm it."

"I know," she said at last.

"I do have one guy in my corner," DeLuca said. "I talked to General Quinn earlier. At least he still likes me."

"What'd you tell him?"

In the aftermath, Actel-Simmons had sent a company helicopter to Vinalhaven to fly the general back to Boston. DeLuca met the helicopter at the Brigham and Women's Hospital helipad, to debrief the general in person. They'd gotten a bite in the hospital coffee shop while they talked, the general listening patiently, chewing his food and nodding. DeLuca told him how his daughter had died, and why, and that the people who'd done it weren't going to hurt anybody anymore. Joe Quinn was able to read between the lines, and offered to attend the briefing in D.C. on DeLuca's behalf, if he needed support. DeLuca politely declined the offer. As Quinn got into the cab to take him back to Beacon Hill, he asked DeLuca for Claire McGowan's telephone number. "Maybe there's time to make things right with her," he'd said. He added, "Call me if you ever need a job. We could send you all over the world, if you're still interested in that sort of thing. I know the press has painted Actel as crooks or idiots, but they're good people—I wouldn't work for them if they weren't." DeLuca said he believed the general, and that he'd keep his phone number, just in case.

"I told him everything," DeLuca told Dawn Massey. "I owed him that. I also told him that if he was interested in pursuing it, his daughter still had frozen eggs stored in a clinic in Northampton. I'll bet Claire McGowan would carry the embryos."

"I'll bet Freddy would be happy to make a contribution to the project as well," Massey said.

"No doubt," DeLuca said. "My cousin Jackie called, by the way. He wants me to meet Gina. He said he thought the two of them and my wife and I should have dinner. A double date."

"Sounds like fun," Massey said, wagging her delicate eyebrows.

"I double-dated with Jackie a couple of times in high school," DeLuca said. "Both times, his dates ended up asking me, 'What's wrong with your cousin?'"

Dawn smiled.

"Bonnie's staying in North Carolina," DeLuca said. "Apparently she has new friends there. I got an e-mail from her asking me if I knew anybody she could hire to get her things. I gave her Freddy's number."

"When's your flight to D.C.?"

"Not until noon," DeLuca said. "I was going to go home, but when I got there . . . I wanted to come here. Unless you mind."

"I already told you I didn't," Massey said.

"Would it be okay if I took a shower?" he asked her. "I haven't had a second . . ."

In the bathroom, he took off his clothes and looked at himself in the mirror. He needed a shave, but the only razor he could find was pink and appeared to have been used recently to shave leg hairs. He looked at his eyes in the mirror. They were red from exhaustion. He looked terrible. He wondered if this was the face that was going to turn up in the newspapers.

He turned the shower on and let the water get hot, weighing himself on the bathroom scale as he waited. He'd lost five pounds. Dawn was right—he was hungry.

He stepped into the shower. He let the hot water pour over him, taking his time. He soaped, shampooed, and rinsed, then soaped, shampooed, and rinsed again. The soap was girl soap, and it smelled like herbs or something. It smelled good. He closed his eyes. He felt the way he usually felt at the end of a fight, where he'd prevailed, but nobody won. He'd been in this position before, not knowing what the future held, but never to this degree.

When Dawn Massey slipped into the shower with him, he at least knew what the immediate future held in store.

That was a start.

About the Authors

DAVID DEBATTO has served in the active duty Army, Army Reserve, and Army National Guard as a German linguist, counterintelligence course instructor, and counterintelligence special agent. He served in Europe at the height of the cold war in the late 1970s to early 1980s and in Iraq during Operation Iraqi Freedom in 2003 where his Tactical Human Intelligence Team (THT) hunted Saddam, WMD, and top Ba'ath Party leaders. He is currently writing further books in this series for Warner Books along with Pete Nelson as well as articles for major publications such as *Vanity Fair*, *Salon*, and *The American Prospect*. He is also a frequent guest on major television and radio news programs giving his analysis of breaking stories in the global war on terrorism. David lives in Florida.

PETE NELSON lives with his wife and son in western Massachusetts. He got his MFA from the University of Iowa Writers' Workshop in 1979 and has written both fiction and nonfiction for magazines, including *Harper's*, *Playboy*, *Esquire*, *Outside*, *The Iowa Review*, *National Wildlife*, *Glamour*, and *Redbook*. He was a columnist for *Mademoiselle* and a staff writer for *LIVE* magazine, covering various live events including horse pulls, music festivals, dog shows, accordion camps, and arm-wrestling championships. He's published twelve young adult novels, including a six-book series about a girl named Sylvia Smith-Smith, which earned him an Edgar Award nomination from the Mystery Writers of America. His young adult nonfiction World War II history, *Left for Dead* (Random House, 2002), about the sinking of the USS *Indianapolis*, won the 2003 Christopher Award and was selected for the American Library Association's 2003, top ten list. His other nonfiction titles include *Real Man Tells All* (Viking, 1988), *Marry Like a Man* (NAL, 1992), *That Others May Live* (Crown, 2000), and *Kidshape* (Rutledge Hill, 2004). His novel *The Christmas List* was published by Rutledge Hill Press in 2004.